Ex-CIA agent Harry Ryder knew that the odds were against him when he agreed to go to Yugoslavia to find the "dead man." Ryder had no desire to get involved with the CIA again, but if he wanted the book he was writing to be published without changes, he had no choice. Don Carlos Bingham, his former boss, had put it to him squarely: "You help me by carrying out a simple mission, and I'll see that the CIA censors don't mangle your manuscript."

This was blackmail, of course, and the mission was not going to be simple. No mission from Bingham was ever simple. Furthermore, Ryder was an old Asia hand; the Orient had been his beat. Now he was to operate in Austria and Yugoslavia. How could he be expected to work efficiently when he knew neither the countries nor their languages?

But Bingham had an answer. "I need you in those countries because somewhere there, probably a prisoner, is the man you once worked with and can still recognize at sight. He is officially dead, especially dead to anyone in the CIA. I can let you know that he is not dead, because I trust you to keep your mouth shut. Your mission is to find that man, free him, and get him out of Yugoslavia. And for operating there, you will be accompanied by a one-time British Secret Service agent whose whole career was spent in Slavic countries. Her name is Melissa Meirion and I expect the two of you to make a team."

(continued on back flap)

ALWAYS
A SPY

Also by Robert Footman

ONCE A SPY

Robert Footman

ALWAYS A SPY

A NOVEL OF SUSPENSE

Dodd, Mead & Company
New York

No part of this book may be reproduced in any form
without permission in writing from the publisher.
Published by Dodd, Mead & Company, Inc.
79 Madison Avenue, New York, N.Y. 10016
Distributed in Canada by
McClelland and Stewart Limited, Toronto
Manufactured in the United States of America
Designed by Erich Hobbing
First Edition

Library of Congress Cataloging-in-Publication Data

Footman, Robert.
Always a spy.

I. Title.
PS3556.064A79 1986   813'.54   86-6218
ISBN 0-396-08840-6

1   2   3   4   5   6   7   8   9   10

Prologue

Shifting a buttock on the rotting dock, the fisherman squiggled his torso, twitched at his line, adjusted his pipe. This was his world. His alone. Well, almost alone. About a mile out—no, now only three-quarters of a mile distant—a tiny sailboat swayed on placid Chesapeake Bay and lulled another fisherman.

He put the glasses on the lone sailor and had the pleasure—the envious pleasure, now be honest, Tibor—of seeing the fisherman reel in a catch. Of what? A striped bass? What did the natives call that? A "rock"? Well, maybe he would get himself a rock, too. He puffed on his pipe and let the feeble March sun bury itself on his shoulders.

An hour later, when he was actually beginning to feel warm, he once more became aware of the sailor. The latter was docking on another hunk of crumbling piling about a hundred yards down the eastern shore. He saw Tibor, waved to him, and picked up his catch and began to trudge up the squishy dirt road. Tibor smiled back, and the stranger wandered over and stood a few feet away. He was tall, about fifty or so, someone who had come to peace with himself and the world. He smiled and said, "Any luck?"

Tibor shrugged and pointed to his empty basket. The stranger nodded. "Well, it's just my lucky day, I guess."

And calmly he reached into his basket and pulled out a pistol, a small-bore automatic. Tibor dropped his fishing line, jerked his head so violently that his skier's cap flopped off his head, and quivered on the dock. "You—what—that's a gun! What do you want?"

1

"You, Tibor. Just you. You don't remember me, I see. Well, I remember you. I've thought of you every day for thirty-five years. Mitra, Tibor. Do you remember her? Ah, I see you do. It's coming back. Mitra Grgić. Yes, Mitra. And I'm Ethan Pickering."

The tall man stepped forward and aimed the pistol at Tibor's right temple. It was covered with thick black hair. Dyed black hair. And he pulled the trigger. Tibor was still trying to say something as the bullet bored into his brain.

PART I

1

Lissa Meirion walked down the worn concrete steps onto the almost deserted Bayswater Station platform. A couple of burly men, but no American. Good. Maybe he wouldn't come. During yesterday's meeting at Sir Alexander James's home, he'd made it quite clear that he wanted no part of her as part of Sir Alex's search mission. If the American was going to help ferret out a missing Yugoslav spy, he wasn't about to do it with her.

Well, the American had no monopoly on dislike. No, that was wrong. On disapproval, rather. He wasn't important enough for her to dislike. He might dislike her; she could do no more than disapprove of him.

If the Putney Wimbledon train came before the American arrived (she knew his name perfectly well, it was Harry Ryder, but if she kept to "the American," she was on safe ground; from "the American" to "the ugly American" was a natural transition, one that needed no conscious thought), anyway, if he didn't come on time, she could slip aboard the train and avoid this encounter. She'd been quite precise. Ten-thirty, she'd said. It was now ten thirty-two. And there came the silver District line train, she could just see it rumbling toward her far down the black tunnel. And there also came the American trotting down the steps.

He saw her. Typically, she thought, he didn't wear a smile or show any more expression than he had yesterday. Uncouth. But on time; he'd join her, and so she'd have to face up to it. "It" being Sir Alex's suggestion: "You're going to the Putney Library tomorrow morning, Melissa, my dear. And Mr. Ryder,

3

you'll be going to Wimbledon for the tennis tomorrow. Why not drive over together in the morning, and perhaps you can have a cup of coffee in Putney or Southfield and see what a night for reflection has dredged up." A smart man, Sir Alex, he'd been quite aware of the mutual frost . . . and why in heaven's name was the American suddenly throwing his hands above his head and starting to run toward her? Run? He was sprinting—and that was her last more-or-less coherent thought in those next kaleidoscopic moments.

They probably had a succession, a this following a that, but at the time they all seemed to happen at once. There were the ugly American's arms and legs churning as fast as they could—his face, she seemed to see then, or perhaps recollect later, his face had indeed turned quite ugly, it seemed one gigantic scowl—and he could have been shouting at her, but if so, his words were lost in the rumble and squeals of the silver train now braking at the tunnel exit. There was also a presence beside her—no, there were two presences, one at each shoulder. There was a violent thrust at her left shoulder, a thrust that started to propel her towards the tracks, a thrust she reflexively defended, not by opposing it but by going with the direction of the push. As a result, as she spun towards the tracks still four feet away (thereby getting a glimpse of the motorman rising up from his seat, one hand flat against the window as if to push her away from the grinding, braking wheels of his train, his mouth wide open as if he, too, were shouting a silent message), her forward motion freed her for a fraction of a second from the assailant at her left shoulder. She took advantage of this by throwing herself at the pres- ence—the male presence—beside her right shoulder. The delay was infinitesimal. The man at her right put both arms about her chest and prepared to swing her full around and back towards the tracks. This motion she once more favored. Going with it, she rolled with the man towards the platform's edge. Reflexes again. And again the right reflex, because this additional infinitesimal delay permitted a new element, a new presence, to intrude on the clumsy, whirling dance. She felt

4

rather than saw him, her ugly American. She never saw how he did what he did, but the results were immediately apparent.

The man originally at her left shoulder was now flying through the air. He landed face down on the tracks, and the train thundered over him. But not before he managed one great scream that could be heard quite clearly above the roar of the train. And the man at her right, thanks to her whirling motion—and possibly because of some help from the American, she wasn't sure—was spinning away from her and stumbling against a silver coach. He tried to brace himself against the slowing train, but only succeeded in having its motion bounce him along until suddenly there was no support, just the space between the first coach and the next. He fell head forward into the gap. His feet, supported by the rear of the first coach and the front of the second, remained visible. He seemed to be walking on his head. At least, that was the impression, since the legs went up and down like pistons, as his head and shoulders presumably bounded up and down between the ties. He was not dragged much farther. The motorman managed to bring the train to a wrenching halt three coach-lengths down the platform. Most of the train was still buried deep in the tunnel. The grotesque scene was too much to bear, and she started to put her hand over her eyes to help block out the sight, but the American distracted her. Distracted—and astonished. Quite wide-eyed, she turned to follow his mysterious actions.

He raced along the coach until he caught up with the now-limp legs that had folded against the couplings. Leaning forward, he wrapped his arms around them, heaved backward and upward, and dragged the man—the body—onto the platform. He paid no attention to the mess above the man's shoulders. He ignored the blood spurting all over the platform and the train and him. Instead, he knelt beside the body and began to go through the man's pockets. The contents of each pocket were pulled out, glanced at, returned. Wallet, passport, cigarettes, cigarette lighter, money clip, handkerchief, diary—

all were inspected and whisked back from whence they came—all except a squat, lethal-looking automatic pistol. This disappeared into his jacket's left pocket. The motion was so fast, she wondered if she had really seen it or was hallucinating. Certainly none of the passengers now streaming from the first three cars—followed by a charging, anxiety-ridden motorman—no one saw the pistol appear and disappear. Squeezing together near the American and the gory corpse, the passengers registered shock in their individual ways. Only the motorman seemed capable of action. He thrust his way through the death-watchers, knelt beside the American, then stood up, took off his cap, shook his bald head, said the obvious:

"He's dead."

Speech prompted more speech, this from a stoutish, fiftyish man in an amazingly loud checked jacket. "Well, so he's dead. How long do we have to stay here? I'm late. I have an appointment in Putney in twenty-five minutes."

She checked her watch. Ten thirty-four. All this—in less than two minutes! She felt an urge to protest that she, too, had an appointment in Putney. She couldn't miss it. Anthony Raines at the Library had assembled for her an armful of photostats of fifteenth- and sixteenth-century documents and maps and street plans of Putney, Wandsworth, and Esher, all of them relevant to Cardinal Wolsey's 1530 stay at Esher and to the protection given him by his assistant, Thomas Cromwell, and she couldn't stand Mr. Raines up, and at that moment she felt an elbow in her ribs. A rather ungentle elbow. The American's elbow. She swung around to face—to challenge—him for his rudeness, but he was not looking at her. His bland, anonymous face—that was the word she'd been looking for yesterday, anonymous—was turned to the distraught motorman, who suddenly found his tongue.

"See 'ere, my fellow"—this to the stout man in the loud checked jacket—"see 'ere, we can't take off just like that. This 'ere's a dead man. And there's another one up there under the first car. Or somewhere down below."

The crowd now gave a low moan. Heads craned to peer at the train. The stout fellow started to heave. He hurried to the side of the train and tried to aim his breakfast between the train's side and the platform. He was partially successful.

The motorman was in command now. "This tryne is stying right 'ere until the police come and me inspector. By now, Fariba up there, she's done it right. She's put in the call. We'll wyte."

And indeed Fariba herself had bustled out of her ticket cage and hustled down the stairs and proceeded to justify the motorman's confidence. "They're coming. The police. They'll be here in a minute. And Inspector Trilby won't take long."

So Fariba. A black-haired, dark-skinned Arab or Lebanese or Syrian or Iraqi or Iranian or Turk or Yemeni or Jordanian or whatever. As Moslem as the corpses. How did she, Melissa Beaumont Meirion, know her attackers were—had been— Moslem? She had not gotten a conscious look at their faces. All she could recall seeing were rather shiny trousers and sleeves and lapels. But she knew without a doubt her attackers had been from the Middle East, a fact that did nothing to make any sense at all of the last few minutes. Maybe the American knew. . . . Maybe he could tell her. . . .

"Yes, they're Syrian. The passport." The American whispered to her without looking at her. He added, "You did well."

Did well? Then he hadn't helped her, is that what his comment implied? She had disposed of her attackers all by herself? But before she could say a word in reply, the police arrived. In hordes. Or so it seemed. They swarmed over the platform. One of them, a giant of a man, a sergeant, came up to the motorman while his colleagues spread out hither and yon to do the things police do.

"Well, my man," the giant said, "what happened, what's this all about?" There was no threat in his voice, no excitement, no passion, not very much interest, either. "Sergeant Giant" was plainly quite inured to corpses and crushed skulls and blood and vomit and crowds.

7

The motorman swung around and pointed to Lissa and the American. "They did it. They threw a man under me tryne. I saw it."

2

The crowd went into a palsied, shuffling motion. (*Did well.* What a switch. Yesterday, the American's every gesture, look, and expression had registered disapproval. *Did well*—now that was clearly approval. Permanent approval? Or only during this grisly period?) The semicircle gradually drew back, reformed around her, the American, the flushed motorman, and Mr. Sergeant the Giant.

While the sergeant cogitated, other policemen administered the crowd. One at the steps prevented anyone from coming or going. Two others began easing the staring onlookers ever further back from the four principals. A fourth policeman clambered up from the tracks. His face was splotchy white. He nodded at the sergeant, pulled out a walkie-talkie, and began whispering earnestly into it. All this time, the sergeant stood there motionlessly. Except for his eyes. They saw everything. Mostly they looked at her and at the American.

Lissa shook herself and opened her mouth, but once again the American intervened. He squeezed her elbow ever so gently. (She hadn't been aware until then that his hand had been resting all this time on her arm; anonymous he was, which, Lissa my dear, was becoming a highly repetitious thought, one with the earmarks of incipient hysteria. Well, why not? What could be wrong with a bit of hysteria?) The sergeant saw all this and, she suspected, probably recognized the pull to hysteria, but still said nothing. He turned his back on them and stared towards the ticket booth. He seemed to be willing something to appear—and appear it did, in the person of a London Transport inspector. The latter—thin, gloomy, long-nosed—talked for a moment to the officer at the steps, walked up to them, and nodded.

"Dykes." This to the sergeant from the inspector.

"Trilby." This to the inspector from the the sergeant.

Inspector Trilby said, "I suppose we'll have to do a bit of switching. How long will you need?"

Sergeant Dykes shrugged. "We've called the ambulance. Also the laboratory chaps. An hour or so?"

"The laboratory? Well, well. All right. An hour. We'll survive. That's more than they did, poor devils. Butler"—this to the motorman—"I'll get your report later. Well, carry on."

Sergeant Dykes nodded. He looked at the crowd, turning completely around so that he caught, or seemed to catch, each person's eyes. "Ladies and gentlemen." His *Ladies* had just a touch of cockney. *Lydies.* Perhaps he heard it, too, because he repeated his salutation. "Ladies and gentlemen." This time the *a* was fully under control; Sergeant Dykes had legitimate pretensions to middle-class veneer. His lapse to an earlier pattern suggested that he was not quite so calm as he pretended. Lissa caught all this automatically. Would the American understand these nuances? She looked at him, but his face was as bland and anonymous as ever. Even his eyes seemed dull and neutral; they were not snapping and flashing like the sergeant's.

"Ladies and gentlemen"—this third try was almost unintelligible; pure mushy Oxonian—"will you kindly take your seats back in the train? Our men will come by and take your names and addresses and any information about the accident you can provide. When you've finished, you can go over to the opposite platform. The westbound trains will be switched over there." And, in fact, this was already beginning to happen. A big silver train was beginning to inch westbound on the eastbound tracks. Inspector Trilby's men were just as efficient as the police. "Thank you for your patience and cooperation."

Only then did the sergeant address the two men and Lissa.

A young officer had come up to stand quietly beside him. He was carrying a tape recorder. He pointed it at each speaker in turn.

"My name is Dykes. Sergeant Harry Dykes of Paddington Station. This is Constable Crabbe." His *H* in *Harry* was a model of aspiration. "May I have your names and addresses, please?"

The American spoke first. "My first name is also Harry. Harry Ryder. I'm a tourist in London." At least he did not say the obvious: *I'm an American.* He apparently understood ten million Londoners could tell his nationality at a glance. "I'm staying a block away at the Terrace Hotel. It's on Inverness Terrace."

"The Terrace. Ma'am?"

"My name is Meirion. M-E-I-R-I-O-N. Mrs. Llewelyn Laurent Meirion. I live at 123 Porchester Terrace."

The motorman's flushed face had begun to resume its normal paleness. The underground look. He now put his hat back on, seemingly surprised to find he had been carrying it in his right hand all this time. "I'm Byley Butler. Nimed after the Old Byley, you know. My dad spent a lot of time there." Mr. Butler had no qualms about his vowels. *Byler* and *nimed* were native, natural sounds. Professor Higgins would have delighted in them. "I live in Stepney at 1185 Monitor Street, and I run this 'ere tryne every week die. I do, and I want to sigh—"

But Sergeant Dykes raised a hand and quelled the torrent. "Thank you, Mr. Butler. We'll get to that in a moment. Now. Mrs. Meirion. Mr. Ryder. What do you say to Mr. Butler's comment? Did you cause this?"

The American started to answer, but he could not head her off this time. "Sergeant, Mr. Butler did not say we caused this. He said we did it. We—he said we threw a man onto the tracks."

"Why, so he did. And I see the difference. All right, Mr. Butler, who caused this?"

"Caused?"

Lissa ran her hand through her hair. "Started, Mr. Butler. Who started this?"

"Oh, they did, ma'am. They kyme at you from be'ind and tried to throw you in front of me tryne, but this gentlemen 'ere kyme rushing up and, neat as you please, 'eaved one of 'em through the hair instead of you going through the hair yourself, if you see what I mean, ma'am, and I didn't see what 'appened to the second man, that one there with a sieve for 'is 'ead, because me tryne went beyond 'im, do you see, and I did my—"

"Thank you, Mr. Butler. Constable Crabbe here will take down your whole story. Mrs. Meirion, Mr. Ryder, will you come with me? This is no fit place to talk. And there'll be reporters here straightaway. May I ask you to accompany me to the station and we'll work the matter out there without having to contend with the reporters?"

"There were three men, Sergeant."

"What?"

The American seemed apologetic. "He was standing up there on that bridge. An observer. A heavyset fellow in a gray, loose-fitting suit. He was—is—a fellow-countryman to the dead men. Or at least a coreligionist. I'm no authority on Middle East nationalities."

"An observer." Sergeant Dykes looked at the corpse. "A coreligionist. Crabbe?" The young officer nodded. "Please, Mrs. Meirion, shall we go?" Suddenly his professional imperturbability seemed to crack. His face hardened, his eyes flashed. "An observer, Mr. Ryder? Or a control?"

But the American looked him straight in the eye without changing his expression or betraying the least emotion. "He stood right up there by that railing, Sergeant. When he observed this man fall against the train, he turned and walked back toward the street. He observed the whole scene, Sergeant. I do not know if he controlled it."

Sergeant Dykes stared gloomily at Mr. Ryder. "If he did control it, he certainly didn't get the results he expected. All right, let's go to the station, and perhaps you two will be

11

able to tell me just what his expectations were."

Lissa felt herself flush with anger. This was outrageous. Why, Sergeant Dykes was practically accusing the American and herself of somehow being implicated in this ghastly business. Ghastly—and incomprehensible. She opened her mouth to give the sergeant a piece of her mind, hesitated.

Was he possibly right? Were she and the American somehow implicated without knowing it? Yesterday she'd met the American for the first time at Sir Alexander James's Mayfair home. Sir Alex and his rabbitlike little American house guest, one Mr. Don Carlos Bingham, had explained why they had summoned Mr. Ryder all the way from San Francisco, and herself all of a mile or so from Bayswater. They'd been summoned because, as Sir Alex had assured them, they were the two best-qualified people in the world to help them find a missing man, one Mr. Peter Trubari, Yugoslavian, a manufacturer of electronic components. He'd been in Vienna on a business trip, was last seen with a beautiful auburn-haired lady with whom he'd gone off to take the cog train up the Schneeberg, near Wiener Neustadt.

On the surface, an open-and-shut proposal: Find Peter Trubari.

It had not been necessary to state the obvious. Mr. Peter Trubari was undoubtedly a Yugoslav agent-in-place for Sir Alex—and perhaps for Mr. Bingham, too. For it was equally obvious that Mr. Bingham, though like Sir Alex some seventy-odd years of age, was still just as much an active part of the American intelligence establishment as Sir Alex was of the British. And it was also obvious that Mr. Bingham had treated the San Franciscan as an ex-employee. Well, why not? In a way she—or, more exactly, her husband and she—they'd from time to time been employees of Sir Alex. The tight little world of Anglo-American spying cousins. But not active spying cousins. At least not on her part. The American might somehow be up to his ears in Moslem thuggery; she wasn't.

So thinking, she came to and found herself with her mouth still opened wide while Sergeant Dykes was staring at said mouth with fascinated eyes. Nice going, Lissa. You've certainly caught Sergeant Dykes's attention. So. . . . So say something. She did.

"Sergeant, I assure you, I'm as curious about this horrible tragedy as you are. And I'm sure I speak for Mr. Ryder, too."

A mealy-mouthed nothing, this—and perhaps an outright if unintentional lie. What did she know about Mr. Harry Ryder? (Mr. Harry Ryder. That *Mister* was a shock—but also only fair. She could no longer dismiss him as "the American"; "the American" he might be, but he also had saved her life, and that deserved some recognition from her. Henceforth, Mr. Harry Ryder it would have to be.) She knew very little of him, only what Sir Alex had said at yesterday's meeting:

"Lissa, Mr. Ryder has had a quite successful career at finding missing persons. And sometimes rescuing them, if they happened to be locked up in prison. Of course we don't know if Peter Trubari is in a prison. We don't know anything at all about his whereabouts. He's just vanished. We want your help, both of you. You, Lissa, are an expert on things Yugoslavian. You and Llew-Llaw—sorry, Mr. Ryder, I should say Llewelyn; Llew-Llaw was the nickname of Mrs. Meirion's late husband—you and Llewelyn spent years in that country; you have friends everywhere, even in the mountains of Montenegro. And you, Mr. Ryder, besides the talent of yours I've already mentioned, you have one advantage, one strength, one qualification I'm not at liberty to discuss. Not, that is, until you and Mrs. Meirion decide to help us. Then, and only then, can I—can Mr. Bingham and I—tell you why Peter Trubari is so important to us. We can outline today all we know of his last few days in Vienna, and as you'll see it's quite a lot. But I must beg your forbearance about the why of all this."

All straightforward enough; and all without the least revelation about any possible connection between Mr. Ryder and Moslem assassins.

And so thinking, she became aware that Sergeant Dykes

13

was still staring at her with fascinated eyes. Why so? Her mouth was shut. Why was he staring at her?

He answered her unspoken question by shaking his head like a dog after a bath and saying ponderously:

"Mrs. Meirion, let me get this straight. You say you can speak for Mr. Ryder? You mean, you and Mr. Ryder know each other? You—you came together to this station? Being here together was no accident? You know each other?"

Sergeant Dykes was a perceptive man, if given to redundancy. Apparently his large size was accompanied by an equally—or adequately—large brain. Sergeant Dykes knew there was no conceivable way for a man like Harry Ryder to be acquainted with a woman like Mrs. Melissa Beaumont Meirion. Not in the ordinary course of events, that is. Mr. Ryder's world and her world were not just an ocean apart, they were a civilization apart.

All of which was very well, but how could she reply to Sergeant Dykes? Should she say, "Yes, Sergeant, Mr. Ryder and I are meeting this morning to find out three things. One, can we tolerate each other? Two, if we pass that test, can we agree to work together? Three, if we do decide to work together, how will we go about finding a missing Yugoslav manufacturer, who probably works for Sir Alexander James, who probably still plays a major role in our secret intelligence service. Yes, in our MI6."

And Mr. Ryder once again came to her rescue. He said: "Mrs. Meirion is conducting research at the Putney Public Library. On Cardinal Wolsey and Thomas Cromwell. She's finishing the monograph on these two great men started by Professor Meirion. There's a man at the Library who's an authority on Wolsey and Cromwell. His name's Anthony Raines, and Mrs. Meirion told me about him when we met yesterday over cocktails. I am also very interested in Tudor history, and Mrs. Meirion very kindly offered to bring me along when she meets Mr. Raines."

What a liar! Meet Mr. Raines forsooth. *She* had been going to meet Raines; *he* had been going on to Wimbledon. What

14

a liar—and how smoothly he rolled out this nonsense, and how sagely Sergeant Dykes seemed to accept it. He nodded soberly, said, "Yes, two great Englishmen. Well worth researching. And what is your occupation, Mr. Ryder? Are you a scholar, too?"

"Not a scholar, Sergeant. Just a writer. A recent writer."

"Recent?"

"Yes, I'm really a business consultant. In Orinda, California. But I've brought in two partners, and I've been turning my business over to them. I've decided I want to try my hand at writing a book. So I'm a recent writer."

"What's the title of your book, Mr. Ryder?"

"It has no title yet, Sergeant. It's at the publisher, and I've left it up to him—to them—to come up with a title."

Sergeant Dykes took his cap, scratched his thick, dark hair, put his cap back on, and said, "Shall we be on our way? We've got a lot to talk about, we three. I can see that. Oh, yes. If you'll follow me, we'll go up to the street by way of the maintenance stairs. By now the press will be very much in evidence at the main entrance on Queensway. Follow me, if you please, and we'll avoid them. And then we can continue our conversation at the station."

"After I've cleaned up a bit," said Mr. Harry Ryder.

The sergeant looked at the gore and slop on the American's clothes and nodded. "After you've cleaned up a bit."

3

The few minutes' ride to Paddington Police Station was hardly the time for her to rehash the morning's events with Mr. Harry Ryder. Not with Sergeant Dykes all ears in the driver's seat a few feet in front of them. But it was a good time to list and catalog the questions mentally that she wanted to ask Mr. Harry Ryder. The acerbic questions. They were:

15

1. Mr. Ryder, who are you, do you still report to your Don Carlos Bingham? (What an extraordinary concatenation: Don Carlos Bingham; why such an unusual combination? But this was not a question for Mr. Ryder, or was it? Why not?) If you do so report, does that make you an employee of the CIA, or if not of the CIA, of what then, and if not of a what then, then:
2. (All of the above was, in her mind, just one question.) Then why did you agree to come all the way from San Francisco to discuss the rescue of a man you've never heard of any more than I have?
3. Did you know beforehand those Moslem thugs were scheduled to attack me? And finally:
4. Is there any possible connection between Peter Trubari and these thugs? That is, we're being asked to go Sir Galahading off to find a lost Yugoslavian. Can Moslem assassins—Syrian assassins—have anything to do with Yugoslavia? Were these Syrians trying to prevent our accepting Sir Alex's mission? They don't want us to embark on a search for Mr. Peter Trubari?

This fourth set of questions was ridiculous. At five o'clock yesterday, Sir Alex had told them about Peter Trubari; she and Mr. Harry Ryder had listened in noncommittal, even glum, silence. They'd agreed to nothing—except a mutual if tacit disapproval of each other, strongly bordering on dislike on Mr. Harry Ryder's part; and then at ten-thirty the following morning an assassination attempt was made. How could there possibly be any connection between a five-thirty meeting in secrecy and a ten-thirty attack in public? And what light could a San Franciscan throw on these matters? None, of course; but ridiculous as the questions were, she'd still ask them. They weren't any more ridiculous than anything else that had happened this morning.

When could she challenge Mr. Ryder with these questions?

When? Not soon, apparently, as Mr. Ryder made clear as they walked behind Sergeant Dykes from the station parking

16

lot. He whispered, "I want you to know I admired the way you forbore discussing the morning events on the way here. Not with Sergeant Dykes and his tape recorder working away on the front seat. I suspect we'll be wise to be equally cautious in the station. There, bugs and one-way mirrors and hidden cameras may very possibly be much with us. We'll get our chance to talk after we get away from here. I know you've got questions of me. I've got questions of you. Thanks for your caution, Mrs. Meirion."

Caution! Bugs! One-way mirrors! Tape recorders! Hidden cameras! What in the world was she getting into? What kind of mind did Mr. Harry Ryder have? (That was a fifth question—and it answered itself: Mr. Harry Ryder's mind was clearly paranoiac.) The London Metropolitan Police didn't employ such nefarious devices. Maybe such methods were a commonplace in the States, where the English common law seems to have suffered a sea change; but it was just not possible here.

Or was it?

Once deposited in a small interviewing room, she had plenty of time to study the decor while Mr. Harry Ryder went off to do his ablutions. Bare gray walls, a plain black plastic-topped steel table, gray steel chairs, a photo of the City of London—was there a camera behind it? How could there be? If ever a room seemed exactly what it purported to be, a place to interview suspects—that is, interview people, interview citizens—if ever a room could be reduced to functional starkness, this was it. Forget the claptrap about bugs and cameras and one-way mirrors. This was London. This was England. Not San Francisco. Not America. When Mr. Harry Ryder came back, she'd explain the facts of life to him.

But she didn't. Mr. Ryder gave her no chance. He gave her one sharp glance that seemed to read her every thought, her every resentment, shook his head, passed a finger swiftly over his lips, started to talk about tennis. About Wimbledon.

Apparently he was a tennis buff. When Sir Alex said he could provide some Centre Court tickets at Wimbledon, Mr.

17

Ryder couldn't resist the opportunity. He was looking forward to seeing the great players facing their greatest challenges. He seemed to know something about all of them. He rattled off their names, told interesting or funny stories about them, about Kriek and Krishnan and Turnbull, about Gerulaitis, Mandlikova, Navratilova, Amitraj, Temesvari, Jausovec, Slozil. An hour-long cacophony of names, no end to them, a recitative kept up until the door suddenly opened and framed Sergeant Dykes.

"Sorry to keep you waiting, but there's been a good deal to do." He stood there, a perfectly enormous man, not quite seven feet tall. He looked reproachfully at Mr. Ryder, who looked back at him calmly. Anonymously calm. Mr. Ryder's features, she suddenly realized, were not unhandsome. She really hadn't catalogued them before, but now she was aware his eyes were gray, his face lean and hollow-cheeked, his moustache neatly trimmed, and his ears not obtrusive. (The moustache was a mistake, a disfigurement even; he'd look much more attractive without it.) He also had plenty of hair; it formed a kind of grizzled, grayish-brown mop. All this evidence said his age was—what was his age? And why was she pursuing such trivial thoughts? Well, his age was probably mid to late forties, though he might be older than he looked. Llew-Llaw had been fifty-three when he died; she was now thirty-nine. And Lissa, she adjured herself, stop this woolgathering, pay attention to the sergeant, who is handing Mr. Ryder something.

"Your passport, Mr. Ryder." He sat down at the end of the table, continued his reproachful, chiding look. Finally he sighed, grunted, looked at her. "Mrs. Meirion, as you requested, I called Mr. Raines at the Library. He won't be in tomorrow, so he'll see you same time next Monday, if that's agreeable. He said that, oddly enough, he also found something about Enrico Dandolo that might interest you."

Safe ground, this. "Yes, I'm trying to finish up two of my husband's monographs. He not only did a great deal of research on Thomas Cromwell and Cardinal Wolsey, but off and on over the years he'd spent considerable time collecting material on the great twelfth-century doge, Enrico Dandolo."

"Yes, remarkable men." So Sergeant Dykes. "At least, Wolsey and Cromwell were. I've always thought them two of the greatest men England ever produced. I don't know anything about the doge."

"You astonish me, Sergeant. The popular view is that Thomas Cromwell was one of England's most renowned toadies. Maybe the leading toad in all our history."

"Popular view. Ah, yes, thanks to Thomas More and Mr. Ryder, this time I'd appreciate the full story."

If he expected this abrupt transition to discombobulate the American, he could hardly have been gratified. Mr. Harry Ryder was imperturbable. "Sergeant, I saw two men grappling with Mrs. Meirion. I rushed up to help. I managed to get hold of one man. He never saw me coming. While I disposed of him, Mrs. Meirion swung the other man into the train. He hit it and fell between the first and second car."

"I swung him!"

"Yes, Mrs. Meirion, you did that all by yourself. That's what I meant when I said you did well. I think you thought I helped you. Believe me, I didn't. I had quite an armful with my own man. You swung your man into the train by yourself. Yes indeed, you did well. You are very athletic."

His tone was kindly. His thoughts were complimentary. But there was no warmth on his expressionless face. Mr. Harry Ryder, rescuer, seemed to approve of her now no more than he had yesterday. Strange, very strange. Well, he deserved a reply of some kind, but fortunately Sergeant Dykes took the bit.

"Yes, Mr. Ryder, athletic she is. A few Olympics ago, Mrs. Meirion represented our country in downhill skiing. You were Melissa Beaumont then. I saw you on television. You won a bronze medal. I still remember the day and Mr. Ryder I think you are holding out on me. Please."

"Sir?"

"Coincidences always bother policemen, Mr. Ryder. Your coincidental presence at the scene of the crime—or was it a coincidence? Oh, I know, you say you had an appointment to meet Mrs. Meirion. But you also used the word *observer*. That bothers me, Mr. Ryder. It's—how do you put it in the States? Ah, yes, a buzzword. You used a buzzword, Mr. Ryder."

"I don't follow you, Sergeant. What's buzzwordish about an everyday word like *observer?*"

The sergeant's face showed his disgust. He plainly thought Mr. Harry Ryder a liar. Well, he was—and devious, too. Mendacious, devious, anonymous, mysterious, this Amer—this San Franciscan. When would she get a chance to hurl her questions at him?

The sergeant gave up on Mr. Harry Ryder, turned to her.

"Mrs. Meirion, this morning your life was threatened. You came within a hair's breadth of being killed. Assassinated. This was a planned assassination attempt. Can you tell me who would want to kill you?"

"Before you answer, Mrs. Meirion, I'd like to ask the sergeant a question. Have you been able to identify the two men?"

"Their passports are Syrian, Mr. Ryder. They'll probably prove false. We haven't identified the men yet, but we think they're Palestinian. We're proceeding on that assumption for the time being."

"Palestinian? PLO?"

"The term PLO covers a multitude of sins and some virtues, Mr. Ryder. There are as many nooks and crannies in the PLO pantheon as there are in the Christian church. We have no idea if they're PLO, and we're not particularly concerned about it. We're more interested in knowing if they were terrorists of some kind, or were they simply thugs for hire, any kind of hire. Those things we do not yet know. But we will. Indeed we will."

Ryder nodded. "I'm sure you will. Thank you."

Both men looked at her. Center stage, girl. She said, "Sergeant, I've of course asked myself who would want to kill me. But even to ask it is somehow silly. I simply can't associate my existence, my peaceful life, with the violence of this morning."

She knew her voice was steady, her face calm, her hands

relaxed. She also knew that she, in the sergeant's words, was "holding out" on him. There were several episodes in her life that could be questioned, most notably a messenger mission she had carried out not long ago for Sir Alexander James. "You know your way around Yugoslavia, my dear." So Sir Alex. "You and Llewelyn made a lot of friends in that country. And you have every right to be seen wandering in and around the monastery of Sopaćani while doing research into the life and times of that ninety-six-year-old doge fellow. Dandolo. Enrico Dandolo. That's the one. After all, his granddaughter, Anna, was Queen of Serbia in the mid-1200s, and her body's buried right there in the monastery. I know that should interest you. And a Yugoslav Army base is only a few miles away from the monastery. That fact interests some of my younger friends. This felicitous merging of past and present has prompted them to ask me to approach you. They wonder if you'll be a courier for them. But before you answer, I must tell you, I'm told there's some danger in this assignment. In essence, it's quite simple. You're being asked to pick up some papers you'll find buried under a rock. Pick them up and bring them to me. But be sure no one catches you with the papers. That's where the danger could come—from being caught. However, if you agree to help them, my friends will see to it you're provided with a rather special suitcase. All in all, Melissa, I do not really expect you to have any trouble. Somebody else might. But not you. Not Mrs. Llewelyn Laurent Meirion, admirer of all things Yugoslavian."

And so she had gone to Yugoslavia, far up in the mountains. She had dutifully found the packet of papers under a rock on a deserted hillside, she had put them in her rucksack, returned to the inn, concealed the inch-thick packet in a trick suitcase and, in due time, had appeared in Sir Alex's Mayfair home. That was it. An episode fourteen months old; certainly no cause for an assassination attempt, and certainly nothing she cared to discuss with Sergeant Harry Dykes of Paddington Police Station.

He stood up, an unhappy policeman. Ryder also rose and faced him. Dykes's body posture bespoke his unhappiness;

his words confirmed it. "Mrs. Meirion, you disappoint me. The assassination attempt was not an idle one. You weren't being used for a practice run. You were the intended victim. Mrs. Meirion, in a moment Detective Chief Inspector Turner and Detective Sergeant O'Brien will be in to take your statement. And yours, too, Mr. Ryder. I hope, Mrs. Meirion, I very much hope that by the time they get here, you'll have thought of something in your life that—"

"Recent life, Sergeant." Harry Ryder smiled apologetically. "Please forgive my interrupting you. But I thought—it seemed . . . well, recent life."

"Yes, quite right, Mr. Ryder. Recent life, Mrs. Meirion. Has something different, something strange, something unusual happened in the last few months, and . . . yes, Mr. Ryder?"

"Ah, thank you, Sergeant. Mrs. Meirion, especially have you seen someone in the past few weeks? Someone unusual, someone you would never ordinarily expect to see in London? Maybe someone from a quite distant past? I don't know how to say it—"

Sergeant Dykes grunted. "You're doing very well, Mr. Ryder. Too well. But your story does check out. Yes, we've already looked into your life in California. The Orinda police confirm that you have a management consulting company there. But that's all they know about you. They can't explain why you would use the word *observer*. They could throw no light on your extraordinary awareness of life around you. Bodies flying in all directions, but you cool enough to spot a third man spotting you. Further, they didn't know anything about your martial arts training. Don't look so innocent, Mr. Ryder. I think you're the most innocent-looking man we've ever had sit in this room. Yes, martial arts. Mr. Butler, the motorman, described how you whirled that thug through the air. Martial arts, Mr. Ryder. And now questions to Mrs. Meirion that I should have put, better questions than I did put. Too many coincidences, Mr. Ryder. They may be as innocent as you look, but if they're not, we'll find this out, too."

"I'm sorry, Sergeant. Sorry I cause you all this uneasiness.

I'm almost afraid to add anything else, but, Sergeant, bear with me. What about Mrs. Meirion's safety? What are you going to do about that? Suppose she's attacked again—but next time there's no one around to lend a helping hand? I don't know London police practices, but it does seem to me you must assume some responsibility."

"Gentlemen, please, Sergeant Dykes, Mr. Ryder, please don't worry about me. One warning is enough. I'll be most cautious. I do not take this lightly. I'll be cautious, I promise you."

Sergeant Dykes nodded. "I hope you will, Mrs. Meirion. I hope you will. Now, if you don't mind waiting a bit longer, Chief Inspector Turner and Sergeant O'Brien will be here shortly to take your statements. And after that, I'm afraid you'll have to face the reporters. We'll pave the way for you. We'll tell them that at this time this looks like a robbery attempt, we know no more. That will satisfy them for the time being. I hope it's satisfactory with you. I'll see you after you give your statements and talk to the reporters."

That took another two hours. When they walked to the front entrance off Edgware Road, Sergeant Dykes was waiting for them. He pointed to a car at the end of the walkway. "Mrs. Meirion, Detective Sergeant Wilkes will join you in a moment and take you where you want to go, and he will be your chauffeur for a while." He glowered at the American. "You don't have to tell us about our responsibilities, Mr. Ryder. We haven't employed you yet as a management consultant. Sorry, that was uncalled for. You're concerned about Mrs. Meirion's safety. So are we. Let's let it go at that."

"Thank you for your understanding, Sergeant. I'll be heading out to Wimbledon. I have the ticket and might as well use it for the rest of the day, but I'll be at the hotel this evening if you need me."

He took her by the arm and walked down the steps to the unmarked police car. As soon as they were out of earshot of the sergeant, he said without looking at her, "The assassins might try again. You understand?"

"Quite. A three-man attack has rather unpleasant implications. Yes, I understand, and I'll be cautious. I'll stay close to Detective Sergeant Wilkes."

Harry Ryder nodded. (She was quite aware she'd just made another transition. From "the American" to "Mr. Harry Ryder" to plain "Harry Ryder." Well, why not? Fair was fair.) Opening the car door for her, he said, "You're going back to see Sir Alexander, aren't you?"

How extraordinary. He did seem to have a really remarkable ability to read her mind. She certainly couldn't reciprocate, not like that.

"Yes."

"Good. But be careful. I don't know about your man." He meant Sir Alex, apparently. "But I know about mine. Birdie Bingham looks like an aging claims clerk. A piece of futility. Don't be misled. He's neither. What he is is the most ruthless devil I've ever known. He may have told us the truth yesterday, but maybe he didn't. Birdie doles out truth like water in the Sahara."

He paused, looked down, then up. This was the first time he'd ever looked her straight in the eye. He said, "Look, I'm not God, no matter how much I may give the impression of wanting to play the role. I know you think I dislike you, perhaps even look down on you. I'm sorry. I don't. As I say, I'm not God. Ask Birdie to explain my reactions to you. He knows."

He paused to watch a thinnish man emerge from the station. Detective Sergeant Wilkes, presumably. "Also make him level with you. Tell him you won't move a muscle until you get the full story about the mysterious Peter Trubari. No, please, wait. Do this. You have a right to know. Those two old warlocks are being devious with us. Mrs. Meirion, believe me, to survive in their world you must learn to be as devious as they are. It's not a question of trust. Of course you trust your Sir Alexander James. Sometimes I even trust Birdie Bingham. But usually no farther than I can see him. And even then I tread warily."

Detective Sergeant Wilkes it was. He introduced himself,

then took the door handle from Harry Ryder. The latter said, "With your indulgence, Sergeant, may I have one more word with Mrs. Meirion? Thank you."

He took her by the arm, moved ten feet away from the car, whispered, "Please, Mrs. Meirion, please ask them. The attack this morning gives you a right to know everything. Ask them about this Trubari fellow. Ask them, too, if there's any connection between today's happenings and their asking us to go look for Trubari. I believe you think there is. I don't. There can't be. The timing's all wrong. . . . But I can be wrong, quite wrong. Ask all these things, please. You won't get the truth. But I think you'll get more than they're prepared to give you. The shock value alone should do that. The attack on your life, that'll shock even them—and believe me, that emotion, shock, is one I know they think they've put behind them, along with all other childish things. They'll be surprised at themselves.

"Ask them, please Mrs. Meirion?"

He helped her into the rear seat. Now she looked up into his eyes. The second time they'd locked eyes. This time she realized his eyes weren't gray at all. They were blue. As blue as her own. She said, "Yes. Yes. Yes, I'll do it. I'll make them stand and deliver."

She still hadn't asked Harry Ryder her four questions. But she would, oh yes, she would. If Sir Alexander James and Mr. Don Carlos Bingham are devious, what are you, Harry Ryder?

Was that a fifth question?

4

Detective Sergeant Wilkes took the key from her hand. "Sorry, ma'am, but let me do this."

Hitching his sport jacket so that a shoulder holster and pistol butt were quite visible, he unlocked her front door, gently pushed her to one side, swung the door open wide, reached in, flipped on the foyer light, and, motionless, crouched there until he had inspected every inch of visible space.

"All right, Mrs. Meirion. But stay behind me. Stay with me."

For the hundredth time that day, she wanted to protest, "Sergeant Wilkes, you don't have to take such excessive precautions." She had already apologized for making him wait until after nine in the evening outside Sir Alexander James's home. She'd told him to go on his way, but he'd steadily refused. She wanted to protest, tried to protest, heard herself say:

"Sergeant Wilkes, I didn't know our police carried weapons."

"Ma'am, times have changed. Some of us do sometimes. On cases like this."

Melissa Meirion, a case like this. Hold yourself together, Lissa; the man would be gone shortly. Hold yourself together, let him do his job. And he did. Room by room, living room, dining room, kitchen, study, basement, connecting garage, upstairs bedrooms, bathrooms. He knelt to peer under beds, he went through each closet, he looked behind chairs, under tables, he searched in and under the silver Porsche, even opening the boot. Detective Sergeant Wilkes was thorough—and quite relieved to find her home without lurking assassins or terrorists or visible explosives.

"Thank you again, Sergeant Wilkes. I appreciate all your help today. Please thank Sergeant Dykes and the others for me, too. And tell him I'm all right now. I won't need your help anymore, really I won't."

"I'll tell them, ma'am. Your light shows on your answering machine. Shall I wait?"

She had seen the light. She was in no hurry to hear the message. She knew who it was. Her intuitive sense was not entirely lacking. It'd be Harry Ryder. Well, he could wait. She was in no hurry to hear him, she only wanted to get rid of Sergeant Wilkes and have a moment's peace to herself. Lots of moments.

And finally, it—peace—was about to be achieved. But not before Sergeant Wilkes said, "Mrs. Meirion, do you know how to use a pistol?"

She knew how. Llew-Llaw had seen to that. As he had also seen to her training in elementary self-defense. "Lissa," he had said, "if it weren't for my work, these skills would not be important for you. I don't ever expect to drag you into a situation where you need to fire a gun or defend yourself against an attacker, but I'm not always—in fact, not usually—master of my own fate. You insist on sharing my travels or as many of them as possible, not only the historical travels but the other kind, too; so if we're going to be together in somewhat tense circumstances, we'll have to learn to function well together." Her reactions on the Bayswater platform this morning, her going with the direction of attack, not against it, were the results of those martial arts lessons taught her years ago by Llew-Llaw. Wouldn't Harry Ryder be astonished to know she knew exactly how she had fended off her thug? Or would he? She said:

"Yes, Sergeant Wilkes, I've had target practice training."

"Good. Do you have a pistol in the house? If not—oh, you do? Sergeant Dykes will be pleased to hear this. He knew you wouldn't let us protect you for long, ma'am. He said he can't protect you if you won't let yourself be protected. But he hoped you might be willing to try to protect yourself. I hope so, too."

And so, once she had dutifully displayed the pistol and set it on the desk by the telephone answering machine, she was alone. Alone with her thoughts and emotions. She was not in shock. She was not hysterical. That had been established fairly early during her visit with Sir Alex. She was not even, surprisingly, really very frightened. A little bit, but not very. Was her calm unnatural, perhaps a mask behind which lurked all kinds of shock and hysteria? Possibly. But she didn't think so. When Llew-Llaw had died after a one week's illness, at that time, as she sat by his bedside twenty-four hours a day, at that time fear had gone out of her. He died, and her life went with him. Probably the children should have counterbalanced this preternatural calm; perhaps they should have generated or regenerated the normal instincts for survival. Ralph and Tim were fine boys, fine young men; but in a way they were unfortunate. Children of lovers get short shrift. And Llew-Llaw and she had been lovers. Which thought somehow, strangely, brought up the subject of Harry Ryder. And she thought about him for maybe one second and stood up.

"Blazes! I'm not ready to think about any Harry Ryder. Or three assassins. Or three more possible assassins. Or Sergeant Dykes. Or Sergeant Wilkes. Or the why of my perfectly impossible situation. Or about this monstrous pistol."

And she stared down at the gun. Harry Ryder had a gun. She had a gun. The literature on hers informed her this was a Fabrique Nationale D'Armes de Guerre. There was no need for the Fabrique Nationale to identify the gun further. Not the Browning 9-millimeter High-Powered, this most famous of all famous pistols. Though smaller than the answering machine, it seemed to dwarf the lit-up telephone device.

"Oh, all right." And she picked up the receiver and listened, not to Harry Ryder—oh, you and your intuitive sense, you!—but to a strange babbling sound, a woman's shrill voice. One does not expect to pick up a telephone in London and have a torrent of sibilant Serbo-Croatian spluttering into one's ears. She really caught only the last sentence: "It won't take a minute." What wouldn't take a minute? She shook herself, braced herself, tuned her ear to hear and understand the national speech of Yugoslavia, her onetime home.

With the second go, the woman's words, though still shrill of tone, were quite lucid and normal. Or were they? What was that strange rasp that seemed to intrude on the sibilants?

"Mrs. Meirion, you don't know me. But I have a message for you. I can't explain on the telephone where I got it or who sent it. But I'll deliver it to you Saturday morning. Please be home tomorrow morning. I'll deliver the message then. It won't take a minute."

Lissa sat down and reversed the tape again, but not before

she observed the red light. It was still on. The machine held at least one more message. That one she had to be right about. That one would be Harry Ryder. But he would have to wait. First she had to rehear, place, and identify that strange rasping undercurrent in the unknown woman's voice. She listened, listened again, listened still again. And understood the message. The real message.

"Fear! Panic! Fear and panic! That woman's in a state of stark shivering panic. She could barely hold her voice together."

And the calm, the preternaturally calm Melissa Beaumont Meirion, Mrs. Llewelyn Laurent—Llew-Llaw—Meirion, bent her head to her arms resting on the desk and began to cry. To bawl, actually. The tears flooded out. Panic? Who was in a panic? She had controlled all emotion during the murder attempt. She had borne with Moslem thuggery, Harry Ryder's aloofness, Sergeant Dykes's unhappiness, Sir Alex's cheery Britain-will-muddle-through-keep-a-stiff-upper-lip routine, Sergeant Wilkes's unremitting caution and tension, the implications of the deadly Browning (now about to rust in the flood); she had absorbed all these passions and dismissed them as inconsequential. And now, the least significant event of the day, an unexpected request from a panic-stricken Serbo-Croatian woman—a Serbian woman, come to think of it; the accent was that of Beograd, not Zagreb—so now, a message from a stranger, and all her self-assurance vanished. Wouldn't Sergeant Wilkes be shook up to see her now—not to mention Sergeant Dykes and Sir Alex and Harry Ryder? Melissa Meirion, the woman with true British pluck.

Tissue paper sopped up the tears from face and desk and gun. A few shuddering deep breaths restored a reasonable self-possession and a partially reasoning mind. She found herself considering coincidences. Sergeant Dykes had said policemen don't like coincidences. Well, this Serbo-Croatian message was a highly unlikely coincidence. Not only did it interject another mystery into a day full of mysteries, it somehow seemed to justify her own musings about her Yugoslavia courier assignment. Her spy assignment. Not to mention Llew-Llaw's assignment in this or that Slavic country, Bulgaria, Czechoslovakia, Poland, and, of course, Yugoslavia. Sir Alex had pooh-poohed her courier job as a possible impetus toward assassination; but he had agreed instantly there was no telling, at that moment, what loose irons Llew-Llaw might have left heating in the furnace of Slavic intelligence. Sir Alex said he would put the wheels in motion, and he had promptly done so. He had made two phone calls. The messages were terse and not repeated. But there was no question about it. Out there somewhere, some younger associates of Sir Alex's were now exhuming and post-morteming Llewelyn Meirion's past. They should be told about this message. Now their research could have a direction, a focus. They wouldn't have to research all his assignments in the Slavic world, just those of or in Yugoslavia.

She reached for the phone to call Sir Alexander James, to alert him about this new development, about the Balkan connection. She reached, saw the red light, hesitated. Well, why not? It was only just past ten. Sir Alex could wait for a few minutes. So why not?

She switched on the answering machine, listened, nodded in approval at her own brilliance. This time it was indeed Harry Ryder. His message was brief:

"Mrs. Meirion, this is Harry Ryder. Would you please do me a favor? Would you call me after your visit with our two ancients and let me know what happened? I'll stay up until your call. My room is 525. The hotel number is 324-2727. Thank you, Mrs. Meirion."

Would she?

She would.

Harry Ryder answered at the first ring, said, "Thank you, Mrs. Meirion. Thank you, and I do hope you were able to snooker those two flimflam artists."

"Snooker? Flimflam artists?"

"Oh dear, oh dear, the English language. Let me see. How's this? Were you able to induce those born swindlers to say more than they would ordinarily say?"

30

"Really? Is that the meaning those words convey? Amazing. Well let me—yes, I'd say I did. Or they did, on their own. You were right. They were quite shaken up to hear about Bayswater Station, so they did tell me things I don't think they ever planned on revealing. Of course, they did keep insisting—I mean, they agreed with you. They can see no connection between today's events and—"

"Mrs. Meirion! Please, I know what you mean. The phone, Mrs. Meirion."

"Of course. Thank you. But they agree with you. There's no connection. And they did answer the questions you raised—and also some I had."

"Identity?"

"Yes, identity. And why you're important, why they asked' you to come. Yes, I think they gave answers to most of our questions."

"True answers?"

"I think so. The answers made sense—even if some of them are quite astonishing. And there's something new—to me, anyway. A new focus is starting to emerge. . . . Well, I can't say any more now, can I? Oh dear."

"There's plenty of time, Mrs. Meirion. Don't fret. But may I ask you another question? I'm only a few blocks from Porchester Terrace. I wonder, would it be convenient for me to come on over and go over all these matters with you—especially the new focus? Or if that's inconvenient, how about tomorrow morning? Perhaps you could join me here for breakfast? In either case, could you tell me about this focus before you pass your ideas on to our two ancients?"

By not asking her one certain question, Harry Ryder really only served to draw more attention to said question. He hadn't asked her if Birdie Bingham had explained Harry Ryder's frostiness toward her, his aloofness, his disapproval. Why hadn't he asked? Because he knew said explanation, if discussed, would only serve to set up a whole set of new tensions, the kind of tensions she hadn't felt in many, many years, not since she'd met Llew-Llaw and fallen in love with him at first sight, thereby removing once and for all the tensions accom-

31

panying male/female courtship rites. She'd been free of all that for almost fifteen years. But no more. Not after Birdie Bingham's analysis of Harry Ryder's attitude. Bingham had said:

"It's my fault. Not that it really is my fault, I couldn't have changed anything. We need you. We need Ryder. The man's a recusant, but useful, most useful for all that. I should have foreseen his reaction to you and at least tried to figure out some way of bucking you both up. But I didn't, and here we are. The simple fact is, Mrs. Meirion, only last year Harry Ryder handled a dangerous mission for us in the Orient. His partner on that mission was a woman. A quite remarkable woman. Her name was Terry Jefferson, and she and Harry loved each other, and she was killed. I don't think Harry's ever recovered from that blow. After all, he was over fifty years of age then, and to love a great lady, a great and much younger lady, and to be loved by her in turn, well, how resilient can you expect a fifty-two-year-old man to be? How much can you expect him to welcome working once again with another great lady and be reminded every day of his previous assignment with Terry Jefferson? I see now I should have realized he'd see the pattern repeating. Not the falling in love, I don't mean that, but the killing. He involved Terry Jefferson and caused her death. He wouldn't relish involving you and causing your death. Oh no, oh no."

Devious, devious, wicked old man. "Not the falling in love." Oh no, indeed. Harry Ryder was right. Sir Alex and Birdie Bingham were warlocks. And here she was, once again back to questions of maleness/femaleness, back to emotions she'd put out of mind lo these several years and never expected to face again. And there he was, Harry Ryder, asking to come to her home at—almost ten-twenty in the evening. The last man to be alone in her home after ten o'clock was Llew-Llaw. How ironic. Llew-Llaw had been fifty-three at that time, Harry Ryder was fifty-three at this time. How ironic, or how—how what? How prophetic?

"Breakfast will be fine, Mr. Ryder. And I won't talk to the

32

ancient warlocks until after we've compared notes. Is eight o'clock agreeable?"

"Most."

"Good. I'll go over everything they said, Mr. Ryder; but there's one thing they didn't say, and it puzzles me. They didn't explain why you consented to catch the first plane out of San Francisco and come do their bidding. Why should you knuckle under like that?"

"Why? Simple, Mrs. Meirion. Very simple. My very own warlock blackmailed me. I'll explain tomorrow."

She put the phone down, went to the dictionary, found the word Bingham had used. "Recusant. One who refuses to comply with some regulation or to conform to some general practice or opinion; a dissenter or dissentient."

5

She dressed with a minimum of fuss. In fact, she made a point of not lingering over her clothes. A dress? A skirt? A blouse? Why not the first thing to hand—a pair of pants, a beige pair, with an absolutely plain white shirt and a red cashmere sweater? Grocery-shopping clothes really, that's all she needed for a breakfast with Harry Ryder.

And she started to trip out the front door and stopped. There he was, Harry Ryder himself, waiting for her on the footpath. He was dressed as casually as she—gray slacks, blue cashmere sweater. He shrugged, flipped his palms upward, said:

"Hope you don't mind. I didn't relish the thought of your walking these three blocks alone."

"How did you know Sergeant Wilkes wouldn't be here to escort me?"

"Well . . . well . . . well. Yesterday I decided not to go to Wimbledon after all. Thought it best—well, I stayed around

33

here off and on and found Wilkes had gone and there was no relief man, so I—well, that's—"

"That's very thoughtful of you, and I appreciate it, and . . . Oh—oh—Did you—you didn't stay out here all night, did you?"

He shook his head. "I thought of it, but I was not up to it. I needed sleep. Sorry."

And she couldn't help laughing, and in a moment he joined in, said, "If you had any school books, I could offer to carry them for you."

"And I'd let you."

Was that any kind of commitment? Of course not. They were just jesting, though what there was to jest about, well, really . . .

Once again he seemed to read her mind, spoke to her thought. "No, Mrs. Meirion, I don't feel that way. The less there is to laugh about, the more important it is to be able to laugh." He grimaced. "That does sound terribly stuffy, doesn't it? But—but—"

"No buts, Mr. Ryder, I quite agree. And I also agree with your underlying premise, which I think I've begun to understand."

"And that is?"

"And that is, anytime one has to try to cope with our two flimflam artists, there's often mighty little to laugh about."

They crossed the street. He did not take her arm, though she could see he considered doing so. She understood and approved. Anonymous, aloof, reserved he was; but not without tact.

"What did you learn from them yesterday?"

"Let's save that for breakfast. First, my question. What did you mean, Mr. Bingham blackmailed you into coming here? What hold does he have over you?"

"You mean, have I sinned, and does Birdie know the dreadful secret? No, nothing like that. It's that book I've written."

"Book? People who write books do the blackmailing, not the readers."

34

"Well, yes, perhaps. But I didn't entirely level with Sergeant Dykes yesterday. It's true my publisher hasn't settled on a final title. But the book did have a working title."

"Which is?"

"Which is *It's About Time Someone Said Something Nice About the CIA*. I'm sure Birdie told you I'm now retired from the spook business, been retired for several years, have recently been a business consultant. I'm sure he also told you about my do in the Philippines last year."

"He did. Or some of it. Including your personal loss."

That was as close as she was prepared to come to mentioning Terry Jefferson's name or her fate. And apparently that was close enough for him, too. (Now that she knew about Terry Jefferson, he suddenly, instantly seemed no longer frosty towards her. Interesting.) He said, "Well, when I got back to San Francisco, I found consulting no longer aroused my passions. I found I wanted to write about my old Company. That's what we used to call the Agency. The Company. With a capital C. The one and only Company. Well, I've read all the books written about my Company, but none of them seemed terribly relevant to my experience. Maybe that's because I served in the Orient, except for one brief experience on the Continent and here in London. So I set about writing my own book, and when the first draft was finished, I submitted it to Birdie Bingham. We have to do that, you know. The CIA has the right to blue-pencil any and all parts of a book written by an ex-employee. If my book had gone through normal channels, it'd probably have been slashed to bits. A lot of things I said in particular are quite ungenerous, but taken as a whole, taken in general, the book is laudatory. The censor hacks would never have understood that balance. So I went way over their heads to my old boss. And I mean way over. Birdie is probably one of the four or five most important men in the agency—so far up and out of sight, most of the employees don't even know what he does. What most of the uninformed know about him is that he is hung up on the question of moles. Birdie makes quite a fuss about moles, and everybody shrugs and says, well, it's just that dotty old fogey, and of course they have no sense at all of how deadly serious my old boss is about the subject of moles. He's already unburied—and buried—two or three already. Anyway, I went to him and he understood—and he let the book go to my publisher without a single excision. Not one."

"Oh. Oh, I see." Somehow it was important Harry Ryder should realize she didn't have to be taken through the ABC's. "Yes, I do see. Mr. Bingham simply told you he'd censor your book to bits if you didn't hop over to London and help him out."

"Exactly."

The Terrace Hotel, complete with Georgian porticoes and stained glass windows above bay windows, was now in sight. And standing on its front steps and looking in their direction— looking reproachfully in their direction, how else?—was Sergeant Dykes.

"Oh dear." So she to Harry Ryder. "He's got that I-want-you-down-at-headquarters-come-along look. Oh dear."

Harry Ryder nodded. "You can also add 'right now!' "

And they were both right—or partially right. It wasn't headquarters at Paddington Station, it was the Yard. Scotland Yard! Sergeant Dykes said:

"Glad I caught you. Something's come up, and I wonder if you can come down to the Yard with me now. My car's around the corner."

Harry Ryder deferred to her. She said, "But we haven't had breakfast yet, Sergeant. We'll make it quick. Continental breakfasts, is that agreeable?"

It wasn't, but Sergeant Dykes couldn't do much about it short of arresting them. After gnashing his teeth—she'd never seen anyone gnash teeth before, but here it was, a fact, a gnash—he said, "I'll be waiting in the car."

The Terrace Hotel dining room looked like—was—a coffee shop. Harry Ryder sensed her implied question, answered it: "I mentioned how I had one European assignment. That was early in my career. Birdie Bingham was my control. He sent

36

me here. I knew nothing about Europe. Then and always I was a predestined old Asia hand. That's why he requisitioned me. I was ignorant of Europe. But Europe was also ignorant of me. My mission began here. In this hotel. I was to meet a German tourist in this room. Over a breakfast table. This table, in fact. He was to tell me where to go next. He did, and I was shunted from city to city, finally ending up in Leipzig before flying home from Frankfurt. Since then, on my infrequent trips to London I've always stayed here. The people are nice, so are the rooms. It's only one block from Hyde Park and one block from Queensway, which I find a charming international street."

Should she tell him she knew about his visit to Frankfurt? In explaining why he had summoned Harry Ryder to London, Don Carlos Bingham had said in his customary, almost inaudible whisper, "I wanted Harry Ryder, Mrs. Meirion, because he is an incredibly resourceful man. Why, once in Frankfurt, five Communist agents tried to kill him late at night outside a restaurant. He killed all five. And collected their pistols before disappearing into the darkness. Harry Ryder is a great one for collecting pistols." As she had already witnessed.

Should she tell him she knew about Frankfurt? She should not. Harry Ryder would not like her knowing about his murderous proclivities.

She said, "German tourists then, German tourists now. Eight out of ten people in here today are Germans."

He nodded. "Nothing's changed. And the Germans themselves haven't changed."

She said—curious how she was able to fill out his cryptic comments—she said, "Surely the Churchillian dictum no longer holds?"

"You mean the bit about the Hun at your feet or at your throat? It no longer holds? Ask the Soviets what they think about the Huns today."

"Ouch."

He looked at his watch, looked at her, raised his eyebrows.

37

She obliged, "All right. The sergeant waits. So what I learned from Sir Alexander James. And from Mr. Bingham. And also about my new sense of focus coming from a mysterious phone call I got last night."

"All of which, I hope, explains what this is all about."

"Let me give you the highlights. Sergeant-free, we'll go over it again later on, and then I'll try to give you the inflections, nuances, gestures, and general paraphernalia."

"Good enough. Fire away."

"I suppose I should begin with a Yugoslavian named Pantić. Žarko Pantić. Does the name mean anything to you? No? Well, he's the key to all this. Or perhaps Ethan Pickering is."

"Ethan Pickering! What do you mean, Ethan Pickering? He's dead. He committed suicide in Chesapeake Bay five or six years ago."

"Apparently committed suicide. What he actually committed was a murder. He's quite alive. He faked a suicide so he could murder a man named Tibor Szentes. A Hungarian diplomat. He murdered Szentes, dumped him in Chesapeake Bay, pushed his own sailboat with personal papers out into the Bay, and disappeared. In due time, Szentes's decomposed body surfaced, and because of the boat and personal papers, he was identified as Ethan Pickering. So Ethan Pickering, suicide, was officially dead. However, he rose from the dead in Yugoslavia as Peter Trubari, thanks to the assistance of his good friend, Žarko Pantić, who happens to be number-one or -two man in the Kontra Obaveštajna Služba, Yugoslavia's military counterintelligence service.

"And now Mr. or Colonel or General Pantić—he was a colonel the only time I met him a few years ago—and now Pantić is apparently responsible for Ethan Pickering's disappearance in Vienna. And Vienna, by the way, is another reason Mr. Bingham wanted you to come over and help out. He can't turn to the CIA station there. The man in charge in Vienna, a chap named Barnwell, knew Ethan Pickering very well. And the last thing Mr. Bingham can contemplate is for a CIA station chief to find out Ethan Pickering did not drown in the Chesapeake Bay."

"Barnwell—Barnwell. I don't know any Barnwell. No reason I should. And anyway, it's probably an assumed name. Standard practice. It confuses everyone except the Russians. They'll know Mr. Barnwell's dossier from teething time."

"Our warlocks, do they have any idea why Pantić has made this move?"

"None whatever. Until now, Pantić has been the great and good friend of the British secret service and the CIA. Of Sir Alexander James personally, and Mr. Don Carlos Bingham personally, and of course of Ethan Pickering Trubari, his wartime partisan buddy." And the only man she'd ever wanted to go to bed with besides Llew-Llaw. But she didn't say that. Wanting was not doing.

"In short, what's up, Doc? Sorry. Not a time for a silly joke." Harry Ryder brooded a moment. "You've thrown me for a loop. Ethan Pickering and I were fairly close. Mostly because of our similar war backgrounds, not because of any personal interests. He was an electronics whiz kid, talked a different language from me, very big with the women, too. Lots of my colleagues had a similar flair. I never fitted in somehow. But we did have something very much in common. In the war, he was a partisan in Yugoslavia. I was a guerrilla in the Philippines. Different names, same job—though his was a lot more dramatic a fling than mine. I counted Jap ships. He killed Germans, lots of 'em. But close as we were, I was obviously not close enough for him to tell me about a faked suicide-murder caper.

"Do you know, did they explain what this is all about? Why Ethan killed that Hungarian? And above all, why Birdie Bingham let him get away with it? This story I've got to hear. For Birdie to do this—well, all I can say is, my old mole-hunting pillar of society must be up to his ears in alligators on this one."

"Oh, sorry. Another silly American joke. Forgive me."

She couldn't help smiling. "Not necessary. I think I understand. And I also think I was right in thinking Mr. Bingham didn't seem to hold anything back. He seemed to lay it all out for me. For us."

"Murder will out. Sorry, another silly joke. Blame Chaucer for this one. What's gotten into me? Look, we'll have to make Sergeant Dykes wait. This is no time for highlights. We're not going to any Scotland Yard until I know everything you learned yesterday. Believe me, we may very well need a united front once we get there."

"All right. Let's see, where do I begin—oh dear! What shall I do about that phone call from the Yugoslavian woman? She asked me to be home at noon today. Oh dear, what shall I do? How can I be certain to be back from Scotland Yard? Oh dear. Well, let me start with her phone call. First things first. First, everything I know, then Scotland Yard. Yes, that's best."

6

But Sergeant Dykes did not take them to Scotland Yard. Its glass structure was in sight down Victoria Street when he abruptly turned right onto Horseferry Road.

Harry Ryder looked at her in surprise, but for a moment she was as nonplussed as he. But only for a moment. She leaned forward, said to the sergeant, "Of course. The mortuary. Is that it, Sergeant?" She pointed for Harry's benefit. "That brick building up there where the road jogs left. Is that it, Sergeant?"

Since it obviously was their destination, the sergeant contented himself with a grunt. He definitely was not in a chatty mood, said nothing even when they drove into a parking lot. There was a discreet white sign near the entrance. She nodded to it. Harry Ryder read the message aloud: " 'Westminster Coroner's Court and Mortuary.' Court?"

"Yes. Our coroners are separate from the police. Coroner's courts are perhaps our oldest courts of law. I don't know exactly, but I think they were established in the tenth or eleventh century. They were originally a check on a sheriff's high-handed ways. How do the police feel about coroner's courts today, Sergeant?"

She couldn't imagine what prompted her to bait the unhappy giant. That was stupid of her. But stupid or not, she knew she'd do it again. The sergeant deserved a little baiting. Yes, and perhaps more than a little.

"Are we here, Sergeant, to see those men from yesterday? Or do you have a new corpse for us?"

Sergeant Dykes stiffened in the front seat, then slowly relaxed, slowly opened the car door, said, "Follow me, please."

She looked at Harry Ryder. He looked at her. He shrugged. She shrugged. They got out of the car, followed the sergeant through a small side door, down a hall, into and through a waiting room. Or what seemed to be a waiting room, because there was someone waiting there, a short, dumpy, frowsy sixty-year-old fellow who was wearing a speckled green suit with a flaming red vest. He looked like a racetrack tout. The three of them got a few steps beyond him, when he suddenly sprang to his feet, called out:

"Mrs. Meirion!"

His words were heavily accented. The accent was . . . was . . . not German, not French, not Spanish, not Italian. It was Slavic. She turned, inspected him, his amazing clothes, his rotund belly, his jowly, anxious face, the bald head. She knew she should recognize him, looked away, looked back, did recognize him. She'd met him once some six or eight years ago. She'd been walking with Llew-Llaw down Belgrade's Bulevar Revolucije near the Savezno Narodna Skupština, the Federal Parliament building. Then he'd been nowhere near so gross; chubby, yes, but trim, as befitted a colonel in the Yugoslav army. For this was he, the very Colonel Pantić she'd just described to Harry Ryder. Only a much-changed Colonel Pantić. He looked now almost as if he were about to ask her for a handout to tide him over rough times. How depressing. Should she admit she recognized him? Why not?

"Colonel Pantić."

He smiled, chortled, shrugged. "No longer a colonel, Mrs.

41

Meirion. Just a civilian. Just plain Mr. Pantić, just a humble trade attaché with the Embassy." Suddenly his face became grave, somber, his tone sepulchral. "Are you here, too, on this tragic matter?"

"Pardon me?"

She was quite aware of Sergeant Dykes's intense interest, Harry Ryder's total disinterest. He seemed barely to have glanced at the fat little man. She was also aware that Mr. Pantić's buffoonish face was quite belied by two sharp, cold, calculating, probing eyes. The Yugoslav spread his hands.

"Tadić? Anna Tadić? Was she a friend of yours?"

Did she look as puzzled as she felt? She hoped so. Whatever was going on here, it seemed only elementarily prudent to display ignorance. And she felt sure she had done just that. She hazarded speech:

"Tadić—I'm sorry, I don't know an Anna Tadić."

She could feel a sudden relaxation in the room. It was as if all three men had let themselves deflate. Pantić shrugged.

"Miss Tadić was an employee in our Embassy. Been there since we moved to Kensington Road. Kensington Gore, actually. Ha, ha. Gore. Always makes me think of our gore. Our mountains. *Gore* means mountains in Serbo-Croatian, ha ha." Mr. Pantić was making a show of himself as a clown, a low-class idiot of a clown. But those unfortunate eyes could not harmonize with the buffoonery. They remained cold, calculating, watchful. "Gore. Well, Kensington Gore is as dangerous as our mountains. Miss Tadić was crossing it yesterday afternoon to go into Hyde Park, and she was run down by a hit-and-run driver and killed."

It seemed to dawn on him that death was not exactly a subject for mirth. Instantly his mobile face rearranged itself into a new caricature, this one the classic mask of tragedy. His shoulders also drooped, and he seemed about to crumble. "She was a wonderful girl, worked with me in the economic section, and I came over to—well, the proper . . . oh, it's so sad, and the police tell me we cannot have her—her—her body. Not yet. There must be an inquest and an autopsy.

42

Autopsy? The police, Mrs. Meirion"—and he pointed an accusatory finger at Sergeant Dykes—"the police tell me this is the English law. For a hit-and-run accident? I do not understand. By authority of my ambassador, I have an ambulance waiting outside. Well, it will wait. I will wait."

The whole charade was just that, a charade. At school she had been very good at charades. She could do her bit.

"Mr. Pantić, I'm so sorry to hear this. I'm sure everything will turn out all right." What in the world did she mean by that? "But Sergeant Dykes is equally firm with me. With us. This is Mr. Ryder. We were involved in an accident yesterday, and there were two deaths. I know how you feel, Mr. Pantić. The English law must be adhered to."

For a moment, Mr. Pantić's face betrayed a genuine emotion—pure bewilderment. She didn't linger to relish his befuddlement. She swept ahead of the sergeant and headed for the door he had indicated as their destination. It opened into a short corridor. The corridor led to an office. A policeman was on the alert in front of the office. She stopped, leaned against the corridor wall, looked up to see a wry expression on Sergeant Dykes's face, said to him:

"Anna Tadić. Is that who we're to see? And that dreadful man back there—did you plan that confrontation, too? Why are we here, what is this all about?"

Did the quaver in her voice convey a proper sense of indignation? She hoped so, though what really made her words loop and falter was the sudden memory of last night's message on the answering machine. The Serbo-Croatian message from an unknown woman. Or was she now quite known? Was she Anna Tadić, now a corpse in Westminster Coroner's Court and Mortuary? Was there no longer any need to get back home by noon?

Oh yes, her voice quavered all right, and maybe said quaver got to Sergeant Dykes just a little bit. He raised a hand as if to ward off her charge, perhaps even as if to apologize. He said:

"Mrs. Meirion, bear with us. We want you to look at Anna

43

Tadić's body. We have a reason—and what that reason is will be clear as soon as we finish this nasty job and go over to the Yard. There, Commander Malmquist will explain everything. Please bear with us, Mrs. Meirion. And you, too, Mr. Ryder. Though I don't think you are involved in this affair, are you? Do you know a Miss Anna Tadić? No? All right, please follow me once again. This way."

The nasty job didn't take long. What was left of Anna Tadić was not good to look at. Even if Lissa had known her, she would have been hard put to identify that battered face. "I've never seen her before, Sergeant. Sorry, I can't help you." He nodded, turned to go. Harry Ryder did not stir. His gaze was fixed on the corpse. Without looking up he said, "What happened, Sergeant? That—that is not your everyday hit-and-run accident, not that."

Sergeant Dykes stopped in his tracks, turned, said, "So I get it once again. Observer. Martial arts master. Expert interrogator. And now an authority on hit-and-run accidents. Do you still say you're just a business consultant turned writer? Is that still it, Mr. Ryder?"

The two men locked eyes. Harry Ryder neutral, Sergeant Dykes hostile; Harry Ryder silent, Sergeant Dykes suddenly loquacious:

"Yes, yes, you're right. It was a messy affair. Miss Tadić was struck at a high rate of speed, carried fifty or sixty feet, run over once, then the car—an estate car, ah, a station wagon, Mr. Ryder, a station wagon. The car backed up over Miss Tadić's body, a man jumped out, grabbed her purse, the car ran over her body a third time, the purse-snatcher jumped into the car, and away they went. Several coworkers from the Embassy got the license number, but it wasn't hard to find the car. It was parked in front of the Lavender Hill Police Station. A rented car. The people who rented it had Syrian passports and claimed to be staying at the Churchill. They weren't.

"Yes, Mr. Ryder, this was not your everyday hit and run."

Now Harry Ryder looked at her. His face, his eyes were

expressionless. But she could read his mind. It was full of expressions, it was thinking, "Your recorded phone message last night; and now a dead Yugoslav lady today. What a shame we don't have a chance to talk with your Sir Alex and my Don Carlos before we see Commander Malmquist at Scotland Yard."

That was what he had to be thinking. And, like her, he was also wondering why she and he had to meet a Commander Malmquist—and just what might a Commander Malmquist be?

7

The sign on the sixth floor door of New Scotland Yard was not in the least illuminative. It said, MAURICE MALMQUIST, COMMANDER. Commander of what?

"Commander of what, Sergeant?" Lissa asked.

But Dykes had reverted to his caveman mode. He grunted, knocked on the door, opened it, stepped inside, and waved Harry Ryder and herself in. Before focusing on the man behind the desk, she glanced around the office. It gave no clue as to purpose. It could have been the office of a senior business executive or banker or diplomat. The furnishings were comfortable, the floor carpeted, the walls paneled, the bookshelves book-laden, the paintings French Impressionist originals.

Commander Malmquist was sitting at his desk as they entered. He stood up, looked them over. He was tall, regular-featured, white-haired; his clothes were impeccably tailored, the dress of an established establishment civil servant.

"My name is Malmquist." He pointed to a swarthy man standing against a bookshelf. "This is Inspector Budim Perpar. He's our expert on Balkan affairs. Please be seated."

Balkan affairs. Of course. Special Branch. Scotland Yard's quite hush-hush, reclusive, and efficient contribution to that world where secrets and secret agents flourish. Commander, indeed. Mr. Commander Malmquist was as close to being in command of all and sundry as any civil servant could ever hope to be. She glanced at Harry Ryder. Did he understand where they were? If he did, he seemed unimpressed. Special Branch, anonymous spy service, meet Harry Ryder, anonymous ex-spy.

The chairs were leather, the kind one associates with private clubs. Well, Special Branch, New Scotland Yard, was about as private a club as one could find in London or anywhere in the world.

Commander Malmquist's face was kindly, his manner benign. He sat down, glanced at the electronic clock on his credenza—it read nine fifty-two—said, "Mrs. Meirion, Mr. Ryder, I know you're curious why we asked you to see the body of Anna Tadić, why we asked you to come here. I'll explain that in a minute. But first about Miss Tadić. The coroner's office phoned to say you could not identify the body. Is that correct, Mrs. Meirion?"

"Yes, Commander. I've never known an Anna Tadić. And I could not identify that body as Anna Tadić or as anyone else. She was unknown to me by any name."

"Mr. Ryder?"

"Unknown to me, also."

The commander pyramided his fingers, ruminated. "Very well. This complicates matters, but before we come back to Anna Tadić, I think it's time to refer to yesterday's events at Bayswater Station. You were attacked by two thugs, Mrs. Meirion. With Mr. Ryder's fortuitous help, you managed to dispose of them. Or was it fortuitous? Was his aid actually planned? Had you two arranged to be there to kill those two thugs?"

The commander's words were like a slap in the face. They were outrageous, false, defamatory, insulting, and—and stupid. But she didn't say so. She kept her voice calm. "Commander, yesterday Mr. Ryder and I were traveling to Putney together. We'd met the day before, and we'd agreed to meet at the station at ten-thirty, ride the underground together to Putney, and have a cup of coffee there to discuss a mutual interest. That was the extent of our planning. We were not meeting to exterminate two rather unpleasant people."

The commander sighed. "Yes. Well. Rather. Well, there'll be a coroner's inquest, of course, but that should be the extent of it. Of the legality, I mean. Justifiable defense, and that's the size of it. However, that leaves the main consideration: What do we make of all this? What indeed?"

"I'm sorry I can't help you, Commander. I—and I'm sure I speak for Mr. Ryder—we were hoping the police could throw some light on yesterday's events."

The commander looked sorrowful. Regretful. "Mrs. Meirion, we—Sergeant Dykes, Sergeant Wilkes, and now Inspector Perpar and myself—we have been and will continue to be quite frank with you. We want you to understand exactly what you're up against. We want you to know everything we know. We do want to see that you stay alive. But you—well, we've asked you, Mrs. Meirion, if you knew anything about the attack on you at Bayswater Station. We have asked you, Mr. Ryder, if you would tell us something about yourself, something about your display of skill at martial arts, your uncanny coolness amidst all that excitement, your use of the words like *observer*, your gift for interrogation.

"We've asked all this, and what have we gotten? Nothing. Not one gesture of cooperation. And yet what happens? Mrs. Meirion, the minute you left Paddington Police Station, you went to see Sir Alexander James and waited until he came in about five. You stayed with him unitl nine in the evening. Now, Mrs. Meirion, please. I know Sir Alexander. I've worked with him off and on over the years. Why should you find it necessary to spend so many hours with one of the most distinguished members of our intelligence establishment? A man you and your husband once reported to. Yes, we know about your husband's work. Why, Mrs. Meirion? Why did you go to Sir Alex?

"And you, Mr. Ryder. We asked you to tell us something

about yourself. You said you've been a business consultant and are now a writer. You would not give Sergeant Dykes the name of the book you're about to publish. No, please. I know that's not quite correct. You said the publisher hadn't settled on a title. You, however, could have supplied its working title. It is"—and the Commander picked up a note pad—"the working title is *It's About Time Someone Said Something Nice About the CIA*. The CIA, Mr. Ryder, for which you worked for over twenty years. Mr. Ryder, Mr. Ryder. You have been less than candid with us. Fortunately our friends at the FBI have been fully candid in giving us an outline of your career and in securing the name of your book from your publisher. Incidentally, we're told your publisher has just about given up in his search for a different title. He now feels your working title may be just, ah, crazy enough to, ah, ring the bell.

"So. Mrs. Meirion? Mr. Ryder?"

She felt her face flush. "I'm sorry, Mr. Malmquist. I was not trying to conceal anything from you. I had nothing to conceal. I didn't know on Friday morning—I don't know now, on Saturday morning—what this is all about. I can't imagine why anyone would want to kill me. Especially Moslems. It makes no sense. But when Mr. Ryder asked me—you were there, too, Sergeant Dykes—but when he asked me to review the recent past, well, I thought of my late husband's past. He—well . . . you say you know about my husband's work. Then you know he wasn't just a professor of history. He helped our government by performing various assignments in various Slavic countries. My husband's father was in the foreign service in Yugoslavia before the war. Llewelyn grew up there, and during the war he worked under General Sir Fitzroy McLean in Yugoslavia and actually, as I understand it, went out on missions with the partisans. One of the partisans was that man we just saw at the mortuary, that Mr. Pantić. They worked together during the war, and afterward, when Mr.— or Colonel—Pantić, as he was once introduced to me—anyway, afterward at different times they worked together, my husband representing our government and Colonel Pantić representing the KOS."

"The Kontra Obaveštajna Služba. Military counterintelligence."

She turned to look at the swarthy Balkan expert. "Yes, Inspector Perpar. Military counterintelligence. And my husband also did similar work in other Slavic countries. My husband could speak Polish, Czech, and Serbo-Croatian like a native, and he was fluent in Bulgarian and Russian. I mean Great Russian, not Ukrainian or other dialects. So naturally, when Mr. Ryder asked about the past, I thought of my husband. I went to Sir Alexander to ask him if possibly something in my husband's past had somehow been resurrected and transformed into a need to kill me.

"I know this wasn't too logical, but it was at least something. So I went to him and put my problem to him, and I'm going back this afternoon to see what he has learned. And that's the story of why I went to see Sir Alexander James."

Commander Malmquist looked at Inspector Perpar, said, "Inspector?" The inspector looked like a Moslem himself. Possibly he was. A Bosnian Moslem. He flexed his stubby fingers, said, "Mrs. Meirion, the commander invited me here because your late husband and I worked together several times. Yes, right here in London. Do you understand?"

Understand? She could hear Llew-Llaw now: "Darling, our country's intelligence effort in Yugoslavia has three major foci: First, how can we help keep Yugoslavia stable after Tito dies? Second, can the country face up to a Russian invasion? Third, how successful are the various splinter groups in their efforts to break up the country, especially the Serbian nationalists, as well as Croatian and Montenegrin and Kosovan-Albanian nationalists, not to mention the Greeks in Southern Yugoslavia and the Bulgarian and Hungarian immigrants? To keep tabs on the Russian threat and on life after Tito, I work in Yugoslavia. To keep tabs on the splinter-group nationalists, I work here in London. Our city today is, as it always has been, the home-away-from-home of revolutionaries from every country in the world. After all, we nourished Stalin here in his youth. And we haven't changed one iota over the decades. London, the City of Revolution and Terrorism."

"Yes, Inspector Perpar, I understand."

"Well, your husband and I were a team monitoring the local Yugoslav dissident cells. These cells are amoebic in nature. Forming, splitting up, oozing back and forth between here and the States and East Germany and France and Italy and Austria and Libya and Syria and God knows where. And now, with the death of President Tito only two months ago, the situation in Yugoslavia—and among these splinter groups— is very dicey. We can never forget what happened in World War II, can we, Mrs. Meirion?" He looked at the commander. "In that war, sir, the Germans killed five hundred thousand Yugoslavians. A terrible slaughter, agreed. But the Croatians killed over eight hundred thousand Serbians. And the Serbians and Bosnians and Montenegrins killed Croatians and each other to the tune of another three or four hundred thousand Yugoslavs. They're all South Slavs—Yugo-slavs—but they've been killing each other for hundreds of years. Nothing's changed, and right now it's anyone's guess as to what will happen. With Tito gone, unity may be gone. Certainly the drive for Serbia to rule the country is as strong as ever. The drive for everyone else to pull away from Serbia is perhaps stronger than ever."

"True enough, Inspector. True enough and perhaps to be expected. Especially the hate between Serbia and Croatia. But why Moslems? Why Syrians trying to kill me? How do they and I fit into these ancient Slavic hatreds?"

"That could depend on your late husband, Mrs. Meirion. We'll be most interested to hear what Sir Alexander turns up, if anything. I know two years have gone by since his death, but, well, some things need time for fruition. Particularly in politics. Do you have any feel about this?"

"I'm sorry, I don't, Inspector. I just don't." Should she tell them about the phone call from the panic-stricken woman? From Anna Tadić, undoubtedly? Who else could it be? She looked at Harry Ryder. At breakfast he had said, "Mrs. Meirion, whatever happens this morning with the police, I'd suggest you not mention this phone call, not until you've had a chance to talk to Sir Alexander and find out if his people

50

have turned up any loose ends left by your husband. Let him counsel you how much to tell the police." Did that recommendation have any merit now in the light of Anna Tadić's death? Did it? She said:

"I was aware of most of my husband's activities, but of course I don't know everything he did. I accompanied him on many of his trips. But not all. Especially not into Bulgaria. Llewelyn was very, very cautious about Bulgaria."

Inspector Perpar nodded. "Everyone is. Even the Soviets."

He looked at Commander Malmquist, retreated to his standing position near the bookshelf. The commander looked at Harry Ryder, said:

"Well, Mr. Ryder, we now come to you." He picked up his notebook. "This is from our friends at the FBI, and I quote: 'Mr. Harry Ryder has a reputation in the trade of being a one-man death machine. No one knows for sure how many people he has killed. Estimates range from ten to twenty. All killings were in the line of duty and with two exceptions were committed in foreign countries. The U.S. exception took place in San Francisco and involved two foreign assassins Mr. Ryder killed before they killed him. Since that was a routine secret war operation, no indictment or prosecution occurred. As to the foreign murders, no one has ever asked the foreign countries how they might feel about Mr. Ryder if they were to find out he was the provider of the mysterious corpses on their sidewalks. At one time, in one episode, there were five such enemy corpses. The host country, an ally of ours, has never ceased its efforts to find out who was responsible for killing our mutual enemy so messily. Most of this took place during Mr. Ryder's years of service with the CIA. After his retirement, when he handled a Far Eastern problem for the State Department, he was up to his old practices, accounting for three more murders, or five, including the two in San Francisco, no one except Mr. Ryder being sure of the exact number. We have no knowledge that Mr. Ryder is at present on any assignment, justifiable or otherwise, in London or Europe. We have checked all U.S. intelligence services to ascertain this fact.' "

51

Commander Malmquist beamed benignly on the American. "Ten deaths. Twenty deaths. And now one or one and a half more to your list. What are we ever to do with you? Well, how is this for a suggestion? We can ask you to tell the truth. Yes, what is the truth, Mr. Ryder?"

Harry Ryder looked at Sergeant Harry Dykes, at Inspector Budim Perpar, at Commander Maurice Malmquist. His facial muscles and jaw were relaxed, his eyes lackluster. Portrait of a dull-witted man. What that fellow Pantić had tried to emulate at the mortuary. He spoke without expression, slowly. "Gentlemen, I told Sergeant Dykes the truth yesterday. There's no need to rehash that.

"As to my work in the CIA and my free-lance assignment in the Far East, no one asked me about them. I saw no pertinence yesterday. I see none today.

"If you want more details about my past, I'll be happy to supply them, consonant with my responsibilities as an ex-employee of the Central Intelligence Agency. I am now and will continue to be as frank as you have been with us."

"Thank you, Mr. Ryder. I'd like to accept you at your word— no, please, I'm not trying to insult you. If I were, I'd start asking many unpleasant questions. Like, for instance, the reason behind the coincidence that an ex-CIA employee should be meeting with and helping protect an ex-British Secret Service courier. Oh yes, Mrs. Meirion, we've been kept briefed on your courier mission in Yugoslavia for Sir Alexander. It's because of your obvious involvement with him that I'm not pressing you or Mr. Ryder at this moment about the real reasons for your meeting yesterday. If there's anything I should know about you two, Sir Alex will bring me up to date, you can be sure of that.

"So I say, Mr. Ryder, I'd like to accept you at your word— from this moment on."

Did a glint of amusement flicker behind Harry Ryder's blue eyes? If so, he kept it out of his voice. "Thank you, Commander. I appreciate your vote of confidence. I also appreciate . . . I mean, I suppose I appreciate your including me in the trip to the mortuary. But frankly, I can't imagine why

I was taken there—or Mrs. Meirion either, for that matter."

Commander Malmquist looked at her, not at Harry Ryder. "Yes. Yes, Anna Tadić. Mrs. Meirion, I wanted you to see Miss Tadić's body for a good reason, which I'll explain in a moment. Mr. Ryder"—turning to him—"I involved you because of yesterday's events at Bayswater Station. Whether Bayswater and Miss Tadić's murder—for that's what it was, wasn't it?—whether those two events are connected is still open to question. But on the assumption they might be, I thought it wise to include you. So—well . . .

"So, Mrs. Meirion, Anna Tadić might very well have been on her way to see you. I don't state that for a fact. All we know is, Anna Tadić had a message for you. We found the message on her body. As you'll see in a moment, the message was intended to be hand-delivered to you, but whether Anna Tadić was on her way to deliver it at the time of her murder, that we cannot say.

"The message was concealed on her body. No casual search would have found it. It was only discovered late last night by a coroner at his work, and it wasn't until early this morning that someone else recalled yesterday's events and your involvement with them and thought possibly that with dead Moslem thugs and a Yugoslavian Embassy employee also dead, the international aspects might make the message of interest to us as well as to the Metropolitan Police. That was very good thinking, we think."

He flipped back the cover of a leather binder, picked up a small white envelope. "Budim?"

The inspector stepped forward, accepted the envelope, said, "The message here on the envelope front is in Serbo-Croatian and written in Cyrillic, the script of Serbia. The rest of Yugoslavia uses Latin letters and Latin script. Obviously this little envelope must have been enclosed in a larger envelope or package. Translated, the message says, 'Anna, please deliver the enclosed card to Mrs. Llewelyn Meirion. It's important. And confidential. So take care. I think they're after me. Please take care. Mrs. Meirion lives at 123 Porchester Terrace. She speaks our language.' It's signed, 'Milan.' "

53

Four pairs of eyes swept toward her—and for good reason. At the mention of the name *Milan*, she had started and gasped. Now four expectant faces confronted her. Commander Malmquist did not say anything, just raised his eyebrows. She obliged:

"Commander, I said I did not know an Anna Tadić. I didn't and I don't. But I do know a Milan Tadić. Or once knew. At the time, he lived in Belgrade and worked in the KOS for Colonel Pantić. On one occasion, Mr. Tadić and my husband collaborated closely on a special project. Whether that collaboration continued, I can't say. Of course, Tadić is a common Yugoslav name, and my Milan Tadić didn't have to be related to Anna Tadić, but I have to assume they are, am I correct?"

"You're correct, Mrs. Meirion. Quite correct. Anna and Milan were sister and brother. We learned this last night when we routinely went to Anna Tadić's flat. She was run over about five o'clock when she left work for the day. By seven-thirty, our people were at her flat, and they found we were not the first ones there. By no means. Her apartment had been thoroughly ransacked. The landlady said a man claiming to be her brother came in about four-thirty—yes, four-thirty, before Anna was killed—and he asked to be allowed to wait for his sister. He gave his name as Milan Tadić. Since the landlady knew that was the right name, she let him in. We have to believe he was not successful in his search. We have to believe he was looking for the card referred to on the outside of that envelope. Budim?"

"Yes, sir." The inspector put two stubby fingers into the tiny envelope and extracted a plain white card, a kind of gift card. He held it up for them to see. "There's one word here. It's also in Cyrillic. The word is *Karadjordje*. In English that's Karageorge, which means Black George. That's all, Black George and no more."

The four pairs of eyes now really bored into her, grilled her. No, not four pairs, three pairs, three pairs of policemen's eyes. Harry Ryder's eyes were still lackluster, his face still relaxed, noncommittal. If his eyes were focused on anything,

54

it had to be on the seconds rolling past on the electronic clock. Good. He at least was not putting any pressure on her. What would he advise now? Should she tell them about Anna Tadić's phone call? No way. It would be too embarrassing. If anyone told Commander Malmquist about that call, it'd have to be Sir Alexander James. Let him cover for her.

"I'm sorry, gentlemen, I can't help you. Karageorge, Black George, that means nothing to me. Oh, the history means something. Every friend of Yugoslavia knows how Black George, son of an impoverished peasant, drove out the Turks around 1800 and became ruler of Serbia. Many years later, his descendants became kings of that country—Karageorge was the Tito of his day. True, nothing that he himself touched was permanent. It took another eighty years or so before Serbia became a truly independent kingdom. But he was the first great leader of a free Serbia, and he's revered and honored in Serbia to this day. That's all I know about Black George. His name on that card means nothing to me. It might have meant something to my husband, but—but . . ."

Silence reigned while everyone ruminated. Commander Malmquist sighed, said, "As matters stand, the message seems to have been the reason for killing Anna Tadić and for trying to kill you, Mrs. Meirion. If it couldn't be delivered to or received by the one person who might understand it, well, then, you see. But the trouble with that, the time is most awkward. Those would-be assassins were waiting for you on the platform, Mrs. Meirion. How would they know you'd be at Bayswater Station at ten-thirty in the morning?"

"Oh, that—I've thought about that. I'd say they'd been watching me this week. Since last Monday I've been going to Putney every day to consult with Mr. Raines, the librarian there. I think you know about that. My husband's and my work on Cardinal Wolsey and Thomas Cromwell. Cromwell was born in Putney and grew up there, did you know that? Sorry, I mustn't get started on Cromwell. He's a thoroughly interesting and unusual man. Anyway, I've been leaving every day at the same time. I know—patterns. But I haven't performed a courier mission for Sir Alexander for over fourteen months. Surely I can afford to live a patterned life now, can't I?"

And the second she heard herself say the words, she knew how silly they were. Perhaps her courier days were over, but what about the proposed search for Ethan Pickering, aka Peter Trubari? How patterned a life would she be living on that mission, if she accepted it? She and Harry Ryder?

And Harry Ryder was the one who finally cut into the only sound in the room, the whirring of the electronic clock. He said—whispered, rather, "You said, Commander, Anna and Milan Tadić were sister and brother. Were, Commander. Were."

8

"You are indeed an intrusive man, Mr. Ryder." The commander looked at his Balkan expert. The latter came forward from the bookshelves.

"I phoned the Belgrade police, Mr. Ryder, and asked how I could reach Anna Tadić's brother. I explained I wanted to report her hit-and-run death.

"I asked. And they said how thoughtful of the London Metropolitan Police to take the trouble to inform the next of kin eight hundred miles away. They also said that, unfortunately, my call was wasted effort. Just the other day Milan Tadić was coincidentally also run over and killed by a hit-and-run driver. The accident took place on a deserted rural road thirty miles from Belgrade. The body was discovered in a ravine only last Tuesday, though death must have been several days earlier. They were very sorry.

"So I said the Metropolitan Police were also sorry, but we still felt it our duty to tell the next of kin. Could they give me the name of either parent or grandparent? They were courteous again. They gave me a number and said they hoped someday I'd tell them what this was really all about. What could I say? I thanked them, called the number, got their mother.

"It was no easy—well, you understand, both of you. This is a bad part of our job. Very bad. But I managed somehow to tell her about her daughter and expressed my sympathy about her son.

"And when I told her someone had ransacked Anna's flat, she said that was strange, because the same thing had happened to Milan's apartment. When she and her husband finally went there, they found it in chaos. Vandals couldn't have created a greater mess."

Again silence. This time, Commander Malmquist broke it. "All right. The Yugoslav connection tightens. Mrs. Meirion, I suggest you get to Sir Alexander James as quickly as you can and brief him on the Tadićs and also on Karageorge. That message upsets someone in Yugoslavia—or about Yugoslavia. Milan Tadić obviously expected or hoped you'd understand the message or at least know what to do about it. Since you don't, it all depends on what Sir Alex's research turns up.

"You did have a set pattern. It was easy for those thugs to try to mess with that pattern. What I suppose we'll never discover is who's been controlling this operation—those murders and this attack on you. Who—or why."

"That's a mystery, Commander." She felt an afflatus well through her, what Llew-Llaw had called her "Welsh gift." "You're pure Anglo-Saxon yeomen stock, Lissa," he had said; "I'm the Welshman; I should have the Welsh gift, the second sight, me, a spiritual descendant of Llew-Llaw Griffes, and generations of Druid bards, but the Welsh gift passed me by and somehow lodged in you. Are you sure you're Anglo-Saxon?" Well, the gift was exploding in her now. She felt all four men now really staring at her, even Harry Ryder; but like a seeress of old she looked past them, past the room, past space. Maybe she wasn't pure Anglo-Saxon; in the Continent, a lot of good Aryan Anglo-Saxon blood had gotten a touch of the Celt. Just witness the Isar River in Bavaria; the Yser River in Belgium; the Isere River in France—Celtic, all of them. And why were they staring at her? Oh yes, oh yes, Yugoslavia and a controller of operations. "No, that's no mystery. The controller is Žarko Pantić."

All four men jumped. The mouths of all four fell open. Let 'em gape, she had more to say.

"Gentlemen, if these unfortunate murders and murder attempts are intended to keep me from learning about Karageorge, I know how to preserve my life. Just take that card over to the mortuary and give it to Žarko Pantić. I guarantee there'll be no further efforts made to kill me."

"Mrs. Meirion!"

Who said that? Maybe they all said it. She favored Commander Malmquist. "Yes, Commander?"

"Mrs. Meirion, that's—that's a most serious—Mrs. Meirion, aren't you aware . . . yes, of course you are, you've already indicated you're aware your husband and Mr. Pantić worked closely together—"

"Colonel Pantić, Commander. Žarko Pantić is as much a civilian as you are. Once a colonel in the KOS, always a colonel. Or more likely a general."

"Yes, I suppose you're right. His new role as trade attaché is a bit out of character, isn't it? Colonel Pantić. Well, Colonel Pantić has long been one of our country's great and good friends and allies—your country's, too, Mr. Ryder. Ask Sir Alex's houseguest if Colonel Pantić is not a valued friend of your country. Oh yes, I'm quite aware Mr. Don Carlos Bingham is staying with Sir Alex. He comes over once a year—we're very much aware of his visits, oh yes indeed. Ask him if there's any way Žarko Pantić could be directing a murder operation against a British citizen. It's just not in the wood, not in the wood."

Since both Sir Alexander and Mr. Don Carlos Bingham had already expressed their suspicions of Žarko Pantić, it seemed to her that Pantić as assassin was very much in the wood. She looked at Harry Ryder—and was surprised to see a glint of approval in his eyes. Why, the American was actually supporting her. Would he speak up for her? Would he confirm that Sir Alex and Mr. Bingham had both fingered Žarko Pantić? They'd both said his asking Ethan Pickering to go to Vienna was quite out of character. Pickering no longer lived in Yugoslavia, his home was Monaco, where he headed up a computer software firm; for him to go to Vienna and see if an electronics firm there should be allowed to build a branch factory in Novo Mesto, halfway between Ljubljana and Zagreb, that was neither necessary nor wise. Pantić didn't need Pickering to perform that kind of task. And for Trubari-Pickering to be openly associated with his wartime partisan comrade, Žarko Pantić, that could well destroy the cover built up over the years. There's no statute of limitations on murder. If Peter Trubari were exposed as Ethan Pickering, back to Washington he'd go on a charge of murdering the Hungarian diplomatic official, Tibor Szentes.

That was the background she'd relayed to Harry Ryder at breakfast. (She hadn't been able to expand the story and tell why and how Pickering had killed the Hungarian; time and Sergeant Dykes had been too pressing; she'd have to brief the American on that before they next called Sir Alex and Mr. Bingham.) But of course Harry Ryder couldn't mention that background now. Commander Malmquist would be most intrigued to learn of Pantić's newfound ill repute. And worse yet, if he ever started to focus his attention on Peter Trubari, well, good-bye Trubari, hello Pickering. Jolly, jolly. Until this week, only Don Carlos Bingham and Žarko Pantić had known about Peter Trubari. Now Sir Alex knew, she knew, Harry Ryder knew. That was too many. Mr. Trubari-Pickering, your cover's close to being blown.

Giving a flicker of a smile to Harry Ryder—he'd know she was thanking him for his support, for that and no more—she said, "Gentlemen, I know I shock you. I'm sorry for that. I believe I have a right to make my request, even if you don't have to accept my reason for it. I have a right, because that message is properly mine. It was intended for me. Here it is. Here I am. Well, I want—I insist, if you will—I insist it now be given to Colonel Pantić. Once he has it, he'll no longer have any need to kill me. I'd like that."

Inspector Perpar did not wait for his commander's permission. He said hotly, "Mrs. Meirion, Yugoslavia has never hired Moslem thugs to perform acts of terrorism. Oh, I know things are dicey there right now. With Tito only a few months dead, they do get at each other a bit. Maybe at outsiders, too. But use terrorists? Never. That's not their way. Furthermore, if I understand you correctly—I hope I don't—you're saying Colonel Pantić killed Milan Tadić and his sister. Killed a KOS member—maybe his own assistant. And also an Embassy clerk, his assistant's sister. That—well, excuse me, Mrs. Meirion, but that's preposterous. That's—what evidence do you have? What!"

What could she say to that? Poor macho males, so sensitive about their masculine superiority. If she argued any further, she'd graduate from stupid female disturber to neurotic bitch. What to do?

And Harry Ryder came to her rescue. Again. He said, "Quite right, Inspector. Evidence is the problem. But, Sergeant"— and he turned to the giant who'd been sitting quietly and almost motionlessly at his side—"earlier you told me policemen don't like coincidences. Well, laymen don't either. Here's a message in Cyrillic intended for Mrs. Meirion. Here's a dead man in Belgrade. Here's his dead sister in London. And also, here's one Žarko Pantić who looks like he's in the spook business. Sorry. I mean in the intelligence community. And said Pantić is eager to carry off the corpse of Anna Tadić.

"Gentlemen, suppose we bear with Mrs. Meirion. Suppose someone gives Mr. Pantić Anna Tadić's effects—including the Karageorge card and the covering envelope, as well as a scribble from Mrs. Meirion, saying, in essence, there must be some mistake because the message makes no sense to her or to all the people she's shown it to. Do this, gentlemen, and then see how long Mr. Pantić and his ambulance hang around the mortuary waiting for Anna Tadić's body.

"My guess is, he'll be gone in five minutes. I'll give odds he'll be gone in ten."

Another silence. A gloomy one for the three policemen. A joyous one for her. Oh, blessed anonymous American spook. Who could have imagined he'd be so gallant? Thank you,

Harry. Thank you—and why just think the thanks?

"Mr. Ryder, thank you." She'd almost said "Harry." Harry! You've come a long way, girl, in two short days. How extraordinary. "It's my turn to appreciate a vote of confidence."

Commander Malmquist harrumphed. "You two do rather make a team, don't you? Well, you give me no choice. Sorry, Mrs. Meirion, but I'll have to phone Sir Alex right now, before you have a chance to get to him. Sorry to be so brutal, but it's quite obvious you two are sitting on something and holding the lid down. Well, I want a peek under that lid, too. Now, right now, before you get to Sir Alex."

And while he picked up the phone and issued instructions to a distant assistant, she flicked a glance at Mr. Harry Ryder, San Francisco American. Was Commander Malmquist right? Did they form a team? Certainly she'd acted at breakfast as if they did. "You," she had said to Harry, "you go out to the car and tell Sergeant Dykes I've gone to the ladies' room and will be right out. I'll go there, yes, but I'll also phone Sir Alex and tell him we've agreed we'll confine the conversation at Scotland Yard to Bayswater. In no way, at no time, will we mention, allude to, hint at, or bring up the name or the fact of the existence of Mr. Peter Trubari." And Harry had smiled and nodded and said, "Smart, Mrs. Meirion, very smart. That way James and Bingham won't be wondering if we spilled the beans. I'm on my way." And he had hied off to Sergeant Dykes, an act of teamwork, indeed. Hadn't she—and he—at that moment committed themselves to teamship? In fact, hadn't Commander Malmquist, with his snide remarks, hadn't he performed an act of kindness? He'd managed to resolve the basic question that had beset her since last Thursday: Could she work with Harry Ryder? (The lesser questions had pretty well unraveled: Harry was no longer part of the CIA, he'd "volunteered" to help Mr. Bingham because that warlock had blackmailed him; and he knew no more than she about the provenance of the Moslem thugs.) Could she work with Harry? She could work. She had worked. And she would continue to work. At this moment, he and she, the two of them, they did make a team. Thank you, Commander Malmquist. And thank you, too, for introducing and thereby clarifying the role, the importance, of Colonel Žarko Pantić.

The good colonel was—had to be—the missing link that bound together all the crazy events of the last few days. He was implicated in the disappearance of Peter Trubari. (Might as well think of the missing man as Trubari, Yugoslav; too many loose thoughts about Ethan Pickering, CIA, could do no good.) He was implicated in the Tadić murders—and presumably in the Karageorge message, too. That left only the Bayswater attack on her. Obviously he had to be responsible for the Moslem thugs. The logic of this assumption might be faulty, but the conclusion couldn't be. Žarko Pantić stood guilty as charged.

Would Harry Ryder accept her deductions? Of course he would. His intuitive sense seemed quite capable of matching and even overmatching her Welsh gift. If there was one firm tie in this newly formed—and as yet unspoken—teamship, it was that neither one of them had to be taken through any ABC's with each other. They were equals—just the way it had been with Llew-Llaw. And what had prompted that vagrant, irrelevant thought?

But there was no time to ponder this question. Commander Malmquist was speaking into the phone. "Alex? Good to have caught you. We've got a little problem here."

9

On this warm, cloudless Sunday morning, Žarko Pantić dressed with particular care. His selection consisted of threadbare, baggy, unpressed gray slacks, a cheap cotton shirt, down-at-the-heel loafers, a thin black nylon jacket. As an ensemble, they were just perfect for Petticoat Lane.

He carried only three things in his pockets: some cash, his passport, and the Karageorge message the police had found on Anna Tadić's body, along with Mrs. Meirion's note saying Anna Tadić and the message meant absolutely nothing to her.

Yuri Yevchenko's bowels would disgorge when he read Mrs. Meirion's statement. Oh yes, poor Yuri would be ready to blow his brains out. The modern Soviet KGB types just weren't as tough as they used to be when Tito and he were traipsing back and forth to Moscow. In those days, it was his bowels— and Tito's—that couldn't stay tight. Of course, nowadays there weren't any Stalins or Berias around, either. Just Yevchenkos. Times do change, they do.

Stefan was already sitting behind the wheel of the black Zastava 101, Yugoslavia's bow to the Fiat 128. Stefan nodded to him, he slipped into the back seat, lay on the floor, stayed there while Stefan maneuvered out of the Embassy garage. Fifteen minutes later, Stefan leaned back and said, "No one's followed us. In a moment I'll pull up, and you can get out normally. There are a few pedestrians, everything's normal, the bus stop's a hundred meters ahead. The 25 bus is a block or so behind us. It'll take you direct to Aldgate. Petticoat Lane starts there. But the street sign reads 'Middlesex Street.' "

Stefan was a pedant. And a good driver. Good drivers can afford to be pedantic. Pushing himself erect, Colonel Žarko Pantić grunted to acknowledge the pedantry, opened the door the instant the car stopped at the curb, swung out onto the footpath, headed for the bus stop—and in another ten minutes was at Petticoat Lane, as Middlesex Street became each Sunday morning. Stefan would have been surprised to learn his colonel had visited Petticoat Lane many times. By Stefan's standard, Žarko was rich, but Žarko Pantić knew better, what with his family obligation to provide blouses, shirts, belts, trousers, jackets, dresses, shoes, underclothes, coats, hats, and gloves for his relatives, for his cousins and nephews and aunts and uncles and children and grandchildren strewn out across Yugoslavia from Skopje to Opatija. Petticoat Lane on Sunday mornings had for sale all these goodies and much more on racks, in bins, on display stalls, four or five blocks of wall-to-wall merchandise all the way from Bishopsgate to Aldgate

High Street. With his shabby clothes—customary Petticoat Lane clothes they were, not a disguise for the modern secret agent—Žarko Pantić fitted right into the thronging crowds. He was the kind of man Petticoat Lane was designed for, the kind of man who'd buy judiciously, try a hand at bargaining, and come away loaded down with gifts for all his tribe.

He'd also be unnoticed, something he couldn't say for Yuri Yevchenko. That worthy, when finally encountered where he'd said he'd be, near the Cobb Street intersection, looked exactly what he was, a Soviet KGB agent living it up in capitalist splendor. He was wearing a Homburg, one a Lawrence Olivier might well covet; his gray pinstripe suit could only have come from Hall Bros. of Savile Row; boots from Trickers or Forter and Son of Jermyn Street. Plainly, Yuri Yevchenko had already managed to endow himself with most of those worldly possessions every up-and-coming Soviet public servant abroad regards as his due. Plainly, also, dressed like this in Petticoat Lane, the Russian came close to making a fool of himself. And a cynosure of every eye. What joy to have to work with idiots like this.

Sighing, he stepped from behind a rack of women's coats, revealed himself to the Russian.

"Good to see you, Yuri." He chose to speak in Ukrainian. He was one of the few people in the trade who knew that Yuri Yevchenko stemmed from the Seret River region, smack in the middle of onetime Cossack Ukraine. He also knew Yevchenko loathed his low-caste Cossack antecedents, prided himself on his impeccable Moscow-Leningrad Great Russian dialect, and could only be thoroughly annoyed to hear his native tongue. Pantić had no motive in baiting the Russian— the Ukrainian. Yevchenko was just the kind of person one can't resist baiting.

Yevchenko scowled, replied in Serbo-Croatian, "You weren't followed?"

"Followed?" Pantić obligingly switched to Serbo-Croatian. "Please, Yuri, please."

"Good. Don't you agree this is a perfect place for a little chat?"

Žarko Pantić thought the choice ridiculous. The Red Lion Pub nearest the Soviet Embassy would have been just as private—and a hell of a lot more pleasant. He said, "A great choice, Yuri. What's up?"

Yevchenko had wakened him at three A.M., said we must meet, said where, and hung up. But even that colloquy had betrayed his anxiety, and his scowl now confirmed it.

"Mrs. Meirion and that Harry Ryder fellow. They arrived in Vienna at midnight last night. They were traveling as Mr. and Mrs. Glen Eliot. They registered that way at the Stefanie."

"You mean"—this was an astonishing revelation, a piece of almost superhuman supersleuthing—"you mean you've had someone tailing those two? After they left me at the mortuary?"

Yevchenko stroked his elegant little moustache. Ordinarily he did that when preening himself. Now it was an act of self-bolstering, an attempt to reassure himself that he really was what he was, a colonel in the KGB, one of its brightest stars, a man on the move. He said, "No, no, of course not. We don't have that kind of manpower. You know that. No, one of my men took a night flight to Vienna and there they were, the two of 'em. On the same plane. He knew I was interested in Harry Ryder, though he doesn't know why I sent the newspaper stories to Moscow Center. Anyway, he called as soon as those two bedded down at the Stefanie. In one room, registered as Mr. and Mrs. Eliot. I didn't get the message until two-thirty. So now they're in Vienna—and what does that mean? Let me give it right back to you. What's up, Žarko? What's up?"

This wasn't anxiety. This was fear. Yuri Yevchenko was close to panic. Pantić countered the question with a question: "Harry Ryder? Have you got anything on him yet?"

"Nothing in London. All the newspaper photos should be back at Center by now. Ryder's obviously a professional. They'll ferret him out. Count on it. Meantime, Žarko, this means they're on to us. Vienna! That means Trubari smelled a rat. He reported your request to his people. He must have known

Vienna was a trap, but he went anyway. What does that mean, Žarko? Are we blown? How else can you see it? Bayswater— look at the facts. Meirion and Ryder are a team. They have to be. Maybe they even knew about our Libyans. Žarko, we're blown!"

Yevchenko had a right to a little panic. Might as well get the worst over with now. The Russian was past reason. Pulling out Milan Tadić's note to his sister and the card with the one word Karageorge on it, he handed them both to the Russian.

"The police gave these to me." He now handed over Mrs. Meirion's note. "And this, too."

Yevchenko's face paled as he read. He reread, then re-reread the message, looked up, said, "Mrs. Meirion's lying. We're blown. We're ruined. Just when things were . . . Ruined. Aren't we? Why are you so calm? What do you know I don't?"

"I don't think it's a lie. They really don't know what Kara-george means. Only Milan Tadić and Professor Meirion knew what that code word signifies—and they're both dead."

"Nonsense. There'll be records. Karageorge has to be on file somewhere. They just haven't dug it up yet."

"Even that doesn't frighten me. What can it tell them? That someone somewhere in Yugoslavia is planning to move Yu-goslavia back into the Russian orbit. What's new about that? Every Russophile in Yugoslavia is tabbed and accounted for by all parties. A plot? Where can they find a plot among them? What's there to plot? Yugoslavia cut its umbilical cord with Mother Russia in 1948. Over thirty years ago. We'll never go back. That's all they can find. Trust me, Yuri, trust me. Milan Tadić was the only one who stumbled onto what's really hap-pening, and he's dead. And his message to Mrs. Meirion is equally dead. Mrs. Meirion was not lying. They don't know its significance. They don't know, they can't know Serbia is about to resume its rightful place as ruler of Yugoslavia. With your help, of course."

Yuri Yevchenko was now stroking his moustache continu-ously. Maybe that moustache was all there was to Yevchenko. A hollow man, alive because his moustache itched. He scowled, said, "They don't need to know details. Trubari has tipped them off about going to Vienna for you. They'll tie his disappearance in to you. And they'll tie you to that girl, too. What was her name?"

"Patak. Arritsa Patak."

Pantić did some quick thinking. Was Yevchenko right? Was his panic justified? Had Ethan Pickering mentioned Arritsa Patak's name to somebody? To somebody! There was only one somebody who knew Pickering and Trubari were one and the same person, and that somebody was Birdie Bingham. Was Bingham in London? When Pickering had left Pantić at the Kensington Palace Hotel, he'd seemed too elated to think of any such mundane reality as his old mentor, Birdie Bingham.

Or had Pickering put on an act for his benefit?

He tried to reconstruct the confrontation. The final moments, especially, when he first mentioned Arritsa Patak's name. That tidbit was only brought up when Pickering had already agreed to go to Vienna and check on the Dyna Disc company. "What I'm asking is trivial, Peter," he had said. "Would you mind going to Vienna yourself and talking to the Dyna Disc people? Talk to them, make up your own mind. I'm not concerned about their ability. They're a good company. We both already know that. You've read the reports. They know all about Winchester-type disc drives and read/write heads and whatever. And they've got money.

"But do they have guts? That's what's really important in life, isn't it? Guts. If we let them set up their proposed plant in Novo Mesto, they'll face rough times with our bureaucracy. Can they take it? Or will they fold up and fade away? Will they?

"We can't afford that, Peter. The whole European electronic community will be watching this move. Hell, the American one, too. All the way from Silicon Valley. If Dyna Disc fails in Novo Mesto, it'll be a mortal wound to our country. No international electronics company will have anything to do with us. We cannot afford that. So. So will you go to Vienna, Peter, and measure them for me? You can do that. You've

67

got the technical expertise; but more important, you have a sense for people. You can tell if they have guts. Find that out, Peter, and send me a simple wire. Yes. Or no. That's all, yes or no."

And then, and only then, after Peter had nodded his acceptance, only then had he brought up the name of Arritsa Patak. He'd said, "You recall that woman you met at Lake Prošce? The one you said looked like Mitra Grgić and claimed her name was Nevenka Hadžić?"

At that moment Trubari's back was towards him, his hand on the doorknob. His face was not visible—or only partly visible—but Pantić did not need to see his face to learn Trubari's reaction. First the tall man's back stiffened as if ramrodded, then his neck began to flush blood-red, flush, and swell. It expanded an inch, two inches, like a pouter pigeon's, and flowed over his shirt collar. It was an astonishing sight. Žarko Pantić felt himself fortunate to have seen it. This was a man in love. This was what love could mean.

And Peter Trubari had stood there motionlessly until his neck swelling had started to subside, then turned around and said soberly, "Yes, I remember."

"Well, her name was not Nevenka Hadžić. She lied to you. I think maybe she was afraid of a too-permanent emotional attachment. A week's romantic fling among the Plitvice Lakes, that was safe. But a man permanently in her life—well, she has a career. And that's what's permanently important to her. Her career."

Trubari had said nothing, had remained standing impassively.

"So she lied to you, and so it took me a little while to find her. There's no Nevenka Hadžić in all Yugoslavia. But the Mitra Grgić clue was enough. The reincarnation of Mitra Grgić, you said. We have many beautiful women, but not many with the beauty of a Mitra Grgić. Certainly only a handful with such beauty—and the red hair. That's how I finally found her. Through the red hair. Her name is Arritsa Patak. She's not married. She lied to you about that, too. Again, I suppose, the career—but you'll have to find out about that yourself. And you can find it out. In Vienna. She's recently been transferred there as an employee, as Austrian financial controller, actually, of Yugo Ex-Import. Amazing combination: a mathematical brain and matchless beauty.

"Enjoy your visit to Vienna, Peter."

And a look of—what kind of look? A look of ecstasy, that kind. A look of ecstasy suffused Peter Trubari's face, and he had departed without a word, not even a thanks.

Where had he gone? Had his training asserted itself? In his prime, no one had ever been better than Ethan Pickering at this sort of game. Had the years as Peter Trubari, as Monaco electronics magnate, had they dulled these feral senses? Or had he spotted the falseness of Pantić's request? Had he known the request was out of line, no matter how plausible it might seem on the surface? Had he, in short, sought out Birdie Bingham—and to do so, he would have had to locate Bingham, wherever he might be, though that wouldn't be too difficult. Ethan could get to Bingham anytime he wanted, just as Pantić could. It would only take a call to Mercy Travel Agents in Washington, D.C. The phone would ring once and a man's voice would say, "Mercy Travel, may I help you?"

And Ethan could have said, "Yes, please. Is Mr. Honeycreeper there?"

There'd be a pause as the call would be switched to Langley, and a computer would work on "Mr. Honeycreeper." The pause would take perhaps a second. In that second, the computer terminus would read, "Honeycreeper, Don Carlos Bingham. Contact: Jack." The operator, incurious, with no sense of humor, not recognizing Birdie Bingham's little joke (one day Dalton Ripples, director of the Smithsonian, had called Birdie out of a National Security Council meeting to tell him a Hawaiian honeycreeper had been sighted on the Big Island, the first such sighting since 1873, and there was a plane to Los Angeles and Honolulu in ninety minutes from Dulles and if Birdie could make it he, Ripples, would save a seat on the plane for him; Bingham had not even made his farewells to his colleagues; he had caught the plane, and he and Ripples got themselves their honeycreeper, a truly big event in the lives of both men; as Bingham had once said to Žarko, "Just think, my boy, how many millions of bird watchers there are in the world who have never seen a Hawaiian honeycreeper. Makes one humble, it does.") the operator would take over the line, saying:

"Sorry, Mr. Honeycreeper is not in right now. May I take a message?"

"Certainly," Ethan might have said, "tell him Jack called. Tell him Žarko Pantić is setting me up in Vienna with a girl named Arritsa Patak. I must talk to Mr. Honeycreeper at this number."

This is what he might have said. But had he? Was Yevchenko right, blast him? Was this really panic time?

And now, recalling that amazing confrontation, he looked at the fearful Russian and tried to hide his contempt, managed to say, "There's no way Patak can be tied in to me. She's just a girl he met at Plitvice, found out she was in Vienna, looked her up when he got there, went with her that first weekend to the Schneeberg—and vanished. With her. The Austrian police have done their best—and their best is very, very good; but Peter Trubari and Arritsa Patak have vanished from the face of the earth, and that's that, so why this concern, Yuri?"

He wanted to say, "Why this panic," but he didn't dare. He had to live with the bastard. Live now—and for a long time to come.

Yevchenko scowled again. "We don't all have it as easy as you, Žarko. I've got to face my Comrade Chairman if this thing has blown up. Although on second thought, maybe you're not any better off than I am. If I have to report to the Comrade Chairman that his thirty-year-long dream of bringing Yugoslavia to heel has been destroyed because of my ineptitude, it won't be just me who's skinned and boiled alive, you'll be right there with me. Your General Jure Kranjc will see to that."

"Two days."

"What's that? Two days?"

Pantić felt he was dealing with a cretin. "Two days. Don't do a thing for two days. If Mrs. Meirion or her people can decipher Karageorge, President Otaronov will know about it in Belgrade in two days. If that happens—well, I agree. We're ruined. Both of us. Just two days. Wait two days before you go crawling to your Comrade Chairman. Or commit suicide, which is what I'll probably do. Can you live with that?"

"Summer maneuvers have already begun in the Carpathians. Hungary, Bulgaria, and Romania. They can be in Belgrade in four days. That's in force. Token troops can be there in a half-day."

"I know. It's in all the papers. The summer maneuvers, I mean. With a focus on Poland. And I've got two thousand orders nearly finished. On July 27, they'll go out to every army base when Kranjc gives the signal on national TV."

"Two days. You're a cold-blooded bastard, Žarko."

"I go back to Beria and Stalin. I'm still alive. I'll live for two more days—and a lot more. Trust me."

"Those stupid Libyan musclemen. Letting a woman out-muscle them."

"A woman, and a very convenient male bystander."

"It's a mess."

"It's a mess."

"All right. I'll wait two days. If nothing happens then, I'll agree with you. We're safe." He brushed his moustache once more, this time confidently, made as if to go, stopped, said:

"Žarko, two questions. One is frivolous, idle curiosity."

"Go ahead. The serious question?"

"Drvar. Things are proceeding on schedule in Drvar?"

"Like clockwork. The whole nation is starting to focus on that town. The statue will be unveiled at eleven A.M. The bomb will destroy it—and probably Otaronov. Kranjc will take over the microphone and give an impassioned speech and call the country to arms—ours and Mother Russia's, too. I know the speech is impassioned because I'm writing it. Yes, we're on schedule. And the frivolous question?"

"Good, very good. Vaseljev will be pleased. Yes. Well. The frivolous question. I'm just curious. Is her name really Arritsa Patak?"

"Oh yes, it really is. And she really did lie to Trubari about her name. The two of them had a spontaneous-combustion affair at Plitvice, and then all of a sudden she sneaked away, fled. I can't imagine why. She's not one of us, you understand. But as a loyal citizen, she did agree to cooperate. She agreed to be transferred from Zagreb to Vienna. She's doing her part in helping us outwit an enemy of the people, and she's prepared to fade away for the time being."

"Fade away?"

"Yes. Very quietly, as long as she causes no trouble. Not so quietly if she does."

"Good." And now the Russian did manage a chuckle. As a model KGB machine-tooled operative, Yuri Aleksander Yevchenko was not much given to laughter. Laughter had been one of the ingredients machine-tooled right out of his system. A chuckle was the best he could do. "Well, at least Mr. Trubari Pickering's last days will have been enjoyable ones. It's good to know he'll die happy."

He turned to go, but Žarko Pantić held up a hand. "One moment, Yuri. My time for a question. Those two in Vienna. What do you plan to do about Meirion and Ryder?"

Yevchenko looked surprised. "Do you have to ask?"

PART II

10

By their second day in Vienna, it was obvious they were being followed.

By the third day, Mrs. Melissa Meirion, known at the Hotel Stefanie as Mrs. Glen Eliot, had had enough. She said:

"Harry, I've had it. I don't like being followed. I don't like the look of the men following us. At least three different cars, each with two men, with each man displaying an Iron Curtain haircut. The kind you'd see in Poland or Russia, I'd say. Not Yugoslav haircuts. But it doesn't matter where they get their haircuts, they're here and shadowing us wherever we go. Who are they? Why are they following us? I don't like it, and it's time we went on the offensive."

"All right," said Harry Ryder, known at the Hotel Stefanie as Mr. Glen Eliot. "Let's offend. How?"

"It's time to do what I said on the plane. We're accomplishing nothing here. The Sacher Hotel confirms that a Peter Trubari did stay there and did check out. All quite proper. He left his business card at the counter with a note to bill his company. All quite routine. And equally routine at Dyna Disc. He came in, talked to them, talked serious shop, apparently got all his questions answered, left. So we've scratched and dug and tried to stir up the natives, but it all adds up to nothing, and so I think it's time to get our pistols—they should be ready by now—and then go up the Schneeberg, talk to Frau Dollwitz, and act on whatever lead she gives us. Because she's our only hope. I refuse to consider the possibility she can't help us. She has to help us."

Her unfailing optimism might be the right approach. For

73

his part, Harry Ryder didn't care if they ever left Vienna, he certainly wasn't optimistic they'd find anything if they did leave Vienna. As for the manpower unlimited trailing them, so long as they kept their distance, let 'em trail. Here in Vienna, he had found what he'd never expected, never hoped to find again. He had found himself besotted by these past three days, besotted with love for this remarkable woman. And oddly enough, it had all begun on a negative note. On the plane. He'd said:

"Mrs. Meirion, here we are Galahading off to Vienna to save the Western world. And maybe find an ex-American murderer on the lam. Has the thought occurred to you we're being set up? We're maybe a trifle expendable in some game, some purpose I know not of? But one very much wist to your Sir Alexander and my Birdie B.?"

"You mean expendable as in Sun Tzu's expendable spy, the one who is deliberately given fabricated information?"

He picked up the refrain. " 'So that when captured the expendable spy will be tortured to reveal the fabricated information and so mislead the enemy.' Yes, Mrs. Meirion, that one. Only please, don't call Master Sun by that dreadful transliteration Tzu. It should be Sun Zi. Written like this, old style."

And he sketched the two-part ideogram out for her. 孫 子 . He was showing off, like a boy whipping a Yo-Yo in front of a girl he wants to dazzle. What for? "And like this, new style: 孙子; the first ideogram is his name, Sun; Zi, the second ideogram, means sun, but two thousand years ago it used to be a fancy word for Master. Mr. Sun, the Master. Yes, Mrs. Meirion, wisdom in our trade begins with knowledge of Master Sun."

Was she amused at his pontificating? Was that what the glint in her eye meant? Was it amused annoyed or amused amused? Certainly she managed to keep her voice and intonation perfectly sober:

"Please call me Lissa."

"If you'll call me Harry."

"Oh dear, I keep forgetting. I must learn to call you Glen, and you must call me Marget."

Besides passports in the names of Harry Ryder and Lissa Meirion, they also had passports as Glen and Marget Eliot, husband and wife, as well as a set with the names of Thomas Edward and Christina Doughty, also husband and wife. These latter were fallback passports and a little joke on Birdie Bingham's part.

"Doughty," he'd whispered to them (the whisper was a speech defect; he couldn't speak any louder), "Doughty was an early Lawrence of Arabia. You, Harry, are a latter-day Lawrence of the Orient. And Queen Christina of Sweden was, of course, one of the great women of all time, a fitting sobriquet for you, Mrs. Meirion. Though I did linger for a while on Eleanor. Eleanor of Aquitaine, you know. Those two women have been my secret lifetime heroines. But Queen Christina had more joy in her life, and you, Mrs. Meirion, strike me as a person for whom joy is a first nature. I hope you two like your names. As to the Eliot name, that's nothing, just a device to get you in and out of Austria." (This was only partially true; the minute Bingham said this, Harry Ryder was quite aware the Eliot name was also a device to get him in and out of the same bedroom with Lissa Beaumont Meirion, or maybe the same bed; he knew this latter was a distinct possibility because he could not detect the slightest protest in her body as the married status was foisted on her, not a frown, not a start, not a quiver; someday he hoped he'd find out why she accepted this role; was it because she was also prepared to accept him, she actually looked forward to bedding with him, or was it because she was simply the dutiful widowed spy on assignment?) "Doughty, however, calls for doughty deeds in Austria or Yugoslavia."

And on the plane, as she said "You must call me Lissa," she had turned full sideways to look him in the eyes. Squarely in the eyes. And his insides had dissolved. Blue Anglo-Saxon eyes. Straight, soft golden hair reaching about to her shoulders and framing a classic Anglo-Saxon oval face. Oval, with a strong jaw, fine white teeth, and an upper lip somewhat shorter than the lower one, an upper lip that normally and naturally pulled open to reveal the teeth and to make her seem as if she were laughing a quiet, almost constant joyous laugh. Such a lady with such a face must have stood at the prow of some Anglo or Saxon ship a thousand years ago, ready to be first ashore to claim some part of Britain for herself and her man.

"Let me say one thing, Harry Ryder, I am not Terry Jefferson. Sorry, I must say this. Mr. Bingham explained about her, how you lost her. Well, you won't lose me. I can't handle a pistol with her skill, but I know the ropes of our trade. Of the spook business, as you called it. I'm a fairly adequate spook. Llew-Llaw trained me, others helped. You do not have to worry about me. Ever. If the going gets rough, well, I'm on my own. Please, I am no responsibility of yours.

"And yes, I have wondered if Sir Alex had other motives in mind. One thinks of everything, doesn't one?"

"And your conclusion, Lissa?"

This was the first time he'd said her first name. He wanted to repeat it—not once, but dozens of times. It was a beautiful name. Exactly what she was. Lissome. Light. Lively. Lithe. Lissalike. In short, Lissa. He couldn't help himself, did say it once more. "Lissa?"

"My conclusion? What it's always been with Sir Alex. He wants my help. That's enough for me. If you'll forgive my old-fashioned mores, it's just a matter of patriotism, isn't it? Sorry, I had to say that, too. And in spite of your professional cynicism, I wonder if you aren't more like me than you care to admit? After all, you're the one who chose your book's title, *It's About Time Someone Said Something Nice About the CIA*. Isn't there a touch of patriotism there, too, Harry? Could Mr. Bingham really succeed in blackmailing you into coming on this quest? Are you that much of a namby-pamby?"

And he had laughed aloud. With joy. Not at her free-flung, intuitive analysis but from simple sheer joy. What a lady she was. What a difference this was, now, from his plane trip to

Hong Kong with Terry Jefferson. Then he'd indeed been the comic namby-pamby, a man in rather abject terror of Woman. With this lady, with Lissa Meirion, there was no terror of Woman. Not even a residual trace. Birdie Bingham had been astute. She was an incarnation of joy. More, she was not only joyful in herself, but the cause of joy in men. Or at least in him.

And recalling that breakthrough—and what it led to, the blissful three nights and long mornings in a Hotel Stefanie bed with this most mature, most delectable woman—he sighed now and said, "All right, I agree. If we're going to go the patriotic route, we won't get far in our delightful bed at the Stefanie. Or," he hastened to add as a tiny frown creased her brow, "anywhere else in Vienna. We've done our best to stir up the natives and gotten nowhere. Okay, let's go get our pistols. Only this time we can't just traipse up to the safehouse. We'll have to ditch our escorts. That'll take a little doing. Any ideas?"

"Yes, I have. But first, a question. On the plane I told you I trust my warlock. What about you? Do you trust Mr. Don Carlos Bingham, that little bird of a man?"

"Bird of a man? Oh, oh I see. His tiny birdlike nose. He does look like a bird, but that's not why he got his nickname. He's called Birdie because he's almost a maniacal bird watcher. As simple as that, in a man who is not at all simple.

"That's one reason I don't trust him. He plays games. He tricked me once into killing a man he wanted killed. Yes, he made a fool of me. How could I trust him?"

"And the other reasons?"

"One other one. I've told you how Birdie is dotty on moles in the Agency. Well, he's made such a fuss about it. I—and not me alone, believe me—some of us can't help wondering if he's not the mole himself. What better way to distract attention from yourself than to focus it elsewhere? Maybe this is irrational, but that's what I sometimes find myself wondering.

"And now, how do we get to the safehouse safely?"

11

It was less than two hours by tour bus from the Intercontinental Hotel in Vienna to Mayerling. To Yuri Yevchenko, the
trip seemed at least three times that long. The stout lady from
Hamburg had severely tested his performance as Gunther
Schwertler, orphaned in '43 by a bomb that killed his mother
in Munich, while Montgomery took care of father Schwertler
outside Tobruk. "My goodness," he said to the stout lady from
Hamburg, "is this all there is to Mayerling? A dingy little
church surrounded by gravel and dirt? Where's that elegant
hunting lodge I've seen in the movies and TV?"

The stout lady laughed. She just loved his soft, slurred
Bavarian accent. "Isn't it always true? The reality beggars the
myth?"

Yuri was careful to be one of the first out of the bus ahead
of forty or so German tourists, including one paunchy fellow
far in the rear who had had a wonderful time with his own
tubby seatmate. General Mikhail Nihailovitch Veseljev, traveling as Dieter Braun, the one man in the service Yuri hated—
the rest were too despicable to hate—the one man who had
seen to it from Yuri's first day of training that Yuri would be
slighted in favor of the sons and daughters of the mighty, the
one and very man who was now his direct boss. He avoided
looking at the general. He was afraid if their eyes did clash,
his rage would show. Why had Veseljev taken this chance?
Why this urgent summons for Yuri to catch the first plane
from Belgrade and hie himself to this ridiculous meeting place?
Why wasn't Veseljev in Budapest, where he ought to be,
making sure Hungarian and Romanian troops—with a scat-
tering of Russian infantrymen—would be ready to enter Yugoslavia on schedule? What could be so important in Vienna
when all the action had shifted to Yugoslavia's borders? And

if this meeting was called for, was justified, why not just meet in the Embassy? Why this rigmarole?

He paid the bent-over Carmelite crone five schillings and waited patiently inside the ornate little shrine until she hobbled behind the altar rail and retold the story of Archduke Rudolf and his baroness, Marie Vetsera. Nothing could be more incongruous than this ancient virgin's recounting that tale of tragic passion. He glanced around to see if anyone else in the tourist group saw the incongruity, but the expressions were rapt. They were Germans, and this was love. *Die Liebe. Ein Liebestod.* Only a Sacher torte could have aroused a deeper emotion. And as the Germans followed the pointed nose of the crone into the tiny room to the right of the altar, he eased back and went outside and stood by the card table, where another crone—this one a villager—was selling worm-filled apples.

He bought one and moved away, and the general stood behind him. "Thank you for coming." He used Serbo-Croatian. Perfect cover for Gunther Schwertler, the German insurance agent from Munich. Well, it was better than coming out in Russian. "I know this sort of thing distresses you. You would have preferred a street pay phone. But just say I like these little deceptions. It's been so long since I had a chance to use them. It brings back my youth. And I also wanted to see your face without anyone in the Embassy knowing I was taking a look at it."

Yuri shrugged and turned and showed it to the roly-poly general. Veseljev had the same jowls and thick neck and obscene paunch that had come into style with Khrushchev. The anti-Stalin look—and certainly anti-Lenin. Fat replacing muscle. The symbol of modern Russian communism. Veseljev nodded. "You've always disapproved of me. You think I've held back your career. You'll never believe I personally picked you for this job. I know you think the Comrade Chairman shoved you down my throat. But you'll never find out the truth, will you? And that's good. The more you disapprove of me, the harder you'll try to please me. What would happen to my plans if you ever decided you liked me? Well?"

"Your plans are coming along as planned."

"If you don't want that apple, give it to me. Worms never hurt anyone. Your little colonel has everything prepared?"

"Yes. Two thousand orders ready to go. The statue ready to explode. Do you want details?"

"You mean, is this why I summoned you from Belgrade for this emergency meeting? No, I don't want details. I want you to hear from me personally what you stumbled into in that Bayswater fiasco." He held up a hand. "No, don't jump, Yuri Aleksander. I'm not criticizing you. At least, I'm not because it's obvious Mrs. Meirion doesn't know what Karageorge means any more than we do. Only Milan Tadić and Professor Meirion could have known what that code word means. It made no difference you failed to kill her. No, I just want you to know your recommendation to dispose of Mr. Harry Ryder is far more significant than you realize."

"Significant!" His tone, he knew, showed stupefaction. Well, he was stupefied, and that was that. "Significant? Why significant?"

"Not just because the presence of Mr. Ryder might imply more than we realized; but because Mr. Ryder deserves to die."

Yuri knew his mind wasn't functioning properly. His hate of Veseljev prevented clarity of thought, impaired his ability to catch nuances, overtones, insinuations. He tried to summon up the yoga discipline taught at the academy, succeeded to some extent, felt himself more or less focusing on the general, said, "Very well. He deserves to die. He'll die."

"He'll die." The general mimicked him. "Yes, he will. And you'll stay here in Vienna and see that he does. There must be no slipup. That's why I wanted to face you, Yuri. There must be no slipup."

Finally, long after Yuri should have caught on, the light dawned. He said, "Ah, Ryder. You've tracked him down on the computer."

"Good. You're starting to think. We've tracked him down. But not on the computer. It took legwork. In Washington. In New York. In Manila. A bit here, a bit there—you know the routine. And now we've got one mosaic.

"The break came in New York. They found out Harry Ryder has just written a book. They managed to get a peek at the galley proofs. You'll like the title."

He paused and peered roguishly at Yuri. The general wanted some stroking. Yuri stroked. "What's the title?"

"The title is *It's About Time Someone Said Something Nice About the CIA!*"

Yuri felt rage sweep over him. He almost said aloud what he thought: "Why in the hell is a CIA connection important enough to drag me to this godforsaken dump?" He almost said it. At the last second, Providence held his tongue. He gulped, said, "The CIA!"

Veseljev mimicked him again, then said, "Patience, Yuri, patience. That's your defect, your Achilles' heel. I didn't summon you to tell you Harry Ryder is one of a hundred thousand CIA agents. I summoned you because I want you to know what I know. Years ago, Harry Ryder killed five of my men in Frankfurt. You don't know the story? Let me tell you.

"The galley proofs made clear Ryder's venue had been the Orient. There he sported a half-dozen names or so. One of them was Warren Sawyer. We did have some films of a Warren Sawyer—a Warren Sawyer who doesn't look at all like Ryder today. Ryder is lean, hollow-cheeked, almost thin. Sawyer was tubby and round-faced with a trace of a pot. But the name Sawyer was all we needed to place Ryder. Sawyer also had another name in Center's files: Ralph Thomson. That still doesn't ring a bell? Well, Thomson was the name of the man who killed my men in Frankfurt. That city was the last leg of a Thomson swing around Europe. Thomson was here in Vienna as Henry Worthington. He stayed at the Ring Hotel and met the Polish underground at the hotel. He went on to Leipzig as Eugene Slater. To the Leipzig Fair. There he picked up a vial of our newest and nicest poison from a Polish sci-

81

entist. By the time we caught on, he was out of East Germany on his way to Frankfurt, where as Ralph Thomson he was to catch a plane home. I sent five men after him and the vial. He killed them all. Outside a restaurant. We of course tried to track him down, but we lost him. He went on the list as a man to be exterminated. And now, today, we have our chance. The galley proofs led to Manila. Someone there with a long memory dredged up the name Warren Sawyer. And with the Sawyer films we were able to identify Worthington-Slater-Thomson-Sawyer as one and the same person, and all of them as Harry Ryder.

"He's on the list. And he's your responsibility. And you will not fail, will you, Yuri Aleksander? You will not fail."

And Yuri suddenly felt himself superior to his superior. It was a temptation to reveal his contempt. God, how this obscene Sir Paunchiness got to him. Prudence, Yuri. Prudence, patience, perspicacity. He said, "Don't kill him. Or her."

"What!"

How he wished he had the courage to mimic the general back. He looked at the church. The tourists were starting to amble out toward the yard. He said:

"Because two CIA men will be better than one. The case will be ironclad then. This is a heaven-sent opportunity. We should take advantage of it. We'll take them here and put them on hold until the twenty-seventh and produce them then. No, not Mrs. Meirion, just Ryder along with Trubari. Two CIA spies—luck, general, sir, sheer luck.

"And as for the lady, well, that's just too bad. But obviously she'll have to go."

General Mikhail Veseljev frowned, rolled the apple between his palms, bit his upper lip, suddenly smiled, and clapped Yuri on the back.

"Genius, Yuri, sheer genius. Wasn't it smart of me to talk to you face to face? Wasn't I even smarter to have picked you for the job in the first place? Yes, do it, Yuri. Do it. Don't go back to Belgrade until you've resolved matters here. Go get a taxi and get hold of Dorlov and tell him you're in charge of the Ryder affair and he is to take orders from you. He and all his men. Obviously you'll want to close in on Ryder and Meirion quickly before they stumble onto something."

The general turned, and in flawless Berlin-German called to his erstwhile seatmate. "Wasn't that just wonderful, Frau Geheimrat Förster? Come, let's get on the bus. Let me tell you some more how we machine-tool rifles."

The general threw the apple away. He had not taken a bite.

12

Harry Ryder stood beside Lissa Meirion outside the restaurant three blocks from the Rathaus, pulled out a cigar, unwrapped it, clipped it, said:

"That beige Volkswagen van about five cars on the right. That's our baby. I don't see the other two cars, but they're around somewhere. Looks like it's pistols away. Are you ready?"

She was. She took his arm, smiled up at him, and her short upper lip, her joyous smile, almost did him in. He'd much prefer to head back to the narrow bed at the Stefanie and immerse himself in its joy. Damn. Keep your eye on the patriotic target. March on to victory. Off to the Rathaus. March. For that was Lissa's stratagem: an unconcerned hike to the Rathaus, the town hall; an entrance into the building, out its Felderstrasse exit; and then an even quicker march to the University, where the process would be repeated. In off Grillparzerstrasse, out onto Universitätstrasse, and thence by a circuitous route to the safehouse two blocks in back of the U.S. Embassy.

It was a shame they couldn't head straight to the Embassy itself and get their pistols and hie themselves away to the Schneeberg. But that would be too simple—and bad manners. "You are nonpersons as far as the Embassy goes," Birdie Bingham had explained in his barely audible whisper. "And anyway, Harry, when you go to get your equipment, I don't want you meeting the station chief. I'll send him to Zürich for some reason or other, but let's take no chances. Because, though he goes by Barnwell, Dwight Barnwell, you know him as James Carter. Yes, sorry, Harry, the very same, the man you loathe. You must know, though, he's not brimming over with kind thoughts for you. And if he were to discover the Mr. Glen Eliot he's doling out armament to is none other than Harry Ryder—well, we can't have that, can we Harry? We can't have that. Just as we can't have Carter or anyone in the Agency finding out you're looking for Ethan Pickering. On no, that would be worse than bad manners. That, I'm afraid, would get me fired—and perhaps even charged with being an accessory to a murder. So stay away from the Embassy and pick up your equipment from Mrs. Jane Fisher at the safehouse. She'll help you. You do understand, Harry."

And that was the moment to strike, and Harry had struck. He'd said:

"Birdie, why did you become an accessory to murder? Why?"

And the old man had whispered a pained and painful explanation. "I was a fool, Harry. I was generous. And also selfish. Perfect definition of folly. But I liked—I like—we can't use the past tense, can we? I like Ethan Pickering. And when he came to me with his proposition, I went along. For his sake and mine, because I confess I saw a way to take advantage of his murdering that Szentes fellow, and so I went along."

"That's hard to swallow, Birdie. Maybe it'd help if we knew why Pickering felt he had to kill a Hungarian diplomat. Something somewhere must make some sense in all this. Tell Mrs. Meirion and me why Pickering killed the fellow, then maybe we'll understand why you protected him and why we're supposed to find him."

And Bingham had told. "During the war, Ethan Pickering became a kind of hero among the Yugoslav partisans. They just loved the man. He went there the first time on a navy assignment. The navy volunteered him to serve at a German

84

radar station near Split. So the PT boat landed him in a cove, and a group of partisans met him. They were a rough lot. Their captain was Žarko Pantić. They took one look at Ensign Pickering's uniform and told him to get out of it. He explained he couldn't. He wasn't OSS. He was no spy. He was U.S. Navy, and the U.S. Navy fights in uniforms. OK, they said, then at least wear a partisan cap and put an overcoat over your uniform. If a German patrol sees you, you might live a few minutes longer. So he did as they said. And at dawn they came to the radar station, and Pantić said, what do you want to do?

"Ethan had no idea what to do. His instructions were to destroy the equipment. At that moment, four German guards came out of the station to perform their morning stretches and Ethan stood up, told Pantić to stay there, and he walked up the hill to the guards. They watched him. He watched them. And when he was a few yards away, he pulled out his navy-issue forty-five and blasted away. That was the first time he had ever fired a gun in his life. He shot four times. Each bullet went right through the heart of a German.

"The partisans went wild. I believe you know much of this, Harry. Ethan was your friend—is your friend—and you know each other's history. But bear with me. It all ties in with the main thread, and that you most emphatically do not know. Anyway, the partisans wanted Ethan to defect and fight with them. Any man who could shoot like that deserved to be a partisan. Ethan said no thanks, went back to his ship, and sent a wire to Admiral King, commander in chief of about everything in sight. Pardon me, Fleet Admiral King, that was King's rank, first fleet admiral in the navy's history. Ethan's wire said U.S. policy in Yugoslavia was stupid. We were supporting Draza Mihailović, and Draza was supporting and fighting with Germans against us. The only Yugoslavs fighting Germans were the partisans under somebody named Tito. Tito was the one we should be supporting.

"When Ethan's captain heard about the wire, he told Ethan he'd probably be shot by King. Ensigns don't wire fleet admirals. He almost was shot. He got a wire direct from and signed by the fleet admiral himself. It told Pickering if he didn't mind his own business, he'd be sent to Omaha and put in charge of prison latrines. And then a week later, he got another wire from King. It said, belay the first wire. Pickering was to locate Tito's headquarters in the mountains and report to and serve with General Sir Fitzroy McLean's British mission at Tito's headquarters. His assignment was to learn all he could about Tito and the partisans and to keep us informed about him or her. Yes, her. Churchill knew Tito was a man, but at that time many others thought Tito was a woman.

"All this came about through Roosevelt's direct intervention, Churchill's really. Churchill kept telling Roosevelt he was making a bad mistake supporting Draza Mihailović. Churchill's policy was always simple: Support anyone who kills Germans. And believe me, Tito and his partisans were killing Germans.

"And thus began Ethan Pickering's love affair with Yugoslavia and a Yugoslavian girl, Mitra Grgić. Their love was against all regulations. Yugoslav women who fraternized with foreigners were sent to the front and kept there until they were killed. But not Mitra. Tito himself took an interest in their romance. He admired Ethan, who very quickly forgot all about King's orders to observe and report and went about the business of killing Germans with the best of them. The best, Mrs. Meirion, included your husband and Žarko Pantić. They were quite a team. Yes, three latter-day musketeers. So Tito condoned the love affair, and it was understood Ethan and Mitra would be married at war's end—except that in the last days of the war, in the mopping-up period, really, Mitra was killed.

"It took Ethan over twenty years to find out exactly what happened. The outline he knew. The murder was the doing of Russian soldiers. When they came through Yugoslavia, the Russians treated the Yugoslavs as if they were Germans. They pillaged homes and raped every woman they could lay their hands on. Mitra was one of them—only she died in the encounter. And twenty-odd years later, a Montenegrin senator came to Žarko Pantić and said he was at a diplomatic reception the night before, and he'd seen the man who'd killed Mitra Grgić. The senator had been a peasant hiding behind a bush as their Russian 'allies' came through. And he'd watched a Russian attack Mitra, kill her when she resisted, and then rape the dead body. Only the man turned out to be no Russian. He was Hungarian and KGB. And Pantić told Ethan, and Ethan's life changed at that point. He divorced his wife and planned his revenge.

"His plan was simple. He set about creating a new world for himself. With his knowledge of science and technology— remember, he was at the cutting edge of the postwar scientific boom—he invested quietly through Swiss banks in growth companies, started his own electronics company, and in time accumulated a fortune. While doing this, he learned every- thing he could about Szentes's life and found out, among other things, that Szentes was an avid fisherman. He learned these things and waited patiently. He knew that, eventually, Szentes would appear in Washington as a local KGB man masquer- ading as a diplomat. And when that finally happened, Ethan came to me and told me what he was going to do. While killing Szentes, he was going to make it appear he, Ethan, had committed suicide, and he would disappear, never to be seen again.

"I will not speak of my dilemma. Nor will I try to condone what I did. I did what I did, and I still don't know what else I could have done. In essence, I did nothing. When Ethan did murder Szentes and did disappear, I told no one what I knew. That was wrong. But I would do it all over again exactly the same way. No, that's incorrect. Not quite the same way. I made one real mistake. I continued my relationship with Ethan Pickering. I took advantage of one thing he told me. He told me Žarko Pantić knew of his plans. Pantić was the only other man in the world who would know Ethan Pickering was not dead, would in fact someday emerge in full flesh as one Peter Trubari, a hitherto shadowy figure whose existence had only been surmised for some half-dozen years. Mr. Trubari would prove to be the sole stockholder and chairman of a quite successful electronics firm, a man with Monacan papers, and also a man with the right to have a ninety-nine-year lease on a home at Bihać near the Plitvice Lakes in Yugoslavia, the place Ethan loved most in the world. That's why he told Pantić his plans. He needed Pantić's permission to lease a home in Yugoslavia. And when I heard of the Pantić connection, I bargained with Ethan.

"I told him his friendship with Pantić was just too valuable, too important, for our country. We must continue to work with Pantić. I reserved the right to ask Pantić's help if it ever became necessary to find out what was really happening on a particular crisis involving Yugoslavia. He resented my pressure. My blackmail. But he had little choice, not if he was going to go ahead with his plan of revenge. So he went along. We've worked together a few times during recent years. We can reach each other through specially set up channels. And last week, I got a message from Ethan. It said he was putting on the dog and would I call him. I did better. I went to see him in person where he was putting on the dog. The Ritz Hotel, of course. And he told me about Pantić's peculiar request that he go to Vienna and check out an electronics firm there.

"It was plain to both of us that our old friend Žarko Pantić was up to his ears in something most peculiar. It was also obvious that his request of Ethan with the bait thrown in of a reincarnated Mitra Grgić, one Arritsa Patak, a woman Ethan had fallen in love with . . . well, this request had all the earmarks of a setup. But a setup for what?

"That's always the problem in this sort of trapping maneuver. In order to unmask a setup, one must walk into the trap and hope for the best. Usually one can provide all kinds of ancillary support. But what could I do? Alert our Vienna station? Hardly. Ethan Pickering did not exist—and he did not want to run the risk of being exposed. He left for Vienna the next day prepared to inform me as soon as he found out why

Pantić wanted him in Vienna. And I must say, he would have gone there no matter what arguments I could have advanced to dissuade him. He was really going there to see Arritsa Patak. For the second time in his life, he was in love. Though really, he assured me, for the first time. He is convinced this Arritsa Patak is the reincarnation of Mitra Grgić.

"I only heard once from him. He called to report he'd found nothing out of line yet. He'd had several productive and up-and-up meetings with the Dyna Disc people, and he and Arritsa were going up the Schneeberg the next day. And that was all. He vanished, simply vanished. With his new love, with this reincarnation of Mitra Grgić, this Arritsa Patak. Vanished, both vanished. Killed? Kidnapped? Killing makes no sense. Kidnapped? But why? What's in Vienna? That's what I hope you two will ferret out. You, Harry, because you know Ethan and you're only at your best under crisis conditions. And you, Mrs. Meirion, because you know Yugoslavia and Austria and their languages. And above all, you know Žarko Pantić and are no stranger yourself to crisis conditions."

Now, as they worked their way to the safehouse, Harry had plenty of time to rethink Bingham's story. Normally the walk from the University to the safehouse would have taken only thirty or forty minutes. They took over two hours, only moving from block to block when they were sure their back trail was clear. They had apparently lost their pursuers at the Rathaus.

"Lissa, with only three cars, it looks like they couldn't cover all the exits from the Rathaus." Was Bingham telling the truth? Was Peter Trubari really Ethan Pickering? Was Bingham setting them up, him and Lissa? Questions, questions, questions—and nothing to trouble his Anglo-Saxon Norfolk yeoman-stock lady fair about. Not now. Play the game out, that was all they could do. "I think we're in the clear. I hope Mrs. Fisher has the right pistols this time. I wouldn't want to have to scurry around like this a second time."

Lissa laughed, snuggled up to him. "After the lecture I gave her?" On their first visit to the safehouse Sunday morning, Mrs. Fisher had turned out to be a white-haired, motherly lady who greeted them cordially, promptly produced two pistols as requested. Only they weren't the type requested. Lissa had asked for Browning High-Powereds; her offerings had been good old American thirty-eights. And Lissa had not been pleased and said she was not pleased, and they would come back on Thursday, and in three days they'd have Browning 9-millimeters for her, wouldn't they? Browning High-Powereds? "No, Harry, Mrs. Fisher, bless her soul, will do the right thing. I'm sorry I spoke so harshly to her. But Llew-Llaw did train me to use the Browning, and well, well, it's best, I think, it's best I stay with what I know."

Was this the time to ask her why her husband had borne that peculiar nickname, Llew-Llaw? Not yet. It would be a long time before he could even hope to achieve equality with the late Llew-Llaw Meirion. Lissa might like sharing a bed with Harry Ryder, might relish their lovemaking, but that didn't give him any rights. Not yet. He said, "There's the safehouse. The way look clear to you?"

"It does."

"Then straight ahead, march."

And they walked up the stone steps, rang the doorbell, heard steps come, watched the door open.

"Damn."

That, Harry suspected, must have been his own voice. The expletive didn't come from the tall, elegantly dressed man standing in the doorway. The man with the Cary Grant face. It wasn't Mr. C. Grant's voice, because it was saying, "Well, I'll be goddamned. Mr. and Mrs. Glen Eliot. Isn't that something! That damn Birdie Bingham. Send me off to Zürich. Who does he think he's dealing with? Why do I continue to work for the bastard? Mr. and Mrs. Glen Eliot, indeed. Hello, Harry. Come on in, both of you. Welcome to Vienna safehouse number three."

"Oh, no you don't." Harry Ryder took Lissa by the arm, started to lead her back down the stairs, said, "Marget, bear with me. This man is bad news, worse medicine. James, see you."

90

"Harry!" Mr. Cary Grant–lookalike plunged down the stairs ahead of them, confronted them from the sidewalk, said, "Harry, the damage is done. I've blown your cover. Spilt milk, Harry, spilt milk. Come on in and get your Brownings. And have some tea or something. Mrs. Fisher knew you were coming today and has tea and scones on hold for you. She said you were English, Mrs. Eliot, hence the tea. Shall I call you Mrs. Eliot? Come on in, Harry, and tell why you need Browning High-Powereds, and what's all this about Peter Trubari?

"Who is Peter Trubari, Harry?"

13

The two Brownings and two boxes of ammunition were on the coffee table next to the silver teapot. Mrs. Fisher served the tea and scones, smiled sweetly, disappeared silently.

Harry turned to Lissa, said, "Marget, let me introduce my old chum, presently Mr. Dwight Barnwell, but previously and always, Mr. James Carter, the man who tricked me and used me to do Birdie Bingham's dirty work for him in the Philippines."

James Carter shrugged. "Mrs. Eliot, Harry's an Ivy Leaguer snob. I'm a corn-fed country boy from Iowa. Does that suggest anything to you? For Yale and Iowa State, substitute Oxford or Cambridge and the University of South Wales. That'll give you the idea. Harry never thought highly of me. Me as a symbol, I mean. Harry much preferred it when the CIA was run by Harvard, Yale, and Princeton. Well, those days are over. Iowa, Missouri, Nebraska, and Kansas, we corn-fed college boys, we're getting our turn now, and he doesn't like it. Snobbery, Mrs. Eliot, sheer snobbery—and no justification whatever for being in my territory incognito, with the gall to pick up weapons from my safehouse. Harry, you can bet Birdie

Bingham's going to hear from me. There'll be an explanation, or I'll raise a stink all the way to the White House.

"What's up, Harry? Why incognito? Why pistols? Who is Peter Trubari?"

Harry Ryder put the teacup down, got up, walked to the coffee table, picked up the pistols, checked to make sure they were loaded, pocketed one pistol, stowed the other pistol and the ammunition boxes in Lissa's ample bag, said, "Okay, Marget, enough's enough. Shall we go?"

"Oh, no you don't, Harry. You 'fess up, or I'll blow your cover. If Birdie Bingham's playing games with me, I can play games with him. I'll spread you out to dry all over Vienna."

"I wouldn't if I were you, James. That I wouldn't. Shall we go, Marget?"

She followed him toward the foyer off the living room. James Carter took two steps after them, said, "Send me off to Zürich on a wild-goose chase. Call up Mrs. Fisher while I'm gone with instructions to deal with a mysterious Mr. and Mrs. Eliot. He's losing his grip, that Birdie. He should be put out to pasture. Didn't it occur to him Mrs. Fisher would call me in Zürich and brief me on all this? Did he think I'd stay in Zürich while someone was messing around my territory, even going to the Austrian State Police and asking for their help?"

Lissa and he turned back as one to stare at James Carter. Ryder said, "So that's how you learned about our interest in Trubari?"

"You bet. And they also told me you've been to Yugo Ex-Import asking about an Arritsa Patak, who apparently has taken a month's vacation somewhere. And you've been hounding people at Dyna Disc about Peter Trubari. Oh yes, Harry, I have friends with the State Police. They've been mighty puzzled by you—but they did find out a Peter Trubari had registered at the Sacher and checked out two Fridays ago. And they also corroborated that he and Miss Patak disappeared during a day's excursion up the Schneeberg. So they couldn't dismiss you as a total crank. They were so puzzled, they wondered if I might be interested in you.

"Might I! Harry, can you imagine what will happen to you if I tell them you've just armed yourself right here in their peaceful city, where no one has arms except terrorists from a dozen nations? Are you one of those, Harry, is that your new role in life, are you a terrorist?"

"James, why don't you get on the phone to Birdie Bingham and ask him those questions? For my part, I assure you—for what it's worth—I'm not here on any mission involving the Agency, your station, the city of Vienna, or the Austrian government. You can check that out with Birdie. I guarantee he'll confirm that. You can reach him at the home of Sir Alexander James in London."

"Ah!" James Carter's face lit up as if he suddenly understood something. For the first time, he focused his attention on Lissa. Said attention seemed to startle him, as he took in her golden hair, her blue eyes, her gentle, incredibly feminine smile, her oval face, her beautiful teeth, her strong jaw, and her obviously limber, lissome athletic build. He said it again, "Ah," only this time it was the *Ah* men do manage to summon up when confronted by some such rare archetypal goddess. Now he nodded, said:

"Sir Alexander James. Maybe this begins to make some sense. Is Harry playing his favorite role, Mrs. Eliot?"

"What role is that, Mr. Carter?"

Her very, very upper-class British intonation was, in its way, as beautiful as the rest of her. James Carter listened to it with frank admiration, said, "You haven't said much, Mrs. Eliot. That's my fault, my loss. I'd much rather talk to you than to Harry. What role, you ask? Why, Perseus, of course, Perseus going around rescuing Andromeda. Are you being rescued, Mrs. Eliot?"

If James Carter had carried a monocle, he'd be using it now to scrutinize her. This was also an archetypal gesture, this scrutiny, the eternal male in his mode of rape. No Roman youth ever ogled a Sabine lass more lasciviously than James

Carter eyed Lissa Meirion. For a moment, Harry was tempted to pull out his Browning and pistol-whip James Carter, but the latter seemed to recollect himself, shuddered, shook himself, said:

"All right, I will phone Birdie. Oh yes, I will. There's nothing he can say now that will cut any ice. I've got the old bird watcher stuck to a goony bird, haven't I, Harry?"

Harry Ryder rather thought Carter had it right. Would Bingham keep his cool, manage to fob off the cover story they'd agreed on? "If you're exposed," Bingham had whispered, "I'll see you're covered. I'll say you're two consultants to an ally of ours who asked for our help in locating a missing man, one Peter Trubari. We have no interest in Mr. Trubari, other than to help an ally find him. Obviously we couldn't involve the Agency in this project, but we could provide our friends with independent consultants who have a certain skill in this sort of endeavor. A bit flimsy, I know, but not any more so than a hundred other cover stories I could point to. The real thing, of course, is not to get exposed. I know you won't, will you?"

So Bingham. Ryder now said, "Don't get too far off base, James, or you'll get yourself thrown out. Call Birdie, do that. If you still have any problems, we're at the Stefanie. *Auf Wiedersehen*, James. Okay, Marget?"

And it wasn't until they were a few doors from the safehouse that he ventured a glance at Lissa. Was she laughing? She was certainly patently demure. "All right, out with it. What are you laughing at?"

"Goony bird and class distinctions. What's a goony bird, Harry, another bit of American slang?"

"Not exactly. More a bit of American erudition. Midwesterners do become rather highbrow. As witness our namesake, for instance, our—or really your—Mr. T. S. Eliot, originally from St. Louis. *Goony bird* means albatross. He was saying, I think, that Birdie Bingham has an albatross around his neck. And what about class distinctions?"

"I thought one could only find such blatant class distinctions in our country. Corn-fed colleges. My word. Tell me, is he right? About the Ivy League? Is—was your boss, was Mr. Bingham an upper-class Ivy League type?"

"Well, yes and no. He is a Harvard man. A Rhodes Scholar, in fact. But he didn't come from Beacon Hill. He came from the rural slums of Tennessee. His parents were white trash, almost illiterate. But his mother did read a book once about Don Carlos of Spain. She thought that was a wonderful name, and so we have our boss."

"Mr. Bingham, then, is both midwesterner and Ivy League. The best of both worlds."

"Mr. Carter wouldn't see it that way. Bingham belongs to the establishment; in no way is he a midwesterner or mountain hillbilly, not like Carter at all. He embodies what de Tocqueville prophesied in 1837. The destiny of the Midwest, he said, is to supply strong men and women to replenish and supersede the effete denizens of the two coasts. That characterizes Birdie, all right—not Carter, who started out effete and stayed that way when he migrated. Only more so. You saw him."

"Two coasts? I didn't know there were two U.S. coasts in 1837."

"There weren't. De Tocqueville, as so often, was writing history before it happened. If you ever want to read a profound history of our Civil War, read de Tocqueville's history of it."

"Also written in 1837?"

"In the book I just mentioned. His *Democracy in America*."

"I'll read it. Shall we walk all the way to the hotel, Harry? It'll give me time to get the taste of James Carter out of my mouth. Inverse snobbery does tend to nauseate me."

"It does. Of course, a walk'll give those cruising cars a chance to pick us up again, but they'll do that anyway at the Stefanie. So let's use this opportunity to mull over an idea I've had. Lissa, do you really think we should take the time to go up the Schneeberg? Why not just skip all that and head for Zagreb and try to track down Miss Arritsa Patak? Where the Patak is, will the Pickering be far behind?"

"That's our last resort, Harry. And maybe the only choice we have. But don't dismiss the Schneeberg in so cavalier a fashion. I think I can find out things there the police couldn't find. I'm a friend of Frau Dollwitz. Frau Dollwitz is no friend of the police. She thinks all police are Nazi scum."

"Frau Dollwitz? Ah yes, the woman who has a food stand up the mountain."

"A pub, really. Or as near a pub as an Austrian mountain house can make itself. Her place is near the top of the cog-wheel train run. Everybody stops there. And that means Ethan and Arritsa stopped there. And Ethan was—is—a real friend of Frau Dollwitz. I only got to know her through Llew-Llaw. She helped the partisans many times. So don't dismiss the Schneeberg so cavalierly, Harry. Let's hear what Frau Dollwitz might tell us that she didn't tell the State Police."

They crossed the enormous Schottenring, headed towards Wipplingerstrasse. Lissa, in a simple cotton frock and good English walking shoes, kept pace with him easily. Or more correctly, he kept pace with her, just barely. Athletic, this lady was. He said:

"All right, Lissa, the Schneeberg it is. Then Zagreb. But we'll have to move fast before James Carter carries out his threats. I don't like having to face Birdie Bingham and confess I blew this simple assignment right off the bat."

"Nor I Sir Alex."

The Swedish Bridge was in sight, with the Hotel Stefanie only a short distance beyond the Danube Canal. "And we have the problem of keeping our Iron Curtain haircuts off our trail. I haven't the least idea why they're tagging us, but somehow I don't relish having them follow us up that mountain and lecture us in some lonely nook as to their purpose. No indeed. And that brings up that car we rented, that Opel Diesel. It doesn't have much get up and go. Maybe we'd better exchange it for a Mercedes or something."

She took his arm as they crossed the bridge. "Don't worry, Harry. I know this is all strange country to you. But Austria and Yugoslavia are second homes to me. I know the back

96

roads. I think I can use those roads to outfox the hounds. And to begin with, I suggest we take off tonight. Right now. We'll check out of the Stefanie as soon as it's fully dark and head for Puchberg."

"Puchberg?"

"Yes, the town at the foot of the Schneeberg. We'll stay there tonight, go up the mountain tomorrow, check out Frau Dollwitz, and take it from there. If that's agreeable to you."

He laughed happily. "You're a wonder, Lissa. And a winner. And a woman. How can one person be all these things in one?" He held open the door of the Stefanie, followed her towards the stairs, waved to Fritz behind the desk, tramped up the two flights of stairs, unlocked the door, stepped aside. Lissa pushed the door back and halted. As well she might. Three men were standing in the room facing them. All three men had Iron Curtain haircuts. All three had pistols extended and pointing at them. "Please come in, Mrs. Meirion." The speaker was the man nearest Lissa, a bulky fellow of medium height. His English was heavily accented. Poles had accents like that. Or Russians. He wore a gray business suit. The suit, the haircut, the accent—they might be Polish. But to Harry the combination spelled Russian. In fact, spelled KGB Russian. The man waved his pistol, said, "You, too, Mr. Ryder. You, too."

All three men more or less ignored Lissa, focused on him. He could feel his own newly acquired Browning High-Powered sagging in his right pocket. Dandy, just dandy. "Very well. Go ahead, Lissa. I'm with you."

14

Did Lissa take his statement as a signal? He would have to find that out later. At the moment, the pace was a bit too fast for progressive, logical inquiry.

With the men's eyes and pistols on him, Lissa brought her bag up from her hip. Weighted with her Browning High-Powered and the boxes of ammunition, her bag made quite a weapon. She swung it with the force of a cricket bowler. Athletic, she was. It struck the bulky fellow's arm just behind his wrist, sent his pistol arcing toward the ceiling. Harry decided it was about time he joined his impulsive lady. He threw his shoulder against the door. It slammed into the bulky fellow now shaking a sore wrist, sent him reeling into the man behind him who, until then, was half in, half out of the bathroom off to the right. Harry did not pause. He dived forward to tackle the third man standing about six feet into the room, right next to the bed.

The dive saved his life, because man number three fired a shot where Harry's head had been. The bullet missed Harry, zinged out into the hallway. The pistol itself made no noise. Or very little. Even as his shoulder crashed into the man's legs, Harry felt himself recognize the pistol for what it was, a silenced weapon. And, as he learned later, it was fired once more. This time, diverted by his tackle, the bullet found a target. It bored into the bathroom fellow. As Lissa explained later, the man in the bathroom had shoved his disarmed colleague out of the way, come charging back into the room to go for Harry, and got himself hit squarely near the right shoulder. He dropped his pistol, grabbed for his shoulder, crumbled back against the man he had just pushed out of the way, his already disarmed colleague.

At this point, as Lissa also told Harry later, she felt she had a choice. Three choices. She could pick up one of two monstrously long pistols dropped by their assailants. (Long, because they, too, had silencers attached.) Or she could pull her own pistol out of her bag and try to get it working. Or she could help Harry.

The third choice seemed best. Harry's man was tackled and down, all right, but he still held his pistol, and he was doing his best to bring it into line with Harry's back. Because of the excessive barrel length and Harry's vigorous efforts to grab his arm, this maneuver wasn't all that easy. But then, it wasn't all that difficult, either. So Lissa acted on her third option. She stepped forward, kicked the gun hand with a sturdy square-toed English walking shoe, saw the pistol go sailing against the television set, then backed herself up to exercise one of her other options. She pulled the pistol from her bag, jiggled the safety off, pointed the barrel at the bulky fellow who was supporting his comrade, then waited for Harry to join her.

He did—after picking up a pistol. He waved it at the fellow on the floor, herded him beside his two comrades, shut the door, and looked at them, then at her.

"Russians, Lissa. At least, they seem that way to me. Genuine, authentic KBG-issue Russians. Shall I kill them?"

Lissa brushed the hair back from her forehead in that quintessentially feminine gesture of hers, shook her head so that her hair rippled over her shoulders. Beauty amidst ugliness. Stunning, just stunning—at least, for him it was. She said, "I don't think so, Harry. I don't think they were planning to kill us, so why kill them?"

"He shot at me, Lissa. Twice." The word *twice* didn't strike him as emphatic enough so he amended it. "Two times, Lissa. Two times."

"I don't think he was authorized to do that, Harry. Did you catch the disgust on the face of that one there?" She pointed her pistol at the bulky fellow, the man she had first attacked. "I don't think he at all approved of the attempt to kill you."

The men—even the wounded one—were staring at her as if fascinated by her words. The Delphic prophetess mesmerizing her dull-witted male audience. As the sense of her words sank in, they let out their breaths. It was now apparent they had stopped breathing when they had heard Ryder's casual death threat. They now turned their eyes on Ryder. With prospects of living now on the rise, they let their eyes and squarish faces assume an unbecoming truculence.

Lissa added one more comment. "The man with the shoulder wound needs medical attention, Harry. Also, blood is starting to stain the carpet."

So it was. "Very well, Lissa. We can't have bloodstains on the carpet. It's unbecoming."

He opened the door, gestured. "On your way, gentlemen. On your way. And don't come back. Next time, I may not let Mrs. Meirion persuade me to be so charitable. Go."

The bulky man held back his comrades. "Our pistols. Give us back our pistols."

"Sorry, gentlemen. I'm a collector of pistols. Just can't help adding to my collection. I've never had one of these. What is it?" He glanced at the fourteen-inch-long weapon in his hand. "What do you know? A PM. A Pistolet Makarov. Russia's best. Well, well. Complete with custom-built silencers. Sorry, gentlemen, I'm afraid you'll have to report your unfortunate losses to your resident chief. Tell him I'll treasure these beauties."

The men trudged out. One tall. One short. One bulky. All wearing strangely ballooning suits. All brachycephalic. All sporting stringy haircuts with minimal, almost nonexistent sideburns. Prison haircuts. Harry stepped out, watched them disappear around the corner. What would Fritz at the desk say when he saw two thugs half-carrying a bleeding comrade?

He returned to the room, shut the door, double-locked it. "They're combat-troop types, Lissa. Strong-arm boys."

"Will they come back?"

"Yes. They or replacements." He studied Lissa's white face. The whiteness set off the blue eyes. She looked like a ghost in a grade-C horror movie. Easing her pistol from her slack hand, he guided her to the bed, helped her stretch out. "May I tell you how much I admire you? Your courage. Your skill. Your speed. Fast. You are fast. You are wonderful. I love you."

He slipped in that *I love you* as unobtrusively as possible. He hadn't dared say it during their lovemaking, even though it deserved saying, since it was the truth. But he'd been afraid to hazard the gambit then, thought maybe he could get away with it now, could go on record, so to speak, and then run like hell. Certainly it seemed to slip by her. She said:

100

"My courage? Why, you said to go ahead, you said you were with me. It was all your idea. I just—"

"Good God, I thought so! Communication. People do say it's the greatest of all human problems." Had he managed to communicate that *I love you*? "I failed to communicate with you and almost got us killed. I just meant to go ahead into the room. We were lucky."

"We were good."

"So we were. Thanks again."

While she closed her eyes and let the tension subside in her body, he got out their suitcases and had one of them half-filled before she came out of her torpor to rise on her elbow and watch him. He looked up, said:

"Why Russians, Lissa? I thought we were dealing with Yugoslavians. Why Russians?"

"Ever since those men in the cars started trailing us, ever since we spotted their haircuts, I've been asking myself the same question."

"And?"

"I may have some answers. But this is not the time to review them. This is the time to move. Harry, a reminder. I believe the Doughty passport has you minus a moustache."

"So it does. I'll get right to it."

"No, finish the packing, if you will, Harry. I've got a little chore to do now, then I'll call Fritz and check out on the phone. I don't want to go down past the desk."

"Right. They'll be watching us."

"And they'll also be watching the back way, too. In fact, they'll be after us no matter where we go. Because that's the name of this game, Harry. They didn't want to kill us, you know that, don't you?"

He nodded. "I know. That fellow you hit, he maybe could have gotten off a shot at you if he'd wanted to. Or maybe he couldn't have, you must consider that, Lissa. After all, there were three guns pointing at us. Men with that advantage really expect obedience. An attack on them by you was the last thing in the world they expected.

"But I agree with you about that cretin who did shoot at me. He was disobeying orders. The other two men were shocked at his action. We were supposed to be taken alive, not dead."

He finished packing, closed the suitcases, stepped back, and looked at Lissa, found her busy cutting up a Hotel Stefanie towel.

"What are you doing?"

"I've always detested people who steal hotel towels. And look at me."

"You're not stealing a towel, you're cutting one up into pieces. And why so, may I ask?"

"Just a precaution, Harry. I'm going to cover the taillights. They'll be following us, but the taillights aren't going to help them keep on our trail. And where we're going, I think the blackout will be a plus. You'll see."

"I'll be all eyes. Now for my moustache. A moment, please."

When he came out of the bathroom, Lissa was just putting down the phone. "Fritz is . . . My, how different you look without that moustache. I liked your moustache, but this— this is better. Shall we go?"

He put the electric shaver in a shoulder bag, nodded, picked up one suitcase. "Will you carry the other, Lissa? I think we both better have a gun hand free for ye olde fast draw. Okay?"

"Harry, I like the way we understand each other without saying a word."

"You mean it's a Pickering-and-Patak story all over again? If they wanted us alive, we can assume they wanted Pickering-Patak alive? Provided, of course, Patak is not herself KGB. If she is, then I'm a little on the lost side."

"She's not. She's the reincarnation of Mitra Grgić. Reincarnations are not KGB types. No, we can assume Ethan and Arritsa were kidnapped. We can assume they wanted to kidnap us. A reasonable assumption?"

"Reasonable, but why?"

"I don't know."

"Why a Russian kidnapping?"

"I don't know."

"Why Russians, then?"

"I may have something on that. Shall we go?"

"We shall. After you."

15

The Puchbergerhof restaurant was off to the left, the registration desk to the right. At that hour, after one in the morning, the restaurant was only dimly illuminated. As Ryder followed Lissa to the registration desk, he glanced into the restaurant, almost stumbled from the shock.

Two men were sitting and fondling half-filled beer steins. They had halted their conversation to turn and watch the late arrivals. They seemed brothers of the men who had tried to capture them at the Hotel Stefanie. Gray, loose-fitting business suits. Brachycephalic skulls. Prison haircuts. One quite blond. One almost dark.

No clerk was at the reception desk. Ryder took advantage of the delay. "Lissa, step back and take a quick look at the men having a beer in the restaurant."

A stoutish clerk came out from the rear office. He was in shirt sleeves and carried a sheaf of papers in his hand. He was annoyed. He didn't like having his accounting work interrupted, even by potential patrons. Yes, there was a room. Yes. They could park their car behind the hotel. Yes, the first cogwheel up the Schneeberg left at eight-thirty in the morning. Was that all? Then please register and here was the key and good night.

"I'll help you carry in the bags."

He noticed that she spoke loudly enough for the men in the restaurant to hear her. Once outside, he stopped and faced her. "Shall we just keep on going, Lissa? Get back in the car and head for Yugoslavia?"

But for once she wasn't quick on the uptake. Just the contrary. Her head and shoulders drooped dispiritedly. She half-whispered, "All that driving . . . thinking we outwitted them . . . and they stayed right with us—followed us to the hotel. Oh, Harry, I'm so tired."

"You've been magnificent, Lissa. And still are. Those slugs didn't follow us here. No way."

He leaned down to look up at her downcast eyes. She hadn't heard a word he said. She was obviously thinking back over their flight from Vienna, asking herself where she had gone wrong. Hadn't she finally gotten away from the trailing Mercedes by pulling off a nifty maneuver? She had raced past a truck right in the face of another truck barreling down at her in the opposite lane. Cutting in front of the two trucks, with both drivers honking madly, she had doused her lights, plunged through a hedge on the right and come to a stop in a Vienna Woods meadow; no sooner had the trucks and Mercedes vanished around a bend, than she had pushed their Opel once more through the hedge and headed back toward Vienna with lights off.

That had been the hairy part. No lights to see by except for a half-moon occasionally peeping through the hedges and trees. But also no lights to be seen by. Their taillights and reflectors had been covered by Lissa in the garage. "Band-Aids aren't the most wonderful of tapes, but they should hold the towel strips. I hope."

"Me, too," he had said. "I understand the effect. Our rear lights and reflectors won't betray our presence. So what?"

"So what? At some point, I intend to drive in the dark. With no lights on. Llew-Llaw and I learned how to do this in Turkey. There, it's illegal to drive at night with your lights on. Not illegal exactly. But unwise. If you hit someone at nighttime with your headlights on, you're obviously responsible for the accident. You should have been able to see the other fellow. But if both cars have their lights off, then obviously no one is responsible. It's Allah's will. Driving there—especially on mountain roads with a cliff on one side and giant lorries coming at you down the middle of the road—that's an experience. But I've done it there. I can do it here. I think."

And her foresight had turned the trick. Watching through the rear window, he had seen the Mercedes come charging back in their direction. Fortunately it had not kept coming; it had stopped at the break in the hedge, then disappeared from sight as their Opel swept around a curve and off to the south and up a narrow lane. Lissa had driven for about five minutes, then pulled once again into a meadow and driven the car into a clump of trees. They had leaped from the car and frantically covered it with bushes and grasses and branches. Not the world's greatest concealment job, but effective. And necessary. Because in about fifteen minutes a car came creeping up the one-lane macadam road. It wasn't the Mercedes. It was a Ford of some kind. And someone in the front seat kept flashing a spotlight to the right and left. "Just like this afternoon," he had whispered. "A team of cars." "Don't worry," she had whispered back. "If they see us, they won't kill us. Just capture us." "Thanks, I'll remember." But they weren't seen, nor captured, nor killed. They had waited in the meadow for over an hour. (And well they had. After about forty minutes, the Ford had come creeping back down the lane, once more going through the spotlight routine.) Then Lissa, car lights still out, had eased the Opel along back roads in the Vienna Woods, kept a generally westward direction, and then, almost to Sankt Pölten, had turned the lights back on, removed the towel strips, crossed the freeway, and gone up into the high Alps, only turning back east toward Puchberg when they reached the high mountains at Annaberg. Altogether it had been a plucky, skillful performance. And a successful one.

"Lissa," he said now, putting his hand under her chin and raising her face, "listen to me. We weren't followed here. Your foresight saved the day. That was the key, your foresight. You lost those cars back in the Vienna Woods. The jolly chaps in the restaurant aren't after us—weren't after us—they're a rearguard action. Covering their back trail."

105

"Rearguard?"

"Yes, rearguard. They're proof that Ethan and Arritsa did vanish around here, around Puchberg and the Schneeberg. They're also proof that the Russians are in this up to their ears. Whatever this is. So shall we try to get the jump on these fellows? I doubt very much if they have any idea who we are, or that their comrades were waltzing all around the Vienna Woods trying to find us. But by now they've looked at the register. Very shortly, Vienna will tell them to hold Mr. and Mrs. Eliot until reinforcements arrive." Maybe they should have used the Doughty passports, but then they'd have no pristine passports in Yugoslavia; Doughty had to be reserved for Yugoslavia. "But they can't hold us if we're no longer here. Shall we take off for the border?"

"Rearguard?"

Hadn't she heard a word he said? Was her mind stuck like a record player needle on the word *rearguard?* What was happening—had happened—to his intuitive, sensitive, Welsh-gifted lady? How does one react to, cope with, a mind apparently bemused by an obsessive train of thought? Humor her? Bark at her? Slap her? He was the man of experience—what did his experience tell him about obsession? Mighty damned little, and that, Harry, is a fact. He said:

"Yes, rearguard." He tried to keep himself from sounding like an adult addressing a thumb-sucking child. He knew he wasn't very successful.

"Harry, if they're guarding their back trail, isn't it possible there's something still here to guard? If we hie ourselves off to Yugoslavia, we'll never find out why they're here. Don't you think it's worthwhile at least to try to find out what's up?"

She was back. Obviously, she had never gone anywhere. Even in the pale moonlight, he could see her great blue eyes flashing and sparkling.

"You're right."

"Then it's agreed? We stay? We've got to stay and find out what they're afraid we'll find out."

"This means trouble, Lissa. Bad trouble. If we think we've seen manpower before, wait until tomorrow."

"So? We're armed. Armed? Harry, we've got five pistols between us."

"Two-fisted gunfighters. Great, just great. Except I'm a terrible shot with my good hand, my right hand. And there's no way I can fire a pistol with my left. Oh. I see. You're the two-gun expert?"

"Me? I'm only an average shot, Harry. I told you that." At least she didn't say she was no Terry Jefferson. "You can't count on me, but you can count on our ally."

"Ally?"

"The mountain, Harry. I know the mountain. It's a beautiful mountain. It's my friend. Our friend."

Should he point out that she was indulging in John Ruskin's detested pathetic fallacy? A mountain is a mountain, not a friend. Should he? He should not. People with Welsh gifts may also be able to maintain friendships with mountains. And, for all he knew, vice versa. No point in being captious. Wiser to say something constructive. So he said it:

"Lissa, I've come to know something. I'm not in love with you. I love you."

16

Perhaps they slept one, maybe two hours that night. Yet curiously, at seven-thirty in the morning, when Lissa and he stood on the steps of the hotel and looked out on Puchberg's central park, neither one felt the least bit tired. Quite the contrary. They were both elated. It had been a big night. A great night. A wonderful night. And somehow it had rejuvenated them. No twenty-year-old could have felt more vigorous—certainly nowhere near as happy—as fiftyish Harry Ryder standing beside his own true love.

He ignored the two Russians sitting on a park bench across the street. He waved at the park. "It's beautiful. It's almost Japanese in effect. A stream, a clear lake, five or six acres of greensward, trees, flowers. It makes me feel as if I were back at home in the Orient. A classic Japanese park in the Austrian Alps."

Lissa was buying none of that. "Why are our two Russians sitting there with their eyes closed?"

"They're enjoying the sun."

"Be serious, Harry. Is it possible they haven't gotten instructions from Vienna? Are we in the clear?"

"Let's find out. Let's go get our tickets before all these Austrians gobble up the seats. If those two follow us, we'll know the answer to your question. Our question."

But they weren't followed. The two Russians, eyes closed, continued to soak up the sun. Lissa and he, hand in hand—marvelous, her touch, marvelous the oneness it created—strolled to the station, got in line with the heavily bundled-up Austrians. When their turn came, he let Lissa do the negotiating for the tickets, turned, and glanced at the cog-wheel train.

It was a pusher. The hissing engine faced into two wooden, green-painted cars sitting before it. The cars were already almost completely filled. The conductor was looking at his watch. And two men in loose-fitting gray business suits with thick heads of hair—both blond this time—were standing by the front car and looking across the two mainline tracks at Lissa and him.

He waited until she had the tickets in her hand, said, "We've got our answer, Lissa. Manpower it is. Those two standing by the first car."

"I see them." She led the way across the regular tracks to the cog tracks. "Business suits, yet. What do they think the Schneeberg is? A stroll around Vienna's Inner City?"

Lissa had strong opinions about the need for proper clothing. As they dressed, she'd said, "We won't be able to match the Austrians. They'll be carrying rucksacks and wearing heavy sweaters or even ski jackets, they'll have hiking boots, knee-length hiking socks, the works. But there's a good reason for all the equipment. This may be July. Midsummer and all that.

108

But that doesn't prevent a sudden snowstorm from coming up. Or equally bad, a wretched freezing rainstorm—or at the least, an equally freezing fog. These are the Alps, Harry. They demand and deserve respect. You can wear your crepe-soled shoes, they'll have to do. You'll need both your sweaters and your Burberry jacket. Me, I'll wear my jeans, my blue jacket, two sweaters also, and an extra pair of hose and of course my walking shoes. We should be able to cope that way."

And he nodded, said, "Good. I'll carry all five pistols in my shoulder bag, plus passports and money. No use leaving them in this room for the inevitable inspection by someone—probably by our Russian friends, but certainly by the maid."

Now they walked past the Russians, went to the second car, the one right in front of the engine. Harry held the green door open for Lissa, scrambled in beside her. Two wooden benches faced each other. Each one extended all the way across the train. There was no central aisle. The benches were filled with eight stout, sturdy, heavily clothed Austrian men and women. Cumbersome, fully packed rucksacks sat on each lap. The Austrians reluctantly rearranged themselves to allow two vacant adjacent seats. Lissa and he faced forward. Eight pairs of eyes watched them settle down. One or two of their neighbors whispered to each other. "Foreigners." Otherwise there was no welcome, no sign of recognition, no courtesy, no greeting. Austrians know no tourist can properly understand or appreciate or value their beloved Schneeberg. They don't deserve a greeting.

The Russians walked down to their compartment, saw there were no vacant seats, walked four compartments forward till they found the first location that offered them two seats facing Lissa and Harry. They seemed unaware of the contempt on the Austrians' faces. Contempt that clearly said these were not just foreigners, intruders, tourists incapable of loving nature and the Schneeberg; they were the worst kind of foreigners, the kind that mountain patrols would have to go up and rescue because they were not properly dressed.

The coughing, steaming pusher engine behind them gave

an extra-loud cough, emitted a blast on the whistle, an old-fashioned train whistle, and they began to chug forward. He turned to Lissa, said:

"How will we be able to talk to Frau Dollwitz with those two goons breathing down our necks?"

Lissa glanced self-consciously at her neighbors, but their discourtesy to foreigners had now become indifference. After the first few moments of stony silence to show how offended they were, eight Austrians were now engaged in animated cross-compartment dialogues and octologues. If the American man and the British lady were talking to each other, were capable of talking to each other, this was a fact to be noted along with other similar facts; e.g., dogs bark, cats meow, cows moo, birds chirp. And given as much attention.

Relieved, Lissa turned back to Harry. "That's a problem. And there's no point in using Serbo-Croatian with Frau Doll-witz, because—"

"Serbo-Croatian?"

"Why, yes. Frau Dollwitz—oh dear, she must be over eighty years of age now. Do you suppose she's . . . that thought's never crossed my mind until now. She just has to be alive, to be there. She *will* be there. I saw her only a year ago. So. So, yes, Serbo-Croatian. She originally came from Rabenstein on the Drau River. That's only a kilometer or so from Yugoslavia. From Croatia. And of course in the old days, when she was a girl, there were no national boundaries between Croatia and Austria. Croatia was part of the Austro-Hungarian Empire. She learned to speak Croatian as a matter of course.

"So as I said, there's no using that language with her. Even if our Russian friends up ahead don't happen to speak it, they should have little difficulty following the gist of any conversation. So . . . so let me think. There must be a way. How do we get a private conversation with Frau Dollwitz?"

Since there wasn't much he could contribute to solving this problem, he immersed himself in contemplation of the mountain. It was beautiful, no question of that. Meadows and slopes and cliffs fell off to their left; mountains tumbled up higher and higher toward the far south; trees—mostly pines but also some spruce and larch and scrub oak—dotted the mountain-side above, below, and around them. Occasional chalets or farmhouses could be seen in the distance, and sometimes near the railroad tracks. Lissa had a point. It wouldn't be difficult to establish a friendly relationship with this mountain.

He turned to her and said as much, and she smiled happily. "I'm glad you like it, Harry. It's not like Kitzbühel, of course. That's high drama. This is a poem. Kitzbühel is the *Eroica*. This is the *Pastoral*."

"Pastoral? What about snowstorms or sleet or fog? What about the menace of the mountain?"

"Beethoven's already answered that. In the storm movement of the symphony."

"Touché!"

"Harry, look at those two up there. They're watching so hard, they don't even blink, isn't that amazing?" And she took hold of his arm, grabbed it really, said, "Harry, I've got it. Here's what we'll do. The train stops for about ten minutes at the Baumgartenhaus so people can buy Frau Dollwitz's delights."

"Buy delights! Look at those rucksacks. They're crammed with delights. Enough food for an infantry company. God, even Austrians must draw the line somewhere."

"Ah, but not when it's a question of Frau Dollwitz's offer-ings. She puts out a spread that's simply mouth-watering. It's her own baking, her own recipes. Tortes, and an incredible apricot bun, six inches high and six inches across. All spread out on a table by the tracks. Wait until you see it. Then tell me how superior Austrians should be to her food.

"Anyway, we'll stop there, and I'll tell Frau Dollwitz we want to talk to her later. We'll stay with the train to the top of the mountain and wander around a bit and then take the yellow trail back to the Baumgartenhaus."

"Yellow trail?"

"Oh, yes, the mountain patrols have marked trails all through the Alps. Each mountain has them, yellow, red, green, white, blue trails, whatever. And when we come down the trail to the Baumgartenhaus, we should be at least a half-mile ahead of those two."

"Baumgartenhaus instead of the usual Berghaus. I like that name. Tree nursery house. That's Oriental, too, you know. A merging and blending, a unifying of man and nature, house and trees. Baumgartenhaus. Very interesting. But how will we be a half-mile ahead of them?"

She explained, and he nodded. "Okay. I understand. Or I think I do."

17

And he did understand, though not at first, not in the hurly-burly of Austrians stampeding from the train. And not while trying to overcome his disappointment at the unimpressive topography at the top of the mountain.

Lissa saw the expression on his face and understood. "Don't let it bother you. If a cogwheel train is going to park at the top of a mountain, then it has to be in a place like this, with an ample flat expanse. Come on, let's go over to the gazebo, and you can enjoy a beautiful view again. And you'll also understand better about how we can get a head start on our leeches."

Obediently he followed her. The gazebo was about fifty or sixty yards due north of the train. When they got there along with five or six other train riders, he looked back at the engine. And at the Russians. They had moved away from the train and taken a seat on a bench by the stone hut that served as headquarters for the train crews. The true peak of the Schnee-berg loomed about a quarter of a mile beyond the hut, rising maybe another four or five hundred feet. The Austrians had begun to disperse, some towards the peak, others to trails around it. None of them was heading north. Towards Puchberg.

"Where are all the Austrians going? Won't they be hiking down the mountain?"

"Most unlikely. They'll stroll around the mountaintop and the next col. They'll picnic somewhere. And then they'll catch one of the afternoon trains down the mountain."

He shook his head. "I don't get it. It's worse than riding a golf cart to hit a golf ball. I just don't get it. They're dressed as if they were going to climb Mount Everest, and all they're going to do is have a picnic lunch. And don't tell me about snowstorms and rainstorms and fog and cold. If it turns nasty, they can go into the railroad hut or sit in a train until departure time."

She laughed and put her arm through his and snuggled up to him. "Forget our fellow travelers. Here, turn around and see what's to see. This is what Nietzsche had in mind, Zarathustra country. *Also sprach Zarathustra auf dem Berggipfel.* Thus spake Zarathustra on the mountain peak."

And he looked. And looked. And looked. She had to jiggle his arm to get his attention.

"That's enough. You'll have to pay your dues another time. Now look toward the northeast. Across that scrubby plateau. See those poles heading to the right, to the northeast? Those mark the yellow trail. That's the way we'll go. You can't see it from here, but the plateau ends abruptly at the third and last pole. From there, the trail goes almost straight down for quite a distance, then hits a new plateau just before the Baumgartenhaus. Shall we go?"

"Not yet. First a misdirection. Let's stroll to the plateau's edge in the opposite direction. Towards the southwest, over there. We'll admire the scenery and point hither and yon and then stroll back in the other direction as if we were going to repeat our sightseeing tour. It can't do any harm to try. Okay?"

When they reached the edge of a cliff, he glanced back at the stone hut. The Russians were leaning forward and watch-

113

ing intently. They were alert enough, but not minatory. Not yet. Whatever he and Lissa were doing, it didn't alarm or threaten them. What would threaten them? The Baumgartenhaus? The yellow trail? "Let's point—say, I see what you mean about the cold and fog."

Lissa acted out her pointing bit, said, "Right. Sunny and almost cloudless up here. Closed in down there to the west. And soaking wet all the way down."

"It reminds me of Muir Woods. In Marin County in California. Sometimes you stand on Mount Tamalpais in the sun and look down at Muir Woods a thousand feet below you and find them fog-blanketed. In fact, this plateau replicates our California chaparral. You don't know chaparral? Well, it covers the Coastal Range for a thousand miles. And it seems to me the spit and image of the flora on this part of the Schneeberg. So? Time to go?"

She nodded and they meandered back to the gazebo and then strolled at a leisurely pace towards the poles. He looked at the first one, said:

"Yellow trail? That's not a yellow swab. That's green paint. Or am I suddenly color blind?"

She laughed. (These were genuine laughs, and as such, the best possible bit of misdirection. Even the sourest KGB ghoul would find it difficult to suspect trickery amidst such patent joy.)

"Just Austrian thrift. One color at a time. The trails branch down below. The green trail to the east and north, the yellow to the west and the north, too. We'll find the yellow paint once we're beyond the restaurant. And yes, Harry Ryder, I love you, too. No, don't stop and kiss me now. But you may tell me you love me."

He complied. Several times. Then added, "It's best this way, Lissa. Maybe it only really happens this way. When neither one expects it. If you go charging around looking for love, well . . . well, I don't think that works. Only like this. Out of the blue. No, wait a moment. Let me finish. I want to say something about something that's been bothering me.

114

I'm not terribly introspective, I just do, and later I might find out why I do what I do.

"So anyway. You accused me of having a latent patriotic drive. I found that awfully hard to believe, Lissa. This is the time of the antiheroic. I've gone along with that, but I've been watching myself, and you know, Lissa, you may just be right. Now I know I'm no Llew-Llaw Griffes, that's for sure." (He at last did know who Llew-Llaw Griffes was, had finally, last night amidst their unreserved lovemaking, had finally dared ask why her husband had been called Llew-Llaw. And she had explained. When Robert Graves's book *The White Goddess* had come out, Llewelyn Laurent Meirion's classmates at Oxford had no sooner read the story of Llew-Llaw Griffes, the Welsh Hercules, than they had transmuted Llewelyn Laurent into Llew-Llaw.) "But I find I do enjoy this sort of thing. And part of the reason seems to be, I think what I've done, what we're doing now, is right. I know that's a selective patriotism. It's not a my-country-right-or-wrong sort of thing. But when the cause is right, when my old warlock asks for my help on a just cause—well, here I am. So."

"So it's probably a way of hanging on to your lost youth."

For a moment he was startled, then he saw her excessively demure expression and found himself laughing with her. She took his arm, said:

"No ABC's Harry. No ABC's, no apologies, no fears. What's happened has happened and will continue to happen, and now let's go."

"Tell me, did you know this was going to happen when Birdie said we'd travel as Mr. and Mrs. Glen Eliot? Did you?"

"What do you think? Come on, another fifty yards, then down we go."

They went the fifty yards and she said, "Five yards more, and we slip over the edge and go as fast as we can run. But not too fast. It's precipitous with loose stones. Awfully easy to sprain an ankle. But we should get the lead time we need for talking with Frau Dollwitz. She got my message all right, I just wish we had gotten hers."

For when the cogwheel had stopped to let the passengers buy Frau Dollwitz's marvelous concoctions—the apricot bun was as vast and tasty and soft and delicious as Lissa had promised—Frau Dollwitz had not only proved to be very much alive, but she had also seen and recognized Lissa at once. She had recognized her, raised her eyelids to show recognition, caught and understood Lissa's mouthed word, "Later!" lowered her eyes rapidly instead of nodding her head, then turned her back to attend to other customers. All of this took no more than a second or so. Lissa had been left standing there, a puzzled frown on her face, but Harry had taken her arm and steered her over to buy a beer from Frau Dollwitz's son, a fifty-year-old, as lean and bony as his mother. If he also recognized Lissa, he gave no sign to that effect. He handed them their beer and, like his mother, busied himself with other passengers. "That was fast," Harry had said to Lissa once they were back in the compartment. "Too fast. She was giving you a warning. What warning?" But Lissa had shaken her head. "I wish I knew. I'm baffled, too. I don't understand it."

Now they sauntered to the plateau edge, pointed right and left as if still sightseeing, eased themselves beneath the crest, and began to jog. She was right. The trail was precipitous, the loose pebbles slippery. They found themselves sliding down the zigzagging path as often as they were able to walk or jog. They hadn't gone ten feet before they were hidden from the Russians. He pointed to the Baumgartenhaus.

"When we reach the flat down there—and assuming they're following us—they'll be able to see us. And we'll be able to see them. They could have us at a disadvantage then. We'll have to walk sedately and maintain an unconcerned front, but they'll be able to run. But no matter what they do, we'll still keep on walking sedately. That's our best bet."

She nodded. "Smart, Harry Ryder. Very smart."

He couldn't say what he wanted to say just then, because they had reached a relatively straight stretch, at least forty yards of gradual slant, and Lissa had sprinted ahead at a reckless speed. However, at the next precipitous zig and zag, while

116

they were gingerly climbing down from brown slate rock to brown slate rock, he caught up with her and made his point. Or tried to.

"Lissa, I'm going to lay the law down. When we get to Frau Dollwitz's—"

But another straightaway beckoned, and Lissa sprinted ahead once more. It took him fifteen minutes to complete his thought. And by that time, they had almost reached the level ground. There the trail paralleled the cogwheel tracks, which proceeded in a gentle slope down to the Baumgarten-haus a couple of hundred yards ahead. As Harry began his peroration, he cast a quick glance back up the mountain. Lissa nodded.

"I see them, Harry. They're slowing down. They're match-ing our pace. We'll have at least five minutes alone with Frau Dollwitz. You were saying?"

"I was saying that, yes, I'm very smart. Smart enough to know this thing is out of hand. I'm laying down the law, Lissa. When we get to the Baumgartenhaus, that's the end of the line. We're not going to take on two armed combat types. Yes, armed. Our two goons are wearing shoulder holsters on the left side. When they get close again, just compare the slope of the right lapel with the slope of the left. You'll see the left one is slightly off kilter.

"And the point is, those two will know a hell of a lot more about handling a handgun than we do. That's unfair compe-tition, Lissa. And it's a risk we can no longer accept. We'll listen to Frau Dollwitz. We'll find out why she was so secre-tive. And then we'll wait right there in the Baumgartenhaus until the cogwheel comes back down the mountain. If those two are bent on abducting us, they'll have to do it down below. If they can. Because once we're at the bottom, I have no compunction whatever about yelling for help from the Aus-trian State Police or even from James Carter. I know when we're licked. We told Birdie Bingham and Sir Alexander James we'd scout around for Ethan and Arritsa. We didn't promise to take on the KGB's First Directorate. I don't care if we've stumbled into some Russian plot with, about, for, or against Yugoslavia. We'll report to Birdie, run like hell, and let him save the world."

For last night, in a lull in their lovemaking, Lissa had explained what she thought might be happening.

"It's simple, Harry. Or it's not so simple. It's not something I could have said while Tito was alive. With Tito, Yugoslavia had a purpose. It was a nonaligned country. Neither West nor East. And it was a genuine country. A united republic. Six republics in one. A true and genuine nation. But no more. I'm afraid the real Yugoslavia is reasserting itself."

"Real Yugoslavia?"

"For a thousand years, Yugoslavia was split. Basically into two countries. Serbia and Croatia. But there were minor principalities. Montenegro. Generally aligned with Serbia, as was Macedonia. Slovenia. Generally aligned with Croatia. And Bosnia-Herzegovina, sometimes aligned with Serbia, sometimes with Croatia, but for three centuries generally with Turkey. Yes, the Moslem influence can still be seen in Bosnia. And finally, Albanian Kosovo, aligned with none of the above, committed only to Albania. So for hundreds of years, there were Serbs and Croats and their allies. And for hundreds of years, one of their chief occupations was killing each other.

"Tito put a stop to that—after the war. He couldn't do much about it during the war. As Inspector Perpar told us at Scotland Yard, during the war these same Croats and Serbs really went at this business of slaughtering each other. It was a bloodbath. Almost a million and a half Yugoslavs killed by Yugoslavs. Outside of the country, this bloodbath was ignored.

"But it wasn't—hasn't been ignored in Yugoslavia. What happened forty years ago can't be forgotten that easily. Nor can the passions of a thousand years be readily dismissed. There are Serbs, many Serbs, who still dream of a Serbian nation that dominates all the other republics. There are as many or more Croats who want no part of Serbia—and hence of Yugoslavia, either."

"I've seen that back home," he had said. "I've seen giant

118

signs painted on cliffs along highways that say, 'Free Croatia.' I've never seen any 'Free Serbia' signs, but maybe Croats are more artistic than Serbs. Sorry. A joke, Lissa. You were saying?"

"I was saying, Tito's legacy may be dissipating. His legacy of unity. Serbs living with Croats, working with them, building with them, a synergistic force that, during Tito's lifetime, made Yugoslavia a uniquely wonderful country. He died too soon, Harry. Too soon. They're starting to split up. And if I'm right, if there are Serbs and Croats who want to set up Serbia or Croatia as ruler, as dictator of Yugoslavia, what better way than to look for allies? Or for one ally?"

"The Soviet Union."

And she had nodded, and now, taking her arm in his, he said, "Please, Lissa. Please. The minute we saw those cars tailing us in Vienna, we should have caught the next plane for London."

And she laughed happily, quite unimpressed by his fears and the causes of them coming down the hill behind him. "Then we wouldn't have had last night. Isn't it good we didn't catch that plane?" She pressed his arm, leaned against him. The Baumgartenhaus was only a few feet away. "That sounds flip. Forgive me. I agree. We won't do anything foolish. We'll hear Frau Dollwitz out, take the train back down the hill, and go to the police. Do you feel better now?"

Lissa pushed past him, embraced the slight, lean, but sturdy old lady, introduced him. Frau Dollwitz hugged Lissa with equal fervor. Her face was wreathed in a happy smile, but there was a frown on her forehead. And after a nod to him, she pulled back and spoke rapidly to Lissa. Her speed—and the Alpine dialect—were too much for Harry's German; but Lissa turned, repeated the old lady's words in slow and simple Berlin-German.

"Frau Dollwitz says those two swine are following us. She saw them from the window."

The old lady nodded, started another torrent of words, backed up, and started again at much slower speed. And now

119

used Viennese German. "Yes, swine. After seven years of Nazi pigs, I and every other Austrian of my time can smell the type."

Lissa nodded. "You're right, Frau Dollwitz. The same breed. Only those are Russians."

Frau Dollwitz had a marvelous serenity to her. Her forehead might frown, but the corners of her lips turned upward. Frau Dollwitz could carry both masks at once, tragedy and comedy. With each one receiving its due. "I know. There was one with our friend. Your friend and mine."

"Our friend? Ethan Pickering? You did see him!"

"Yes. At first I didn't recognize him. He had a beard and long hair. And he was with a redheaded Yugoslav lady who was obviously very much in love with him. As he with her, maybe even more so. And two steps behind them, but never talking to them, just watching them with pig's eyes, was one of those swine. I didn't recognize Herr Pickering, not even when he did a strange thing. I should have understood, should have remembered. He moved his eyes. Like this." And Frau Dollwitz shot her eyes quickly from right to left, left to right. "With the Nazis, we all learned to do that. We learned the trick from the Yugoslav partisans. You couldn't shake your head when trying to warn a friend. If you did, you'd end up in a concentration camp. You shook your head at me, Frau Meirion. You didn't have to. I saw the two swine watching you.

"But sit down, let me get you a beer. And I just baked some fresh apricot buns. They're still warm. Here, sit down."

But Lissa put her hand on the old lady's arm. "Thank you, Frau Dollwitz. But we haven't time. Those swine up there are after us. Tell us why Herr Pickering waggled his eyes at you."

For the first time, Frau Dollwitz seemed to recognize the tension in their faces and bodies. She appraised them, nodded. "I begin to understand. Before, I was just puzzled. Now I understand."

"Understand what?"

"When Herr Pickering and that woman came on down—they were going to hike back down the mountain—they came in and ordered a beer. And after ordering, Herr Pickering, he—but you understand, I hadn't yet recognized him—he turned to that woman and spoke in Serbo-Croatian. He said, 'Arritsa, it's wonderful news, that phone call you got this morning. They're granting you your vacation. Marvelous. At last I'm going home. No more delays. I can't wait to see Plitvice again. I want to show you my home. Žarko Pantić got me the necessary permission to build it, and I know you'll love it. And it's not far from Bihać, either. All the joy of mountain living with a beautiful town nearby.'

"When he said that, that's when I recognized him. Years ago he told me his dream was to have a home near the Plitvice Lakes, not too far from Bihać. He used almost the same words—even the reference to Pantić. I know Pantić. Herr Pickering brought him here once and introduced us. Oh yes, I finally recognized him."

"And then?"

"Why, then this Arritsa, she said, 'Peter, that old lady is looking at us. You make me self-conscious. I think she understands what we're saying.' And Herr Pickering, now apparently Herr Peter also, he said, 'Nonsense, Arritsa. This is just an ignorant old mountain hag. She barely knows German, much less Serbo-Croatian. God, how wonderful it is for us to use my real language. Home! Home at last!' "

"What then, Frau Dollwitz?"

"Well, then they had their beer, and I went back into the kitchen. I couldn't lurk around and eavesdrop, could I? Even though it was clear Herr Pickering wanted me to hear everything. But anyway, after a while they left. With that swine only two hundred meters behind them. He waited over there at the foot of the cliff until they left, then he followed them. I've thought about that meeting ever since, but since I didn't know what to do, I did nothing. I thought of calling the police, but if Herr Pickering had wanted the police involved, he didn't have to act like that. He could have used that telephone right there. No, he wanted me to do something—and I didn't know what until you came along. He wanted me to tell his story to the right people. I have done that."

"How did they go, Frau Dollwitz? By what trail, the green or yellow?"

"Yellow."

Lissa looked at him, brushed her hair back from her forehead. "Harry?"

He knew what he was supposed to say, said it: "You want to go down the yellow trail and see what you can see."

"They were never seen again, Harry. Suppose . . ."

He supposed. It was easy to do. Two bodies rotting in some hidden mountain ravine. Still, he owed it to the gods of sanity to protest. "What about the men behind us, Lissa? I can't go along with Frau Dollwitz. Maybe Ethan didn't want the police brought in. Maybe we don't either. But it's got beyond him and us. It's an open-and-shut police matter now."

Lissa looked at the old lady. "Forgive us for speaking in English, Frau Dollwitz. Herr Ryder and I are debating whether to go down the yellow trail or call the police." She turned back to him. "Harry, it seems we have only two real choices. Calling in the police—at this time—is not one of them. We can either take the train down the mountain, somehow duck the men following us, and head for Yugoslavia. For Plitvice and Bihać. Or we can go down the yellow trail, keep our eyes open, take our chances with the men behind us, and then go to Yugoslavia. This is not a police matter. Your Birdie Bingham asked you to help, not to turn to the police. I know you think I'm impulsive. Well, I am. And my impulse is to take our chances. I'm not really afraid of them, Harry, not with you with me."

He wanted to embrace her there and then. Her simplicity made his insides melt, as it did last night when she had dismissed his one feeble attempt to be totally honest with her. "Lissa," he had said, "one thing. I've never told you my age. I know I look younger than I am. I'm one of those men with a baby face. In our twenties and thirties, we look like teenagers. And that makes it tough for us with our peers. But in our fifties, the baby face pays off. We look forty-five or so. I'm not forty-five. I'm fifty-three years old. I'm fifteen years older than you. That's an enormous gap." And she had leaned on his chest and looked down at him and run a finger along his lips. "Silly. I wouldn't care if you were seventy-three years old. People count, Harry. Not their years. You and I count. As we are."

Now he didn't embrace her. He said, "I don't think they're lying somewhere down there beside the trail. I think your original premise still holds. They weren't killed. They went down the trail and got themselves kidnapped. And there's no possible way we can find any trace of a kidnapping. Let's take the train down."

"Harry, you're exasperating. No wonder I love you. You see everything so clearly. Of course you're right. We're not here to take on the entire KGB First Directorate, however many that might be—"

"About fifty thousand spies, plus hundreds of thousands of agents, that's how many."

"But at the moment, only two of the fifty thousand concern us. You remember what Bingham said? In trapping situations like this, one has to walk into the trap and trip it. If they do want to kidnap us, let's give them their opportunity. Maybe we'll get a clue as to what happened to Ethan and Miss Patak. And anyway, it's a lovely hike, and I wouldn't want to miss it."

He walked to a window and looked back towards the mountain. "Our Nazi swine are dawdling back there. The way Frau Dollwitz said the first one did with Ethan and Patak. They're practically inviting us to continue down the mountain. Nazi swine. Frau Dollwitz is right. Josef Goebbels used to say Communists make the best Nazis."

Lissa's eyes glowed. She turned to the old lady. "Frau Dollwitz, thank you for your help. We're going down the yellow trail. We'll find them. Down there or in Yugoslavia. We'll find them. And please don't tell anyone of our talk. If

123

someone comes, the police or anybody, if they come and say we're missing, don't tell them anything. Wait until they've gone, and then call this number." She took out a pen and wrote swiftly. "That's a London number. Ask for Sir Alexander James. He speaks perfect German. Tell him everything. Will you do that?"

"I will, Frau Meirion. I will. Herr Ryder, I am happy to know you. And I'm very happy for both of you. You remind me of how we were, my Franz and I. God bless you both, and good luck."

Lissa embraced Frau Dollwitz and listened to a final torrent of mountain dialect, not a word of which Harry Ryder understood; when Frau Dollwitz finished, Lissa nodded, turned, and followed him out the screen door. They waved to Frau Dollwitz and began to stroll down the path to the right of the railroad tracks. After a short distance, the tracks rose twenty yards above them as the path first sloped downward, then leveled off. In a few seconds, they were out of sight of the pursuers, but only for a few seconds. The two men suddenly hurtled into sight, running so fast they had to brake themselves by throwing their legs stiff-legged before them, their heels grinding into the path, loose stones shooting into the air and spraying the ground for yards around them.

"Don't look," Harry said. "They've taken the bait. They've stopped again. They're worried. But not yet alarmed, not yet minatory. Easy does it—until we start down the mountain."

Lissa handed her handbag to him, put her arm through his. "Here, put my bag in your shoulder bag. You see that white stone with the yellow arrow about two hundred yards ahead? The yellow trail turns there and goes up over the railway embankment. Once we're across the tracks, the trail goes through a meadow, past a chalet, and then into the forest. The minute it reaches the trees, the trail starts down. For at least seven or eight kilometers."

"Good. I understand. When we get across the tracks, we'll run like hell. I hope we can reach the forest before they come charging after us. They can't kidnap us—or, God forbid, kill us—if they can't get near us. We'll go down the trail for a kilometer or so, and then we'll set about alarming them."

She looked up at him. "Harry, when we get out of sight, in the forest I mean, hand me my Browning. Maybe I'm not much of a shot, but I can certainly create some confusion."

"Good girl. You not only are good at the ABC's, you're not bad with the XYZ's."

18

One of the Russians had a thick neck. The kind of neck a wrestler could have envied. The other's neck was more or less normal, but his torso was, if anything, more substantial than his thick-necked colleague's. However, heavyset as they were, they came down the trail with a peculiar grace. Their feet inched and uncoiled before them like snakes in motion. First one foot forward, then the body over it, then a quick forward slither to the other foot. But no matter what movements their feet made, their right arms were in rigid balance by their side. Each right arm ended in a pistol. Each pistol had an extraordinarily long barrel. A doubly long barrel. A barrel with its silencer attached. No wonder their left lapels had been off kilter.

Harry glanced swiftly back at Lissa. She was crouched behind him, her eyes enormous, one solid cobalt blue mass. She held the Browning in her right hand. It was pointed at his shoulder bag by her feet. If she raised the Browning on a straight line, its muzzle would poke him in the small of the back. But that was all it would do, poke. She had forgotten to release the safety.

He started to mention the safety to her, but the Russians distracted him with their abrupt, noiseless, stealthy slithers. He could just make them out through the fog. They settled some thirty yards above the ten-foot-high boulder that concealed Lissa and him. He had found it after a breakneck dash of a half-mile or so down the trail. He did not dare run any farther or seek a better cover. Not with the Russians so close behind them. For when Lissa had led the way over the railroad embankment, the Russians' alarm point had been reached. They immediately charged down the slope from the Baumgartenhaus. And simultaneously pulled out their weapons. Small cannons, they seemed. "Run, Lissa, run!"

And run she had. Her stride, free and unimpeded in her jeans, was short but swift and powerful. What a skier she must be. If they ever got out of this, he would bring her back here and go skiing with her. Fine thought, that, but meanwhile he had all he could do to keep up with her. (Of course in skiing he could never keep anywhere near her, not with a former Olympic champion. Maybe he'd better forget the skiing idea.) For the longest while, until they had raced past the unoccupied chalet and almost reached the forest, a good hundred and fifty yards from the embankment, they had the meadow to themselves. Then, just before they plunged into the trees and began their descent, the Russians sprang atop the embankment like cosmonauts launched into space. They hit the ground, steadied themselves, raised their pistols, and fired. At this distance there was no sound at all, no typical *phut* of the silenced weapon. The only sounds had been a whine of one bullet as it pinged off a nearby stone, and a crack as another split a branch by his head.

This had been the worst part, the plunge down the mountain. Lissa had been right about the path. It seemed to go almost straight down.

"Ankles be damned! Follow me. We've got to find cover."

The scenery went by as if they were looking out a train window. A confusion of lofty pines and some kind of berry tree with blossoms and ferns and boulders and bushes and swirling fog and more pines. And always sharp zigs and zags.

"Don't take the zigs. Straight down. Straight across. On the diagonal. It's our best chance."

A fall here would have been disastrous. Perhaps fatal. Once

she ran up his back and almost knocked him on his nose. But by accelerating, by running with his body almost straight down the mountain, he managed to stay on his feet and was able to turn in time to catch her if necessary. But it wasn't. Her ski training was operative. She was running bent well forward as she used the fall line. "Great, Lissa. Just great. Let's go."

And she had nodded and plunged after him. As best he was able, he tried to find a resting spot. One with cover. They could hide behind a couple of pine trees. Or cower in some bushes. But bushes couldn't shield bullets. And the trees weren't all that thick. Once he paused to look up the mountainside to the right. Would that do the trick? Go above the Russians so as to be able to fire down on them? This had been a favorite tactic against the Japanese in the jungles of Leyte. But the Schneeberg was no jungle. The mountainside offered no real cover. He started downward again, but not before he heard the Russians above him. One of them seemed to have taken a tumble, because there was a volley of words, unmistakably oaths, and then silence.

He had grabbed Lissa's arm, pulled her nearer, whispered in her ear, "That rock twenty-five yards ahead. Two zigs down. That's our spot. Follow the path. It's tippy-toe time, Lissa. Nary a sound. Okay?"

This wasn't difficult. The mulchy path formed a natural carpet. The only sound came from a slight squish as water bounced up under their feet. In fact, as he had now become aware, the whole forest was not only damp but dripping wet. And the fog swirled about them like a San Joaquin Valley tule fog. Visibility was only for twenty or thirty yards.

A finger on his lips, he had led the way down and to the right, then left, then right again. Indians couldn't have done it better. The silence seemed a palpable substance, as thick as the fog. The Russians had not moved. They, too, seemed to be assessing the significance of the silence. Probably they had been stopping every few yards to listen for the sound of flight before them. The silence told them the story. Flight

127

time was over. Shooting time was at hand. Or did they truly know that? Had their colleagues in Vienna tipped them off that he and Lissa were armed and dangerous? A finger still on his lips, he had guided Lissa to her knees behind the boulder, knelt in front of her, and taken stock of their defenses.

The boulder was really two boulders. The large one, by his left shoulder, bulked ten feet above his head. The short one, off his right shoulder, formed a triangular mass, a natural pyramid. A space, a sliver of space, separated the two boulders until about five feet up, where they pulled apart. By putting his eye to the sliver of space, he had been able to see snatches and portions of the trail above them. By placing his Browning High-Powered in the sliver, where it was firmly braced by the walls of the two boulders, he had found he could enfilade exactly two stretches of trail. One about twenty-five yards up the mountain. The other only ten yards away. He had been pondering these options when the Russians snake-footed into sight.

With each slither and slide forward, their caution seemed to increase. They tried to keep close to a tree trunk as they glided downward, preferably lingering behind the trunk before advancing. What did this caution mean? That they expected to encounter armed opposition? Or were they just naturally the cautious type?

At about twenty-five yards away, they became aware of the boulder. They pointed it out to each other and nodded. Could they see him through the sliver of space? Possibly, but not likely. The boulders created a natural shade between them, a darkness; the fog swirled in and around the stone, making visibility difficult; and there was at best only three inches of open space, and this space ran for a depth of over two feet.

The Russians looked at each other, nodded, and slid ahead with their snakelike glide. And in so doing passed out of his line of sight. And line of fire. They would have to descend fifteen yards before they came back into sight again. How long would that take? And what would he do when they did appear? Because of the nature of the boulders, he would only be able to get off one or two shots at only one of the Russians. Anyway, if he hit that one target, then what? (If he missed, there wouldn't be much point to this whole mental exercise.) Should he rise up to where the boulders pulled well apart? At that point, about two feet above his head, there was over a foot of space. Would that be sufficient for him to see and cover the other man? Or should he spring back into the path and take his chances in an open shootout?

He heard his pistol fire even before he became consciously aware that he had a target before him. One moment his mind was rationally assessing alternative possibilities, at the next moment his finger had squeezed convulsively. Squeezed twice convulsively. And the narrowness of the space was his salvation because the shoulders of the rocks braced his Browning and kept it from kicking. The bullets went precisely and directly to the target. The Russian—the thick-necked one—bounced backward and downward, his arms to his chest, his pistol dropping silently into the pine needle mulch.

All of this he saw without really comprehending it. What he did not see was the other Russian. Hauling the pistol from its stone cradle, Ryder shouted a great, long, drawn-out "Eeeah" and sprang to the trail below him. And in so doing he tripped and rolled twice on the trail. It was wet. But his Burberry jacket, though not waterproof, was, as advertised, quite water repellent. An excellent jacket. However, water bounced up from the pine needles and sprayed his eyes. Blinking and struggling, he tried to aim his pistol. And now saw the other Russian before he could raise his pistol. The Russian had fallen to one knee. He had raised his weapon to eye level, brought his left hand up to help the right; both of them held the pistol and helped aim it at the hapless Harry Ryder.

Cringing and retracting his skull as far as it could go into his neck, hardly an adequate defense against a bullet into the top of that skull, Harry tried to point his pistol before death ended his share in the proceedings. But just as the Russian started to squeeze his trigger ever so gently, Ryder heard a series of barking roars above him. Lissa's doing. Lissa's shooting. At the first shot, the Russian was lifted half to his feet, at the second, he was propelled one step backward and towards the cliff, and at the third, he was knocked over its side. He disappeared in a kind of dive, body following head, feet pointing upwards and arcing after head and chest.

Ryder struggled to his feet. He walked to the man he had shot. Blood—not much blood—had begun to stain his shirt. The left lapel was no longer out of kilter. He was quite dead. Ryder picked up the pistol. It was also a PM, a Pistolet Makarova, a 9-millimeter automatic with custom-built silencer, a copy of the three he already carried in his shoulder bag. Manpower unlimited. Gunpower unlimited. He went to the edge of the trail and looked down. The barrel-chested Russian lay sprawled in a clump of ferns. Henri Rousseau should be here to paint the Russian in the ferns. He turned and looked back at the boulders.

Lissa was leaning against the tall rock. Her eyes were shut. The Browning hung in a limp right hand. It seemed about to slide to the ground. It did slide to the ground. He climbed up beside her, picked up the Browning, placed it, his own pistol, and the PM on a ledge of the boulder, put his arms around her, and held her tight.

"Thank you, Lissa. Thank you."

She nodded, her head against his shoulder.

"Your safety, Lissa. When I looked, you hadn't released it. I thought you'd forgotten about it. Obviously you remembered. What made you remember?"

She began to shake and twitch against his shoulder.

"Lissa"—and he reached and lifted her chin—"for Christ's sake, don't cry. Don't cry for yourself, don't cry for those bastards. Look at me. Tell me about the safety. Here, take this handkerchief and blow your nose and talk to me."

She blew hard and shook herself and looked up at him. "I didn't release it earlier because I was afraid I would shoot you in the back."

"Well, I'll be damned." He bent down and kissed her on the lips. This was a brotherly kiss. There's a time for a brotherly kiss. This was the time. "And how did you know what to do?"

"You went to the right. So I went to the left."

"Yang and yin. And then?"

"You saw it."

"No, I didn't, Lissa. I was rolling in that muck. The water bounced into my eyes. I saw nothing."

"Why, the Russian, the one on his feet, he first started to run when you came flying out like a madman. Then he suddenly turned back and started to aim at you. So I let my pistol aim itself. I . . . I . . . here, this ledge. I rested it on this ledge, and the rest just happened."

"Thank you again."

"You've said that."

"You haven't said, 'you're welcome.' "

"You're welcome."

"Good. I'll cart these chaps off to the bushes, and we'll be on our way."

"The noise. The shots. Won't someone hear them?"

"I don't know. I don't think so. Maybe if they're only a short distance away. This fog—it blankets sound as well as vision. Here, you rest here while I do my chores. There're thick ferns below. I think I can conceal the bodies down there. At least until we're off the mountain, and maybe, if we're lucky, until we're out of the country. Into Yugoslavia." He started to leave her, turned back. "One more thing. We aren't finished yet. This is only a start. I suspect there may be some surprises waiting for us down below."

He watched her play with that idea, nod, look up at him. "These two were just shepherding us? Did they miss us on purpose when they shot at us up above the meadow?"

"Possibly. Maybe these two weren't all that eager to catch up with us. I don't know. But the fact is, they did shoot. Us Western gunfighters, when we get shot at, we shoot back. Do you accept this . . . this . . ."

131

"Rationalization?"

"This analysis."

"Yes, Harry, yes, I do accept your analysis. Maybe they didn't care if they brought us in wounded. Anyway, they did shoot. And if there are others down below, they'll be prepared to shoot, too. Or at least threaten to shoot. I see that. A sandwich, that's what this is. We're the tasty tidbit in the sandwich."

19

"Describe the yellow trail to me, Lissa. What's it like down below? The terrain, I mean. Foresight's the name of the game. What can we expect to find the rest of the way?"

"Why, it's like this."

"Like this" was a scene of enchantment. Or on a different occasion, it would have been a scene of enchantment. Today, at this time, he was not enchanted. The lofty trees, the fog wreaths swirling about them, the soft, springy, mulchy path, the moss-covered rocks, the tumbling prolific bushes and ferns, the jewellike drops of mist and dew on leaf and branch, the quiet, the churchlike omnipresent silence, a silence so oppressive it dampened even the sound of an occasional rivulet gurgling from the cliff on their right toward the chasm on their left, these were not gifts of God to be treasured and admired, they were a constant reminder of danger. He would have liked to exclaim and proclaim over their beauty. Instead, he examined each natural wonder with the dispassionate, unsympathetic cataloging eye of the soldier. This bush was harmless. That one could conceal a machine-gun squad. As the trail cut back and forth down the mountain, he had made Lissa pause as each new vista opened up. Not to admire, but to reconnoiter. To stand immovably and patiently until their normal senses had evaluated the situation, until their sixth sense—

132

or whatever sense it was—told them the scene before them was free of lurking danger.

"Good. We can handle this. This is guerrilla warfare. I had twenty-odd months at this sort of thing. In the Philippines. You learn guerrilla warfare builds on illusions. Their illusions. Our illusions. They must not control ours. They must never know we're here. We must always know when they're there.

"So much for the mountain. What's it like at the bottom? No, no, stay here. No walking while we're talking. Pause awhile and tell me what it's like at the bottom."

Lissa shut her eyes and thought. She nodded, looked up at him.

"I remember. The Schneeberg, it's a national park. Look—all the trees are intact. See that fallen tree over there? It fell naturally, and it stays there naturally. But down below, just where the trail reaches level ground, lumbering is allowed. Under park supervision. One moment you're in the forest, the next you're on cleared-out ground. The trees have been removed. Only stumps remain.

"The path goes maybe a hundred yards or so down through the stumps. That last hundred yards will be muddy. Real mud, not like this mulch. That's because dozens of little streams criss and cross there in the cleared-out portion. It's mud up to your ankles.

"When the path levels, there're about twenty or thirty yards of even ground. And then a substantial creek. Almost a river. It collects all this water from the Schneeberg's western complex. The creek runs for maybe five or six kilometers before it reaches the Puchberg River. A dirt road parallels the creek. There are no farms until the dirt road meets the Losenheim-Puchberg Road. That's about three kilometers down the valley. The hills on the opposite side of the road go straight up. But on this side, there is that space of thirty or forty yards before the mountain starts up.

"Lumber trucks use the dirt road. They don't haul out big trees. It's not big lumbering like you're used to in your West. Little lumbering. They're restricted now to clearing out saplings and small trees. All these are stripped and piled up along the creek, and at intervals truckers come up and haul them out. At least, that's the way it was last time I was here."

He tried to picture the lay of the land, nodded. "I think I understand. We'll be exposed at the bottom. There's no cover for us. They could be waiting for us behind boulders. We could never spot them. And we'll be sitting ducks for over a hundred yards. That's a tough one. Let's get going and think about it."

As they started down again, they both shivered. The pause and their slow pace had cooled off their heated bodies, let the chill get to them. Fog and damp and cold. Burberry jacket and sweater combined could not keep out the chill factor. He rotated his arms to generate some warmth, and Lissa nodded and followed suit, but the windmilling did not accomplish much. The cold was not only external; the cold formed a chilling around their hearts, a freezing reaction to the Russians freezing under the ferns far up the mountain above them. He remembered now. He recalled the dead Japs on the jungle trails in Leyte. He had been this cold then—in a hundred-degree jungle heat. Death brings its own chill factor.

They did not come to a stop for over an hour, then he touched Lissa's arm, and she looked back, halted close to him.

"Am I right, Lissa? Every so often when the fog lifts, am I seeing the valley below us and the opposite mountain? And have I heard an occasional cowbell?"

She nodded. "It's not far now. Maybe a quarter of a mile. Less. You can tell from the terrain. It's not so steep. Have you worked out what we should do?"

He squeezed her shoulder. "Good girl. We. But this time, it's got to be me alone. That cleared space you described—that's a special consideration." He raised a hand as she started to object.

"No, please hear me. You've been wonderful. You saved my life. That was teamwork. We needed each other together. Here, we need each other apart. From here on it's a guerrilla operation."

134

"Guerrilla operation?"

"Look, I'm not trying to keep you out of the action. It's not that. It's . . . It's . . ."

"Harry, that's enough. I believe you. We are a team. Together or apart. Frau Dollwitz was right."

"Frau Dollwitz?"

"Yes. When I said goodbye to her, she whispered to me that you have a kind face. She said you obviously belong to the same world as the two Nazi swine, but you have a kind face. She was happy that you were with me to protect me. She said she never thought I'd find a man as fine as Professor Meirion, but God has been kind. And so He has been. I know better than anyone how kind He is and you are."

"Even though I'm like the Nazi swine? Now it's my turn to be sorry. I shouldn't be so stupid. Of course I belong to that world, I've always belonged to it. Since I was a nineteen-year-old guerrilla fighter in the Philippines. Okay. Okay. I accept Frau Dollwitz's comment as well-meant. And—"

"Frau Dollwitz also said you're an impressive man."

"Impressive. And kind. So be it. So let me kindly impress on you the gravity of this situation. It's guerrilla warfare in microcosm. We must create an illusion that we're not here. That means you'll have to stay up here on the trail. Or off it. Up the mountainside a bit, so you'll be concealed. I'll keep going past you across the mountainside." He pointed to the right. "I'll go a quarter of a mile or so and then sneak down there, cross the stream, and come from the rear at anybody who might be lurking there."

Lissa shook her head. "That won't work."

She pointed. "The mountain down below has no cover that way. The trees have all been cleared out years ago. It's just a hillside meadow now."

"All right. What about the other way?"

He pointed to the left, down the chasm, where trees and bushes and ferns and rocks seemed to form an impenetrable barrier.

"It's like that all the way. If you go down and follow the bottom, you'll reach the creek about ten or twenty yards

135

above the point where this trail crosses it. There's a little wooden bridge there, and the road starts on the other side of the creek. But I don't see how you can go below. You'll sound like a bulldozer going through all that brush."

"That's a problem. But Leyte was tougher, Lissa. This is almost bare land compared with the Leyte jungle. So, let's go ahead. We'll go another hundred yards and split there. I'll take one of those PM's with me if you'll take my shoulder bag. Please go up the hill and find a tree to hide behind; meanwhile, I'll go down the hill and hide behind a hundred trees."

"That's just dandy, Harry Ryder. What do I do if you don't come back? That would be a dirty trick. We find each other. We lose each other. What then?"

"Have faith, Lissa. Have faith. I'm not going to get myself killed. I won't play any dirty tricks on you. I promise."

He waited patiently while she thought this through. Her body, from head to toe, proclaimed her unhappiness. And disgust. But she finally, reluctantly, angrily, disapprovingly, nodded. He grabbed her, pulled her close, kissed her.

"Good. And be patient. It's going to take me an hour at least to go through the thickets and brush. Give me an hour before you even start to consider what to do next. One hour. Promise?"

"I promise."

20

"Look at that!"

"That" was a complete surprise. Two men were washing and polishing a car. A nondescript black Ford Consul. Parked near the wooden bridge Lissa had mentioned. Two men— the same two men last seen sunning themselves on a park bench across from the Puchbergerhof.

"Well, what d'you know, it's their cover. If a forest ranger happens to wander by, he would be a bit startled to see two men crouched behind rocks or tree stumps with silenced Pistolet Makarovs pointing up the trail. He would not be surprised to see two men taking the afternoon off to wash and polish their car amidst a national park. Of course, he might think they were stupid and illogical to choose a damp and foggy place, when they could easily find a cloudless sunny spot to wash their car, but whoever said logic rules human existence?"

He sat back on his haunches, adjusted his body so he could see through the fern thicket, looked at his watch. Nearly forty minutes had elapsed since he had left Lissa concealed behind a boulder far up the hillside. Forty minutes of—and he now recognized his emotion with amazement—of wild, exhilarated lust for and absorption in life. He hadn't felt like this since 1945. Time must have a stop. Time had stopped. Once again he had lived each second with a passion and intensity he had long since thought himself incapable of recreating. To crawl and inch his way from rock to rock, tree to tree, bush to bush; to measure each pebble, each blade of grass, each leaf and twig; to stretch forward noiselessly, with infinite patience; to hear and be aware of and merge with each breath of air, each bird's chirp, each squirrel's chatter—this was living. The sort of living that made each second, each fraction of a second, a vital, episodic, isolated drama.

He shook himself and brought his mind back to the present. He waited until passion subsided, exhilaration retreated, heart ceased pounding. He might be fully alive again. The object of the moment was to stay that way.

The car was forty yards away. To approach the men, he would have to cross the stream twenty yards or so above the bridge, follow the contour of the opposite hillside until he was directly above the men, and then come down upon them. Could he do all that? Could he do it in twenty minutes?

"No way. That's another hour's work. If I was careful before, now I'd have to make myself invisible. Sure, they're keeping their eyes up the trail and not in this direction. But they've got their antennae out. They'll pick me up somewhere along the line. And meanwhile, Lissa will be fretting away, and God knows what she might do. She's not much on the patience rumble. What else can I do?"

And to ask was to answer. He began to move ahead again, straight along the bottom of the gorge. It was a difficult maneuver, but not the least bit impossible. Only time consuming. It took him twenty minutes to achieve his objective, a tree stump only a few feet from the bridge. "God damn it, why didn't I say ninety minutes! Lissa, keep calm. Keep calm. Don't move. Don't come charging down the hill. Don't do a damned thing."

The last ten feet to the tree stump were in the clear and up a slight slope. His only cover was the stump itself and two scrawny, scraggly bushes projecting above and around it. If one of the Russians stepped five feet from the car, he would be in plain sight.

But they didn't move five feet. In fact, when he saw them again through the scraggly bush, they were both half-sitting on the hood of the car. He was close enough now—only ten or twelve yards away—to see them clearly. One, a blond, bushy-haired fellow, was sliding a piece of cloth back and forth through his fingers; the other, the one with a dark brown crew cut, held and squeezed a sponge in his hand. Terrible haircuts. And terrible clothes. Baggy, ill-fitting gray business suits with the trousers almost touching the ground. The official uniform for flunky KGB thugs.

Carefully he pulled his PM from his belt, raised it to his eye, pushed down the safety, drew his knees up, and stood up. He held the pistol at his waist, took one step forward.

"You. You two." He used English. If they didn't understand, then what did he do? "Lie on the ground. Face down, Now!"

The bushy-haired man and the crew-cut man looked at him carefully. They computed their chances at a thirty-foot distance, apparently found them excellent, for the man nearest the windshield, Mr. Bushy-hair, snaked his right hand toward his left shoulder. Ryder pulled the trigger. He did not aim carefully; he had no desire to kill anyone. Only to intimidate. The silenced Makarov phutted, kicked, and Mr. Crew-cut spun around against his comrade. He put his left hand on his right arm and doubled over the hood.

Ryder took another step forward. "No more nonsense. Down! Down where I can see you."

Lissa had put it succinctly, "Let the pistol find its target." Only this time the pistol had found the wrong man. It had missed Mr. Bushy-hair, the aggressive one, the man he had aimed at. But his errant aim didn't matter. The sight and sound of his wounded comrade proved more intimidating to Mr. Bushy-hair than the weapon in Harry Ryder's hand. The Russian slowly pulled his right hand away from his chest and helped his wounded comrade stretch out on the ground. Mr. Crew-cut lay there, sobbing and choking like a child. Well, why not? Once upon a time he had been a child. And no doubt had a mother who'd cooed and ah'd over her lovely tyke.

Ryder walked over and stood two paces away. He examined the Ford Consul. Its keys were in the ignition. Mr. Bushy-hair squinched his head around and scowled at his captor. His sense of being intimidated was barely skin deep. He continued to snarl and grimace until his eyes fell on and recognized the pistol in Ryder's hand. Then he gasped and seemed to cringe and collapse, to become suddenly inches shorter.

Ryder nodded. "Yes. They're dead. They won't be coming to the rescue. But that's enough dead for today. I have no desire to kill you. Tell your friend to shut up. For Christ's sake, he's only got an arm wound. We'll take care of him in a minute. We'll fix a tourniquet. Tell him."

Mr. Bushy-hair nudged Mr. Crew-cut, and the latter obediently repressed his moans by biting his lips. Well-disciplined sorts, these fellows. Orders are orders. And must be obeyed. From friend or foe.

Ryder knelt down and carefully pulled Mr. Bushy-hair's

jacket halfway down his back. One arm at a time. Mr. Bushy-hair lay there in the handcuffed position, with the jacket serving as handcuffs. Ryder did not touch the wounded man. From the blood now flooding out the hole of his jacket and spreading down its arm, it was quite obvious handcuffs were not required. In fact, if the wound were not dressed quickly, nothing more would ever be required for him. Mr. Crew-cut was a bleeder.

"Let me get your pistols, then we'll walk up the mountain, and a good Samaritan and I will do the best we can to dress that wound. As I say, two in one day is enough killing for anyone. We don't want a third."

The Russians' weapons were companions to his. "In the last few years," he mused, "I've collected maybe two dozen pistols. What a shame to have to keep throwing them away." But after removing the cartridges and stowing them in his jacket, throw them away he did, as far up the hillside as he could heave them. "All right, on your feet, march! Up the trail we go."

The going, especially in the muddy part, was difficult. Mr. Bushy-hair, with his arms pinioned, could not help his comrade. "Tell him to put his good left arm around you. Help the man! If we don't get another fifty yards up there out of this muck, your friend will never get anywhere else. Do it!"

And they did and continued to lurch up the hillside. When they passed the last stump and emerged from the mud, Ryder threw back his head to call Lissa's name. But it wasn't necessary. She stepped out from behind a pine tree. While stuffing her Browning back into her jacket, she trotted down toward them.

Ryder looked at her disapprovingly. "You didn't wait."

"Oh, yes I did. Until just a minute ago. Then I came down very carefully. I really did. I came down to that thick tree up there, and I was very careful. They couldn't see me. I made sure of that. But I saw you. Oh, Harry you were just marvelous. My protector. My impressive, kind-faced protector. Just marvelous."

"Marvelous? If you say so. I give the credit to your mountain. You said it would be our friend. It is. But now I need your help. We've got to dress this fellow's arm. If you'll keep your pistol on Mr. Bushy-hair here, I'll try to bandage up this fellow with his undershirt. I guess the belt will have to do for a tourniquet. He's in a bad way. Much worse than he should be. Maybe I've hit a main artery or something. It doesn't look good."

Lissa nodded, took out her Browning, pointed it steadily where it needed pointing. Ryder did his task as efficiently and quickly as possible, ended by draping Mr. Crew-cut's shirt and jacket around his shoulders, then pointed down the dirt road toward Puchberg, said to Lissa, "We've got no choice now. We've got to have time to catch the first plane out of Vienna. I don't care where it goes. I just want us to get as far away from these fellows as we can possibly get.

"I'm going to cut up Bushy-hair's jacket into strips with my jackknife and use the strips to tie these two to saplings. It won't be the best binding in the world. These two will work themselves free. But by that time we'll be on a plane out of Vienna. We'll drive their car back to Puchberg, pick up ours, and scoot away. Make sense?"

She brushed her hair back from her forehead in her characteristic gesture and stared at him. Damn it, would he have to wink at her?

He didn't. Not at his ABC-XYZ lady. She nodded, stood by him as he herded Mr. Crew-cut and Mr. Bushy-hair off the trail into a cluster of saplings.

Fifteen minutes later, he stepped back, surveyed his handiwork, shook his head. "Gentlemen, I'm sorry I can't tie you up any better. But maybe that's best. This way you won't be here all night and run the risk of freezing. Good luck."

Mr. Crew-cut was only half-conscious. Mr. Bushy-hair was fully conscious, and his hate and rage had set him to scowling and grimacing again. With that kind of energy, he'd be loose in a couple of hours. But even then it would take him several more hours to reach Puchberg, especially if he attended to Mr. Crew-cut. That should give them enough lead time.

"Come on, Lissa. Let's get out of here."

141

They did. But carefully. This was no time to have an accident, to drive off the dirt road and fall into the stream or bounce off a pothole and break the drive shaft or do any one of a dozen silly things. And certainly no time to attract the attention of the forest ranger parked in his green Volkswagen by the entrance to the park. They waved to him, and he waved back.

"Do you suppose he was parked there and saw two men drive up? And a man and woman drive back?"

Lissa shrugged. "Maybe he thinks I'm a transvestite."

Harry looked at her. Her face was sober, her expression thoughtful. He laughed and patted her knee, and she let herself go and enjoyed her own joke.

"By God, Lissa, I like this. No matter what happens now, even if the worst comes to worst, let's go down laughing."

"I prefer not to go down at all. In fact, where are we going?"

"To Yugoslavia, of course. To Plitvice, wherever that is."

"In this car? Oh, of course. Manpower unlimited. We can't go back to the hotel. Not with Russians crawling all over the place. But we'll have to go buy all the things a traveler usually carries."

For the last few minutes they had been going past cultivated fields. Once they went by a man. A blind old fellow, holding a white cane in one hand and leading a horse with the other. Lissa pointed beyond him. "The paved access road to the Losenheim-Puchberg highway is just ahead. By that white farmhouse."

"I've been thinking, Lissa. Or rather, asking myself questions. Perhaps you can answer them. Here's the first. Do Yugoslav customs officials go through luggage, or does common-market practice hold?"

"Yugoslavia is no different from Austria or France or Germany or Italy. They just wave you through. Though if you are a Yugoslav citizen, they do open the trunk of your car. Not to go through luggage, but to make sure you're not carrying machine guns or boxes of jeans or something. The duty on jeans exceeds their sales price."

"Then when we rent our own car somewhere, we'll have to make sure it doesn't have Yugoslav license plates. Next. Where do we get the clothes and luggage? Is there a fair-sized city where we can buy a couple of suitcases and enough junk to fill them so we can pass as tourists?"

"Graz is the biggest city. About three hundred thousand people. It's fifty kilometers from the border."

"How long will it take to get to Graz?"

She looked at her watch. "Goodness, it's after one. Let's see, it's, oh . . . about a hundred and fifty kilometers to Graz. Slow going from here to the A2 motorway, which only continues twenty or thirty kilometers and then becomes a two-lane highway. With lots of lorries. Ninety miles, but it'll take a good two hours, maybe three hours to get there."

"Okay. Say Graz by four o'clock. That wouldn't be too late. Stores would still be open. But suppose we're delayed by a flat tire or something. Where else can we get luggage and clothes?"

"Wiener Neustadt is the only place I'm sure of. It's got at least forty thousand people. We'd have to backtrack five or six kilometers."

"Wiener Neustadt it is. Now. Where can we rent a car?"

"Graz will do. Once with Llew-Llaw, our Hertz car broke down at Koflach, and we had to be towed thirty kilometers to Graz, where Hertz has an office. And I remember that Avis and Europa had offices nearby."

"All right, I get the picture. While you shop in Wiener Neustadt, I'll phone Graz for a car. Whichever promises to stay open and hold a car for us till six or later—Hertz or Avis or Europa—that's where we'll do business. Assuming of course that the State Police are not on a carhunt for a Ford Consul last seen leaving the Schneeberg National Park. Or assuming that we don't accidentally run into another Mercedes full of combat-type goons. A lot of assumptions. But all we can do is try. Agreed?"

She agreed.

"Good. And one more thing, if you don't mind—and don't

laugh at my middle-class morality—when we get to Wiener Neustadt, we'll drop a postcard to the Puchbergerhof and settle our bill. I hate leaving unpaid bills. Okay? Okay, then direct me out of Puchberg on back roads to Wiener Neustadt. This is the tricky part. If we can get to Wiener Neustadt without being spotted, I think we can get to Yugoslavia. Direct away."

PART III

21

Any customs inspection—even when one is pure of heart and blameless in thought—any customs inspection tends to make one's muscles tense up a bit. When one approaches a Communist country and has buried under the rear seat two Browning High-Powered pistols, three Pistolet Makarovs with custom-built silencers, two sets of passports, along with two nearly full boxes of 9-millimeter cartridges, plus an assortment of subsonic 9-millimeter cartridges for use in silenced weapons, one particular muscle, the heart, not only tenses up but goes into an irregular and audible beat.

The sign above the customs station read ŠENTILJ. Pronounced something like *Shentilye*. Lissa had given him a brief course on the Serbo-Croatian alphabet. "Just learn the S's, C's, and Z's. The other letters pose no problems. There are two S's. S pronounced naturally. As in said, sap, sack. And S pronounced *sh*, as in shock, shade, shadow. There are three C's. One has a distinct sound, the other two seem to have the same sound to most non-Slavs. The distinct C is spelled C and pronounced *ts*, as in cats, hats, mats. Thus, Plitvice is Plitvitsa. The two similar-sounding C's are spelled Ć and Č. To our ears, they both sound like the *ch* of itch, church, chapter. And there are two Z's. The natural Z sound, as in zounds, zonk, zap. And the Z*h* sound, as in pleasure, azure, Žarko Pantić." Now he pointed to the uniformed officer strolling along the line of cars.

"You ready?"

"Ready."

The officer leaned in, smiled at them, flipped through the

two passports in the names of Thomas Edward and Christina Doughty, smiled warmly, and stalked off to a one-story gray office on the right. Ryder raised his eyebrows.

"He's being courteous. He's taking our passports over to be stamped. But I'll have to go get them. Courtesy goes just so far."

Lissa slipped out of the car while he studied the scene before him. Surely Žarko Pantić or the Austrian State Police or somebody would have agents there to pounce on Harry Ryder and Lissa Meirion, murderer and murderess. Surely they would—if they had discovered the two corpses beneath the ferns near the yellow trail on the Schneeberg. He looked at his watch. Almost eight in the evening. What about the two they had left trussed up? The wounded man—had he survived? Had his comrade managed to help him stagger to town? What about the forest ranger and the green Volkswagen? Did he stay by the park entrance? If so, what did he do when he saw the wounded man? Questions, questions.

Lissa came back with the two passports, nodded, put them on her lap. They inched their way to the customs gate, tried not to look around apprehensively for lurking police or military intelligence types, waited interminably while a youthful guard opened the trunk of the car ahead of them, a Yugoslav car occupied by a Yugoslav family: mother, father, two children. ("Probably back from visiting relatives in Graz," said Lissa.) There were no jeans in their trunk, no machine guns. The guard closed the trunk, waved the family on, waited while they slid up to him, his eyes very busy, his face noncommittal. Lissa started to hand him the passports, but his face suddenly broke into a big smile. He stepped back, gestured them forward, said *"Geradeaus."*

Geradeaus. Straight ahead. Ryder felt an absurd urge to protest: "My dear fellow, just because this Hertz Ford Fiesta has Viennese license plates, that doesn't make us Viennese. Mrs. Doughty is a loyal British subject, and me, I'm an American citizen." Instead he smiled meekly, said *"Danke,"* and eased the car towards the gray buildings on the right, one of them a bank, another a general store. When he had changed dollars to dinars, he handed Lissa her half; twenty thousand dinars, the equivalent of one thousand one hundred dollars, followed her to the store, watched her buy three Yugoslav newspapers, one from Belgrade, one from Maribor, one from Zagreb. Was that a mistake? Should she proclaim to a nosy world that she could actually read this mysterious language? Of course it was a mistake. And of course he wouldn't say a word about it. He had learned better than to criticize Lissa's impulses, her impulsiveness. So far they had brought their team nothing but luck.

While she studied the newspapers, he drove them to Maribor, some ten miles ahead, with Zagreb another ninety miles beyond that. It would take over two hours to get to Zagreb. Zagreb, Arritsa Patak's home. Lissa was convinced they could track down Miss Patak, find someone who would know somebody who would know where Patak would go for a vacation. "From me to the Queen of England is just one person," she had said. "One person who can arrange the introduction. If it's that easy to see the Queen, should Arritsa Patak prove any more difficult to meet?" And his reply had stopped her, but only for a moment. "Suppose Arritsa Patak works for Žarko Pantić? Suppose she's military intelligence all the way? Suppose she's the real villain, the one really responsible for trapping Ethan Pickering?" And Lissa had tossed back her hair, looked off into space, said, "No. No. I don't think so. I think she's as much in love with Ethan as he is with her." Once again, the Welsh gift. Once again, wisdom from him, the wisdom this time consisting of silence. She was a marvel to him, a marvel and a treasure. No wonder, with women like her in the world, no wonder men write books about White Goddesses.

And pondering these matters, he drove for a good five miles before he started to become aware that he was no longer in Austria, that Yugoslavia was not Austria. The differences were not blockbusters. Small things. Weeds along the road. An occasional tin can or scrap of paper on the shoulder of the road. In Austria, that just didn't happen. And though the farmhouses, now only dimly glimpsed in the gloaming, though they seemed solid and substantial enough, their paint jobs were often past their prime. And further, a surprising number of them were incomplete. There would be the framework of a house, but it would have only one or two rooms.

He nudged Lissa, distracted her from her newspapers. "Lissa, I've never seen so much new building going on in my life. Yugoslavia must be enjoying an extraordinary building boom."

She laughed. "It looks that way. But those aren't new houses. It's their credit system. They don't get enough credit to build a whole house at once. Just enough money for a room at a time. When that loan is pretty well paid off, they can tap the bank for more. It'll take a typical family five to ten years to complete their home. Not prosperity. A shoestring economy." Upon which, he slammed the brakes so suddenly, Lissa almost hit the windshield, seat belt notwithstanding.

"What's that for?"

"Look." Ryder pointed off to the right, brought the car to an abrupt halt on the shoulder. "That wreck. Down there."

"What about it?"

A blue police car, roof light revolving, siren abruptly shutting off, pulled up behind them. Two policemen sprang from the car and plunged down the hill. A crowd had already gathered around the wreck, a tiny white car, upside down, its wheels still spinning. It looked like a bug on its back waving its limbs and trying to right itself.

"It's impossible."

"It's not impossible. It's a Zastava. Yugoslavia's contribution to the auto industry."

"Funny. I meant the wreck was impossible."

"Oh, that! Think nothing of it. You'll get used to it. To the wrecks, I mean. Yugoslavs are always running their cars over cliffs."

"Lissa, how many times in your life have you seen a car go over a cliff? Cliff, hell! You could barely ski down that incline. It's not even steep enough for a beginner's slope. Is that the

148

answer? Are they beginners at driving? Or just macho drivers? Can we expect to have speedburners running us off the road? Well, whatever it is, we've been warned."

Once under way again, Lissa tapped the newspapers. "Harry, the papers are full of ominous overtones."

"Like what?"

"Well, the papers have column after column about the need to carry out Tito's legacy. And a few discreet references to the riots in Kosovo."

"Kosovo. Ah, I remember. The Albanian part of the country."

"The gist of it is that Beograd—sorry, Belgrade—no, Beograd. In Yugoslavia we'll use the right names, if you agree?"

"I agree."

"Good. In Beograd, they profess not to know what the riots are all about. Do the Albanians in Yugoslavia want Kosovo to annex itself to Albania? That seems incomprehensible to everybody. Probably even to the Kosovans. No sane person could conceivably want to immure himself in Albania."

"No sane person."

"All right, your turn to be funny. But the general feeling is that Kosovo probably wants to stay in Yugoslavia but will only do so if it gets independent status. To become a seventh and an equal full-fledged republic, like Serbia and Croatia and the rest. It doesn't want to continue suffering the indignity of being labeled a mere province. But whatever they want, they have set up ripple effects everywhere else in the country. Today Yugoslav unity is a shaky business. Maybe that's why they're making such a fuss about the unveiling of Tito's statue in Drvar on July 27, two weeks from tomorrow. That's Bosnia's national holiday, celebrating the day Bosnia-Herzegovina rose against Germany in 1941. Each republic has its own national uprising day. Serbia's, for instance, is July 7, twenty days ahead of Bosnia's. Apparently the people of Drvar have commissioned a statue of Tito, and everybody who's anybody from everywhere will be there to see the unveiling and honor Tito and his legacy of unity and success. Incidentally, it's a re-

149

markable statue. Apparently it shows Tito in his marshal's uniform and—"

"Marshal's uniform?"

"Yes. It's quite a story. Both Llew-Llaw and Ethan Pickering were part of the story, and so was Žarko Pantić. That's when Ethan rescued a five-year-old girl from the Germans and—"

"Sorry, Lissa. Maribor dead ahead. Excuse me while I concentrate. Save the story until we're back on the highway to Zagreb again. Tell me now how to find a hotel in Zagreb— and where to find Arritsa Patak."

"Zagreb's simple. We'll stay at the Sava. It's not much, but some of the rooms have baths. And we should be fairly inconspicuous there. As to Arritsa Patak, that's also simple. We'll look up her address in the phone book and take it from there. But before we do any of those things, don't you think we'd better find a pay phone here in Maribor and report in to Sir Alex?"

"And Birdie Bingham?"

"And Birdie Bingham. We don't want the Austrian police asking their Yugoslav counterparts to round us up. I think our two warlocks can head them off."

"They can, if we can trust them. Sorry, not trust them, trust him, Birdie Bingham. Well, what choice do we have? If he's playing games with us, we'll find that out. If he's the mole I've suspected he might be, we might find that out, too.

"Meantime, here and now, let's find that pay phone. *Morituri* et cetera."

22

Žarko Pantić patted the redheaded woman's hand, walked with her to the door, maintained his avuncular mask, tried to keep his voice dispassionate.

"Thank you for coming, comrade citizen." He risked a confrontation with Arritsa Patak's eyes. They were a grayish blue. Good Slavic eyes. But there was nothing Slavic about her abundant red hair. That betrayed a possible Jewish intrusion somewhere in the Patak family tree. And come to think of it, wasn't there something Semitic about her slightly slanted eyes, her astounding beauty? Avuncular mask indeed! Žarko, you're not all that superannuated, not any more so than Pickering, and yet the girl was clearly in love with the horny American. There was a time, Žarko, there was a time . . . "You have done a great service for your country, and it will always be deeply appreciated."

"Good. I was happy to be able to help." She had a mellow, throaty voice. Voice, eyes, hair, beauty. The effect was staggering. How could all that overpowering femininity be muted and confined by a mathematical, financially oriented brain? Beauty as bookkeeper. Sickening. Just sickening. A mockery of God's will. She continued, "I simply wanted you to know I'm still willing to contribute, if there's any way I can be of further assistance."

He beamed as hard as he could, now patted her shoulder, as he let his hand slide, just once, ever so gently, across a ripely rounded breast, shut the door behind her, stood there, eyes closed, did not turn his head when the Russian came in from the next room.

"Well?" Yuri Yevchenko's *well* was harsh. "She's dangerous. She knows too much. She's obviously in love with Pickering. You'll have to do something about her."

"Do something?" He turned around, examined the lean, handsome Russian, gestured toward the inner office. They walked past Korta and Dimitrije, who didn't look up from their labors. They had completed the last of over two thousand orders to all army contingents in the country, all ready for instantaneous delivery on the twenty-seventh. A magnificent piece of work. On that day the country would be safely under martial law. General Jure Kranjc could whisk in his Russian allies, Serbia once more would be where it belonged, the absolute ruler of the whole nation. Every radio station, TV station, and newspaper would be under army control, and all would be spouting the common message: "The United States and its CIA had attempted to force Yugoslavia apart from Mother Russia, but the danger is over, and as proof, Russian soldiers are even now entering the country to support the nation against the vile CIA's attempt to take over the country." Yes, his two aides deserved and would get rapid promotion. He would see to that. "Do something? I've done it. She's under a twenty-four-hour-a-day surveillance, and I've got her phone tapped. No, don't say it, I'm well aware Pickering could have enlisted her aid, given her numbers to call. Her visit here was a lie from start to finish, I know that. Give me some credit. No, I wasn't asking your opinion about Patak. I can't wait to hear your report on Ryder and Meirion. What happened, for God's sake? Where are they? Why don't you have them in tow, as you promised?"

He went behind his desk, a cheap plastic affair. Yevchenko picked the least uncomfortable of the wooden chairs, eased himself down, visibly braced himself.

"You won't like this. I don't like having to tell it to you. But . . ."

The *but* was a dismal story, so dismal it was comic. The almighty KGB foiled and thwarted by a middle-aged, retired American spy and a British housewife who dabbled in historical research on the lives of Enrico Dandolo and Thomas Cromwell. It was comic, all right, but he couldn't tell Comrade Yevchenko so. Instead, he was all sympathy, clucking soothing sounds as Yevchenko lived out his anguish. Apparently the story had three chapters.

The first chapter was an opera bouffe attempt by three men to kidnap Ryder and Meirion at the Hotel Stefanie. "You understand, Žarko, my men could not shoot. They had strict orders to bring the two in alive. Of course one of these men, Boris, he did risk a shot, but he wasn't trying to hit Ryder, just scare him. We need . . . The more I thought about him, the more I realized we need Ryder at Drvar. The CIA uses two-man teams in cases like this, everybody knows that. Pickering and Ryder would be an overwhelming self-evident proof of CIA complicity. So my men couldn't shoot. I have to have Ryder."

Pantić clucked his sympathy and heard the second chapter.

This one was not at all comic. Oh, maybe, viewed in the light of some higher metaphysical sense. But not as far as everyday down-to-earth reality went. Two men had been killed on the Schneeberg. Two good men, Yuri insisted. (If they were good men, what did that make Ryder and Meirion? Pantić forbore asking.) Georgi and Aleksei had been killed and hidden under ferns on the slopes of the Schneeberg. And the other two men at the bottom of the mountain, Pavel and Anatoli, well, they had, or one of them had, Pavel, he had been wounded. And both had been picked up by a forest ranger and delivered to the Austrian State Police, who had kept them incommunicado for four days, from last Sunday to yesterday, Thursday. The third chapter was composed of those four days.

They had been frantic ones for the KGB staff at the Embassy. At first no one had gone to the police. The chief had sent men to Puchberg. They had scoured the Schneeberg, learned nothing, absolutely nothing. On the fourth day, yesterday, an Embassy secretary had finally gone to the police, reported four underclerks missing. The clerks had gone hiking over the weekend on the Schneeberg and disappeared. And then the story came out. The secretary learned that the police had Pavel and Anatoli in custody, had been quizzing them incessantly. For the first two days, the police had gotten nothing. Or rather, they had gotten a wild tale of an attack by two burly thugs, who had calmly shot Pavel, taken their car, and driven off. That lie didn't hold up too long, because the forest ranger reported the two burly thugs were a man and a woman, and when confronted with this, Pavel and Anatoli began to dribble out the whole story. The police proceeded to find their guns where Ryder had tossed them up the hillside. And they found the bodies of Aleksei and Georgi under some ferns.

The police at first accused Pavel and Anatoli of killing Aleksei and Georgi—or at least that was the excuse they gave for keeping the two incommunicado. What was so amazing about the whole thing—alarming, actually—was that the police had been lying to Pavel and Anatoli the whole time. They had actually found the bodies and guns last Monday, within one day of the murders. This was finally learned from an informant. Obviously the police were covering for Ryder and Meirion, giving them time to disappear into Yugoslavia. For that, too, was obvious. The stolen car had been found on a street in Graz. Graz, fifty kilometers from Yugoslavia. Ryder and Meirion had undoubtedly rented a car in Graz and disappeared inside Yugoslavia, and what did the comrade colonel propose to do about that?

The rotund little colonel wanted to say, "I guarantee I'll do a hell of a lot better than you did." Once again, he forbore, instead said, "Yuri, my friend, from what you've learned, it'll be a simple matter to track down Ryder and Meirion. I'll have all the border entries checked at Šentilj, and it shouldn't be too difficult to find out what names they're traveling under. Of course they've had a five-day head start, and from what you've told me about Ryder's love of disguises and name changes, there's no guarantee they've kept the same names they used when crossing the border. But think nothing of it. Think nothing of it. We'll find them. You'll have the CIA team you want. Let me get Korta and Dimitrije working with the border people, then you and I will go over Kranjc's speech. We've got to hurry, Kranjc will be here in"—he glanced at his watch—"in twenty-two minutes and thirty-two seconds. The general wouldn't like it if we hadn't done what he commanded. And I wouldn't want to fake it. I think I've done a good job, especially when I have Kranjc quote our good President Miodrag Otaronov's words to the Labor Congress last month at Ljubljana, when he indicated Yugoslavia would always feel a filial bond to Mother Russia. Those words alone would justify the CIA killing Otaronov, but the ending's dynamite. Listen:

" 'Comrades, comrades, comrades, please give me your attention. Please.' There's going to be all hell to pay, Yuri, and if I didn't put this in, Kranjc would barrel right ahead in his speech, and no one would hear a word he said. Then he goes on like this: 'Thank you and great news. There is no need to panic. We've caught the perpetrators of this vile deed, the destruction of the so-beautiful statue of Tito, this foul murder of our heroic president. They are—yes, you already know who the guilty parties are, they're the slinking detestable black-arts dogs from the CIA of the United States. The world's greatest villains. We've got them, we've caught them—and they've already confessed—and I want the whole world to hear this. You out there in television land, hear this: They've confessed. They've told us why the CIA acted. Those criminals acted because they feared Yugoslavia under its great leader, Miodrag Otaronov, would turn its back on the Western plutocrats and take its rightful place with the socialist future. Yes, with Hungary and Romania, with Czechoslovakia, Poland, and Bulgaria—and with Russia, our own Mother Russia. Well, the CIA won't stop us. We know our destiny. We don't care even if we learn Western troops are massing on our border, prepared to invade us, prepared to force us away from our friends and brothers. No. No. We are Socialist. Thanks to our beloved founder, thanks to Tito, we are Socialist. We are Socialist now, and we will be Socialist tomorrow, and we will be Socialist forever. We are one with Russia, one with our neighbors, and we welcome them with open arms. Yugoslavia! Yugoslavia! Yugoslavia!' Stunning, what?" And he looked at Yevchenko for reaction, at the same time saw the light start to blink on his phone. "What's this? Korta knows better than to interrupt me. Unless . . . do you suppose? Kranjc? Is he here already?"

He punched the intercom button, but before he could lift the receiver, Korta himself poked his head into the room. He was a handsome twenty-two-year-old. Very efficient, but still shy in the presence of brass. He cleared his throat, said, "Sir?"

"Yes, Korta."

"I have a phone call for you. I know what you said, but— but—"

Korta was also very intelligent. "Yes, Korta?"

"The lady was insistent. She talked Central Exchange into relaying her call and—and—"

"She also talked you into relaying it to me. All right, who is this mighty persuader?"

"She says her name is Meirion. Spelled M-E-I-R-I-O-N. She speaks perfect Serbian, sir. Her name is foreign, but . . ."

"But?"

"But she said she's with a Mr. Harry Ryder and you did know her and would want to talk with her and they're at Plitvićka Jezera, in the Hotel Plitvice, and—"

"And she's right. And you're right. Thank you, Korta."

His face a portrait of relief, the young soldier pulled his head out of sight, closed the door behind him. Pantić inspected the white light on his telephone, raised an eyebrow at Yuri Yevchenko. The Russian waved an arm vaguely. "Do they know about you?"

"They know."

"Then they've failed to find any trace of Pickering. They're trying to spring a trap. That means they're not isolated. They've got backup. Be careful."

Pantić punched the white button, picked up the phone. He used English. "Mrs. Meirion? This is Colonel Pantić." He saw no point in keeping up the fiction he was no longer in the army. He obviously hadn't deceived anybody at the Westminster Mortuary, and he certainly wasn't deceiving Mrs. Meirion now. "What can I do for you? And for a Mr. Harry Ryder, if I got the name right? I understand you're together."

"Yes we are, Colonel. Thank you for taking our call. Mr. Ryder is on an extension in the lobby. He's the man you saw with me at the Westminster Mortuary."

"Colonel."

"Mr. Ryder."

It was Mrs. Meirion, then, who would carry on the conversation. That figured. Ryder might once have had fine cre-

156

dentials, but it was Mrs. Meirion who knew Yugoslavia. And knew Ethan Pickering, too—or did Ryder also know Pickering? Had they ever worked together? Damn, he should have checked that out. Too many things on your mind, Žarko, you're letting balls slip through your fingers—or are you just getting too old for the game anymore? He tried to picture the American in the Hotel Plitvice lobby, shut his eyes, recalled the incredible opulence of the mountain resort hotel, the great overstuffed brown chairs, the thick carpets—and the telephone exchange. Clever, no one was listening to their conversation. Clever. And Žarko knew he could be clever, too; as soon as they hung up, he would check to see what calls, if any, they had made from the hotel.

"Colonel, Mr. Ryder and I need your help."

"Just command me, Mrs. Meirion. I'm at your service."

"Mr. Ryder and I were on vacation in Vienna when we got a request from an old friend to help locate a missing friend of ours. And of yours, too. You'll recall him. Ethan Pickering, one of the original partisan musketeers. You, Ethan, Llew-Llaw. You do recall, Colonel?"

"I recall. But what do you mean, locate?" Should he pretend he didn't know Ethan Pickering hadn't committed suicide? Hardly. "I last saw Ethan in London. He, of course, goes under the name of Peter Trubari. He has a very successful electronics firm in Brussels. I asked him to do me a business favor in Vienna. He went there at my request, got the information I needed, relayed it to me, and that's the last I've heard from him. Why should he need locating?"

"Because he's vanished. He was killing two birds in Vienna, Colonel. Besides helping you, he was also performing another commission, but he never reported back on that one. Since Mr. Ryder and I were planning a vacation in Vienna—after those exciting times in London, well, we wanted a change of scene, didn't we, Harry?"

"We did."

"So our friend in London asked us to see if we could find anything the police might have overlooked."

"Did you?"

"No. Only that Ethan—Peter Trubari—was last seen with one of your compatriots, a Miss Arritsa Patak. We came here, Harry and I, to see if we could locate Miss Patak, but she's disappeared, too. She's on vacation, and no one seems to know where she is. Harry—Mr. Ryder and I—we talked it over and decided to ask you for help. I know this is an imposition, but, well . . . you and Llew-Llaw and Ethan—the three partisan musketeers—well, I thought . . ."

"You thought quite rightly, Mrs. Meirion." How many lies had she managed to crowd into her little speech? It would take a computer to unravel their permutations and combinations. Was this a natural feminine gift or a trained intelligence agent's? Was she capable of carrying on her husband's work in ways he had never suspected? Come to think, he recalled having wondered why Llew-Llaw brought her along so frequently. At the time he had thought her a hindrance. Had he missed her role entirely? Žarko, every day in every way, you keep finding the world is getting more and more complicated, and you more and more simple. Suppose he asked her what friend in London had sent her to track down Ethan Pickering? What name would she give? What name? Why bother, Žarko, you've heard enough lies already. From her. Well, now it was his turn. "I'll be glad to help, Mrs. Meirion. Just tell me what I can do for you. After all, the three musketeers, what?"

"What indeed. Thank you, Colonel. Mr. Ryder and I were hoping you could help us locate Miss Patak. She will know where Ethan Pickering is. They've become very close. You understand?"

"I understand. But I don't understand why you call on me. I'm not a policeman. Of course, I'll try to help, but—"

"But, Colonel, you located Arritsa Patak when she was using a false name. Nevenka Hadžić, wasn't that it? So I was hoping you could perform an equal miracle for us—or perhaps even a lesser miracle, now that she's using her real name."

In spite of himself, Žarko heard himself laugh aloud. She

was quite a woman, this Melissa Meirion. "You win, Mrs. Meirion. I'll go to work immediately. This will take a while. She's on vacation, you say? Well, I'll start looking. You—you and Mr. Ryder—you just sit tight in Plitvice. Give me four days. I promise I'll call—no, better yet. I have reason to be in the mountains over the weekend. I'll come see you to report in person next Tuesday. Four days. Is that satisfactory?"

"Most satisfactory. Oh. One point, Colonel. We're staying here under the name of Doughty. We had a little problem in Austria. We'll explain it to you when we see you. I'm sure— anyway, I hope you'll approve. Christina and Thomas Doughty. Thank you, Colonel, thank you."

And she hung up. Slowly, Žarko restored the receiver to its cradle, rubbed his chin, looked up at Yevchenko. "Yuri, I underestimated Mrs. Meirion all those years. She's obviously British intelligence. She knows all about Pickering and Patak. Even knows the name Patak used when she wasn't sure of herself with Pickering. She—she and Ryder—they are traveling under false passports." He recounted the conversation, concluded, "So now we know what we suspected. That canny Pickering did go to his people about this. Well, enough of him. As for Meirion and Ryder, I'll send Jovan to take care of them." Jovan was his chauffeur; at times he had other duties. Yevchenko was quite aware of his supplementary talents.

But apparently those talents didn't impress the Russian. His disapproval was patent. It was almost disgust, as if he were saying aloud the thought Pantić had been whispering to himself: "Pantić, you're slipping." Obnoxious man. Obnoxious Russian. He had already forgotten his humiliation over the Schneeberg incident, was his usual impatient, domineering self.

"Yes, Yuri?"

"You forgot their backups. We've got to isolate them. We have just ten days. We can't tolerate a mistake. We can't have unknown enemies blundering around out there and stumbling across Drvar. We can't."

159

"All right, we can't. And so?"

"And so it's time to activate our mole. I think it's the time, anyway. I'll have to get approval. From Veseljev. In person. This is not a phone matter. I'll go to Budapest and see the general."

"So it's true. The stories. You do have a mole in the CIA."

Yevchenko's disgust became vocal. "Žarko, my friend, aren't you being just a bit naïve? We've got moles in every service."

"Including ours?"

Yevchenko ignored him. Tito's words came back to Pantić. They had been uttered in Drvar in February 1944, just after a particularly trying confrontation with General Kornieiev, Moscow's condescending gift to the Yugoslavs. Tito had grimaced wryly, said, "No matter how many different words a Russian uses to cry his support of communism, he's always saying just one thing. To support communism, you must support Mother Russia. Just once, I hope to live to hear a Russian say he'll support Yugoslavia. Just once." Damn, Tito was right. Then as always. Why, oh why had that American secretary of state turned his back on his Kranjc, insulted him publicly? Kranjc did not take insults from any man—certainly not from any American secretary of state. And so history is made—and you, Žarko, who loathes Russians and loves Americans—ah, poor Ethan, I'm so sorry, but I had to do it, have to do it, lovely American blood brother, partisan musketeer, hero. I'm so sorry. My general was insulted, and empires topple, and who are you and I in such a mess, what do we matter? Sorry, Ethan, sorry.

He beamed roguishly at Yevchenko, wanted to say, "You supercilious bastard. How many moles do you think we have in Moscow?" Instead he said, with a nice touch of awed humility. "Your mole, he's available on short notice? He can come to Beograd?"

"He'll come."

"In a position of power?"

"Of course."

"And who will he report to once he's here?"

"To you, of course. You coordinate his work. We've got to

know all Ryder's contacts here. He'll find them. Oh yes, he'll find them."

"Then you'll have three CIA villains to unveil at Drvar— Pickering, Ryder, and Mr. Mole. Excellent."

"Mr. Mole? What are you talking about? Our moles are honored heroes. This one will do his job, retire to a dacha in the Crimea, live in style for life. You know our policy."

"Do I?"

He had the satisfaction of seeing a flicker of doubt in Yevchenko's eyes. Maybe Jure Kranjc was right. "Don't worry about them, Žarko." So the general. "The tougher the Russians think they are, the easier they'll be to control. You'll see. Trust me."

What other choice did he have?

23

James Carter, aka Dwight Barnwell, CIA station chief at the plushest post in the world, knew he should be one of the happiest men in the world. Instead, holding Birdie Bingham's cable in his hand, he knew himself to be, if not the unhappiest, then close to it.

He stood at the third floor Embassy window and stared down at Boltzmanngasse. At first it was an unseeing stare. But gradually the motion on the one-way street caused his eyes to focus. Two American tourists stopping at the police kiosk across the street. The policeman pointing to the Embassy. The tourists craning their necks to see over the cars flowing to his right past the Institute of Physical Chemistry, monument to Ludwig Boltzmann, nineteenth-century Viennese physicist supreme—a suicide at the height of his fame, a fact he did not relish remembering, not at this time, not since that astonishing phone call five days ago from Birdie Bingham reporting the grisly events on the Schneeberg.

Then, at that moment, he had first noticed the peculiar

constriction in his chest. It hurt to breathe. Was this what happened in cases of cardiac arrest? Perhaps. But be honest with yourself, James. Had the pain truly begun five days ago? Hadn't the strange vise, the panic response, begun to clamp his lungs when Harry Ryder first appeared on his mysterious mission in Vienna? What mission? Why hadn't Bingham briefed him on it? Was he Ryder's—and Bingham's—target? Did they somehow suspect something? Had someone observed that fateful, that horrifying conversation seven months ago, in Rock Creek Park, just before he was posted to Vienna?

Certainly when he'd called Bingham to raise hell about Ryder and Meirion, he'd done his cause no good. "James," Birdie had said, "I sent you to Zürich to keep you out of mischief. And out of trouble. One more word out of you about Harry Ryder, one more word to me or anybody, and you've had it, James." Was Bingham's brutality a tip-off that he somehow knew about Rock Creek Park? Damn that Birdie Bingham.

He turned from the window and walked to an adjacent bathroom. (For the first time in his life, little things had begun to register on him, the little perks, the office with its own bathroom, the suite at the Embassy, dinners any night he chose at the Drei Husaren; those were good things, they were things very hard to come by in this uncertain world; was he about to lose them?) He stood before the mirror and inspected himself critically. Were his worries beginning to show? Gray hair at the temples, a fleck or two of gray amidst his full naturally wavy brown hair. Nothing critical there. Nothing critical either about his lips or cheeks or neck. No lines, no signs of tension. God, he was good-looking. (Now that fact— or the perks stemming from it—had nothing to do with the Agency. How many women had he bedded in Washington? Ten? No, at least twelve. Mary Jane, Betty, Mary Lou, Diana, Ginger, Jacqueline, Cynthia, Patricia, Babs, and—and—well, the other three had kind of faded in a happy mist, especially since he'd met Frau Amalia Klesl here in Vienna, a woman just as neglected and deserted as her counterparts in Washington, D.C. Wonderful women all. And all safely married.

162

All with totally indifferent husbands. Power-hungry men and neglected wives. And how much better he had handled himself than that stupid lecher Junius Oakland, glowing pink at his forehead every time he saw a pretty or even a halfway pretty woman. How stupid to be a lecher, when it was so much easier to fall into a charming and gracious and—usually—exuberantly sexy love affair with a frustrated married woman.) Somehow, as long as he could maintain this marvelous Cary Grant face, he would go through life as the happy survivor.

The phone began to ring. The red phone. The scrambler-equipped phone. He let it ring a few times more while he drew strength and courage from the handsome face in the mirror.

"James, my friend," he said aloud, waving to himself, "your panic is unbecoming. Birdie is not after you. If he were, he wouldn't be phoning you. Don't be stupid."

He laughed ironically, composed himself, glanced at his watch: six thirty-five P.M. Birdie was good as his word. The cable in his hand read, "Sorry I missed you this morning. Must talk to you today. Will call you this evening before seven, so you won't have to cancel any dinner date." Misplaced thoughtfulness, that. He had no dinner date. He was going to eat as usual at the Drei Husaren. They expected him about eight-thirty almost every night, sometimes alone, sometimes with Frau Amalia. Tonight he would be alone. They would find a place for him. What a restaurant.

He picked up the phone. "Barnwell here."

"Ah, James. Glad I caught you." The familiar whisper was so faint, it didn't seem possible that even the most modern science could carry its vibrations seven hundred miles or so across sea and mountains. But it could. And did. "I need your help."

Carter felt his ironic laugh threaten to break out again. All that needless anxiety. Christ, the man just wanted his help. "Yes, Birdie, of course. What can I do for you?"

"Your time, James? What are your time commitments?"

163

"Nothing I can't get out of."

There was a long and lengthening silence. Christ, had the equipment failed to pick up the vibrations? Was Birdie whispering away, his voice lost somewhere over the Black Forest? He pressed the phone receiver tightly against his ear. Nothing. He started to speak, to shout into the phone. It wasn't necessary. Birdie's voice trickled faintly against his ear. He spoke so softly, it almost seemed as if he were trying to foil any eavesdroppers, scrambler notwithstanding. And also obvious he didn't like what he had to say.

"James, I want you to help Harry Ryder and Lissa Meirion. They're in Yugoslavia. They're in over their heads. In real danger, I'm afraid. I want you to go help them resolve their problems and then shepherd them out of that country."

Carter had visited Yugoslavia on two different weekends. Once to Belgrade. Once to Zagreb. What he knew about Yugoslavia wouldn't fill one page of his desk calendar.

"Yes, Birdie. Yugoslavia."

"James, please. Don't try to sound so alert and intelligent. I know you don't know enough even to read the Cyrillic street signs in Belgrade. Too bad you're not going to Zagreb, where they use the Latin alphabet. But you do know something. What you do know are Harry Ryder and Lissa Meirion. No one at the Belgrade station can identify them. No one in secret intelligence at the British Embassy. But our people and our British cousins do know their way around the country. You will work with them and coordinate their efforts. I want Meirion and Ryder out. Safely out. Along with Ethan Pickering."

"Ethan Pickering!"

James Carter held the phone away from his ear and stared at it. This was unheard of. Without precedent. Birdie Bingham was breaking security. He was destroying a cover story. This was against all rules, was never done. The world had come to accept Ethan Pickering's suicide. He himself had come to accept it. Now Birdie Bingham was lifting Ethan Pickering from his mythical watery grave in Chesapeake Bay and plunking him down in Yugoslavia. Presumably on his feet. Presumably on an Agency mission. Presumably in danger.

What mission? What danger?

The silence continued. Carter shook himself. Was he now supposed to add something to his cry of shock? How about: "Birdie, it's apparent, then, that Pickering murdered someone and dumped him into Chesapeake Bay? Who was it, Birdie? Who did Pickering murder?"

A good question, but not one he had the courage to ask. The best he could do was:

"Do you have any suggestions where I should start?"

"Yes, of course. With a man called Žarko Pantić. Colonel Pantić. I'll spell it." He did, complete with appropriate diacritical marks. "He's military intelligence. Not the UDBA. Not the Služba Državne Bezjednosti, or as it used to be called, the Uprava Državne Bezjednosti. Not, in other words, the secret police. This is the KOS. The Kontra Obavještajna Služba. Military counterintelligence. Do you follow?"

"I follow. Why Pantić? Why military counterintelligence?"

"I don't know the why of the KOS. The why of Pantić is that he's the one who has undoubtedly kidnapped Ethan Pickering, whose cover name is, incidentally, Peter Trubari. I couldn't tell you that before now, James. Anyway, Pantić and Pickering have been lifetime friends. Patience, James, patience. I'll explain all that. Let me give you the whole story. It includes a *cherchez la femme* angle. Her name is Patak. Arritsa Patak. This'll take a while. Do you have any engagements?"

"None, Birdie. But before you start, one question. An overview question. If Pantić is the opposition, the villain of the story, why go to him? Why not go to the president or minister of the interior or somebody we can trust?"

"James."

The whisper was like a lark's trill.

"Oh, of course. Pantić is not operating on his own. We can't tell friends from opposition. Perhaps he's even working for that president fellow—"

"Otaronov. Miodrag Otaronov."

"Yes. And so—"

"And so you're to put the fear of God into Pantić. The whole resources of the Central Intelligence Agency and the secret intelligence service are being directed against him. He is to cease and desist. And in so doing, he is to free Pickering and help you get him and Ryder and Meirion out of Yugoslavia. Make it quite clear to him we know this is some kind of Russian plot—no, patience, James, I'll explain that, too. That's your overview. Satisfactory?"

"Quite. Here, let me get a pad and pencil and I'll take this down."

"Good. No tapes. All right, here's how it all began. It started at the Bayswater Underground Station sixteen days ago, on July second, and ended with the phone call I got from Harry Ryder five days ago. . . ."

24

By eight forty-five, James Carter had completed the forty-minute walk from the Embassy to the Drei Husaren restaurant. He was in an expansive mood. He smiled at the crowds strolling along the Kärntnerstrasse and they smiled back.

"Shadows of Iowa, it's just like high school!"

And in this expansive, happy moment, when he knew his anxieties had been meaningless, he was still Birdie Bingham's boy, James Carter had a sudden vision of his high school days in Waterloo, Iowa. Every morning before class, the student body paraded around the block-long marble-floored lobby. The parade went to the right. Up one side to the end of the lobby, back the other. The pace was almost a lockstep. Groups of boys, groups of girls, all focused on their own sex, with only an occasional glance at members of the opposite sex. What a happy time that had been! What a happy time this was! A better time, actually, because here the sexes did meet, did parade together, did share their happy chatter and laughter and joy. Quite a city, Vienna. The spirit of Johann Strauss had never really left it. Empire gone. Power gone. Wealth gone. But Johann Strauss remained. One could almost imagine that the parade up one side of the Kärntnerstrasse and down the other was to waltz time.

A block from St. Stephen's Cathedral, he turned up Weinburggasse, walked the short distance to the Drei Husaren restaurant, pulled open the heavy wooden door, and found himself in the nineteenth century. Dark paneled woodwork, flowers and plants, ornate chairs, substantial tables, glittering impeccable table settings, a maître d' in a well-tailored dinner jacket, and beyond him, music from a gigantic grand piano.

"Hello, Karl. Can you handle me?"

"I've only got a table by the kitchen door, Mr. Barnwell. But one out here"—and he nodded to a kind of antechamber to the main dining room—"will be free in another fifteen minutes. They're already late for the opera. *Fidelio.*"

"I'll wait at the piano, I'm in no hurry."

Karl nodded and went past him to greet a group of four. Marvelous-looking men in their fifties, expensively dressed, with well-preserved wives. What a city. What a restaurant. He strolled a few steps and leaned his waist against the grand piano, smiled at Gunther, the stoutish pianist who seemed half-asleep as he rippled through a Debussy piece.

There was a Chinese bowl on the piano. Patrons had already tossed in ten- and twenty-schilling notes. Carter started to do the same, changed his mind, switched to his wallet, and pulled out a twenty-dollar bill, held it up so Gunther could see it, and tossed it into the bowl. Not twenty schillings for James Carter, not tonight. Tonight was a two-hundred-and-forty schilling night.

Gunther's eyes were no longer half-closed. He smiled and nodded and looked inquiringly at James Carter.

"When you've finished the Debussy—what is it? The *Reflets*?" He rather liked that touch. Anybody could say *"Reflets dans l'eau."* The abbreviation—and his flawless German— somehow brought him into the center of sophisticated Europe's cultural life. And that is about as far as one can get from Waterloo, Iowa. "I thought so. Well, when you've finished, how about trying *Die Fledermaus?* Just say it's for a

167

romantic expatriate who is madly in love with Vienna. Old Vienna. New Vienna. Future Vienna. Tonight's the night for *Die Fledermaus*."

Gunther nodded and smiled as if he were responsible for creating the night, Europe's cultural life, the Viennese musical world, and, indeed, Johann Strauss himself. And as the familiar melodies began, James Carter leaned forward on both elbows and let the music flood through him, saturating him with visions of the Imperial Court and Francis Joseph whirling his Empress Elizabeth past the dignitaries lining the great hall at Schönbrunn, while Maestro Strauss himself conducted. So rapt was James Carter that he was three songs into *Die Fledermaus* before he became aware that someone, a man, was leaning on the piano beside him and sharing his music and appropriating it and, by crowding him so closely, ultimately disrupting his music-drugged fantasies.

Annoyed, he swung around as if to push the intruder an arm's length away and found himself almost nose to nose with an elegantly dressed, truly handsome man. A man as good-looking as James Carter himself. He had a lean, dark face, a most attractive moustache, and gray, good-humored eyes. They crinkled as he smiled at James Carter and said:

"Sergei sends you greetings."

It was fortunate James Carter had one elbow still resting on the piano. The support kept him from collapsing. But only just barely. His insides seemed to hollow themselves out, leaving him boneless and spineless. The stranger took in the stricken expression on James Carter's face and, repressing a fleeting twinge of distaste on his own, leaned nearer and said quietly, "He's sorry he could not meet you here himself, but he asked me to look you up. I'm so glad I found you here. There's nothing like Johann Strauss, is there? Absolutely magnificent."

He spoke so softly that there was no way Gunther could hear his voice. Carter, even in the midst of his despair, accepted the professionalism, the marvelous tonal control. He pushed himself erect and turned his back on the pianist and shook himself like a dog flipping water off its back.

"Sergei."

He must have breathed the name aloud, because the stranger nodded. "Yes, Sergei. My name is also Sergei."

It would be. James Carter closed his eyes for a moment and saw the other Sergei, the Rock Creek Sergei. A fat, untidily dressed little man who, seven months earlier, had seated himself beside him on the bench along Rock Creek in Washington, D.C., and changed—no, destroyed—James Carter's lifestyle. "I'm so glad you could come," the dumpy creature had said. "It's been so many long years since the first Sergei entered your life. Long years and good years. You have done well, better than any of us dreamed or expected or even hoped for when you first told us, told Sergei, at the Simpli Club in Munich, how you wanted to serve the cause of freedom and justice and asked what could you do to help. Yes, I'm glad you could meet me, because now we have a need for you. At long last, we have a need for you. The time has come when you truly can help."

That had been a harrowing moment. Just how many years had it been since that night at the Simpli Club in Munich? Twenty-two years. Twenty-two years since, in outrage and disgust, he had sought out the first Sergei and said he could no longer tolerate a world ruled and usurped by power-mad, hypocritical, greedy capitalistic tyrants. The more tyrants there were, the fewer there seemed to be, as they concealed themselves behind facades of democracy and opportunity for all. Opportunity for all! How he had writhed and raged at the hypocrisy of the Western world, with its iron fists in velvet gloves crushing into nothingness the miserable billions in the Third World. Third World? The Fourth, Fifth, and Sixth Worlds—although in all truth, the docile sheep in the First World were really no better off. Oh, he had been bitter, and the first Sergei, a man in his sixties, with a flashing, happy smile and a kindly face, had soothed him. "No, no," he had counseled, "you don't have to do anything. We have plenty of people who want to do something. We want you to do nothing. To live your life, keep your principles, but keep them to yourself. Someday, there will be a great and glorious task

169

for you. I promise you. Enough glory to satisfy any man. Just be patient. Finish up your graduate work here in Munich, and let life take its course. You will never see us or work with us. We don't need spies. There are always plenty of spies. We just need you as you are, a man truly committed. Just be patient, and your commitment will have its opportunity. When that time comes, another Sergei will contact you. Wait for Sergei's call, and do nothing desperate in the meantime. Patience, James Carter. Patience. Let your numbered bank account in Zürich grow, or use it as you see fit, and think nothing of it. You will earn it in time. I promise you."

And Carter had thumped his mug of beer onto the wooden table and said, "I don't buy that. I will not drift through life, hoping, expecting, waiting for some glorious moment that may never come. I'll put myself in a situation where such a moment will be bound to come. I'll join the CIA." And the kindly old man had shut his eyes, sighed, and said, his eyes still closed, "You can do that?" "I can do it. I have connections. I can do it."

And he had done it, for twenty-two years he had done it, his commitment as real and fervid as ever. The more he had served the unprincipled wolves at Langley who manipulated America and all the rest of the world in the benign name of intelligence, the more committed he had become. Or so he had thought, until he sat beside the fat, untidy little man in Rock Creek Park and suddenly realized that his easy, irresponsible life was about to end. What would they want of him? What world crisis existed that demanded that they, the Sergeis out there, should activate their sleeper, activate him and risk him—and in so doing force James Carter to contemplate a life without the perks the capitalist tyrants had so freely bestowed on him? What could the Sergeis want? And the reply had astonished him with its triviality, or rather with its contrast to his expectation of derring-do and cloak and dagger.

The fat Sergei wanted nothing glorious from him, nothing— thank God—dangerous. All he wanted was to prepare James Carter, to alert him. "My friend," he had said solemnly, "great events will be happening. You will be part of those events.

You are being posted to Vienna. And Vienna is at the epicenter of those happenings. From Vienna you can touch and follow sensitive developments in all the focal countries." "Focal countries?" "Look at the map, Mr. Carter. Look at Vienna—and then draw lines to Warsaw, Prague, Budapest, Bucharest, and Belgrade, even to Sofia, Athens, and Istanbul, and certainly to Berlin and Bonn. Vienna is like a giant central telephone exchange. From your new post, you'll be able to tap calls to and from all these critical cities. You can hear every conversation everywhere." "And that is all you want? Information?" Not action, not violence, not danger. Just information, thank God. And the dumpy Sergei had seemed puzzled. "Of course. Information. What else do we ever want? I don't understand your question."

He had been trapped, and being trapped, had blustered. "I was—I am—I am prepared to do more." And the moment he spoke, he knew he had made a great mistake. But the fat man had only shrugged. "Of course. We all are. We always are. If it comes to that, well . . ." And he had risen, started away, turned back. "You'll be contacted in Vienna. By another Sergei. Meanwhile, your account in Zürich continues to grow, and that is good, isn't it? We have to trust something in this world, don't we?"

Twenty-two years had not diminished James Carter's commitment, but it had taught him a few facts about the way of the world. One of those facts is that blind trust in the Sergeis of the world is not necessarily conducive to a long life. At this stage of his career, James Carter valued his life above all things, even above the substantial tax-free secret numbered account in Zürich. But this new Sergei would never learn that. James Carter was no fish from Waterloo.

"What can I do for you?"

Not the sharpest reaction to the ambiguities and uncertainties of the situation. But at least his question of this new Sergei would serve to open up, and at the same time delimit, his options. Right now he was a man who wanted every option he could lay his hands on. Maybe, somehow, he could find one that would permit him to retreat to his sleeper's nest—

a nest he could continue to feather with discreet, wonderful, grateful, neglected wives.

Sergei smiled benignly, moved to the end of the piano, and by a slight gesture suggested that James Carter come nearer.

"The pianist is too curious. He's playing the *Chacun à son goût* much too softly, don't you think?"

Carter shrugged but moved to the end of the piano. Sergei's tongue dripped honey, but his eyes were no longer good-humored—they had become quite frosty. Even the friendly crinkle at their corners did not soften their hardness. This Sergei was no kindly old man of the Simpli Club, no slovenly clerk in Rock Creek Park; he was hard mentally, hard physically, the kind of man who belonged in the arena with the Harry Ryders of this world, not with the James Carters. He was not just a classic intelligence agent; he was that specially trained field man prepared to kill casually, indifferently, efficiently, and often. An arrogant Russian James Bond. And as the implications of this thought reverberated through James Carter's head, he could not repress a shiver. If this Sergei should ever become displeased with James Carter, he would waste no time in discussions at a grand piano. Not when a mighty once-blue Danube could whisk an unwanted body on a long journey toward the Black Sea.

"You're right. This is better."

Sergei nodded. "Good. Here I can answer your question. We want you to go to Yugoslavia."

"Yugoslavia!" His incredulity was magnificent. And probably quite genuine. First Birdie Bingham, now Sergei Number Three.

"Not so loud. Yes, Yugoslavia. We want you to help us neutralize Harry Ryder. And Mrs. Meirion. Lissa Meirion. They called on you a week ago at the safehouse. They're in Yugoslavia now. Using false names and making a decided nuisance of themselves."

"Neutralize?" How had this Sergei learned about the safehouse? "What do you mean, neutralize?"

A look of distaste crossed Sergei's face. Had he sensed the panic behind the question? Could he detect the constriction in Carter's chest, the pain in his windpipe? Careful, James, careful. This is a different ball game. He might not be a Harry Ryder spewing bodies over hillsides, but he'd better learn to maneuver in Harry Ryder's world. And learn fast.

"Nothing violent, Mr. Barnwell. Don't be alarmed. We know violence has not yet been your métier. No, let me explain."

And he did. Carter was to get permission to go to Yugoslavia and, once there, contact Ryder and Meirion—or Thomas and Christina Doughty, as they now called themselves. The contact would be accidental, if necessary; but preferably it would be official. Get Langley's blessing to assist Ryder and Meirion. After all, as Barnwell well knew, those two had killed two of our men (the *our* made Carter's stomach do a little flip-flop), and Ryder and Meirion would expect Langley to take an active interest in their fate. That active interest would come from Dwight Barnwell. That was correct, wasn't it? (It was.) In the course of his interest—and this was the sole purpose of Barnwell's assignment, to show interest—he, Barnwell, was to find the names of the operatives supporting Ryder and Meirion. This was critical. He must use the Agency station in Belgrade, use Langley, if necessary. But Moscow Center had to know the identities of the Ryder-Meirion team. Did he understand? He did? Good. Having learned the identities of the support staff, he was to finger them, then make one phone call to Ryder and return to Vienna and go on as before. Simple, nothing to it, no danger, no violence.

James Carter ignored the only slightly tempered contempt in Sergei's voice. He felt new powers rising in him. (Not of rebellion. The fat, rumpled Sergei of Rock Creek Park had taken care of any notions in that direction. He had played a cassette for James Carter. The tonal quality wasn't the best. Noises of singing and laughter and shouting by university students occasionally blotted out the foreground voice, James Carter's voice. But it was all there, his whole declaration of newfound faith made at the Simpli Club in Munich twenty-two years before, ending with the ringing declaration, "I'll join the CIA.") No, not powers of rebellion, but of deceit.

173

The third Sergei hadn't said a word about the purpose of Ryder's and Meirion's excursion to Yugoslavia. Not a word about Peter Trubari, once known as Ethan Pickering, one-time director of science and technology at the Central Intelligence Agency of the United States of America. If Sergei wasn't leveling with him, why should he level with Sergei? Why tell him he already had full authority to go to Yugoslavia and work with the local people there? Why? Foolish question. He said:

"You understand my problem?"

"I understand."

"But do you? Do you really? I have no jurisdiction in Yugoslavia. I can't wander into the Embassy and look up my counterpart and ask him to brief me on Ryder and Meirion. Hell, I don't even know his name." This was another lie, of course. An Iowa lie. One made with an open, corn-fed frankness.

"It's Johnson. Merritt Johnson. His real name is Archibald Pettibone."

"Pettibone. I know him. He's from Iowa University. I'm from Iowa State. I know Pettibone. That'll help. But only barely. Only barely."

Sergei nodded. (Was there a flicker of amusement as he contemplated Iowa's contributions to the straight-faced lie? Was there? Let there be. Sergei might suspect a lie, he could never know exactly what it was.) And after a moment, while he beat time to a *Fledermaus* waltz, Sergei looked squarely at James Carter. He seemed almost a mirror double. His face was just as open and handsome as the American's. "I understand. I know you can't work alone. Or blindly. And I know you'll face all kinds of problems trying to get permission to operate in Yugoslavia—and once there, trying to operate intelligently. You don't know a word of Serbo-Croatian. You have no idea what agents are being run in that country. But fear not, Mr. Carter, we can help you in many other ways."

Sergei listened a moment to the music. "So. Two problems.

174

How to justify your going to Yugoslavia. And once there, how to work efficiently. All right, how will this do?

"For justification, you can say you received a call from Ryder. He's at the Hotel Plitvice with Mrs. Meirion. Look at a map. At the Plitvice Lakes. In Serbo-Croatian, that's Plitvička Jezera. They're staying there under the name of Doughty. Thomas and Christina Doughty. You can tell Langley that Ryder wants your help. He wants a liaison with Belgrade. He's hot on the trail of that Trubari fellow, yes, the one they were scouring Vienna for. You know about Trubari, you checked the police about him." At this revelation of Sergei's knowledge of his doings, Carter barely refrained from wincing. But he did refrain, did manage to focus on Sergei's next words: "Anyway, that's why Meirion and Ryder are in Yugoslavia. To find Trubari. Your story will do the job. It will have to."

"Yes. I see. Trubari. Well, I can try. I know, I know. This is my problem. All right, I'll work it out. What about operating efficiently once I get there?"

"That, too, is basically your problem. You'll have to find ways and means of discovering the cast of characters supporting Ryder and Meirion. That is essential. Nothing else matters. The names and identities and whereabouts of the support team. You understand?"

Carter disdained any acknowledgment. He said, "And when I learn the names, what do I do with them?"

Sergei took out a cigarette, found a matchbook, struck a match, lit the cigarette, left the matchbook lying open in front of James Carter. The latter glanced at the name written inside the cover, the name and phone number, and found himself gripping the top of the piano to hold himself erect. He straightened his back, pulled his hand away, watched the sweat mark of his palm and fingers slowly dissolve. Keep calm, James, keep calm. The hell with the sweat. Let Sergei try to figure out if the sweat was from panic or shock—or the warm room.

He shoved the matchbook back, kept his disingenuous, corn-fed mask intact. Sergei raised his eyebrows. "You have it?"

"I have them. The name and the phone number."

Oh, he had them all right. Had had them for two hours, ever since Birdie Bingham gave them to him: *Žarko Pantić. 863-1174.*

"Good. That's a Belgrade number. Phone as soon as you arrive there. Someone is always there. A meeting will be arranged. At a safehouse. No, that's the wrong English, sorry. At a place safe for you to meet in."

Carter felt a peculiar elation beating through his veins, listened to it, identified it, forced his face to stay calm. The elation came from a whole new concept. Birdie Bingham and Žarko Pantić. Sergei Number Three and Žarko Pantić. What a perfect setup for the double, even the triple cross. Hadn't Bingham put himself in his hands with the revelation about Ethan Pickering? Foolish old man. He'd practically admitted his complicity in a murder. Threaten him, would he? Bingham was in no position to threaten anybody who knew about Pickering. Oh, did he have Bingham over a barrel, but did he! And as for Sergei Number Three, he was just a source of money, no more. And with his newfound hold over Bingham, the money would be big money. Oh happy world, where one smart Iowa boy can manage to dupe the best. Hail James Carter. He said calmly:

"And my phone call to Ryder? What do I say?"

"You'll learn that at the meeting in Belgrade. What to say—and when to say it."

25

Birdie Bingham had it right. James Carter couldn't even read the street signs in Belgrade.

"Number 19 Čika Ljubina. Just off the Terazije." So Žarko Pantić on the telephone. "You're driving? There's a garage just across the street from the entrance to Čika Ljubina. You can't miss it."

Can't miss it. First he drove around for fifteen minutes, trying to find the garage, finally located one a half-mile from the Terazije, Belgrade's great central avenue, "the nerve center of the city," as the guidebook proclaimed. Then he had trouble locating any street signs. They were often plastered discreetly on the sides of buildings, part of the building, advertisements for all he knew. But once he did find a sign, the problem of interpreting it became intolerable. He tried asking passersby, but they only smiled politely, shook their heads, and hurried on. English, the universal language. Who dreamed that up? (Not that French or German was any better; Yugoslavians obviously felt no need whatever for any language other than Serbo-Croatian. No need, no shame, no embarrassment. It was his problem, not theirs.) But finally a ten-year-old child, very solemn, came up to him.

"May I help you, sir?"

He almost embraced the lad. "Thank you. Thank you. I'm trying to find a street. Čika Ljubina Street."

A look of shock? Of disbelief? Of amazement? Anyway, a look spread across the boy's face. He was wearing tennis shorts, tennis shoes. A little old boy in tennis shoes. He essayed some words, found none, finally pointed. Above Carter's head.

Carter craned his neck around, saw nothing, backed up into the sidewalk, thereby discommoding a horde of rushing Belgradians (no one moved slowly in Yugoslavia, this was the original land of hustle), finally located a sign. Letter by letter he worked his way through the Cyrillic: ЧИКА ЉУБИНА

He had to say something. If only to unfreeze the boy's frozen look of dismay. He said it. "Ah, I'm standing on it. Čika Ljubina. Thank you. I can find number 19, thank you. The number 19 is 19, even in Serbo-Croatian. Thank you."

Number 19 was the American Library. Colonel Žarko Pantić had suggested they meet there. "At two in the afternoon. A good safe place for a Yugoslav to meet an American." He had stressed the word *safe*. Obviously he had a word-for-word report of Sergei Number Three's conversation with James Carter. The street itself was only a few blocks long. It contained, he saw, the Australian Consulate and a school, probably a university, probably a humanities branch of the University of Belgrade, since he had already walked past the Technical Faculty branch located on the Bulevar Revolucije, a block or so from his hotel, the Metropol.

Number 19 was a doorway. The doorway led to a stairway. The stairway led to the American Library on the second floor. A modest affair, it had two rooms—or rather, one longish room split down the middle by a ceiling-high bookshelf. To his left was a long reading table. At the far end sat a chunky little fellow wearing an unpressed, ill-fitting, shiny suit. As prearranged, he was reading an American newspaper. *The International Herald Tribune.* To Carter's right was the librarian's desk, presided over by a white-haired, pleasant-faced American lady. Carter walked up to her, smiled, said:

"I came to read some newspapers, ma'am. All I've seen on this trip is the *Herald Tribune.* I was hoping you'd have some real papers from back home."

She sprang to her feet. "Indeed we do. Follow me."

She led him past the rotund, balding little man, pointed. *"The New York Times. The Christian Science Monitor. The Washington Post. The Wall Street Journal."* Her voice was proud. These publications were America incarnate, her justification for existence and job.

For a moment, James Carter forgot his mission, gave way to idle curiosity. "Who generally uses your library, ma'am? Many tourists like me?"

"Oh, some. But not many. No, we mostly provide service to the students and professors from the University. Across the street."

He looked around at the bookshelves. She understood, said, "Oh, not with our facilities. We work with the Library of Congress and with American universities. The professors here use us as a branch of the American library system. Otherwise, how would they get books?"

How indeed? "Thank you, ma'am." He took *The New York Times*—it was five days old—carried it to the reading table, sat down near the rotund fellow, smiled.

Colonel Žarko Pantić smiled back. It was an extraordinary smile. His whole face, from ear to Adam's apple, seemed one vast crease. He said, "You are American, no?"

"Yes."

"Good. Then maybe you can explain this to me. I like American sports." He shoved the *Herald Tribune* over to Carter, stuck a stubby forefinger against a headline: NFL AN-NOUNCES RULE CHANGES.

National Football League? Mid-July, and football already beginning? Was there some esoteric message in the squib that he was supposed to pick up? Or was the message Žarko Pantić's voice? Just like Sergei Number Three, Pantić had marvelous tonal control. Without whispering, speaking normally, he managed a sound that reached Carter's ears and no farther. Damn, these fellows were professionals. James, you'd better remember the Camp Peary training of years ago, remember the exotic field techniques you've never had to use, never intended to use. Well, you'd better start intending now.

He read the article, looked at Pantić; the Yugoslav said:

"It talks about 'line of scrimmage.' What is a 'line of scrimmage'?" This time the voice carried farther. Mrs. America at the librarian's desk heard it, nodded approvingly. The Slavs were being indoctrinated with American culture. Good for America. Good for the lines of scrimmage.

Carter explained as best he could. Žarko Pantić beamed, hunched closer to Carter, kept pointing at the article. Carter nodded, also hunched himself forward. Now their heads were almost touching. Pantić said:

"You got permission to come?"

"Yes. From Langley."

Pantić's face reshaped itself into a look of admiration. Now it was one vast beam of approbation. "Good. I was told you were good. You are. That is."

"That is? Ah, that is good. Thank you. I try."

"How long will the try take? When will you identify the support team?"

"I already have. There is none."

179

"None!" Now the face was incredulity incarnate. (That, by God, had been the expression on the ten-year-old boy's face. Not shock. Incredulity. The boy's expression had at least been genuine.) "How do you know?"

"They told me. I didn't have to get permission to come here." How was his tonal control doing? "They ordered me here to help our two friends. They're on their own. Two misfits trying to track down Ethan Pickering and his girlfriend, a Miss Arritsa Patak."

"Ah." Now the face was granite. "Ethan Pickering. They told you about Ethan?"

"Yes. Everything. Chesapeake Bay. The murdered man, Tibor Szentes. Peter Trubari. Everything. How did you know they hadn't told me before?"

"Your questions around Vienna made that quite clear. You are rather a public figure, you know."

It was time to go from skirmish to battle. "They also told me you kidnapped him."

Granite dissolved to outraged innocence. "Kidnapped? Me? Nonsense."

"Nonsense?"

"Nonsense. Pickering—or Trubari—simply fell in love with Arritsa Patak and came here to be with her. He wants to marry her. Kidnapped? How extraordinary. Your Agency reads too many spy novels."

"Then there is no problem."

"No problem at all."

"Why am I here, then? Why do two intelligence services both send me to work with you? The KGB tips me off to come see you. And my boss orders me to come see you. Why?"

Outraged innocence vanished. The mobile face became a portrait of wounded self-esteem. "Why? It's simple. So simple. Mr. Ryder and Mrs. Meirion kill two Russian employees and come here under assumed names. They purport to be looking for Peter Trubari. For Ethan Pickering. What's going on? When our friends in Moscow reported what's happened on the Schneeberg, well—what could we think? Is there some concerted move against us? Can you blame us for being alarmed?"

James Carter had it now. He was being lied to. Almost shamelessly lied to, as if he didn't matter. And the next question underlined his insignificance in Pantić's eyes.

"Why, Mr. Barnwell, why did your bosses send you to me? They have this monstrous charge against me, that I'm a kidnapper of my lifelong friend, and yet they send you to me. Why?"

Now a crazed glint flashed from Pantić's eyes. And the Danube remained the Danube, only here in Belgrade it was much nearer the Black Sea, quite handy as a vehicle for carrying a bloating corpse to that cold, that Russian burial disposal.

"Why, Colonel? Because I was ordered to come to threaten you. To make you cease and desist. To release Pickering, to escort Ryder and Mrs. Meirion out of your country. That's why."

Pantić nodded. Now his face was sad, the concerned parent grieving over an errant child. "Strange. Very strange. Like your poet says, much ado about nothing."

"Nothing?"

"Nothing. You're a hero. Take them, Mr. Barnwell. Take them all with you. Pickering, Ryder, Meirion. Of course, what happens to Mr. Ryder and Mrs. Meirion when they get out of our country—well, that's none of our concern. They are murderers. Let them face the consequences on their own time, in some other country. Yugoslavia is not a target-shooting range."

"Take them? How?"

"Pickering and Patak are out of the city. In Sutjeska. You know Sutjeska? A great battle was fought there. A very great battle. Three partisan divisions against twelve German. Yes, Sutjeska. We won. By running away as fast as we could. Oh yes, we won. Well, they're at Sutjeska, and they'll be back by Wednesday, possibly Thursday. So until they get back, call up Mr. Ryder and ask him and Mrs. Meirion to join you here. You can all leave together by plane, car, or train. You can report back to Langley how clever you've been. Call up Ryder tomorrow, or call him today. Any day you want. Thanks, Mr. Barnwell. Thanks for all your help."

James Carter could still hear Birdie Bingham's whisper. "And so, Dwight, when Ethan came down the Schneeberg, he and Miss Patak were followed by a most unsavory type. A Nazi type. That's the description Frau Dollwitz gave Ryder and Meirion. Very apt. Nazis and Communists, both the same side of the same coin." He recollected the whisper and knew himself in trouble. Bad trouble. Pantić was plainly, almost nonchalantly, lying to him. But had Birdie Bingham told him the truth? Was Birdie setting him up? Was Sergei setting him up? (No need to ask about Pantić, he'd already finished his setup.) Who could a man trust anymore? Double crossing and triple crossing were both fine concepts, James, as long as it was you doing the crossing. Keep cool, James, keep your cool. He said:

"I'll call Ryder tomorrow. They're still at the Hotel Plitvice? Good, let them enjoy their holiday. After the Schneeberg, they need it."

This would also give him one more day to do some very fast shuffling. What about Pettibone, CIA chief of the Belgrade station? Could he help? Or was Pettibone just another Birdie Bingham tool, prepared to trap and destroy James Carter, Russian mole? Was that it? James Carter, it is obvious the only person you can rely on is James Carter.

And that, a small voice deep down inside him murmured, and that isn't much.

26

He opened the door for Lissa, stepped back. She started into the room, jackknifed, picked up a sealed envelope, held it up.

"The girl downstairs was wrong, Harry. We do have a message."

Every two hours they had returned to the Hotel Plitvice lobby, received the same negative headshake from the girl at the front desk. (She also handled the switchboard, was fluent in several Slavic languages plus Hungarian, German, English, French, Italian, and Spanish, and in her spare time served as resident psychiatrist and tour guide to the busloads of Europeans come to visit the Plitvice Lakes region, one of the world's scenic wonders.) The headshakes were sympathetic, but they were accompanied by a speculative look in her eyes. "Like a relative waiting for a sick, rich uncle to die." So Harry, growling. Lissa could not dispute his analysis. The girl clearly expected bad things to happen to Mr. and Mrs. Thomas Edward Doughty.

"Open it."

Lissa lifted her great blue eyes from the envelope, confronted him. (As always, when she did this, he felt his insides churn; even now he could not help glancing at the bed lying defenseless and inviting.) She saw his expression, smiled, ripped open the envelope. The message was on a hotel memo sheet. It was in German. Lissa read it aloud: "Meet me at the trestle by Lake Prošće tomorrow morning at nine A.M. Make sure you're not followed." There was no signature.

Lissa and he spoke simultaneously. He said, "Miljana Dragan in Zagreb." She said, "Arritsa Patak." They meant the same thing.

At Zagreb, they had failed in their efforts to find Arritsa Patak. (The first night, at his insistence, they had acted as tourists. He could not get over these Croatians, their vitality, their youth, their exuberance. Perhaps it was the contrast with Austria, where everyone, in retrospect, seemed old; even the children there seemed miniature grown-ups. Here, in Zagreb, in this university city, the capital of Croatia, Tito's homeland, the streets and shops and restaurants seemed inundated in a tide of youth. He had been so excited by these first impressions that, once booked at the Sava Hotel, he had insisted Lissa follow him from bar to bar to bar. Wherever they went, they were welcomed by laughing university students who punctuated their welcome with songs, great roaring choruses. Lissa wanted to join, she knew the songs, everyone in Yugoslavia knew the songs, but he wouldn't let her. "You're a tourist. It's English or German or nothing." Some students had taken them to their apartment, the informal party had continued to almost dawn. What a day. Murder on the Schneeberg. Wine and song in Zagreb. Not bad for one aging codger and a woman old enough to be the mother of their hosts. Not bad.)

They had found Arritsa Patak's name still in the phone book, had gone to her former home, an apartment in a giant housing complex south of the Sava River. (He had never heard of the Sava River; it was wider than the Golden Gate; Harry Ryder, the experienced world-traveler; though, on reflection, he saw no need to be chagrined at his ignorance; no one in Zagreb had ever heard of the Song Hua Jiang, the Pine Flower River; that Harbin river was also wider than the Golden Gate; things balance out; egos are preserved.) But at the apartment they had learned nothing. In fact, they had been treated rather rudely by a thin-faced neighbor. She hadn't liked Lissa; she was annoyed by Lissa's fluency in her language—this time there had been no alternative; Lissa had had to use her Serbo-Croatian—and she obviously didn't think much of Miss Patak, was glad she no longer lived next door. She made quite clear she considered Miss Patak no better than she should be. "Men, always men." That with a sniff. "When she went away, it was good riddance."

Lissa and he had fled in silence and in defeat. But they got a reprieve as they reached their car. An old gentleman, the thin-faced lady's husband, it turned out, was waiting for them. "Don't let my wife bother you. We lost both our sons in the war. Things have never . . . well, you understand. I'd like to help you, but I don't know where Arritsa went. But she has a good friend at the University Library. Miljana Dragan. See her. She'll know where to find Arritsa. Wonderful woman, Arritsa. And so is Miljana."

This time they were cautious in their approach. They said they were friends of Arritsa Patak and they had a problem and could they have dinner or a cocktail after hours because they needed Miss Dragan's help. Cocktails it was. And they had leveled with Miss Dragan, telling her about Arritsa and Peter Trubari, their disappearance, and she had shaken her head and said she, too, had lost track of Arritsa, but—brightening—some of her other ball-breaker friends might— And Lissa had interrupted. Her what? And Miljana had blushed. "We're all divorced. Arritsa. Me. Lots of us. We married young. And always for a short while. Men call us ball-breakers. We're all smart, not unattractive"—no question about that— "and ambitious. Men in Yugoslavia aren't used to that. They aren't used to the modern woman. Remember, only a few generations ago the Turks ruled much of our country. The change has come too fast for many of our men to accept—in spite of Socialist equality of the sexes. So men are afraid of us. Oh, they'll sleep with us, but then they run away, afraid somehow we'll destroy their manhood. Ball-breaker. That's me. Anyway, there are a lot of us here and in Beograd and other northern cities, and I'll ask around."

"Good," Lissa had said, "we'll be at the Hotel Plitvice. We have no particular reason, except that Peter Trubari did promise Arritsa to take her to his home in Bihác, near the Lakes. Or so we were told. Anyway, we'll wait there. Please let us know what you find out, even if it's nothing. Please. And thank you."

Now, his eyes still on the note, he eased the door shut, nodded. "Patak is here. Miljana Dragan found her." He put his arms around Lissa, held her close, stroked her hair, came out of his reverent reverie as the phone clanged. "Damn. Pantić. He's here, too. Now what do we do?"

But it wasn't Pantić. It was Dwight Barnwell. James Carter. Lissa handed him the phone. He placed it so she could hear the conversation. "Dwight?"

"Yes, Dwight. Harry! Forget that Doughty crap. It doesn't matter anymore. Nothing matters. We've got our boy."

"Our boy?"

"Peter Trubari, Harry, Peter Trubari. Or do you prefer Ethan Pickering?"

"Dwight!"

"Don't be so damn cautious, Harry. The game's over. Birdie sent me down here to find you and Pickering and I've done it and we can all go home. Tomorrow. Come join me here in Belgrade, you and Mrs. Meirion, and we'll go pick up Ethan and get the hell out of here."

"How did you find him, Dwight?"

"Birdie sent me to Colonel Pantić and—"

"Pantić!"

"Oh yes, Harry. Pantić. Pantić said he promised to phone you, but in view of the circumstances he asked me to do the honors. Birdie told me all about the little colonel. All. London and before that. The war. Mitra Grgić. Tibor Szentes. Chesapeake Bay. Arritsa Patak. Everything. But it's all been a comedy of errors. Ethan will be back in Belgrade tomorrow. He doesn't have a phone where he's living, but he'll call me from a pay phone as soon as he gets back to town, probably about noon. I'll set up a time to go see him. Him and Miss Patak. Yes, they're together, and we can all leave on Thursday. If he wants to leave, which I rather doubt. Ethan came here of his own free will, and I rather suspect he'll stay of his own free will. That's if I understand what Arritsa Patak means to him. So come on up. I'll reserve a room for you here at the Metropol. Chalk one up to Birdie, Harry. The Whisperer knows all."

"Pantić told you where we are?"

"Of course he did, but so did Birdie. Your phone call to Birdie from Maribor, remember? Now don't go off into one of your paranoiac fits, Harry. This is a simple business. Can I expect you?"

"Yes. We'll drive up after breakfast tomorrow. Would you ask Ethan to have us for dinner? Say about nine. We'll probably make it by seven or eight, but give us leeway, okay?"

"Okay. See you."

Ryder put the phone down, looked at Lissa. "What does your Welsh gift tell you about that conversation?"

"It tells me you were right to call Pantić. Harry Ryder's credo: Stir up the natives. Our phone call to Pantić has succeeded in doing just that."

He tapped the message still held by Lissa. "And this?"

"Let me see. Ethan and Arritsa are together and will be in Beograd tomorrow. Arritsa is near here somewhere and will see us at Lake Prošće tomorrow. I would say the truth is not in Mr. Carter."

"Maybe we're wrong about Arritsa. Maybe it's somebody else who's here."

"Do you believe that?"

"No." He pointed. "And the second part of the message: 'Make sure you're not followed'?"

"Arritsa thinks someone is following us."

"Who?" An unfair question, that. The Plitvice, and the companion hotels, the Bellevue and Jezera, had seven or eight hundred guests. But perhaps not so unfair. The person or persons following them would not be Hungarian or German or English. He—or she or they—would be Slavic. Would probably be Yugoslavian. How many Yugoslavs were vacationing here? How many? Over half the crowd, that's how many. Lissa had explained it to him. "Yugoslavs are madly in love with their own country, Harry. Not just because it's beautiful and well worth seeing. But also because of the historical associations. Here, for instance. In the Plitvička Jezera. Terrible battles were fought throughout the Lika—these western mountains. The winters were like your Valley Forge winter. When a Yugoslav hikes around the countryside now, he's reliving some of his country's most heroic moments." All right, there were too many Yugoslavs. So his question was unfair. He started to apologize. But Lissa ran her hand through her hair, her eyes began to flash.

"I've got it. Mr. Gat-tooth."

"Mr. Gat-tooth?"

"Haven't you noticed him? He eats alone. He's the only

187

Yugoslav in the place who's here by himself. He eats alone and he never, never looks at us. Never."

He shook his head. "I'll watch for him." He hugged her again. "Have I told you recently? You are something." He started to ease her toward the bed. She did not resist. She did look up at him.

"What is really happening, Harry?"

"As you put it, I haven't the foggiest. We'll start to find out tomorrow. If we have to avoid Mr. Gat-tooth, we'll skip breakfast, slip out of here by six, hike our way to Lake Prošće. But that's tomorrow. This is now."

"It's been four days of nows."

But that was not an objection. She demonstrated that. She was something.

27

They dressed warmly. Fog blanketed the mountains, a chill fog, reminiscent of the Schneeberg. Well, why not? This was an extension of the same mountain range and, in fact, almost due south of the Schneeberg.

"We'll go out through the basement past the restaurant. We can't let the girl at the front desk see us. Okay?"

"Okay."

Lake Prošće was more than an hour's brisk hike away. Sixteen lakes in all, with waterfalls cascading from one lake to the next. A scene for Oh's and Ah's. And not just because of the lakes and waterfalls, but also because of the trees and, in some places, the rank, oversize vegetation, great ferns and gigantic bushes and weeds. Leyte had not been lusher. Or more beautiful.

They crossed the national park highway and descended to the paths and trestles and bridges that skirted the lakes. No one saw them. Or at least, they saw no one who saw them.

They walked at a leisurely pace, stopping frequently to admire the views, took more than two hours to reach their destination.

"Damn, it's cold. We'll freeze when we get there. We'll still have to wait forty-five minutes."

"No we won't." Lissa pointed through an opening in the trees. He saw her, too, a tall woman with flaming red hair striding down from the highway. They picked up their pace, reached the trestle at one end as Arritsa Patak arrived at the other end. For a moment she hesitated, then strode across the logs. She had a shy smile on her face, her marvelous face. (Why marvelous? he asked himself. Because of her beauty? Because of the reddish glow on her cheeks? The gleaming teeth, the exotic slanting eyes, the Rita Hayworth hair? Maybe. But not really. It was the serenity that radiated from her. The serenity of a beautiful woman who has learned to accept herself for what she is, whatever that is. No mean accomplishment in any human being, extraordinary in one like Arritsa Patak.) She came up to them, ignored him, took Lissa's hand, smiled.

"Miljana said you are wonderful. She is right. You are."

She used German. That was her only concession to his presence. From then on, she ignored him. In fact, both women ignored him. They were absolutely taken with each other. Two beautiful women. Two brainy women. Two equal women.

"Thank you for coming, Miss Patak. We're here at the hotel under the name of Doughty, as you know, but my name's really Lissa Meirion, and this is Mr. Harry Ryder. We are both friends of . . . of Peter Trubari."

"Yes. Peter Trubari. But I know his other name. Ethan Pickering."

"So. So he told you."

"Yes. Everything. On our way down the Schneeberg. With that terrible man behind us. And two more in front of us. And over them all, that . . . that—"

"That Colonel Žarko Pantić."

She nodded. "Ethan . . . Peter—that's how I really know him. As Peter. He told me his story, and I said let's escape, let's cut across the mountains and escape, and he said no. He

189

had promised to see this through, to find out what his lifetime comrade in war and peace wanted with him. And he made me promise not to reveal to Colonel Pantić or anyone what he had told me. He gave me a telephone number in London, but I've been afraid to call. My aunt's phone—I'm staying with my aunt in Beograd—my aunt's phone has been tapped, we can hear the breathing on the line, and I'm followed wherever I go and—"

"Followed?"

"Oh, not here. A friend told me Miljana Dragan wanted to see me. In private. So I went to the Robna Kuća on the Terazije—you know it?" (The Robna Kuća, Harry learned later, was a department store, Yugoslavia's largest.) "I went there and out the back way and borrowed a Zastava from a friend, drove to Zagreb, talked to Miljana, and she told me about you. Both of you. She was impressed by you. She was right."

"Thank you. We came here because of Frau Dollwitz at the Baumgartenhaus on the Schneeberg. You remember?"

"I remember. Peter hadn't told me his story yet. I wondered why he spoke so frankly. I thought that old woman understood everything he said even though he used Serbo-Croatian. She tried to hide it, but the gleam in her eyes— you understand?"

"I understand. Peter was simply leaving a trail behind. He mentioned Bihać. So we went to Bihać, found his home, but it was locked up. Our only hope was Miss Dragan. We thank Miss Dragan."

Arritsa's face clouded. "You know you are being followed?"

"We know. After your message came, we worked out who it had to be. Mr. Gat-tooth."

"Gat-tooth? Ah, I understand. His name is Jovan. I don't know his last name. Sometimes he chauffeurs for Colonel Pantić. He scares me. He's the one who led the capture of Peter on the Schneeberg."

And tears came from her eyes, great bubbles. Lissa embraced her, patted her tumbling red hair. "Don't cry, Arritsa." It was no longer Miss Patak. Woman's world. "We understand. You did what you thought best. And don't worry. We were careful. We were not followed."

Lissa reached into Harry's shoulder bag, pulled out a handkerchief, an oversize red and white ski affair. Arritsa blew her nose, buried her face, looked up.

"I was wrong. I know that now. I didn't know it then. Colonel Pantić said he needed my help. An enemy of the state. Of the people. They wanted this enemy in Yugoslavia. To make him confront the evidence. That was all. A confrontation. And then I found out . . . found out . . ."

"That you loved Peter."

"Yes."

The two women were lost in each other, in their mutual sympathy and admiration. Should he break in? Try to get the conversation back to current issues? Outsider males don't break in. At least, outsider males with any modicum of common sense don't.

Lissa smiled. "But he found out, too."

Arritsa nodded. They beamed at each other. Apparently Ethan's discovery of her love for him solved the problem, justified everything. Woman's world.

He started to clear his throat, to do something, but Lissa's words rode over his feeble gurgle. "Do you know where Peter is now? Where they have him?"

Arritsa Patak shook her head. Water falls; red hair cascades. "I went to see Colonel Pantić. I intended to challenge him to—"

"You what!" Ryder's bellow was witless. The two women looked at him with annoyance. Lissa turned back to Arritsa.

"Mr. Ryder is simply concerned for your safety. If Colonel Pantić suspects you might challenge him, you could be in great danger."

"I know. I lost my courage when I got there. I said stupid things and got out. I have no idea what's happened to Peter."

Lissa's tone became even gentler than before. "We have a friend in Beograd who called us and said Peter will be in Beograd today."

"Beograd! Today!"

191

"And he also said you would be with him. We would all have dinner together tonight."

Arritsa suddenly laughed. She tossed her hair. It flamed around her, latter-day sun goddess, present-day Amazon. "A lie, of course. What does it mean? What do we do?"

Now Lissa looked at Harry. Arritsa looked at him. Damn, what was the outsider male supposed to come up with now? "Lissa, will you translate for me? My German's not good enough for this." She nodded. He said, "Miss Patak, we don't know what the lie means. We just know it's all bad. And no place for you. Please stay out of this from now on, especially stay away from Colonel Pantić. Mrs. Meirion and I will go to Beograd today and see our friend and play the game out."

Arritsa nodded. "I checked out of the Plitvice last night and stayed in Bihać. I couldn't take a chance Jovan would see me." She pointed. "My car's up there. On the highway. I'll leave for Beograd now."

He raised a hand. "One moment, Miss Patak. What London telephone number did Peter give you?"

"Number? Ah." She looked off into space, nodded. "It's 016–5472. Yes, that's it."

He looked at Lissa. She said, "Sir Alex's number."

"Don't try to reach it, Miss Patak. Keep out of trouble. We know that number. We may have to call it, but I don't see what good London will do us right now. London is a very long way away. And Beograd is very near. But . . . but how can we reach you? We can't phone you. And your home is under surveillance. Suppose we have to talk with you?"

She thought, ran her hand through her hair, a gesture almost identical with Lissa's habitual, unselfconscious motion. "Ludmila. Mrs. Meirion, call my aunt Veda. Veda Lukac, she's in the phone book. Call and say you're Ludmila. No more, just Ludmila. She's another aunt in Novi Sad. Say you'll be in Beograd next weekend and could you and Veda have lunch at the Seher Restaurant? Aunt Veda will say fine, but come by the house first. And that will mean you and I will meet two hours after your phone call. We'll meet at the merry-go-round in the park off Naradnog Fronta Street. Near the Terazije. I'll try not to be followed, but—"

And she shrugged and Lissa said, "Good. Ludmila. Veda Lukac. Naradnog Fronta merry-go-round. I'll remember. Goodbye, Arritsa, and thank you for coming."

Harry cleared his throat. The women came out of their absorption in each other and looked at him. He said, "You can do one more thing, perhaps, Miss Patak. Your women's network?" He started to say comrade ball-breakers, but backed off. "Perhaps they can help. Perhaps they can find out what Colonel Pantić is up to, what he's devoting himself to, what's his assignment? He's a fairly public figure in military circles. What's said about him? His work? You understand?"

"I understand. I'll see Miljana on the way back. I'll ask her, and if we meet at the merry-go-round, I'll pass her news on to you." And suddenly she broke into a torrent of Serbo-Croatian, blushed scarlet, face framed by scarlet hair, hugged Lissa, listened to Lissa's murmured reply, also in Serbo-Croatian, nodded, laughed, and turned and fled.

He watched her, watched Lissa. "What was that all about?"

"She said one reason she held back with Peter—with Ethan— was because he was so much older. Over twenty years difference. Her first marriage had been to an older man, a professor. It was awful. But when she saw us, you and me, she knew she had made the right choice. Age differences don't matter. Love matters. Our love for each other is the most beautiful thing she's ever seen. Except for her love for Peter. That's what she said."

"And what did you say?"

"I said it takes men like you and Ethan not to be terrified of ball-breaking women like us. Just the contrary, we seem to bring out the best in their balls."

"Well, I'll be damned. I didn't think she even noticed my presence."

"Oh, she noticed all right, she noticed. All women notice. Haven't you seen their eyes as we walk down the street?"

"I have. They're all looking at you."

"Oh, Harry. Don't you understand anything? They look at me because they're curious to see what I've got that attracted a man like you. This is quite elementary, Harry, and doesn't require any Welsh gift. Or are you just fishing for more compliments?"

He hugged her. There was no bed present. The trestle was hardly comfortable. The ground was thoroughly wet. "Okay. If you say so. It's elementary. But Beograd is not elementary. What does your Welsh gift say about that? And about James Dwight Barnwell Carter and Žarko Pantić?"

"It says—it says exactly what your paranoiac sense says: it says we can't trust either of them, they're all liars, and we're going to have problems with Jovan Gat-tooth, Mr. Pantić's hatchet-man. And the problems will be right here, not in Beograd."

"So they will. I think it's time we go retrieve our pistols. We'll miss breakfast. It'll take us a couple of hours to hike up to the highway, find the bush they're buried under, and hie ourselves back to the hotel."

"Good. We'll be in time for lunch. Or do you plan to shoot Mr. Jovan before lunch?"

"You mean, before he shoots us? Let's keep on playing out the game. We'll take it as it comes. Sooner or later we'll find out what the rules are."

28

It was fortunate they had retrieved the pistols before returning to the hotel. They could never have picked them up later. Jovan Gat-tooth was all over them the moment they returned. He no longer pretended to ignore them; indeed, he made no attempt to conceal his interest, his absorption, in their doings.

"Damn, Lissa. I am slipping. How could I have missed him before? This is not surveillance. This is attack."

194

When they checked out—they didn't wait for lunch; they wanted out of there—Jovan was standing right behind them. His check-out consisted of a return of his key, a wave of his hand, a nod from the all-powerful girl at the desk. Now her eyes did not look at Lissa and him with speculation. They looked with, yes, commiseration. Such a nice couple they had been.

While they packed their Ford Fiesta, Jovan sat in his car and stared, no, glared at them. He leaned on the steering wheel, mouth open in a kind of feral snarl, gat-tooth quite visible even at this distance.

"A Mercedes, Lissa. Damn again. His car outruns us but good. Let's take a last look at the map."

Over three hundred miles to Beograd. The fastest route would be to go north towards Zagreb and then take the express highway to the capital. But they had decided to go the mountain route. Bihać. Bosanski Petrovac. Ključ. Jajce. And then Banja Luka to the express highway that followed the quarter-mile-wide Sava River to its conjunction with the Danube at Beograd. "It's a scenic highway until we get into the Sava plain," Lissa had told him. "If you like wheat fields, I imagine you could fancy the Sava plain. But up here the mountains are a natural wonder. And lonely. One can go miles without seeing a car."

"Lissa, maybe we should opt for the heavily traveled express highway up to Zagreb. But the more cars there are coming at us and going around us—and from what you say, on the expressway they're all going ninety miles an hour or better—well, the more cars there are, the less control I'll have. I think I can handle a car better in a lonely stretch even though that stretch will take us along some pretty hairy cliffs. I want to be able to give Jovan Gat-tooth individual attention." And after much weighing of pros and cons, they had finally chosen the mountain route.

She had agreed, and now they eased down the long plateau towards Bihać, with the Mercedes a discreet hundred yards behind them. (Jovan, he saw in the rearview mirror, still kept his mouth open. Was he singing? Or snarling? Either way, there was no mistaking the hole between his upper teeth. The black hole.)

Once again, he rehearsed various cliff-hanger scenarios. The Mercedes riding the Fiesta bumper to bumper. The Mercedes pushing them over the cliff into the Una River far below. Or maybe they would land by one of the little marble war memorials local citizens had installed on their onetime battlegrounds. Thin, gray marble slabs, each with a half-dozen, a dozen, two dozen names of war dead and each with fresh flowers. Every day, forty years later, every day fresh flowers out here in the wilderness. Of all the sights and sounds of Yugoslavia, all the words and thoughts about Yugoslavia, these mute monuments and their fresh flowers moved him most. But not to the point of growing sentimental about Jovan Gattooth and his Mercedes.

If he couldn't cope with the Mercedes, how about pistols? At Bihać he could let Lissa drive; he could get in the rear seat; and when they climbed into the mountains, he could lean out the window and blow Jovan away. Would that be better? How about skipping the whole thing? How about going to Bihać, parking the Fiesta, taking a bus to Beograd? What could Mr. Gat-tooth do about that? No heroics. The hell with heroics. Better to live and fight another day. He tried it on for size.

"Lissa, I've been thinking. The hell with heroics. Better to live and fight another day. Let's take a bus in Bihać. Our friend back there can't attack us in a bus."

"Why not?"

Why not. That took care of that. Woman's logical mind.

"No spy has ever committed a murder on a bus. The Orient Express, yes. A bus? Impossible."

But he knew he didn't sound very convincing. Lissa plainly wasn't convinced. He sighed, eased the car to a stop at the main highway. Karlovac and Zagreb north to the left. Bihać and Banja Luka south to the right. He looked in the mirror. He couldn't see the front of the Mercedes. It was almost smack against their Fiesta. He could see Jovan. His looks hadn't improved in the last fifteen minutes.

He turned right onto the main highway, said, "Lissa, as I recall, once we get beyond Bihać, the Una River turns off to the right. At that point, we'll leave the river and head east up into those clouds yonder. Is that right?"

She checked and nodded. "Yes. The river turns off at the village of Ripač. The road goes into a ten percent grade. And once up there, we'll be going on tricky mountain roads. With deep gorges and ravines to the right. Does that mean what I think it means?"

"We'll see. If we can see, that is. That mist seems pretty thick. It reminds me of that day on the Schneeberg."

"Some memory." Lissa checked their seat and shoulder belts. "They seem sturdy enough."

"Good. Jovan is now keeping a couple of hundred yards back. Hang on. The minute we get past Ripač and start up the hill, I'll give this little baby all she can take. We can't outrace a Mercedes on a straightaway. But mountain roads are different." And twenty minutes later: "Ready? Here goes."

The Fiesta was a little marvel. When it was time to go, it went. It scooted up the mountain, took the curves in stride, hugged the road with a minimum of torque. The mist enveloped the car and slicked the highway and splattered the windshield. He started the wipers and saw that the Mercedes had done likewise. It was creeping up on them, no question about it.

"I was wrong, Lissa. This guy's a master. Anything I can do, he can do better."

And the bump jolted both of them so their necks snapped. Whiplash at—and he cast a glance—at eighty-five kilometers on hairpin curves alongside deep gorges with no protective railings. After the bump, the Mercedes dropped back a few feet but caught up almost immediately as Ryder had to slow to sixty to maneuver the next curve. The blow came just as he swung sharply left. For a second, the Fiesta seemed about to reject the turn and proceed straight ahead over the cliff.

197

But the front wheels held while the rear ones tossed up mud and gravel at the edge of the cliff.

"Good baby. Good baby."

The next straightaway went for three hundred yards or so, before turning to the right. The Mercedes was no more than two feet behind them. Jovan had thrust himself against the steering wheel as if he wanted to plunge over it and through the windshield.

"He won't hit us at the right turn, Lissa. That would just drive us into the mountain wall. It'll be the next left turn. Hang on. I've never tried this before. I've seen it done. Here's the curve. Hang on. Hang on."

They hurtled to the curve. Fifty yards or so ahead. The road vanished to the left behind the mountain wall. The sky continued straight ahead into infinity. He pressed the gas pedal to the bottom, got a three-foot lead on the Mercedes, and then, just before the road veered sharply left, pulled the emergency brake full back, slammed the brake pedal, and twisted the steering wheel full left. The noise from the shredding tires was appalling, the stench foul. The rear of the car whipped around in a frightening skid as the car careened backward, while the front of the car, now facing back toward Ripač, seesawed so violently, the car rocked back and forth and threatened to tip over. But as he let the brakes go and slammed the accelerator, he felt the spinning, shrilling rear tires finally catch the dirt on the shoulder nearest the mountain. For a moment the right rear fender struck the mountainside, then they were moving back the way they had come.

He looked at Lissa but she had turned totally around in her seat to look out the rear window, her right hand to her open mouth, her blue eyes enormous.

"God. God. God. Did you see that?"

"See what? What happened? Tell me, for Christ's sake. What happened?"

"Over the cliff. Like an airplane. The Mercedes seemed to sail right over the cliff. Like an airplane."

"Okay. An airplane."

He drove a half-mile back towards Ripač until he found a

place where there was room to turn around. This time there was no shrieking of tires and shrilling of brakes. Back and forth he went like a little old lady driving an electric brougham. But finally he made it, and they started back to the fateful curve. He did not stop but did drive to the edge of the cliff so Lissa could look down.

"Can you see it?"

She nodded. She had now lowered her right arm to rest on her chest.

"Well?"

"It's gone straight into some boulders. Its rear is sticking up. Harry, it's all crushed together. The Mercedes is a tiny bundle. Half the size of this car. That could have been us."

"So it could. Well, that's the way the car bounces. Just another of these silly Yugoslav macho drivers taking his car over a cliff." And then he began to snicker. "I wonder if James Carter will be surprised to see us?"

"You mean, you think he planned this? He's working hand in glove with Žarko Pantić? Well, if he is, he shouldn't be surprised. He knows you, Harry Ryder. Just as I know you. No, he won't be surprised."

29

James Carter wasn't surprised, he was astonished. He said as much. "Harry, I'm astonished. I told you I've a room for you here at the Metropol. Why are you staying at the Intercontinental?"

Should he tell Carter the truth? "You slime, you set us up. There's no way we'll walk into your parlor." He said, "Lissa told me about the Intercontinental. Built last year. The finest hotel in Yugoslavia. And convenient, James. This side of the Sava. You know I'm a tourist at heart, I just had to see it. Okay? You'll come pick us up, then?"

He put the phone down. Lissa was looking at herself in the

mirror. He raised his eyebrows. She laughed, said, "I don't do this very often, Harry. I'm not given to narcissism. But you keep telling me how beautiful I am, and I just had to take a look."

"You accept my verdict?"

"No. No, not really. My jaw is too big. I'm just another healthy, wholesome British lass. That oval face in the mirror, I've seen dozens, hundreds of British women with oval faces just like it. No, you're the typical man in love. Someday you'll start seeing the reality, the defects. Then what?"

He went over, stood behind her. "That's the face I'll always see. Exactly that. No more. No less."

She turned around, put her arms around his neck, looked up at him. "This is a dead end, isn't it, Harry? Stalemate?"

"Possibly. Possibly. We've got a half hour or so. Let's do some heavy talking before Carter gets here. And let's start with the conclusion first: Whatever Carter and I decide to do tonight, you're not part of it. Not this time."

So it wasn't really a discussion. It came close to a shouting match. And they were still at it when there was a knock on the door. He walked over to it, called out, "Yes?"

"For Christ's sake, it's Dwight, Harry. Open up."

Ryder pulled out his silenced Makarov, crouched down away from the door, flicked it open. James Carter stared at the gun staring at him. He was astonished. There was no need to say so.

"I see, Harry, I see." He stepped in.

"What do you see?"

"I see how you've kept alive all these years. Hello, Mrs. Meirion. No, Harry, there's no one out in the hall. No one has followed me. You're safe, you really are."

Ryder closed the door, stuck the pistol in his belt, gestured. Carter glanced at himself in the mirror, seemed to preen a moment, refused a seat.

"Let's go, Harry. I'm ready, if you are. Ethan's waiting for us."

"With Arritsa Patak?"

"Why, I assume so. Colonel Pantić said—what do you mean?"

"I mean, Arritsa Patak visited with us this morning at the Plitvice Lakes. She's not with Ethan. Or Peter Trubari, as she knows him. She's not with him because she helped Žarko Pantić capture him. Ethan is a prisoner somewhere here in Yugoslavia. In a country the size of Oregon."

James Carter's Cary Grant face lost its look of flippant superiority. The ruddy cheeks seemed to shrivel; they definitely turned ashen. He took—he groped for—the chair. "No. No. No. It can't be."

Harry looked at Lissa. Should he say something? She shook her head. Let James Carter wrestle with himself. By himself.

"Pantić told me it was all a mistake. Pickering wasn't kidnapped. He came here of his own free will. To be with Arritsa Patak."

Carter still had a lot of wrestling to do. The silence continued. Carter shook himself, said, "She lied to you."

He saw the problems with that. "But . . . but you say she's not with Ethan? Pantić said—he said they were in Sutjeska together. . . . A great battle was . . ."

His voice trailed off. He got up, walked to the mirror, stared at himself. (Strength through narcissism. Lissa nodded. She had had the same thought.) The ashen look vanished. The flippant superiority did not return, but at least James Carter's face had recovered its normal good looks. He turned to face them.

"I talked to Ethan an hour ago. Or . . . or . . ."

"Or you talked to someone who said he was Ethan. Do you know his voice?"

Carter shook his head in misery. "I never worked with Ethan. I saw him around. In the halls. At conferences. But . . . but—but no, I don't know his voice."

He went back to his chair, leaned back, shook himself like a wet dog. "I've been lied to. Why? What's this all about? Why is Pickering a prisoner? Why are you after him? What's Birdie up to? Are we being set up by that devious, cunning, whispering devil? What do we do? Harry!"

Interesting. Carter was in a state of panic. His was a simple cowardice. Ryder said calmly, soothingly, "Good questions, James. Especially the setup part. Are you setting us up, James?"

"Me? You? Setting up?"

"We get a phone call at Plitvice from you, James. A big jolly happy phone call. Come see me, one and all. And then we're attacked on the way here and—"

"Attacked! Did you—?"

"Did I kill anybody? I didn't kill anybody, James. I didn't have to. He killed himself."

Carter could only manage a whisper. Birdie Bingham wouldn't do it any more faintly. "Killed himself? What are you talking about? This is crazy. Let's get out of here, Harry."

He was right. Any sensible person would pile in a car and head for the border, any border, as fast as he could. Ryder said, "Where did your Ethan say he is? Where are we to meet him?"

"He said he's behind the Red Star Stadium. On Ronko Street. A corner house. Number One, Ronko."

He looked at Lissa. She nodded. "Stadion Crvene Zvesde. Red Star Stadium. I know the neighborhood. The Voždovac district. Small homes. Quiet streets. It's a plausible place for Arritsa Patak. For Ethan? I don't know. From what I've heard about Ethan, the Dedinje district would seem to be more his style. The Dedinje is only a half-mile from the Voždovac, but it's like the distance from Notting Hill Gate to Embassy Row. In fact, your American ambassador lives in the Dedinje, so did Tito. I'd say Ronko Street is possible, but . . . but—"

"Not plausible?"

"Exactly."

Ryder turned to Carter. "There you have it, James. It's another obvious setup in a long line of setups. Who did it is one question. Žarko Pantić? You?"

Carter shook his head. A denial, presumably.

"But the other question is: What do we do about it?"

"Nothing," Carter said. "Be sensible, Harry, we do nothing. This is some damned Oriental game, and we don't belong in

202

it. We do nothing. We get out of this trap and run to the American Embassy and yell for help."

Oriental? What did that mean? The Slavs? Their migrations centuries before from the Russian steppes? Hence the Oriental? Or was it just another way of saying a Russian plot?

"Are you armed, James?"

"Armed? Of course I'm not armed. What do you think I am? For god's sake, Harry."

"Good. But just to make sure—Stand up, James."

"Stand up? Harry! You're crazy."

But he stood up. He had told the truth. He was unarmed. "Good, James. I really couldn't trust you with a weapon. Come on. As you said, let's go."

"Harry, you really—you think I'm involved in this? You don't trust me?"

"I've never trusted you, James. As far as I'm concerned, you represent all that's unsavory about our profession. You set me up in the Philippines. You've set me up here. I don't know whose orders you're following. It might be Birdie's, as it was in the Philippines. Or it might be Žarko Pantić's orders. Don't blink, James. If one were to seek a prime candidate for a mole in the Agency, he'd find your psychological profile the perfect fit. To begin with, you're an arrant coward—"

"Coward!"

"Don't jump like that, James. I've killed many better men than you for less. I had no emotional involvement with them, not one way or the other. You I dislike, James. One of my recurring fantasies is the picture of my bullet blowing your head in half. Don't make these sudden moves." Carter's face was not ashen. It was green. A phenomenon, this. Green with jealousy apparently does not cover the possibilities. Green with cowardice. He would have to ask a psychiatrist about that sometime.

"But I'm not going to kill you, James. I need you. You're going to prove me a liar. You're going to be a hero."

"Hero! Like hell I am. Mrs. Meirion, stop him! He's a maniac."

"Leave her out of it, James. This is between you and me. You'll do what I say. Or I'll blow you to bits right here. You're going to prove me a liar."

"Prove? How? How?"

"Simple. We're going to Ronko Street. We'll case the neighborhood. We'll park a block or so away from Number One, Ronko Street, and you'll walk to the house, and you'll bring Ethan Pickering out with you. In a minute's time. If you don't come out with him in a minute, I'm long gone."

James Carter gripped the back of the chair. He half-leaned over it. "You're . . . you're sentencing me to death. I won't do it."

"You won't? Why? Because you know what's waiting for us in Number One, Ronko? If you go in alone, will that be an admission of failure to produce me? Will you be chastised for that failure, James? Killed? Terrible word, *killed*. Killed, murdered, dead. Let's go, James. No time to dawdle. And remember, be very, very careful. Don't try any quick moves in the lobby. I really would like a good excuse for shooting you, James. Any excuse is full justification, as far as I'm concerned. Let's go."

They went.

PART IV

30

Was she angry? Annoyed? Put down? Lissa stared out the window of the Intercontinental. Her eyes wandered from the Sava River bridge two blocks away to metropolitan Beograd lighted up in the distance across the river, thence to the black parking lot below, but they saw nothing. She tried, not too successfully, to convince herself that Harry had been right.

"Look," he had said, "you can't come with me. If anything goes wrong, you'll have to play Horatio for me. You'll have to tell my story to the world and report me and my cause aright. Please, Lissa. Please understand."

Well, she did understand. Intellectually. But not emotionally. Her impossible American had rejected her, and that after all they had been through together. And this, Lissa, was pathetic childishness, and you had better take hold—and that was that!

Her eyes focused. There was something in the parking lot. The light, get the light. And she raced to the switch, turned off the light, leaped back to the window. Now it was all plain. Plain to her. But not to Harry Ryder and James Carter. As they strode to Carter's car, they could not see what she saw: five or six men crouched behind fenders of cars. Men in dark suits. Men holding something in their right hands. She turned to grab a chair, smash the window, scream a warning. But it was too late.

As Carter opened the car door, the six men sprang out and jumped her Harry and James Carter. It was all over in a trice. She saw them take Harry's gun, clamp handcuffs on him and Carter, start to hustle them toward a black limousine. There was a moment's delay, some altercation. Carter swung around to one of the men, protested or said something or did something. The man replied with a violent blow to the face. A pistol whip. Carter crumpled, two men picked him up, carted him off.

Carter carted. Not funny, Lissa. Especially not funny when one of the men pointed up toward her window. Toward her. And two men split from the limousine and sprinted toward the lobby entrance. Tell Harry's story aright! If she didn't make a move, there'd be no felicity in Beograd tonight.

She picked up her purse, grabbed the brown shoulder bag. (For the first time she noticed the insignia on it. A very faded red star. Some Chinese characters. Then "*Zhong Hua Renmin Gong He Guo.*" Then the translation, presumably: "The People's Republic of China." Where had Harry gotten it?) A quick look inside. Her passport. Her passports. Christina Doughty and Melissa Meirion and Marget Eliot. Passports and two pistols, one of Harry's Makarovs, her own Browning; money—dinars, schillings, pounds, dollars; a Fodor's Yugoslavia Guide; some maps, sunglasses. Was that enough? Think, Lissa. Slow down, make haste slowly. (That's what the old teacher had said ominously to the students at St. Margaret's, ominously and mysteriously; the silly phrase had bothered her all her life, curious how now it came to her as a saving grace.) Clothes! Get some clothes. Get a slip, hose, panties. Anything else? Yes, toothbrush, toothpaste and . . . and that was it. Now make haste hastily.

She ran to the door, opened it, peered down the hall. Good. She was in time. Pulling the door shut behind her (damn, wouldn't Harry be annoyed with her; she was going to sneak out of the hotel without paying the bill), she raced to the stairway door, opened it, stepped into its gray concrete coldness. As the door swung to, she saw the distant elevator doors begin to open. Good. She was still in time. But just barely.

Down seven floors she plunged. Recklessly—even more recklessly than in the flight down the Schneeberg. At the bottom, on the lobby floor, she saw the sign: КУХНИЈА — kuchinja, kitchen. Two steps and she was in a corridor that ran the whole length of the kitchen, with open doors showing glimpses of white-capped chefs and shouting waiters and flaming stoves and gleaming dishes. So far, so good. So far—and then a cart materialized in one of the doors, with a waiter bent over behind it. He saw her. He straightened up. His eyes grew wide as he took in her costume. Blue jeans. Shoulder bag. Dark blue jacket. Golden hair. He was starting to speculate, perhaps to challenge her.

She swaggered up to him, her hips wiggling provocatively (too bad he didn't see the wiggle from behind; Sophia Loren couldn't have done it better), got her own challenge in first. "Cheap lays. That's all I ever get in this dump. Cheap lays. Haggled over the price, didn't even give me a tip. How about you? Down there in that storeroom, huh? How about it? Will you give me a tip?"

Now the eyes were owlish. The waiter shuddered, backed into the kitchen, pulling the cart behind him. She sneered, swaggered down the hallway to the rear door. The wiggle wasn't wasted after all. Watch it, Lissa. You might get the flustered waiter steamed up enough to chase after you.

But he didn't. Once outside, she took stock. Or tried to. It was quite black here. She could sense a wing of the hotel over her head. Some tool and electrical worksheds lay to the right and left. And straight ahead, maybe twenty or thirty yards distant, an earth wall rose some twenty feet high. Beyond the wall was—was what? Mostly space, as she recalled. This was the new section of Beograd. Novi Beograd. Only recently a swamp—now the center of Beograd's largest hotels, tallest office buildings, biggest apartment complexes, all of them set off by parks, beautiful parks stretching for miles west along the Sava and north along the Danube. In one of those parks about two miles away, fronting the Danube, was Beograd's largest hotel, the Yugoslavija. It had a Hertz office.

She didn't linger. Trotting tippy-toe, she glided to the earth wall, raced up it a few steps, then went to hands and knees to scramble the rest of the way. Once beyond the top, she turned to look at the Intercontinental. In the daytime, its almost continuous windows were sky blue. Tonight, except for a few occupied rooms, it was a black blankness.

Nowhere was there a sign of two men searching for a missing Englishwoman. Missing English spy.

Good. Now to the Yugoslavija Hotel and a car; tomorrow . . . tomorrow . . . tomorrow to the British Embassy, and . . . and what? What could they do? Hear Harry's story? Hold her hand? Shrug? Embassy rules, madam: spies are on their own. England officially has no spies. Especially not once they're caught. And anyway, your man's not British, he's American. That makes it really too bad, sorry, ma'am, come see us again anytime, always glad to help.

She trudged along, head down. She didn't straighten up until she was a block from the Yugoslavija. "Of course! Arritsa Patak, Ludmila, Aunt Veda. Veda Lukac. I'll call first thing in the morning, give the Ludmila signal, and Arritsa and I'll meet two hours later at—at the merry-go-round, in the park off Naradnog Fronta Street. And I've got to tip Arritsa off about Harry. How? Aunt Veda—I'll tell her Rajko won't be able to join us. Will Arritsa understand I've lost Harry?"

And what would Harry say to this? She could hear him now? "Lissa, poor Arritsa knows even less about this mess than we do. I know I asked Arritsa to use her old girls' network. But I didn't ask her to risk herself. You'll just be getting Arritsa into trouble. Don't do it. Solve your own problems your own way."

So much for Harry. Man of little faith. He could give lip service to woman's world. But what could he ever really know about it? What could any man know?

31

By noon, just as the merry-go-round started, Lissa was in the park off United Front—Naradnog Fronta—Street. Arritsa would—should—arrive in a half hour.

The problem was, how could Arritsa recognize her? She would expect to see Christina Doughty, with shoulder-length golden hair and wearing blue jeans, a white shirt, and sturdy English walking shoes. She would not expect to find a middle-aged lady with nondescript brown hair, glasses, a flowered print cotton dress, cheap black sandals, and on her lap a needlepoint flower design, which she would be assiduously stitching, just one of a dozen Yugoslav matrons passing the time while her children played in the sand pit or rode the merry-go-round. Harry would admire her getup. Don Carlos Bingham had told her Harry put great store in disguises. They kept enemies at bay. But also friends.

There was only one hope. She rummaged in her great straw bag, pulled out an oversize ski handkerchief. She had purchased it—and bag, wig, needlepoint set, print dress, sandals, sunglasses—at Robna Kuća, Merchandise House, as soon as the huge department store had opened. The handkerchief was, as near as she could get it, a red and white affair like the one she had given Arritsa at Lake Prošće to blow her nose. Squaring off the handkerchief, she draped it over her hair, tied the ends under her chin, Yugoslav style. Four other women in the park had also covered their heads with handkerchiefs, none of them, fortunately, red and white. She could do no more. Arritsa would interpret the handkerchief. Or she wouldn't. In which case, in which case—back to square one.

Forty minutes later, she spotted Arritsa. She was coming up Kamenička Street, which dead-ended into the park. Presumably she had parked her car in the same garage as Lissa, three blocks down the hill. Presumably she and her companion—another girl, a brunette, dressed like Arritsa, like Lissa wearing the Yugoslav uniform, the flower print cotton dress—presumably she and her friend would walk up through the park toward the Terazije and its central shops a block or two above them. But. But would they pick the right path? There were three different paths. Lissa's bench was along the middle one directly below the merry-go-round. A poor choice, she saw now. The northern path skirted the merry-go-round, led directly to the Terazije. Would Arritsa and her friend take the northern path? If they did, there could be no turning back. Not with a man ten paces behind them, obviously matching his stride to theirs. A rugged man, in his twenties, wearing a sport jacket, sport shirt, and slacks. He was making no attempt to conceal his purpose.

Even at this distance, a full block away, she could sense Arritsa's eyes sweeping the park, scanning, examining each person in it. Left to right. Right to left. Back again. All the time she was laughing and chatting with her friend, a younger woman, perhaps twenty-two or -three. After the third search of the park, Arritsa turned all her attention to her friend. Their conversation was animated. Neither woman so much as glanced back at the man behind them. Looking at each other, seemingly unaware of their surroundings, they left Kamenička Street, crossed Naradnog Fronta, entered the park, strolled up a path. The middle path.

Lissa concentrated on her needlepoint, head bent forward. How many years since she had last coped with a needlepoint design? How many? Certainly before she had met Llew-Llaw. Curious how the skill stayed with one—and the interest, too; she had forgotten what fun needlepoint is. But fun and interest notwithstanding, she was quite aware of Arritsa's progress. Quite aware, too, of how neatly Arritsa handled the situation. Just as they came abreast of her, Arritsa's young friend fell slightly behind and so blocked the view of their pursuer. The maneuver only took a second but that second was long enough for Arritsa to reach into her purse, whisk out an envelope, and stuff it in the gaping opening of Lissa's straw bag. Neither woman paused in her progress or animated conversation. Lissa's right hand dipped and pushed and pulled wihout abatement. Madame DeFarge in Beograd. It was neat, very neat. But not over yet, not while the rugged young man was strolling steadily toward her.

Panic, or anyway a trace of panic, swept over her. She wanted to lean over and ease her bag shut. Surely the white envelope would betray her, would signal her complicity and guilt. Surely the young man would reach in, sweep it up, snap her up. Surely he would.

But he didn't. He barely glanced at her. His eyes were focused on his prey. He had an assignment. He was carrying it out. Able man.

Panic subsided. Impatience took over. Time to go. Time to pack up her wares and get the blazes out of there. And once again the ghostly echo: Lissa, make haste slowly. Stay there, tend to your stitching, wait. Wait and wait. And, sure enough, wait not in vain. For a block away, a second man, also in sport clothes, came trudging up toward the park. He was carrying a walkie-talkie. Every so often he whispered into it. Of course. The first man had been wearing an earring. What was her old teacher's name? McCarthy. Helen McCarthy. Thank you, Miss McCarthy, wherever you are. I'll never forget. I'll always make haste slowly. In this case, she needled away another half hour before she packed up her things and headed for her garage three blocks down the hill.

32

If Lissa were ever commissioned to write a training manual for female spies, she would insist that every student become adept at needlepoint.

It—needlepoint—acted like a magic wand able to create a zone of invisibility. No one had really seen her in Naradnog Fronta park. And now, on the bus from Jajce to Drvar, no one showed the least curiosity about her past or present. The women clucked over her work, recounted their own experience—or lack of it—with needlepoint, but otherwise gave her no heed. Even some of the men, the fierce-looking mountain men of Bosnia, a few with Moslem headdress, even they could not resist leaning over her shoulder to admire her handiwork. But that was the focus. The work—not her. She was invisible and hence quite free to think her own thoughts and plan her own plans.

The thoughts weren't much. A mishmash of memories— Harry Ryder at Bayswater Station, trousers riding too high and thus exposing his socks; the Schneeberg; dead bodies; Anna Tadić and her mysterious Karageorge message; Žarko Pantić; James Carter; Ethan Pickering; Tito's uniform. "How awful! I haven't told Harry about the marshal's uniform and the fateful events at Drvar on Tito's birthday in 1944 or about Ethan's heroic rescue of five-year-old Anna Stupica from the Germans." And at the thought, she felt tears start to come. "If I'd only told Harry, he wouldn't be a prisoner now."

Since that thought made no sense at all, she concentrated on her plans. They were based on Arritsa Patak's note. "Pantić spends much of his time in Drvar." Of course. When she had talked to Pantić from the Plitvice Hotel, he had said he would be up in the mountains. She should have figured this out by herself. What had happened to her Welsh gift? "He's in charge of security there. For the unveiling of Tito's statue. If you decide to go to Drvar, you'll have trouble finding a room. Every hotel, motel, even the private rooms, are taken all the way to Banja Luka, Jajce, and Bihać. So I've enclosed a note to a friend of mine in Drvar. Her name is Olja Jaka. She's a schoolteacher. One of us. She'll help. Good luck. And remember, you can call on me anytime. I can always slip away from my guards. Don't worry about my safety. I worry about Peter's. God bless you."

God in atheistic Yugoslavia. Brave lady. A whole world of brave ladies, come to think of it.

The note to Olja Jaka was in a separate envelope. "Dearest Olja. This is to introduce my friend, Christina Doughty. Please put her up for a few days and give her any help she needs. Just as you would for me. Thanks." The signature read, "The girl two seats over."

Two seats over. Presumably a code or a proof of identity. Miljana Dragan in Zagreb. Arritsa's younger companion in Naradnog Fronta park. Olja Jaka in Drvar. How far did this network of ball-breaking women extend? How much should she use it? Could she really expect to walk up to a stranger in Drvar and say, "Olja, my name is not really Christina Doughty. It's really Lissa Meirion. Only now I'm going under the name of Marget Eliot. See, here's my passport. My forged passport. And all I want you to do is help me expose a nefarious Yugoslav villain. This villain, Colonel Žarko Pantić, just happens to be the man in charge of security at the ceremonies tomorrow, the man here to protect the life of your president, Miodrag Otaronov, and the lives of all other members of the presidency and of your cabinet ministers, not to mention the lives of dignitaries from the world over. And having exposed him, I want you to help me rescue my lover and Arritsa Patak's lover as well as the head of the United States CIA station in Vienna. How about it, Olja, are you on?"

Thanks for trying, Arritsa, but no go. She could not ask those questions of a stranger. She couldn't go to Olja Jaka. But she could go to a friend, could ask that friend for a place to stay. And even pick up discreet support. This she could do. From Ethan's friend, Anna Stupica. But whether Anna Stupica would respond to her request for support—well, how much gratitude did Anna feel toward Ethan Pickering because he had saved her life when the German soldier grabbed her to ask the one question asked of each citizen in Drvar in 1944, "Where is Tito?" Anna, even at five years old, would have lied. Every man, woman, and child in Drvar had lied, had said, "I don't know," and saying it, was instantly shot. The Germans had parachuted into the Drvar valley that spring morning, Tito's birthday, the day he was to receive the colorful marshal's uniform so lovingly crafted for him by the townspeople; the paratroopers had floated down in division strength, resolved to exterminate Tito; they had failed—and were exterminated themselves after three days' fighting, but not before they had massacred most of the townspeople. Most of them, but not Anna. Ethan had charged the soldier, stabbed him, slung the girl over his shoulder, carried her off to the British mission's camp. He had protected her through the

213

battle, seen to it that she was cared for afterward, helped her career subsequently, and at her graduation from medical college had been present with Žarko Pantić and Llew-Llaw and herself. Cause for gratitude, certainly. But was it also cause for trusting Lissa Meirion? Especially a Lissa Meirion who hadn't the foggiest notion of how to go about exposing Žarko Pantić and rescuing her Harry, Arritsa's Ethan, and, well, Mr. Don Carlos Bingham's James.

The needlepoint flower design showed two big, bold sunflowers, one with red petals, one with yellow. After driving to Jajce and turning in her car there, she'd taken a bus, pulled out her design, and begun work on the central dark stamen, which she'd completed by the time the bus trundled down the mountain into the Drvar valley. But she kept fussing with thread and needle until the time when the bus driver, unable to budge his vehicle one inch amidst seemingly thousands of stalled hooting cars, had opened the bus door and let the passengers walk the rest of the way. Only then did Lissa relinquish her wand of invisibility, stow her materials, retrieve the Chinese shoulder bag from the rack, hoist her straw bag, step out into the cars and thronging pedestrians. The cacophony was deafening—not only from cars and crowds threading through them, but from police whistles and bullhorns as police and military tried to unscramble the mess. But it was a happy noise. The shouts were shouts of laughter. The hoots were chorus accompaniment. The whistles and cries of soldiers and police were good-natured. This was celebration time. The people celebrated. Lissa celebrated. Laughing with the rest, she eased her way out of the downtown mob and headed north down the Unac River. She looked at her watch. Six-thirty. Would Anna be home? Still at the hospital? Downtown watching the fun? If she weren't home, would neighbors get suspicious of a middle-aged lady fumbling around their doctor's front door?

The house was a good mile out of town amidst scattered farmhouses. She had been there once with Llew-Llaw. At that time, Anna and her husband, Miloš, had only completed two rooms, the kitchen and a bedroom; the rest of the house had been stark lumber framework. Now, ten years later, it was fully assembled, an attractive two-story white farmhouse with a porch and a flower garden in the front and a vegetable garden in the rear running down to the river's edge. (*River* was a bit ambitious. The Unac barely qualified as a stream; it wasn't much more than twenty yards wide and only about two or three feet deep; it moved sluggishly along the almost-level valley floor; and it had somehow, even far up here in the mountains, only a few miles from its source, it had somehow managed to become thoroughly polluted; perhaps the careless crowd had caused this; perhaps when the crowd dispersed in two days after Sunday's ceremonies, perhaps the river would once more become sparkling clear and even potable; right now, one wouldn't use it to irrigate the vegetables.) Pausing only a moment to take this all in, Lissa walked up the gravel path, climbed four steps to the porch, pushed the doorbell, heard the bell tinkle at the rear of the house, waited.

Nothing happened. No footsteps could be heard. Anna was not home, Lissa had better retreat before some neighboring farmer started to get curious. Half-turning away, she reached forward to ring once again. Before she could press the button, the door suddenly, noiselessly, was pulled open. A tall, big-shouldered, big-busted woman stood there and stared at her. It was Lissa's move.

33

"You don't recognize me?"

Dr. Anna Stupica shook her head doubtfully. Her loose, abundant straw hair flopped in vague directions. (Anna Stupica had never put much store by looks or feminine charm; that had not prevented her from marrying and keeping a husband, a magnificent hunk of manhood, one Miloš Stupica, a civil engineer, which profession kept him usually shunted off to places like Iraq, Bangladesh, Saudi Arabia, Afghanistan; he had been home long enough to father two or three children, they would be teenagers now. Would they be around the house? Dear God, what kind of complications would that cause?) Anna Stupica said, "Your voice, yes. But . . . but—"

"But I'm changed. Only outside, Anna, I'm Lissa inside. Lissa Meirion. I'm a widow now, and I need help. May I come in?"

Anna's big blue eyes—they were as blue as hers—grew bigger. Obviously she heard something, caught something in Lissa's tone. She reached forward, took Lissa's bag, stepped aside, pointed. "Back there to the kitchen. I'm still a farmer's daughter at heart. I live in the kitchen—and you must be hungry."

Lissa hesitated, looked around. She wasn't taking in the decor, and Anna Stupica seemed to understand. "Miloš? He's in Kuwait. The children? Rada and Rajko are enjoying the festivities in town. We'll have time."

She didn't add "to make up our story." She didn't have to. Her heritage was a thousand years of Balkan flair for conspiracy. No point in being obvious or hurrying. She put a bowl of *pileća čorba* before Lissa, a thick tangy chicken soup. It was delicious, as was the solid, dark bread. Lissa had two bowls of soup, leaned back, sighed, reached up, took off her wig, shook her golden hair down to her shoulders.

If Dr. Stupica's eyes were large before, they were enormous now. "Ah," she said.

"Yes, ah. I'm here as Marget Eliot. Or if you like"—and she reached into the shoulder bag, pulled out the passports, dropped them onto the white Formica table—"I'm also Christina Doughty. I've used them all on this trip. I'm in trouble, Doctor, trouble all the way. If the police—or rather, the KOS—if they knew I was here, you could be ruined. No, correction. If Žarko Pantić knew I was here, you'd be ruined. I'm not so sure if the police or the KOS are really involved in this. I'm not so sure of anything. Only of Žarko Pantić. The

216

third musketeer. The friend of my dead husband. The friend of your benefactor, Ethan Pickering."

Anna Stupica pushed the passports back, watched Lissa pack them and restore her wig, said, "Tell me."

And Lissa did. All of it, including the truth about Ethan Pickering. Finishing, she said, "Before I came here, I made a resolve not to tell you any of this, not to implicate you, not to endanger you. Not much of a resolve, was it?"

The big lady shrugged. "I'm a physician. I'm used to it. I'd have been insulted if you hadn't told me. My professional competence, you understand? All right, the children first. I can't tell them you're Marget Eliot. You know our laws. I have to report overnight guests to the police. That might be all right. It might not be. I'll say you're a friend from Niš. Sister of one of my medical school colleagues. If you don't speak too much, this will work. Your Serbo-Croatian is good, very good, but you never know about children. They have sharp ears for the latest slang. They'll expect some of it from you and won't get it. No, I'll say your name is Svetlana Llubeb— she really does live in Niš—I'll say you're Svetlana and you're here for the festivities and you'll be out seeing the sights tomorrow. So. What can I do to help?"

"I was right. I shouldn't have told you."

"What do you mean?"

"If something happens to me, if Žarko Pantić learns you've tried to hide me—knowingly tried to hide me—you, a Yugoslav citizen—well, don't you see?"

"So what?"

"So it's not right. No, you tell the children I'm Lissa Meirion. The police—well, you'll report my visit after the unveiling of the statue. I'll either be out of Drvar by then, or captured, or dead."

"Or, please, or successful."

"Or successful. But you won't be implicated. You have no reason to know your old friend, Mrs. Llewelyn Meirion, is wanted by the authorities. Stay with the truth. Only delay it a bit. Do it my way, Anna. Please."

"You have brought me the best news I could have. My benefactor is alive. After all these years. There is no way, there's nothing I won't do to help the marvelous Ethan Pickering. Look, I'm a good friend of the chief of police, Veljko Kaja. Well, all right. He's been more than a friend. Well, all right. Is still more than a friend. I can go to him."

"We'll both go to him. I insist. We'll go."

"Maybe. Maybe. Let's sleep on it. Tomorrow we'll decide. Me alone. Or the two of us together. Okay?"

"Okay."

34

The rectangular blue sign above the door used Latin script; this was Western Yugoslavia. It read MILICIJA: Police. Two men were standing under the sign, both in uniform. The one in army gray—a colonel—was Žarko Pantić. The other in blue was . . .

"Yes, Veljko Kaja. My chief."

"Keep walking, Anna. I don't want Pantić seeing me."

"In this crowd?"

Overnight, the traffic controllers had established order. No autos were allowed on Drvar's few downtown streets. They were now parked in the fields surrounding Drvar to the north and south. And as new cars and buses came down the mountain into the valley, they were shunted even farther out, well past Anna's house. It was Wimbledon ten times worse, if that was conceivable. But no one minded. The Saturday crowd swarmed like an army of ants in the downtown squares and the memorial park. Swarmed and ate and drank and laughed and shouted. They were part of history, and they were proud of it, gloried in it.

"You've got a point. Let's go up there. We can keep an eye on Pantić."

"There" was the war memorial on the hill above the main street, a futuristic assemblage of concrete pillars slanting into the sky, forming V's and H's and I's, in no particular order. Somehow, especially with the thousands and thousands of flowers bedecking the pillars and flashing in the brilliant morning sun, the memorial was impressive. How Tito would have loved the display.

"I'm sorry, Lissa. Seeing those two together, well, I'm afraid my chief of police can't be trusted. The masculine mind. Duty before adultery."

Lissa laughed. Anna laughed back, said, "Good. I didn't know if you knew how to laugh. And no, he's not the father of either Rada or Rajko. Yes. I saw you looking at them."

"More physician's insight? Yes, you're right—and wrong. The thought did cross my mind, but what I was really thinking . . . Well, I just realized I haven't given my children—I have two boys, Ralph and Timothy. A bit older than yours, but like them, beautiful people. And I just realized I've barely given them a thought in the past few weeks. I did phone them at school to say I was going to Vienna for a vacation. Rather. I should have told them the next time they see me, I might be in a coffin. So."

"Yes. So. Now what? We can't go to the police. We can't go to the army. I might be able to get to President Otaronov. He'll arrive tomorrow morning to unveil the statue. I could call my professor at the medical school. He could arrange a meeting with the president. I think."

"How do we know Otaronov is not responsible for all this?"

"I can't believe that, Lissa. Miodrag Otaronov is not terribly bright. I sometimes feel he's overly sympathetic to the Russians. But he's not wicked. A good, simple soldier who loves his country and adored Tito. He wouldn't kidnap your Harry or my Ethan. Not even the bad James. He might shoot him. Never kidnap."

Pantić and Kaja shook hands. Kaja went inside the police station, Pantić turned and began to ease his way through the throng.

219

Lissa patted the big lady's arm. "Thanks, Anna. We tried. Now it's my turn. I'm going to follow him. Foolish, I know. He won't lead me to his prisoners, if they're here. I know that. But . . . it's something to do and . . ."

She zigzagged down the hill through the crowd, master British detective on the hunt. What would the giant Sergeant Dykes think of her technique? Not much, probably. Sergeant Dykes generally had not thought much of any of her talents, except skiing. Well, it was the best she could do. And all things considered, not too bad. Pantić turned east off the main street, toward the river two blocks away. There was no difficulty in following him. Traffic on the side street was no less formidable than on the main street. Beer drinkers offered him beer; accordion players serenaded him; singers shouted folk and war songs at him—and at her, too. Once or twice she simply had to accept a bottle of beer, once or twice she had to stop and join in a rousing First Proletarian Brigade camp song, known to every Yugoslav. (The First had been here on Tito's birthday in '44; it had been given the assignment of killing the German paratroopers, and kill they had.) Keeping a discreet street or so behind Pantić, she trailed him to the river's edge, followed him north down the river toward the bridge across the Unac.

"Of course. He's going to the statue. To check on security. That's his job, isn't it?"

With that clarified, she no longer tried to keep Pantić in sight. It wasn't necessary. For much of the crowd, in spite of its pauses and starts and retreats and weaving, was also heading for the statue grounds. Rather than oppose its kaleidoscopic groupings and regroupings, she let herself merge with it, follow its glacial pace across the highway bridge, meandered with it into the Tito Memorial Park.

Here the crowd's motion was almost nonexistent; only the fact that the mass had a purpose kept any forward motion at all. And this purpose was to see the veiled statue of Josip Broz, Marshal Tito. Everyone wanted a look, got a look, and then had to yield place. Thus, in time, she had her moment to view that statue some thirty yards away.

The first thing she saw was Žarko Pantić. The colonel was standing at the foot of the statue, inside the restraining ropes, talking to some of the soldiers and guards. The statue loomed fifteen feet or more above the little group. A canvas drape concealed the statue itself, which, as everyone knew, was a marvel of ingenuity—or actually of derivation. The sculptor, Radule Sumi, had gone back to the Egyptians and Greeks for inspiration. Though no one had yet seen the statue, everyone knew Radule Sumi had used marble, and had also painted it in lifelike colors. Blues, reds and greens and blacks and silvers for the uniform and the sword, with flesh tones for the features. Praxiteles would have approved of the decision to use colors. Lissa took her look and was then eased away toward a new objective. This was Tito's cave, a hundred feet or so up the cliff behind the statue. Two unending lines were climbing up and down the cliff. For a moment, she let the crowd push her toward the climbers, but only for a moment. Pantić had ducked under the ropes and was slicing through the pack toward the river. He passed only ten feet from her. She followed as best she could, managed to keep him in sight, saw him do a peculiar thing.

He went right to the edge of the Unac and stared down at the muddy, almost stagnant stream. Then he looked up, glanced across the river at a row of houses on the opposite bank, turned back into the sun for one last look at the veiled statue—and in so doing squinted right over Lissa's head. She eased herself behind a man and his wife, and when she dared peer out again, Pantić had vanished. So much for her report to Sergeant Dykes. "I'm sorry, Sergeant, I lost my man." Now what do I do? Take Doctor Anna's suggestion? Have her try to communicate with President Otaronov? Stand here on the bank of the Unac and start screaming how Pantić is a villain?

Better not ask Sergeant Dykes. He might well advise her to drown herself. "And once again, Lissa, you're starting to dither. Where's your famous Welsh gift? Or if that's a lost gift, at least take a look at what Žarko Pantić looked at. The river? It's muddy and impenetrable. The statue? It's veiled.

The houses across the river? There are three of them. Two are fully built. And one has only two rooms finished. The cellar, the second floor, and half the first floor remain unfinished, except for the wooden framework. Altogether a typical Yugoslav tableau."

And then it happened, then it came to her. "Oh, blessed Welsh gift, please, please do not mislead me now."

Her face flushed, her pulse racing, she slipped through the crowd, away from the statue, up the river, until she was directly across from the three houses. The two complete houses were obviously occupied. The unfinished house was deserted. Its two rooms had drawn shades. One room was, must be, the kitchen; the other, a bedroom with probably an adjacent bathroom. Again a typical Yugoslav tableau. Turning, she ran her eye over her neighbors, found what she wanted—a couple in their late fifties sitting on the bank and sunning themselves, faintly superior looks on their faces. Superior. Precisely. They were local people. The world had come to pay homage to their local glory. There was no need for them to push and shove their way through the thronging crowd. Every day for the rest of their lives they could see and admire Tito's statue.

Drifting near them, Lissa looked down, smiled, pointed. "Lovely houses. In a lovely city. You must be very proud."

The man and wife were both old enough to have been here in 1944. Somehow they had escaped the general massacre. Or had they moved here after the war? Why not ask?

"Were you here the day the paratroopers came?"

"We were. Or rather, my father was. He was a partisan. With the First Proletarian. My mother had taken us children to live with friends in Martin Brod. That's how Anton and I met. In Martin Brod. And that morning we all got up before dawn to walk here and see the presentation of our uniform to Tito. Oh, it was exciting for us children. And then, just as we reached the end of the valley, we saw the paratroopers."

She had a sense of the value of understatement. She shrugged, looked modest, sat mute. Lissa picked up the conversation, worked it back to the unfinished house, said, "I wonder. Drvar

222

would be a wonderful place to have a home. Is that house for sale?"

The husband—this was business, man's work—shook his head. "No, it belongs to Nikola Vuković. He's building it for his parents to retire in. Nikola's off somewhere. Iraq, I think. He's a draftsman. A good man. No, I don't think he'd sell, do you, Nada?"

Oh, great moments of history. Of her history, anyway. Her Welsh gift had not deserted her. It had come from the void and pointed the way. For whatever reason—and already her mind was assessing possible alternative reasons—for whatever reason, Ryder and Pickering and Carter were incarcerated in this ostensibly empty house. For whatever reason, the shaded windows were significant because they fronted the Unac River, the Tito Memorial Park, and the great man's veiled statue.

That was why Pantić had squinted over her head to see the statue. Not for a last look, but for a last confirmation that the statue and the windows were truly on a direct line, that no obstruction blocked a view from windows to statue. Even before she said her farewells to the Drvar couple, she knew what she was going to do. And what she would not do.

She would not let Dr. Anna Stupica get involved in any part of her plan. Not any part. Harry Ryder would approve of this decision. No innocent third parties. You and me, Harry, just you and me.

35

At twelve-thirty, in blackness, Lissa slipped from the bed and began to dress. There was no need to adjure herself to make haste slowly. There could be no other way. The teenagers' bedrooms were on either side of hers, she did not dare awaken them or her hostess down at the end of the hall.

Nor did she. When she eased open the bedroom door—it

was at least twelve forty-five—the house was still. She stood there a moment, analyzing the silence, analyzing herself. Both were in order. She was once more wearing her blue jeans, a blue jacket, and a dark shirt. Her natural hair hung free. Whatever happened this night, it would be as Lissa Meirion. Any failure would be hers. Any success, too.

In stockinged feet, straw purse in hand, she crept out into the carpeted hallway, down the carpeted stairs. The Chinese bag was slung over her shoulder; its central pocket held her sturdy walking shoes, the Browning High-Powered, and one of Harry's confiscated Makarovs, as well as some old newspapers and a can of lighter fluid; the side pocket contained the items usually carried in her straw bag—her cosmetics, passport, wallet, money, keys. The straw bag itself held all the accoutrements once worn by Mrs. Marget Eliot or Christina Doughty: sandals, print dress, wig, false passports, red and white ski handkerchief, half-finished needlepoint. She was careful, most careful, to keep the bag from striking a banister or the stairs from creaking.

She was successful. She reached the front door, put her hand on the knob, started to turn it.

"Good luck, Lissa."

No Welsh gift had alerted her this time. Its powers were becoming entirely too haphazard.

"Anna!"

"Yes, I knew you'd be on your way tonight."

They were both whispering. Lissa said, "Once more, physician's insight?"

"No. The look in your eyes at dinner tonight."

Anna clicked on a flashlight, beamed it at the floor, took in Lissa's costume, said:

"I see. Mrs. Lissa Meirion. A latter-day Joan of Arc. Well, your hair will burn nicely. Do you really need that purse?"

"No, not really. I'll hide it in the bush somewhere."

"No, you won't. Why leave it lying around for someone to find and ask a lot of questions? Let me take care of it. I'll burn it."

"Don't look for your lighter fluid. I took it."

"Oh. That way."

"That way."

"Take care, Lissa. But remember, if things go bad, well, women like myself and Arritsa Patak and Miljana Dragan and the woman Arritsa recommended to you, Olja Jaka—I know her, she's good people—well, don't count us out. And remember, there are many more of us, and we can be heard. Here, take the flashlight. Follow the river path. Cars and caravans are parked all along on both sides of the road. True, some people are also in sleeping bags along the river, but you can't have everything. Good luck."

Life in full circle. The five-year-old girl repaying her debt almost forty years later.

They embraced, Lissa slipped out the door, adjusted her eyes once again to the darkness (and that was quite dark indeed; a valley mist blotted out stars and moon, transmuted Drvar into a Welsh moor), eased her shoes on, and headed for the river path.

Anna Stupica was right. There were people in sleeping bags, but they weren't all sleeping. Some sensed her presence, even in the blackness, and raised their heads inquisitively. But she was convinced none could recognize her or identify her sex. She was wrong.

"Hey, beauty, come brighten up my boudoir." So one Don Juan. The other: "I got it all, kid. All the comforts of home. How about it, hey?"

No replies seemed called for, and since her wooers made no further advances, Lissa continued to drift ghostlike through the mist. Once inside the town, her problems multiplied. Even at one-thirty in the morning, celebrants were still pouring out—or in—their homage to Tito. They stood at corners, in streets or footpaths, and toasted their soon-to-be immortalized leader—when they thought of him. Most of the time they just toasted. All the world loves a party. Now her movements were furtive. She had to avoid the random, infrequent streetlights. A bad scene this; anyone seeing her slink from

225

black hole to black hole would yell for the police instantly. Maybe she should walk boldly through them. Maybe. If she did, maybe she would run into Žarko Pantić or some minion of his who might be able to identify her. No, it was slink time, and she slunk along the river's edge until she knelt below the "deserted" house.

She sat down behind a river bush, pulled out three newspapers slowly, gently disassembled them, then crumpled them into three balls. Her torches-to-be. She wouldn't douse them with lighter fluid until she was in the unfinished cellar. She had its layout memorized. The cellar had the slight hill slope as a back wall; the kitchen was toward the rear of the house; the bed and bathrooms, to the right rear and right front, toward the street; the open cellar ended halfway under the kitchen and bedroom. She would put the torches in three places. One in the center of the building, one each to either side, north and south. They should have the wooden framework in flames in an instant. It should be—must be—a roaring blaze before anyone inside would even know he was in trouble. (Of course, if no one was inside, her heroic effort would turn out to be a wretched piece of arson; but either way, heroism or arson, she begged the forgiveness of Nikola Vuković in faraway Iraq: "Forgive me, Nikola. If I survive this, I'll see that your house is rebuilt. Completely. And, Harry, I'll also pay the bill at the Hotel Intercontinental. Won't you be proud of me?") Altogether, it was an excellent plan. Or at least the best she could devise. Once the fire was out of control, Harry and Ethan and James Carter would scramble from the holocaust along with their captors.

She refused to let her mind contemplate the obvious question: Suppose they were bound and immobile and therefore were simply incinerated by her fire. Anna Stupica had said it: You can't have everything.

She took out the Makarov pistol with its silencer, put it in the side pocket of the shoulder bag, where it was accessible, stuffed the balls of paper into the central pocket, began to crawl toward the cellar. It was two-twelve in the morning.

36

The air was downright chilly. Yet sweat bathed Lissa's face, matted her hair. Her thoughts were:

"There's many a slip betwixt cup and lip."

"Don't count your chickens before they're hatched."

"Beware of, had I but known."

"Look before you leap."

"Don't bite off more than you can chew."

Because that was pretty much what she had done. "I've jumped in where angels fear to tread." And with this last dither, she leaned back against the dirt rear wall and wondered whether to weep or flee. That afternoon it had all seemed so simple. Slip over here. Set the paper by the wooden framework. Douse the paper and the wood with lighter fluid, light the fire, slip away, and await the happy results.

So the plan. The reality was different. In the first place, getting the crumpled newspaper out of the shoulder bag was—or seemed to be—out of the question. Every time she took hold of a paper ball, it began to rustle and rattle, to make a simply horrendous scratching sound. Even if the people above her head were all asleep—and how likely was that?—they would promptly awaken when they heard the brittle noise. Why hadn't she brought a knife? With a knife she could slit the side of the plastic shoulder bag, lay it open, light the newspaper without a sound. But she didn't have a knife. And anyway, even if she did, her problems wouldn't be solved.

She would still have to put lighter fluid on the balls of paper and place them at three locations. One above her head. One in the center of the cellar. And one at the opposite side, the south side, of the house. Then she would have to light one of the balls, race to the other, light it, race to the final one, light it. All this would have to be done quietly and expeditiously, a dubious proposal even in bare feet. And finally, having gotten the fire going, she would have to scramble away.

Fine, just fine, all of it. What would Harry say about my foresight on this one? Say? He wouldn't say anything. But he'd have some thoughts, oh yes he would. Think it through and rethink it through and then, maybe, then maybe do it. That's what he'd think and not say. Well, I certainly didn't think this through. I didn't allow for noise. Noise of the paper. Noise of the flames, noise of my racing across the cellar floor, noise of my trying to scramble away. Don't bite off more than you can chew. If, Lissa, if you can manage to get the fire going, you certainly won't be able to scramble away. You won't get ten yards before someone will be looking out the window, spotting you, disposing of you. No, there will be no scrambling. I'll get the fire going and stay here. Then we'll all incinerate together. Harry and Ethan and James above, me below.

"Well, at least I'll foil their plan." This she whispered aloud; half-aloud. "They won't be able to use any of us for whatever they want to use us for."

With this brilliant conclusion, she should have picked up her bag and shoes and gone home. Instead, she wiped the sweat from her forehead, eyes, and cheeks, reached into the bag, once again took hold of the top paper ball, started to ease it out of the bag. And froze, as she heard a noise. Someone was coming up the path from the street. Someone in tennis shoes or gym shoes. He—she presumed the someone was a he; this was macho Yugoslavia—was truly noiseless, except that in her present condition she had no trouble hearing him. He was breathing. And that she heard, his breathing.

She also heard a knock on the kitchen door, on the south side of the house, away from her. The gentlest of knocks. Knock once, a pause, then two quick knocks. Footsteps—the first sound she had heard from above—beat across the floor. The door opened. A muttered colloquy, then something she could make out.

"Ha, sandwiches and salad. Did you include beer, too?"

"Of course. Karlevac beer. Like you said. I had to go to

228

Bosanski Petrovac to get it. This town doesn't have a bottle of beer left for sale."

"Good. Maybe they'll sober up in time for the unveiling."

"See you."

"See you."

As the bearer of food and beverage turned back toward the street, Lissa acted. (A dim part of her mind could hear Harry Ryder: "My, you are the impulsive one." Well, so she was. Harry Ryder also had a message about that: "Your impulses are always good." Were they? Always?) She reached into the shoulder bag, slipped the Browning High-Powered from under the balls of paper, thrust it beneath her jeans, then hoisted out the silenced Makarov, flipped off the safety, and, pistol in hand, took advantage of the footsteps on the floor above her to tiptoe across the cellar floor. Peering out from behind a wooden beam, she tried to locate the messenger. But it was too dark. He had vanished. He might be standing on the dirt footpath; he might be all the way to the next corner. So be it. The darkness worked both ways. If she couldn't see him, he couldn't see her. Except maybe her hair would glisten even in the night. Why hadn't she buried it under a dark handkerchief? Why? Because when Harry Ryder saw her, she wanted him to see her natural hair, even though it was slicked down and matted by sweat. He liked her hair. What a time to be vain.

Drawing a deep breath, she flitted up the easy slope, stepped onto the porch, tiptoed to the kitchen door, knocked once, very gently, knocked twice, quickly.

Footsteps again and the door flung open.

"What the hell do you—" and silence. A wide-eyed silence as the soldier—he was a noncom, a sergeant—goggled at her but mostly at the pistol. She waggled the barrel up and down. The sergeant understood the message, refused to obey it. Instead of retreating, he lunged for her. She shot him. Squarely in the chest, near the heart. The Pistolet Makarov's 9-millimeter cartridge, though not as powerful as her High-Powered 9-millimeter parabellum, and though slowed by the

229

silencer, was still powerful enough to lift the soldier off his feet, send him crashing into the counter on top of the sandwiches.

Ignoring the racket, not lingering to watch the soldier slump and cave to the floor, she whisked the door shut, sprang with two barefoot steps all the way across the kitchen to the open bedroom door. Skier's legs, skier's leap. Two soldiers were visible. And three trussed-up bodies on the bed. Three little lambs, they. Ignoring them, she leaped once more so she could have both soldiers in line of fire. One was waking up. The other was jumping up and going for his automatic rifle.

"Don't." She used Serbo-Croatian. "I've killed one of you." Had she? No time to find out. "That's enough. Don't."

He didn't. The other—no longer asleep and not the least sleepy-eyed—also didn't. The two did sit up alert and tense.

"Hands over your heads."

Hands rose slowly.

"Higher. All the way."

They went all the way.

"Now up and face against the wall. Feet like in the movies. Do it."

They did it. She reached forward gingerly, abstracted each soldier's pistol, tossed each across the room. Now she turned part of her attention to the men on the bed.

They were handcuffed and footcuffed. Their arms were above their heads and draped over the bed frame, where the handcuffs held them. The position must have become excruciatingly painful. If so, they couldn't comment on their situation. Masking tape covered their jaws and mouths. Or rather, covered Harry's and Ethan's mouths. James Carter had no gag. His jaw was clearly broken. It stuck out at a strange angle. And whereas Harry's and Ethan's eyes were snapping with excitement, James Carter was not really aware of her or of what was happening. She didn't need medical training to recognize that Mr. Carter was a sick man. Sweat covered his forehead, nose, and lips. Shivers went up and down his body. Little moans ricocheted past his battered jaw. He was quite sick.

What to do? The two soldiers, although temporarily im-mobilized, radiated a constant threat. If they both sprang at her, one of them would surely overpower her. Somewhere down the line, this thought would occur to them. And that line wouldn't be very far distant. What to do?

She became aware of Harry Ryder's eyes. They weren't just snapping with excitement. They were looking fixedly at some-thing, then back at her, then at something. At what? At the soldiers' legs, that's what.

She saw. She understood. She fired. Twice. The Pistolet Makarov coughed its distinctive *phut*, both soldiers crumbled, grabbing for their right upper legs. One of them screamed. The other gave a long wail.

She looked at Harry. He blinked approvingly, then frowned. No, it was not a frown; it was a look down at the gag.

She saw. She understood. She reached forward and jerked.

"Kee-rist!" So Harry.

"Sorry. I thought it would be easier that way."

"Don't do it that way with Ethan. His face will come off with the beard."

Now she looked at the cause of all their trouble, the one man who once had the power to make her think bad thoughts, to think of betraying Llew-Llaw. God, but he was good-look-ing. And—even shackled and gagged—still a dynamic force. No wonder he had stirred her once. Had she held herself back—or had he simply refused to respond because of Llew-Llaw? Whatever, thank God she'd never let things go any further. What a contrast he was with Harry Ryder. Harry Ryder, all understatement and anonymity. Ethan Pickering, alias Peter Trubari, all manifest animal dynamics. It would be so very easy to submerge oneself in Ethan Pickering's ego. Submerge—and drown. With Harry Ryder, there was no sub-mersion, rather flight together. Joint flight. And enough of that—eyes front. Eyes, in fact, to the kitchen.

But Harry put off squishing and squeezing his lips, inter-rupted her progress toward the wounded soldier. "Watch out for that fellow. He might be harmless. But if he's not dead, remember he's still armed."

"I know, Harry. Foresight. Believe me, I've learned the lesson. I'll take care."

She did. The soldier seemed unconscious. He was certainly badly wounded. Blood had spread all over his shirt. Cautiously she reached down, pulled out his pistol, a standard Yugoslavian 760-millimeter, model 57, stuck it beside her Browning, found a washcloth, soaked it, came back, and headed for Ethan.

"Not yet, Lissa. Forget the gag. Get us out of here. The keys. They're on that table over there. The keys."

"Lady, help us." One of the wounded soldiers, clutching his leg, had rolled over onto the floor to face her. "We're dying. Help us."

That was a possibility she hadn't thought of. Not from a leg wound. Maybe.

"In a moment. First, I must help my friends."

She got the keys, six sets of them, trialed and errored her way through the locks.

"Kee-rist!" So Harry. He sat there as if stunned. "Kee-rist. Help us get our arms down."

Now Harry and Ethan were sweating. Beads burst out on their foreheads like soap bubbles. Only James Carter did not show any additional reaction; he was already soaked in sweat.

She eased their arms down, helped Harry and Ethan sit up and bring their legs over the side of the bed, then dampened and gingerly removed Ethan's gag.

He smiled at her. "Thanks, Lissa. Somewhere along the way Harry told me you'd be along."

"Took her a while." So Harry.

She started to protest, saw the gleam in his eyes, joined him—and Ethan—in a flicker of a smile.

"What about Arritsa?" So Ethan.

"She's not here, but she did help me get here. So did the girl you once rescued."

"The girl? Ah, of course. Anna St—sorry. No time for names."

She looked at the soldiers. "We've got to do something about them. I suppose their belts will make the best tourniquets. I'll find some towels for bandages. I don't know what we'll do about the one in the kitchen. He looks—"

"Right, he's dead," said Ethan. "Well, we can doctor these two and make that fellow decent and get the hell out of here."

"I don't know," said Harry. He pointed to a black box sitting on a small table under a window with a drawn shade. A window that faced out across the Unac River to the Tito War Memorial Park and Tito's statue. The black box had a conspicuous red button. "I don't know. What are we going to do about that? I mean, if we go getting the hell out of here, where do we take the box? And once there, what do we do with it?"

37

"Now I think I know where we are, Lissa. Drvar, right? The five-year-old girl gave me the clue." Ethan strode to the window, started to raise the shade.

"Don't!"

He halted midstride. This left him leaning forward like the needle nose of a Concorde. Nothing had changed. The same Ethan, even behind the mask of a beard and under the near shoulder-length burst of hair. When walking, he had always plunged ahead like this, leaning forward, face eager, eyes flashing, nose sniffing ahead of him, a wild animal on the prowl.

Ethan looked his question. She explained:

"This house is supposed to be empty. Žarko's men are outside. If you raise the window shade—"

"Fair enough. What's up? Why all the noise outside? We were blindfolded when they brought us here. What's with Drvar? Why here, why the mobs? Why the loudspeaker being tested—one, two, three, four? Why this black box?"

"The Drvar's simple, Ethan. Everyone's here for the celebration of the unveiling of Tito's statue with the marshal's uniform. Tomorrow, President Otaronov unveils the statue at eleven. Sorry, today. When he does that . . . well, the red button. At least, I think that's the place and time for the red button. But before we do anything about it, please, let's help these men. Please, just look at them."

"Right. We'll help." And they did, Ethan the while musing aloud: "So. Blow up poor old Miodrag Otaronov. I've met him. He wasn't in Drvar in '44. He commanded a brigade over towards Niš. Blow up Otaronov, destroy Tito's uniform. Tito didn't get it alive, isn't supposed to get it dead. Why not? Who's done this? For what purpose? For what advantage? How do we fit in? No, belay that. It's pretty obvious how we fit in. We're going to be fall guys, though I don't see . . . No, wait a minute. Those were Russians who did me in on the Schneeberg. Žarko set me up with Russians. What about you two? Russians?" Harry nodded, she nodded. "Right. Russians. Maybe KGB. Maybe Army Intelligence. Either way, Russians, though what Russia can gain from all this, I can't imagine. Russians and Pantić. That's an odd combination; Žarko never held the slightest admiration for things Russian, not any more than Tito did. Russia to both of them was a tool to be used when advisable—and only very cautiously. So it's Žarko, yes. But he's not on his own, not for a caper like this, he's a tool to be used in his own right. Someone's diddling him. Someone in Yugoslavia. Who? Why?"

There was silence. Lissa broke it. "The who we don't know. But I think I know part of the why—and that all comes back to the significance of Karageorge." She explained how they'd stumbled onto the mysterious message. "You'll recall your history, Ethan. When things went bad for Karageorge, when finally the Turks got to him, he turned to Russia for help. The very Russia he loathed. That's what Milan Tadić's message was supposed to mean to me. Only Llew-Llaw never told me about it. It took quite a while for the obvious to become clear. Yugoslavia is turning back to Russia, someone here is undoing all that Tito created. Someone is putting Yugoslavia once more back behind the Iron Curtain."

"*Was* putting, Lissa. Was." So Ethan. He pointed to the black box. "As long as that thing doesn't go off, the Russians won't be coming. Is that how you two see the scenario? Kill

Otaronov, blame the warmongering CIA, call in the Russians, happy Socialist paradise again. That it?"

She nodded, but Harry was motionless, had gone into his anonymous phase. Even his eyes had assumed their protective dullness. Why this reaction? Where was the danger? What was he suspicious about? She challenged him.

"All right, Harry. Tell us."

He pointed to James Carter lying on the bed, arms folded across his chest, eyes closed, sweat beading his face. "Pantić and Russians, yes. But also James Carter. He fits in there somehow, doesn't he, Lissa?"

Ethan grunted, said, "So our James is not all he's supposed to be, eh, Harry? Never liked the bugger. Only met him once or twice, but that was enough. Too oily. Doesn't at all surprise me."

"James." Ryder shook Carter's shoulders, brought the sick man's eyes open. "James, what did you mean in the parking lot when those thugs grabbed us? What did you mean: 'Colonel Pantić wouldn't—' Colonel Pantić wouldn't what?"

A whisper, a garbled whisper, little better than gibberish. But still interpretable. "Go to hell."

"James, I know you're sick. Your jaw's a mess. But concentrate, James. Concentrate. Here's the situation. Along about eleven today, the men in here were going to push that red button, blow up Tito's statue and maybe the president of Yugoslavia, then they were going to kill us. Ethan and me and you, James, yes, you, too. We were to be fall guys. Three CIA men caught red-handed killing the president of Yugoslavia. Why, James? Why the CIA? Why the killing? What's the game? Tell us, James. Tell us. You've got a chance to get out of here alive, thanks to Lissa. Why Žarko Pantić and Russians? Who's Žarko working for?"

Carter's eyes flickered, then closed. The sweat poured out, a stinking sweat, almost like urine. He groaned, shivered, said, eyes still shut, "Don't . . . don't . . . know."

Ethan and Harry Ryder looked at each other, locked eyes, ignored Lissa. No wonder women have been forced into Wom-

235

en's Lib. With two men like these around, she would join Miljana Dragan's network of ball-breaking women. She said, "Then, gentlemen, what do we do about the red button? And ourselves?"

The two men's necks swiveled toward her. Harry smiled. "You tell us, Lissa. You know more about this than either of us. Your turn."

Good for her Harry. Wrong of her to write him off. She'd apologize later.

"My turn. Well, how does this sound? We can't just walk out of here, can we? Maybe Mr. Carter is not highly regarded by you two, but he is yours, isn't he? I mean, still yours? We can't just leave him here, can we?

"So I suggest you two stay and guard the fort. When the red button is not pushed on schedule, you'll undoubtedly have some irate visitors. And among them will be Colonel Ž. Pantić, and who knows how many more. Of course, you may have visitors before then. In that case, I hope you'll be able to bundle them up with those two over there."

"You say 'You'll.' " So Harry.

"Yes, you, not me. Me, I think it's best for me to try to go get some help."

"Help? Where will you turn? Who can you trust?"

"Trust? How about Miljana Dragan's ball-breakers?"

"What's that?" So Ethan. "Pardon me, Lissa, but did I hear you say—"

"You did. They got me into Drvar. I'm hoping they'll get the four of us out of Drvar. Harry will tell you about Miljana Dragan. I'd best be going now. And I'll take the black box with me, I think. I'll hide it safely. You won't be able to tell anyone where it is if . . . if . . ."

"If we foul things up here." So Harry. "Smart lady, very smart." He went to the table, picked up the box, handed it carefully to her, walked with her to the kitchen door, said softly, "Lissa, your hair is glorious. It's so beautiful, I want . . . well, you know what I want. But—well here, put this on, no need for me to share your hair with the whole world, is there? Not now, anyway?"

And as he spoke, he was plucking a dark napkin from the kitchen table and using it as a scarf to cover her hair.

"There. You look like a good Bosnian hausfrau." He leaned forward, kissed her cheek gently, slid the door open, held it as she slipped outside, watched her a second, then eased the door shut.

Lissa stood still a moment until she had adjusted to the darkness. To her left, down toward the sluggish stream, there were occasional flashes of light. Cigarettes. After three A.M., and still cigarettes. Toward the right, toward the main street and the Hotel Park and the police station, she could see a dim street light and, possibly, some people standing under it. Right ahead to the south, more sensed than seen, was the neighboring house. Beyond it, a block and a half away, was her objective, the home of Olja Jaka. Terrible to bring her into the melee, but Anna Stupica's home was just too far out of town, there wasn't time to struggle her way out there, she needed help now—and Arritsa had picked Olja Jaka as the one ready to help. Well, that would be determined shortly, but not yet. First the box.

Swiftly but cautiously, Lissa crept back into the cellar, went to the top of the earth wall where it joined the kitchen flooring, scooped out a hole, buried the box in it, making most sure the red button was supported by earth on all sides, not pressed down by it—then crept back below, put her shoes back on, picked up Harry's Chinese shoulder bag, and put her pistol back in the pocket, slung the bag over her shoulder, and crept back down to the river, followed it upstream until she reached a path that should lead up the slope toward Olja Jaka's house, followed the path, came to the house, stood at the gate a fraction of a second, unlatched it, pushed it open, skipped to the front porch, located the door, located the doorbell, reached her hand toward the bell, and froze in that position as the door suddenly swung open, revealing a woman in the doorway. Revealing Arritsa Patak.

"Come in, Mrs. Meirion. We've been sitting here hoping you'd come. Hoping . . . and I see I did understand your message about Rajko not being with you. It meant your Harry is not with you, is in trouble, no? All right, come in and meet my friend, Olja Jaka."

And she did. She grasped Arritsa's hand, was guided by it to another hand, heard a disembodied woman's voice say, "We're so glad you came. We're ready to help. We want to help. What can we do?"

During these exchanges, Lissa stepped inside and shut the door behind her. She said, "I do have a plan. It involves danger, but I think it has a chance of working. I can't ask you to go along with my thought, but—"

"Tell us, Mrs. Meirion. Arritsa has explained everything to me. About the man she loves and the man you love and I do want to help. There are many of us who I know will want to help. Tell us what we can do."

Lissa again heard the refrain: "There are many of us who want to help." Exactly what Anna Stupica had said. "Very well. I will tell you what I think we can do."

38

By nine o'clock, over a hundred thousand people—maybe two hundred thousand, a lot of people—were massed for the day's ceremonies. Harry and Ethan took turns peeking at the crowd from the space between the window shade and the window. While one watched and reported, the other sat in the kitchen and kept an eye on the locked door lest visitors should come knocking.

No one did. And when they gave water to the wounded soldiers and let them crawl to the toilet, one of them confirmed no one was expected. As Ethan trussed them up again, he nodded, said:

"And then once you pushed the button, you were going to kill us."

The two soldiers shrugged, said no more. Ethan said, "Fortunes of war." He translated the episodic conversation for Harry, explained what was going on outside.

"People are everywhere, Harry. They're even in the river fully clothed. The cliff opposite us, up where Tito's cave is, the cliff is a wall of people. They're up trees, in bushes, on rocks. Hardly like 1944."

"1944?"

"Yes, that's when the events they're celebrating took place. Harry, this Drvar Valley resembles your Napa Valley. Mountains on the east and west. A long valley, with additional mountains to the near north and far south. Only it's not wine country. *Drvar* means lumberjack. There's still some lumbering here, but mostly now it's sheep and row crops and light industry. The events they're celebrating took place on Tito's birthday in '44. On that day, the people of Drvar were going to gift Tito with a fancy new marshal's uniform. That morning, Tito came out of his cave hut in the eastern cliff, went out on the porch about six A.M., and saw German paratroopers coming down, north and south. We saw them, too, Llew-Llaw and I. We were both with the British mission in the western hills, with General Sir Fitzroy McLean and Randolph Churchill. Yes, the very one. We hied ourselves to the nearest partisan contingent—it was the First Proletarian, great fellows, great fighters. While we were doing that, Tito's entourage at the cave told him to forget the marshal's uniform, made him climb up over the mountain and hike sixteen kilometers inland. One of our planes picked him up and took him to the island of Vis. Say, the Italians call that island Lissa. Curious. Anyway, he went there, and we stayed here and had a busy three days. I think those days were the high point of my life."

"And this," Harry suggested, "is this the low?"

"We won't know about that until eleven o'clock, will we?"

"Or until we hear from Lissa."

"There's that, yes, there's Lissa. A great lady, Harry. Is she the one who got you into this?"

"She's the reason I stayed on. But credit your old boss and mine for the inspiration."

"Boss? Bingham? Birdie?"

"None other. He blackmailed me. Typical Birdie. The minute you disappeared in Vienna, you and Arritsa Patak, he put the screws to me. Let me bring you up to date with my side of the story. I think I know yours pretty well, thanks to Birdie and Arritsa."

"I gather he told you all about me."

"Told Carter, too. Here, while I play nursemaid to James and tell about Lissa and me, will you watch the door? I'm sure Mr. Carter, sick as he makes out to be, will also manage to follow my dissertation. Won't you, James?"

But neither then nor in the ensuing discussion that lasted until after ten did the once-urbane Vienna CIA station chief open his eyes or otherwise show he heard a word. Perhaps he did twitch slightly when he found out how Arritsa Patak by her mere presence at Lake Prošće had exposed his lies to Lissa and Harry. Otherwise, he maintained silence and immobility until ten-fifteen, when the loudspeakers went into action. A military band let loose a march that shook the house and made them all jump, including the two handcuffed prisoners and James Carter. Apparently the nearest loudspeaker was not far away. Going to the window, Harry spotted it on a tree near the house north of them. People under the tree scattered before the blast. The crowd began to roar in protest, two hundred thousand people began to roar—and they were heard. Some engineer somewhere turned down the volume so that the music was endurable. And in a moment, enjoyable. The band started playing folk songs, the crowd responded. Every man, woman, and child sang them. It was most impressive—and more than Ethan could take. He joined Harry at the other side of the shade, peeked out on the multitude, joined them in song. Startled, Harry pulled back from the window to protest.

And said nothing. Tears were in Ethan's eyes. He shrugged. "Sorry again. This is my home. These are my people. Sorry."

The band suddenly switched to the national anthem. "Ah," Ethan said, "the brass arrives. Twenty, thirty . . . well, as far as I can see nothing but big black Mercedes, all the way up the north mountain highway. God, where'll they put them? Where? Nowhere, that's where. Lord, Harry, they're all stuck."

Harry joined him at the aperture, saw the debacle. It was chaos all the way. People—generals, admirals, dignitaries, both male and female—poured from their cars and began to struggle through the throng toward the viewing stand.

"There's Miodrag Otaronov." So Ethan. "He's president this year. Officially, President of the Presidency. There are six presidents representing each republic—Serbia, Bosnia, Croatia, and the others. They rotate the top spot each year. This year it's Otaronov's turn. He's a Serb. What a mess out there. A terrorist's paradise, except a terrorist couldn't get through that mob any better than the brass can."

It was well past eleven before said brass were ensconced in the stands. Then there were a series of speeches by the Mayor of Drvar, by assorted members of the Presidency, and finally by Otaronov himself.

He didn't go to the podium at the front of the stands, he left the stands, walked toward the veiled statue of Tito. A microphone stood by the statue. He lifted the microphone, carried it to the statue, turned, faced the TV cameras, and addressed the crowd—and all Yugoslavia and much of Europe. He didn't pick up the theme the other speakers had harped on: Tito as symbol and inspirer of Yugoslavia's unity. Instead—and Ethan translated for Harry's benefit—Otaronov told the story of Tito's marshal's uniform, how the people of Drvar had happily designed and crafted it for the great man in their midst, how the Germans, finding it in the tailor's shop, had shot it full of holes—they couldn't shoot the man, so they shot his uniform (laughter)—and that original shot-up uniform was preserved in the museum at the entrance to the Park, but ever since 1944 the comrades in Drvar had wanted to do something to commemorate that great day. And so, finally, they had commissioned Yugoslavia's internationally

241

renowned sculptor, Radule Sumi, to create a statue of Tito wearing his marshal's uniform, said statue to be ready for unveiling on Bosnia's Day of Uprising, today, July 27, and so, without further ado, lo and behold, Tito at last wearing his marshal's uniform.

The crowd roared, the president yanked a cord, the canvas fell to the ground, and now the crowd really went wild. Laughter, tears, shrieks, applause, a repeated susurration: *Tito . . . Tito . . . Tito . . .*

Watching from the other end of the window shade, Harry said, "When the rope was jerked, that was probably red-button time. Boom. No statue. Boom. No president. Boom. Boom. No free Yugoslavia."

Now the crowd's chant shifted from Tito, Tito, to Sumi, Sumi. And the chanters kept it up until a lean, bearded man stood up in the stand, walked down the wooden steps, went over to Otaronov, and bowed his appreciation of the admiration. And that admiration was, Harry thought, well justified. The statue was magnificent. It loomed high enough above the crowd so everyone could see Tito standing there, arms upraised as if in benediction, a serene smile on his face as if he was delighted with his gaudy new uniform. For, using the ancient Greeks as model, Sumi's statue was a vivid splash of colors: green, blue, gold, silver, the gamut.

Moving back to the kitchen and peering out behind the window shade, Harry said, "Quite a show, Ethan, quite a show. And along about now, Colonel Pantić's heart should be in a fancy state of fibrillation."

"But nevertheless coming our way. Any sign of him yet? I can't see hide nor hair of him out this window. You?"

"Nothing."

"Wait a minute, Ethan. Out there beyond the mob, three soldiers. With automatic rifles."

"And?"

"And they're staring at this house. At this door. Come take a look."

Ethan did. He came to the window, leaned over Harry's shoulder to put his eye to the window, said, "I see—"

And could say no more. A crash from the bedroom cut him short. A crash, a thump, three or four thumps, and a voice:

"Put those pistols down."

The voice was that of Žarko Pantić. Colonel Žarko Pantić. In full uniform. With two soldiers to his right and left, each with an automatic rifle, each with a target, Ethan and Harry.

"You shouldn't have left the window, Ethan." So Pantić. He sprang across the room, unlocked the kitchen door, stood aside as three more soldiers filed into the room. They were the same three Harry had spotted from the window. And they also held automatic rifles and also proceeded to focus them on the two Americans. "Where's the box? The box, dammit, where's the box?"

Ethan walked to the door to peer into the bedroom. Harry followed him. The bedroom window was a shambles. The table under the window was tipped sideways. One leg was broken. Ethan shrugged. Harry shrugged. Pantić slugged Ethan with his pistol butt. Ethan crumbled to the floor, managed to shrug again, then lay limp. Pantić glared at Harry, raised his pistol to strike again, changed his mind, glared at the corpse under the blanket, inspected the two bound soldiers, said, "Later I'll find out how this all happened. Right now . . ." And he went to the bedroom window, peered out, said, "Right now, there's still time. Otaronov's still at the statue."

Swinging back to one of the three late-arriving soldiers, he barked out a command in Serbo-Croatian. The soldier unslung a knapsack, put it on the floor, started to undo the straps.

While this was going on, Pantić looked at Harry, said— rather, snarled, "You think you've won. Don't you think I'd have a fall-back position? Look."

Harry looked. Ethan, coming alive again on the floor, looked. The soldier was pulling out a container. He set the container on the floor, opened the top, and looked inquiringly at Pantić. The latter barked out another command in Serbo-Croatian, said to Harry, "You—you're going to push the button. Yes, that's another trigger. A spare. You're going to blow up Tito and Otaronov. You."

And the soldier picked up the box, carried it to Harry, held it in two hands so Harry would have no problem pushing the red button. Harry stared at the button, glanced at Pantić. The square-jawed, pudgy colonel's face still maintained a snarl. His pistol, an enormous American-made .45, was being maintained five inches from Harry's ear.

Harry had time for one thought, the thought of Lissa and the way she'd whipped her purse through the air and sent the KGB Russian's pistol flying up towards the ceiling. A good thought, he thought. One worth a try again. He'd snatch the box from the soldier's hands, whip it up to dislodge Pantić's pistol, then heave the box out the window. There was a chance the button wouldn't be depressed. Yes, there was a chance, and it was worth a try, and he reached forward to grab the box—and at that moment, the kitchen door was flung open and a woman sprang into the kitchen.

The woman had red hair that seemed to fly through the air as she bounced into the room. The woman was Arritsa Patak. Behind her was a buxom blonde, and behind her a horde of women. As everyone turned to face the shrilling, screaming intruders, Harry continued his motion. He gripped the container, tugged it away from the soldier, shut the lid, buried the whole package under his folded arms—and couldn't move a muscle thereafter. The women saw to that. They crowded into the room until all the men were imprisoned by female flesh. The soldiers couldn't even budge their automatic rifles. Žarko Pantić's pistol was resting on the buxom blonde's head and pointing to the ceiling.

When any further motion was clearly impossible, when no additional women could press into the room, a silence fell. Harry swiveled his head around to focus on the only woman he recognized, Arritsa Patak—there was no sign of Lissa, although in this pressure cooker she could be two feet from him and he wouldn't be able to spot her. Arritsa was jammed up against Pantić. She leaned her head back so she could look down at the shorter man, said in German:

"When I last saw you, I told you I wanted you to know I was still willing to be of assistance. I still am. Let me assist that pistol out of your reach, Colonel."

She dislodged one arm, reached up and slid the weapon out of the colonel's hand, handed it over toward Harry.

He shook his head, summoned his reluctant German, said, "No, Miss Patak, you keep it. I'm holding a . . . a . . ." He couldn't think of the word for detonator, tried an oblique approach. "I'm carrying a button for the bomb, do you understand? Yes, another one. I don't dare move a finger, okay? Lissa—is Mrs. Meirion with you?"

"I'm here, Harry—about three rows over. I'm here, but where's Ethan?"

"I'm standing over him, Lissa, straddling him. He's okay. Explain all this to Arritsa and the others, will you? About the bomb, too. I'm holding a detonator. Pantić wanted me to push the button and kill the president and destroy Tito's statue. Explain all this, will you?"

Lissa did. The women groaned. Lissa said, "We've sent a delegate to bring the chief of police here, Harry. Dr. Stupica and two other doctors went with her. Even if the chief's part of the plot, he can't do much to further it now, can he, not with all Miljana Dragan's ball-breakers here."

A sepulchral voice rose from the floor:

"Lysistrata strikes again."

Žarko Pantić's expression of shock had begun to subside. He said, half-groaning as he spoke, "I begin to see. It was Mrs. Meirion all the time. That's how—"

"Yes." So Harry. "When your thugs failed at Bayswater Station to dispose of her, you doomed yourself. You should never underestimate the power of a woman, Colonel. Never."

245

Epilogue

The wedding and the reception were held in the Mayfair garden of Sir Alexander James's home. Peter Trubari, arm around Mrs. Peter Trubari, guided his bride from their host's side, came over to Lissa and Harry, said:

"Your turn next, you two. Your turn."

But before either Lissa or Harry could speak, Mr. Don Carlos Bingham materialized beside them, saying: "I'd like you to meet someone. You four, all of you." And he shepherded them to a corner table. An already occupied table. Lissa reacted first.

"President Otaronov? Sergeant Dykes!"

The sturdy President of the Presidency of Yugoslavia rose and bowed. The giant from Paddington Station uncoiled himself, rose, towered above the whole group, said: "I was right, wasn't I? You two do make quite a team, don't you? Commander Malmquist and Inspector Perpar send their regards. They asked me to come and hear the post mortems. Sorry. That's too close to home, I mean—"

"We know what you mean, Sergeant." So Lissa. "And we're glad you're here. Thank you for coming."

Don Carlos Bingham introduced the bride and groom to President Otaronov and the sergeant, waved everybody into a chair, beamed, whispered, "I suggest we use German, since I believe Mrs. Trubari is not at home in English. Sergeant?"

The giant nodded. "I can follow you, I believe, provided you speak slowly."

"Good. German it is. Well, to begin with, as you've probably read, President Otaronov is in London on a state visit and he kindly consented to slip away from the Embassy and join us on this happy occasion. In fact, it was his idea. He has two reasons for wanting to meet all of you."

"Four reasons, Mr. Bingham. Four reasons. The first is to express my best wishes to you, Mr. and Mrs. Trubari. I understand you'll be living in Bihać a good part of the year."

Peter Trubari said gravely, "Yes, and we'll schedule our visits so our children are born in Yugoslavia."

"And my second reason for coming is, well, quite personal. I'm here and able to talk to you only because you saved my life. What can I say, except thank you, thank you all?"

"Well, yes, well, yes. And that leads to the third reason, our country's thanks. We want you to know our country's appreciation for the way you protected the statue of President Tito. I'd like to broadcast our thanks to the world, but well, you understand, yes? Nothing ever happened, did it? However, we do want to give you something tangible, we do think it's appropriate to present you with, well, here, here they are."

And he reached into the briefcase at his feet and brought out four gold plaques, each one with the same message, and the name of the recipient. Harry's plaque read: "Our country's everlasting thanks to Mr. Harry Ryder, a great friend of Yugoslavia. Miodrag Otaronov, President of the Presidency." As he passed the plaques around, the President added: "Of course, I've already delivered Mr. Carter's, sorry, Mr. Barnwell's, I've delivered his plaque to him in Beograd. We're all delighted he's been transferred to our capital. For that, we all thank you again, Mr. Bingham. Mr. Barnwell is a truly heroic friend of our country."

Lissa gasped. Harry Ryder scowled. Peter Trubari chuckled. Arritsa Trubari and Sergeant Dykes were puzzled. Seeing the reaction—savoring them?—Mr. Don Carlos Bingham beamed at all of them, whispered, "I know we are all delighted you are delighted, Mr. President. We think Mr. Barnwell's achievements do truly reflect the bonds of friendship between our two countries."

"Exactly." President Otaronov's face now became grave. "And his achievements and the achievements of all of you have prompted our government to permit me to tell you the outcome of our efforts. In short, what we found out. This is the fourth reason I am pleased to be able to talk to you in person.

"To begin with, the statue. There were indeed, as you told us on July twenty-seventh, explosives at its base. When I unveiled the statue, that was to have been the signal for detonating the explosives. And, of course, me.

"A word, if I may, a word about me. I—we Otaronovs—we are Serbian. But we are not thereby anti-Croatian. We are Titoists, we believe in one Yugoslavia. One Yugoslavia with six equal republics. But there are other Serbs who still hold on to the old beliefs. Just as there are Croats who want to pull away from Yugoslavia and remain an independent country, as Croatia once was. Institutions die hard. For Serbs. For Croats.

"The leader of the plot against you and me was a Serb, was in fact one of Yugoslavia's three senior generals and hence able to control the army as he wished. His name was General Jure Kranjc."

"Kranjc!" So Peter. "Sorry. I just remember seeing an article about an automobile wreck. General Kranjc and his chauffeur, Colonel Žarko Pantić, were killed when the brakes of their Mercedes-Benz gave out and they went over a cliff in the Sutjeska mountains."

"Yes, so they did. A great shame. But the two men of course were buried with full military honors. After all, they had done great deeds for us in the war, they deserved our thanks for that."

"And," this time Lissa, "and, General Kranjc turned to Russia, did he not?"

"He did. He did not approve of Yugoslavia's lapses from strict Marxist-Leninist communism. In his eyes we had become too capitalistic. Yes, he turned to Russia. That morning, July twenty-seventh, over two thousand orders were ready to be delivered to our troops all over the country. Pantić prepared those orders over many months. The army would take over all radio and TV stations, all newspapers, all magazines, all telephone communications. And Kranjc himself was going to go on television and proclaim martial law and denounce the United States as perpetrators of this great crime. The United States, he would say, feared I was leading Yugoslavia back into the Russian orbit, so the CIA killed me to prevent this.

"There was a grain of truth in his analysis. I am nowhere as anti-Soviet as Tito was. I want to enjoy friendly relations with Russia as with all the world. So it would be easy to make me look pro-Russian.

"And with equal plausibility, Kranjc would have announced he was asking Russian troops to enter our country immediately and help protect us from any possible invasion led by or inspired by the United States. Oh yes, he would have pulled this off and today we'd be like Czechoslovakia and Poland and the rest. Yugoslavia, as we know it, as you and I love it, Yugoslavia would be dead."

The President stood, shook their hands, said his thanks again and strode off, followed a moment later by a pensive Sergeant Dykes.

They all watched them go, then the eyes of Lissa Meirion, Peter Trubari, and Harry Ryder bored into Birdie Bingham. Arritsa Trubari once again seemed puzzled by the trio's hostility.

"You bastard," said Peter.

"You manipulating devil," said Harry Ryder.

"You ancient warlock," said Lissa Meirion.

"Why do you say these cruel things?" said Arritsa Patak Trubari.

Birdie Bingham coughed, beamed deprecatingly at them, said in his faintest of whispers, "They're talking about James Carter, Mrs. Trubari. They do not approve of my making him the new CIA station chief in Belgrade. They—especially Mr. Ryder—they loathe James Carter. Right, Harry?"

"You made him into a double agent!"

"Of course, Harry, of course. Wouldn't you? We expect him to become an inexhaustible pipeline into the KGB apparatus. He's a national treasure, is our handsome James. The mole becomes a supermole."

(continued from front flap)

Bingham's prediction was correct. Harry Ryder and Melissa made a team. It was that or perish when unknown persons try first to assassinate them and then to kidnap them. They are suddenly thrust into the middle of a Soviet plot to take over Yugoslavia. By the time Harry and Melissa understand what they are up against, it is almost too late. How they devise a daring plan and carry it out leads to the startling denouement of this immensely exciting story.

ROBERT FOOTMAN lives in San Francisco. For a number of years he has been an admirer of Yugoslavia and its determination to make its unique way perched between the Soviet Union and the West.

Mr. Footman is the author of *Once a Spy*, the first novel of suspense about Harry Ryder, former CIA agent.